I0590128

COURTING SIN

A SEVEN DEADLY SINS
NOVEL

CRYSTAL CRIST

This work is self-published.

Copyright © Crystal Crist, 2024 Cover design by Crystal Crist
Cover by Crystal Crist
Edited by Nicole DiPatri Sheldon

All rights reserved. No part of this book may be reproduced in any form or by any electronic or mechanical means including information storage and retrieval systems—except in the case of brief quotations embodied in critical articles or reviews—without permission in writing from its publisher, Crystal Crist.

The characters and events portrayed in this book are fictitious or are used fictitiously. Any similarity to real persons, living or dead, is purely coincidental and not intended by the author. Any similarity to specific religions is purely fictional and no offense is intended by the author.

Author notes:

Thank you for choosing my book. This is a debut book, and I am a new author. As such, I apologize in advance for any typos you may find, and I ask that you do not judge me for them. If you would like to report them to me, my email is Crystalcrist.author@gmail.com

CONTENT WARNING:

This book contains mature content and is only recommended for readers over the age of 18. This book includes content that may be seen as triggering, such as:

- Physical assault
- Graphic depiction of murder
- Graphic depiction of blood
- Alcohol abuse
- Torture
- Blood play
- Forced marriage
- Bullying
- Childhood abuse

While this book isn't what I would consider "dark," the rest of the series will be. So, please keep that in mind when beginning your venture into the "Seven Deadly Sins Series." I caution you to know your triggers and read cautiously. This book is LGBT friendly and contains LGBT scenes. We don't yuck anyone's yum. If LGBT scenes are not for you, then this series may not be either and I completely respect that.

Playlist

Leaves of Yggdrasil by Myrkur

The Water Is Fine by Chloe Ament

Your Heart Is As Black As Night by Beth Hart and Joe Bonamassa

The Songcord by Mack Lorén Caroline by Xxelia

Spinnin by Madison Beer

What Was I Made For? By Billie Eilish

I Did Something Bad by Taylor Swift Bloodsucker by CIL

Iris by Tommee Profitt and Ruelle

Could Have Been Me by The Struts

Zombie by The Cranberries

Blue by Billie Eilish

Who's Afraid of Little Old Me? By Taylor Swift

Vampire by Olivia Rodrigo

Courting Sin

Crystal Crist

Turn the page.

That's my good little

dove.

Prologue

Long ago, the gods ruled over Andonia.

Aisha, the goddess of life, and Ryuk, the god of death, reigned as their King and Queen. They lived peacefully among their people—mere mortals that worshipped their very *existence*. Society thrived, and the people of Andonia were happy in their small, little world. But nothing truly lasts forever. All life must meet its inevitable end. And for every *good* that resides in this world, there is an evil that feeds from it… A darkness that *drains* the light from its source until it's consumed.

The gods were all-powerful beings—the energy of their magic living within the very essence of their blood. Because of this power, the gods had strict rules that were unanimously agreed upon amongst them. The most important rule being that they could not be *together*—could not *love* one another. Their powers were too great, too dangerous, and the bitterness and hate brought on by love could not be risked. They *were* allowed to mate with mortals, and could even bear their children, but to have a child with another god... That would have been considered an *abomination*. The power that child could wield... They deemed it best to avoid the problem altogether.

Rosina, however—the goddess of earth—fell in love with Ryuk. In a world that Ryuk too often saw as dark, Rosina introduced a light he had never known. He shared her affection, but he knew that their feelings were wrong. After keeping their relationship a secret, he confessed his wrongdoings to his fellow gods—for the good of Andonia. He begged for their forgiveness. Not only for *him*, but for *Rosina* as well.

But, when Rosina learned of this, she saw his actions as a form of betrayal. Bitterness clouded her heart that had once shone with love. She targeted her anger at Ryuk for destroying their relationship and stealing her happiness away from her. So, when the gods decided it was finally time for them to ascend, she took actions of her own in rebellion. Using a magic so dark, so full of hate, she cursed the lords that the gods had chosen to rule over Andonia.

This act of defiance ignited a violent war between the gods. In this war, Rosina created vicious monsters that fed on the innocent lives of mortals. Without the strength to defend themselves against the evil roaming in the dark, thousands of lives were taken. And the seven lords did all they could to protect their people from the monsters that Rosina had manifested. In the end—with the help of the gods—the lords managed to kill Rosina, ending the terror she cast out into the land.

A prison was then created in another world, used to harbor these evil souls once they passed on. It trapped them there for all eternity, ensuring they would never reach Eden, their place of everlasting rest for the gentle souls of Andonia. In this *new* world, their souls would be tortured in penance for the lives that they destroyed.

Though the war had ended, people continued to live in fear. The land filled with dread at the idea of what could happen if the lords, too, grew angry with each other and decided to revolt against one another. So, to ease the tension before their departure, Minerva, the goddess of fate, declared a prophecy. Using a dagger made of the darkest material known on earth—obsidian—each of the gods offered a single drop of blood. They then painted a seven-pointed star in blood on a scroll blessed by Minerva herself. A queen had been promised. One born of pure blood, with the same star branded into her skin. This queen would be given to the people as protection, and would ward off any evil that threatened their world.

But what truly defines *good* and *evil*? Who decides *right* from *wrong*? What happens when truths become lies and those lies threaten to tear down an entire kingdom? What do you do when the ones who created you, and promised to protect you, become your enemies? In a game of lies and deceit, how can you truly know which truth to believe… and which one will get you killed?

Chapter 1

Tiptoeing quietly, I tried to keep the weight of my feet light against the wooden floor beneath me.

I passed *her* door and peeked inside. Her body seemed relaxed against her bed, her chest rising and falling slowly. With the luck of the gods, she hadn't woken when I descended from the attic. Making my way to the stairs, I grabbed the wooden railing as carefully as possible before walking down. The oak held my feather-light weight without making a sound, another prayer thankfully answered. When I made it to the front door, I unlatched it dreadfully slowly and slid outside. In a small effort to prevent *more* sounds, I twisted the handle before closing it. When it latched with barely a whisper, my body slumped over in relief.

Now, all I had to do was sneak past the guards.

Tying my hair back, I wrapped my curls with the thick fabric band in my hand and crept past the garden, toward the wall. The small clearing only took a few seconds to sneak through before I reached the bushes that bordered it. They hadn't always been there. The garden had always looked so dull to me. Close to five years prior to *this*, I had planted them and tended to the shrubs on my own. Little did I know just how handy they would come to be. The shrubs created large enough pockets of darkness against the back wall that could hide a petite person, such as myself, from the light of the moon.

The cracked stone came into view in front of me, but the sound of footsteps nearby caused my body to still. Quickly, I crept forward and pressed my back against the wall, hiding within the shadows my garden offered me. I held my breath as two guards passed me by, making their usual rounds. While, yes, I may have been weak, at least my small frame had been good for *something*. As long as I kept quiet within the darkness, the guards couldn't have known my presence there. After a few agonizing seconds, they disappeared up ahead without a sliver of suspicion. As an extra precaution, I held fast for a moment longer before moving quickly to the spot that I was looking for.

A couple of days before my most... *recent* escape attempt, I had come across a crack in the stone during one of my walks. Though it wasn't very large, I had been just small enough to fit through if I really tried. I had even portioned my meals for good measure, just in case. I *would* make it through. I *had* to. There were no other options. This would be my last chance to flee the future they had planned for me, and the death that would surely follow it.

With one more glance behind me, confirming no one lurked nearby, I turned to the side and pushed into the gap. Shoving my arm through first, I reached until I felt an exit. A premature smile stretched across my face at the thought of my escape being successful this time. As the feeling of freedom brushed against my fingertips, I began pushing the rest of my body through. But just as my chest grazed the inside of the gap, my other arm was grabbed from beside me, yanking me back through the wall. The stone scratched my arms and chest, leaving a stinging pain in its wake that didn't come close to the ache I felt, knowing my final attempt had now failed.

"What do you think you're doing, *Morrigan*?" Her words sounded more like a snake hissing as she turned me to face her. Then, I stood eye-to-eye with the woman that haunted every one of my nightmares.

While she may have been youthful on the outside, with beauty seemingly unmatched, there had always been an ugly cruelty in her eyes. Something in the way her brows furrowed together, causing a deep line in her perfectly smooth skin, felt like a peak into the real monster beneath the mask. When she would look at me, her lips would instantly purse into this permanent scowl that no one else seemed privy to. She always seemed so unhappy being my caretaker, which made me wonder why she ever volunteered to begin with.

The look she graced me with now, however, had been forged from the very depths of the anger I had spent years fueling. So many futile attempts at escaping, but I couldn't stop. I had to try one last time with my twenty-first birthday looming over my shoulder like a parasite waiting to consume the last of my courage.

"It is *well* past midnight, and the Unveiling is in a week." If you stared hard enough, you could practically see the smoke steaming from her ears. "You will march back up to your room, *now*. If I have to come out here again, you *will* be locked up." Letting go of my arm, I rubbed the spot where her fingers left a deep, red imprint.

I had no energy to argue. The flame had been extinguished by my failure, and sleep seemed to be the only thing left that I could do. So, with a quick roll of my eyes, I turned to walk away, but she stopped me with a cold, unwelcoming grip. *Idiot*, I thought as I willed myself to disappear with the wind. I wasn't against praying to the gods to just take me now and save me from my own recklessness.

"Did you just roll your eyes?" she asked, leaning her head close to mine.

I tried not to give away just how frightening her eyes looked in that moment. "I'm sorry, Priestess. It won't happen again." *At least not tonight.*

"You're lucky I'm tired." Lips pushed together, she let go of my arm and allowed me to make my way back to the house.

Priestess Maeryn was one of the only two women in my life. As a baby, my mother had given me to the priests and priestesses who claimed me to be *chosen* due to the mark on my arm. They brought me to this godsforsaken wasteland and never actually explained what that meant. Being *chosen*. The only thing I knew was that I would be given to the seven lords of Andonia on my twenty-first birthday.

Passing Maeryn's bedroom—on the second floor—I heard another door slide open. When I turned, Lady Guinevere leaned against the wall with her arms crossed over her chest. On the list of things that hurt me more than Maeryn's punishments, seeing disappointment on the Lady's face happened to be at the very top. But she didn't understand the freedom I craved so badly. Once they gave me away, she would be relieved of her duty. She could *live* her life still.

"My Lady," I whispered with my head down in shame. "I'm going back to my room. I'm sorry for disturbing you."

Sighing as gentle as ever, I heard her footsteps approach me. She placed a soft hand on my arm and I looked up at her. Her brown hair that normally covered her head, pinned up like a crown, now lay across her shoulders. The small waves shaped her face beautifully. She didn't look as young as Priestess Maeryn, but her beauty stood mountains above that witch in *my* eyes. Lady Guinevere had been tasked as my caretaker. While the priestess helped *shape* me, the lady helped *raise* me. The lady was the only mother I had ever known.

Her brown eyes pierced mine with a polite smile. "I'll walk with you," she said, her voice as smooth as silk.

I still remember the days that she would sing me to sleep as a child, drowning out the nightmares that kept me awake most nights. Without her songs, I likely never would have slept. Though, sometimes when my nightmares were bad enough that I couldn't wake from them, I would hear a voice—a man calling my name, commanding that I follow him. Using him as my anchor, I'd let his voice guide me until I would finally open my eyes. I had always assumed it to be my father's voice and never dared to tell anyone of it.

Walking arm in arm, we made our way down the hall to the stairs leading to the attic. "I've been stuck on these grounds for almost twenty-one years. The walls are so high I don't even know what it looks like beyond them."

Lady Guinevere always listened to my whining. I had always wondered if she, too, missed the outside. When she volunteered to be my caretaker, it meant forfeiting her freedom as well. But even if *hers* was only temporary, that didn't make it any less hard to give up your life for someone else. I used to ask her if she regretted her decision to raise me, but she would never humor such a statement. *"There isn't a place in this world I would rather be, Morrigan,"* is what she would tell me.

"The Unveiling is in a week, and you'll be allowed to leave then," she said, trying to sound reassuring as we reached the bottom of the stairs.

Free to *leave* really meant free to *die*.

Looking up into the attic—my *room*—I stared into the dark abyss waiting to swallow me whole. Priestess Maeryn would have loved to lock me inside of it until the Unveiling, if only to save herself of the troubles I caused. She always made sure to remind me just how much of an inconvenience my existence really was to her.

"At least I'll be free in Eden soon enough," I sneered.

Before Lady Guinevere could respond, I let go of her arm and climbed into my void.

My sleep had been disrupted by the same nightmare that haunted me for the past few months.

My limbs were being held down, and pain shot across my skin as they fed from me. My blood felt like it had been lit on fire—like poison ran parallel to my blood, pumping straight into my heart. It always ended the same. I would feel my body drain and then I would fall into darkness, burning as if I had been consumed by flames.

Sweat dripped from my forehead as I sat up from my bed and walked to the window. I cracked it as much as it would allow, letting the Fall air into my room. Bars had been placed over my window, just in case I tried breaking it to escape. Not that it would matter. The house was two stories high, *three* if you included the attic, and I would likely die from jumping off. Though, that death may have been quicker than the death I was destined to face.

The morning breeze found its way through the small opening and helped ease the tension at the center of my brows. "Morrigan!" *Oh look... the tension's back.* "It's time for your studies. Just because you decided not to sleep, doesn't mean you can slack off!" Maeryn's voice sounded no more soothing than that of nails on a chalkboard.

I rolled my eyes and moved to the closet, pulling out the same blue gown I wore every day. It was the plainest hue of blue that had ever been invented, and exceedingly dreary to the eyes. While it clung nicely to my body, it covered my arms and legs. The only skin showing was the small part of my chest that remained bare. Priestess Maeryn always reminded me that showing off was meant for *whores* and I didn't need to impress anyone when I was *chosen.*

Making my way down the stairs, I walked to the ground floor. We had a room for our studies in the back part of the house. It didn't actually *look* like a home. Or at least what I *thought* a home should look like. No paintings hung on the walls that were made of a plain, dark wood. The halls felt cold, not due to the insulation, but because they lacked the warmth of love within them. We had a kitchen, a bathing room—that we all shared—our bedrooms, and the study where Priestess Maeryn *taught* me every day.

The room consisted of two tables, one for me and one for her. We mostly worked on writing and reading together, but she wasn't the most patient teacher. If I stumbled over any words, or my writing looked too sloppy for her taste, it earned me a… lashing. She would make me place my hands on her desk and would strike my fingers with her cane. The number of blows usually correlated with how angry she was with me that day. Sometimes I could get away with two or three. But one time, I had angered her so badly that it earned me *ten* lashes. My fingers began bleeding by the eighth strike, but she didn't stop until she felt satisfied with my punishment.

I was *twelve.*

Sitting down, I watched her sip her tea as she stood from her desk. She inhaled a long, slow breath and closed her eyes, like teaching me was the worst part of her day. Her white gown was long, the hem trailing to the floor. Jeweled necklaces hung from her neck, and on her head lay a golden crown of leaves. Although the *chosen* couldn't show off in any way, priestesses, apparently, *could* in every possible way.

"Write your sentences," she ordered, placing a paper and pencil in front of me. "Your penmanship has been sloppy lately and I don't think the lords would appreciate a dull-witted maiden."

I rolled my eyes at the thought of it. I didn't know how being intelligent would serve me when I wouldn't be alive much longer. It felt like a waste of everyone's time. A quick, sharp pain shot across my fingers and I pulled them back, recoiling.

"Stop with the eyes. That won't be acceptable where you're going. And they'll do far worse as punishment," she warned.

I wrote until my hands cramped and Maeryn seemed satisfied enough with my work. She then handed me a textbook to read a passage from before allowing me to tend to my daily chores. Lately, all of my studies had been about *etiquette*—how I should act, what I should and shouldn't say. Gods, if that's how women were forced to live, I would accept the death waiting for me with open arms.

When we had finally finished for the day, I ate a quick breakfast and started in the kitchen, preparing tea for the priestess and Lady Guinevere. Then, I grabbed a brush to clean the floors. I scrubbed the kitchen, hallways, and rooms upstairs, including my own. With the guards filtering in and out all day, the floors would quickly be tracked in mud from their boots. So, deep cleaning them became a daily chore. After cleaning the floors, I took a brief lunch break and made my way to the garden—the only part of my day that brought some happiness. Once I finished clipping all of the dead leaves and petals, I watered the rest of the plants in the front and back gardens. With my chores behind me, the savory scent of supper curled through the air like a promise.

This had been my routine every day for nearly *ten years*.

Walking into the dining area, I saw Priestess Maeryn already seated at the head of our small, rectangular table. I sat across from Lady Guinevere, beside the priestess, and said nothing as I began to eat my food. Our meals consisted mostly of freshly grown vegetables from *my* garden, and a small amount of meat that the priestess would acquire each week. *"They won't want a* fat *maiden,"* is what she had said to me once when I asked for seconds. Though, I would likely taste far better if I had more meat on my bones. I didn't look *starved*, but no one had any plans handing me a sword and calling me Commander either.

"You're to be fitted tomorrow for your ceremonial gown," the priestess said as she placed her utensils on her plate.

She then tapped the plate, a silent order for me to clean up her mess. I stood with my head dipped down, as she preferred, the perfect picture of submission, and moved her dish to the sink.

"When the seamstress arrives, you will not speak unless I give you permission to do so," she reminded me.

Allowing myself a single roll of my eyes without her seeing it, I finished washing her plate. "Yes, Priestess Maeryn," I replied, though a touch of conviction might have sold it better. Turning back toward the table, I clasped my hands low in front of me. "May I be excused?"

Just as the priestess turned around, as if to say something more, Lady Guinevere quietly answered, "You may."

Chapter 2

The seamstress arrived the next day and I made sure to do exactly as the priestess ordered as she took my measurements.

I had been on my best behavior to try and avoid any problems for the next couple of days. There were too many things I needed to think about with the Unveiling approaching so quickly. Before I knew it, my time had run out. No more useless attempts at escaping. I had one more night before they would hand me over to the *"Lords of Sin,"* a nickname I heard the guards say one night. Naaz, Dormius, Cain, Cassius, Eris, Dez, and the most ruthless one of them all... *Kaiden*. One night, as the guards were playing a game of cards, I could hear them whispering, *"That poor girl is going to be their next meal."*

In my textbooks, I learned of a ceremony that took place once a month in each of the seven territories. A villager would offer themselves to the lords. The lords survived off of their blood, and, for some reason, I would be handed to them on a silver platter. The guards would make little comments as the Unveiling approached about how the lords were going to "eat me up" and I *knew* that couldn't have meant anything good.

I sat on my windowsill, looking through the barred glass at the stone wall of my prison when a soft knock sounded from the attic door on the floor. "You can come in," I called out.

The door pushed up and Lady Guinevere emerged from the stairs, smiling softly at me as she made her way to the end of my bed. As she patted the spot beside her, I moved from my seat and joined her.

"I know you're scared. I know you have these crazy thoughts in your head about what's happening tomorrow. And I want to ease your mind as much as I'm allowed to." She pulled me into her, and I laid my head on her shoulder.

"When you were born, you bore the mark of the *chosen*. The gods had promised a girl to be given to the lords." With a gentle touch, she pushed my curls behind my ear and caressed my hair. "They've waited centuries for you, Morrigan. It is not my place to tell you why or *what* will happen when you leave, but know that you will be safe." *Safe.* I had never known Lady Guinevere to tell such lies through her teeth.

"I heard the guards speak of them, of what they do to humans," I whispered.

"Don't listen to those small-minded men. They know nothing of the lords, my love. The offerings are voluntary. No one is forced to participate. They do it purely out of love for their lords. You will be safe Mor, I promise."

Looking up at her with every ounce of sincerity, I made one final plea. "Don't let them take me," I begged. But she ignored it, shushing me before laying down beside me.

She began humming her lullaby, a song she only ever shared with me. There were no words to it, but the melody soothed me, nonetheless. The idea of sleeping sent a current of fear through my body, knowing that, when I woke, I would be sent to a new prison. But, in Lady Guinevere's comforting arms, I fell asleep listening to her beautiful voice and prayed that it would be enough to keep the monsters at bay this time.

When I woke, Lady Guinevere was gone, and I could hear voices downstairs.

They were likely preparing for my departure. Against my better judgment, I got dressed and made my way downstairs, where Lady Guinevere and Priestess Maeryn were waiting. With barely a *"good morning"* from either of them, they escorted me to the front of the house to a carriage outside. I stepped inside and the two women joined me. And after a couple of agonizing minutes, the carriage began to move.

In the absence of small talk, the carriage shrank around me, and my hands trembled from the weight of the silence. In an effort to soothe me, Lady Guinevere grasped my hand with hers and squeezed it. This had been my first time ever leaving my home and, of course, the windows had been covered from the outside, preventing me from actually seeing anything. All I craved was a glimpse of what I had spent so many years trying to escape to. With the help of Lady Guinevere, some of my tension seemed to melt away, but I didn't miss the way Priestess Maeryn would glare at our interlocked fingers.

I never truly understood her anger toward me. She treated my misery like it was her life's ambition. I would have thought that someone *chosen* for something would be treated with basic kindness at the very least.

As a young child, Lady Guinevere would tease that Maeryn's menacing actions were rooted in jealousy over *me* being *chosen*. Such implications would have gotten Lady Guinevere in heaps of trouble if the priestess had ever heard her accusations. But it didn't make any sense to me. Why *choose* to die? Especially when you've been gifted with eternal life and beauty.

The carriage came to a stop, and my entire body stiffened like a board. I looked to Lady Guinevere, and she squeezed my hand with reassurance. *"You will be safe, Mor,"* she seemed to repeat once more with her eyes. Reaching beside her, she pulled out a black veil and placed it over me. I could barely see anything with it on, just outlines and shapes.

"No one is allowed to see you before the lords do. You can remove it after the Unveiling," she spoke softly, squeezing my hand once more before the carriage doors opened.

Both women exited first, and one of them helped me out, though I couldn't see which one. Two hands linked with my arms on each side as they escorted me forward. The vague structure of large doors were visible through the thick fabric of my veil, and guards greeted us as we entered. Shaking again from my nerves, the force of fingers digging into one of my arms distracted me enough to stop.

"Stop shaking," the witch hissed at me.

"Yes, Priestess," I whispered in return, trying everything to settle the nerves that continued to stir in my chest.

We were then escorted to a room where I could finally remove the veil from my face, only for me to change into my gown. This gown looked completely different than anything I had ever worn before. The sleeves fell around my shoulders, revealing my bare skin, and the neckline almost dipped between my breasts. Though the hem of the dress fell down to the floor, there was a thin slit that ran up both of my thighs, partially revealing my legs when I walked. A small part of me wanted to glance at the priestess, knowing she would be giving me a snide look with a crude insult hiding behind her teeth.

Lady Guinevere had pinned my curls to my head, with a few strands clinging to my ears. Against the dark, black dress, my skin somehow looked even paler. But one quick look at my face and I... I dared to think that I may have actually looked... *pretty*. Slipping into the heels they provided me with, I stumbled trying to find my balance. I couldn't fathom why women would want to *torture* themselves in this way.

"Sit," the priestess ordered as she approached me with two diamond earrings in the palm of her hand.

Without warning, she placed the sharp end of the jewelry against my ear lobe and forced it in, piercing my skin and ripping a hole into it. Sucking in a sharp breath, I snapped my head toward her and grabbed my injured ear.

"Don't be so *dramatic*, Morrigan. My ears are pierced, as are Lady Guinevere's. Turn your head so I can do the other one," she insisted as she rolled her eyes at my hesitation.

I followed her orders and tried not to flinch as she stuck the other earring in. With a cloth, she wiped the blood from my lobes and then had me stand from the chair, placing the black veil over my face again. They were all going through an awful amount of effort to make me look good before my inevitable death. I wondered if, perhaps, the lack of material on my dress had been devised to expose more skin for them. Maybe it would be easier to rip off of me in the process as they mutilated my body.

Linked together again, both ladies escorted me to another room. I could barely see the doors open in front of me. With it so dimly lit, my vision had been almost completely obscured. The faint sound of hushed conversations seemed to stop altogether when they noticed my presence. *Great. Well,* that *was welcoming.*

The priestess let go of my arm, but I could still feel Guinevere's calming presence beside me. "I have brought the *chosen one* to you on her twenty-first birthday. With your permission, I will begin the Unveiling," she announced loudly. The room had to have been large because I could hear her voice echo against the walls.

No one verbally answered, but they must have gestured for her to begin because Guinevere began walking me forward. Unfortunately for her, I couldn't seem to move. My feet were stuck to the ground, even as I willed them to walk. Guinevere gently tried to usher me forward again and a lump began to form in my throat.

What if I run? How far can I get? Would the death be quicker that way?

"Morrigan. Come," the priestess demanded, but I *couldn't.* When I didn't move, she hissed, "Morrigan, *now.*"

The temptation to run was so great that I could feel myself starting to turn, when a sultry voice called out to me, "Are you scared, Princess?"

Heavy, but somehow also *light,* footsteps approached me with a slow confidence that only frightened me more. Acting on pure instinct, even with the veil covering me, I kept my head down like it would hide my fear. Two perfectly polished black shoes stopped in front of me. The pants he wore were a deep, blood red. With my breath quickening, my pulse seemed to match its tempo.

"Finish your speech and leave," he ordered her.

Through the fear that rose in my stomach, a droplet of humor blossomed from hearing someone order Priestess Maeryn around. I almost smirked a little, until I remembered they were likely growing impatient. And the moment the Unveiling was finished, my death would be next. With any luck, it would follow immediately after Lady Guinevere and the priestess took their leave. Unless they planned to drag it out... To get *every* possible use of my body...

It took the priestess a moment to speak; she seemed unsure of how to respond. Such a *new* feeling for her. "The *chosen* will now be unveiled. Allow me—"

"I got it," he interrupted her.

Long fingers curled under the tips of my veil and I held my breath as it lifted with a slow gracefulness that didn't seem human. I didn't have the heart nor the courage to look up with the light finally filtering back into my eyes. But against my own will, his fingers touched my chin and raised my face. When my eyes finally met his, that breath I had been holding escaped my lungs without warning. Standing before me was the most beautiful man I had ever laid eyes on. Though the only men in my life were the guards that patrolled the grounds, I knew that something in his beauty seemed unworldly. Like it had been created, not born.

His blonde locks were pushed back, tucked behind his ears, and his mesmerizing blue eyes shot into my soul. It pierced my chest with invisible arrows. He had a strong, but soft, nose, and his smile matched the twinkling of his eyes. It lifted his cheek bones that were painted the perfect shade of pink, causing my own to flush as his thumb caressed my skin.

"She's a twig," called a voice from behind him. But I didn't look away from the man in front of me as he held me in a daze. "Did you starve her for twenty-one years?"

"She's beautiful." If his fingers weren't touching my skin, my knees might have buckled beneath me. His voice felt like a trance that I couldn't escape, and his lips seemed to call my name.

Clearing her throat as if to remind them of her presence, she began to say, "If I may…"

"Leave," he chimed in, the sound of his words like an unsung melody playing in my head. "You may leave."

"My lord," she scoffed, "I haven't even started."

"This all feels very… *archaic*. We know her purpose and are no longer in need of you," said the same man who had called me a twig seconds before.

Priestess Maeryn cleared her throat once more and I could feel Guinevere walk behind me, making her way toward the priestess. "We will retire to our quarters then, my *lords*. If we are needed just—"

"You won't be," the blonde man hummed as he took another step toward me, pushing our bodies closer together.

What is wrong *with you, Morrigan? Gods, snap out of it and stop drooling at this man who's* literally *about to* kill *you.*

Doors closed somewhere nearby, and the man in front of me dropped his hands instantly. Like a tidal wave, my body had been overcome with a dreadful emptiness in the wake of his touch. Like he stole every bit of energy that I had conserved. I tried blinking away the confusing sensation, but even my eyelids felt heavy now. The sound of steps around me had my eyes shooting up and I noticed two other men approaching. They were both tall—They were *all* tall. One of them had short brown hair and strikingly blue eyes, darker than the first one. He wore a black suit with golden accents that he seemed to flaunt without any humility. Fixing the cuff on his wrist, he seemed unbothered by my existence and I noted the large, similarly golden rings that decorated his fingers.

I might have been sheltered my entire life, but I knew a *prick* when I saw one.

"Do you know why you're here?" he asked, blinking slowly as he looked at me like he had far better things to do.

"No," I lied.

"The gods have *chosen* you." An uncomfortable feeling washed over me as his eyes roamed down my body and back to my face—his expression unreadable. "Before the gods ascended, they decided that having seven lords ruling Andonia only caused more divide. But they couldn't have just *anyone* sitting on the throne. They promised a *chosen one* who would select one of *us* to ascend to the throne. A woman created by the gods themselves." The way he spoke the last part sounded almost as if he mocked the very idea of it.

"I'm sorry," I said, confused and still a little overcome. "Why am *I* choosing who's going to become king?"

"Because, Princess," the blonde one purred as he reached out and placed my hand in his, "*you* will be our *queen*."

My body seemed to heat under his touch, a feeling I wasn't used to, and my mouth felt painfully dry. "I don't understand."

"I think we can *both* agree on *that*," the prick muttered, unamused. "Nevertheless, you are the first person to have been born with the mark." Looking around, I could see the rest of them still seated in their thrones. One in particular had my stomach turning. Too far away to actually see him, his looming presence made him all too obvious. I knew exactly who that darkness belonged to. The man in front of me cleared his throat, reclaiming my attention. "You will spend seven weeks with each of us, and by the end of the year, you will make a decision. You, and whomever you *choose*, will be crowned."

My head now felt ten pounds lighter and I placed the back of my hand above my brows to cool the heat rising above them. "This doesn't make any sense."

"Now *that* we can most definitely agree on." Without another glance, he walked away with his hands in his pockets.

"Don't mind Eris. The only thing he cares for is his gold," the blonde one whispered. "I'm Dez." His smile seemed to somehow brighten the room around us, but my head still reeled from what Eris had just said.

While the other four men that sat on their thrones began to leave, the bigger one that walked down with Eris ran up to Dez and me. He had copper red hair with curls that bounced as he moved. He wore a tight-fitted dark orange suit that barely seemed to fit over his muscles. His frame would have been frightening enough if it wasn't for the broad, contagious smile that stretched across his face.

"I'm Cassius." After every nightmare I had through the years, these men were nothing like I expected them to be. Well... *Eris* came close enough.

"So..." I whispered nervously. "You're... *not* going to eat me?"

Dez and Cassius shared a look and the former leaned in until his lips brushed my ear. "Do you want us to?"

Before I could even process the conflicting emotions I felt at that question, Cassius threw his head back in a deep laugh. He slammed his hand down on my shoulder, causing me to almost jump out of my skin as he sighed.

"I like you." He turned his head to look over his shoulder. "Alwin! Take us home!"

A man jogged toward us and immediately extended his arm. When Dez and Cassius each placed a hand on it, I foolishly followed with my own. Within seconds, darkness surrounded us, swallowing every ray of light until I could no longer see. My body felt as though invisible ropes were pulling me in multiple directions, like it didn't know which way it wanted to go. It didn't hurt, but it was far from a pleasant experience. Thankfully, it didn't last long. A few seconds later, light filtered in with a blinding shock and a strong wave of nausea had the bile in my stomach bubbling toward my throat.

I covered my mouth before it could rise any further and I felt Cassius's large hand against my neck. His palm started out cold but began to warm rapidly, turning almost *hot*. The sickness retreated as quickly as it came, but now I felt left with more questions than answers.

"How did you do that?" I asked him, stepping back from his embrace. His laugh appeared to be the only response I would get as he placed his hand against my back and gestured for me to walk beside him.

They escorted me to a room that was roughly the size of my entire home... Well, my *old* home.

I guess I'll have to get used to saying that eventually.

Floral designs painted the walls and there were portraits hung *everywhere*. I had never been inside of such a vibrant room. The only things that hung within my attic were the few drawings that Maeryn allowed me to keep from my childhood. It had only been due to Lady Guinevere convincing her that I might go crazy without something to look at during my downtime.

In this room, the bed *alone* seemed almost the size of my attic—four beautiful wooden pillars connected to a large structure that hovered over the bed. Even the headboard had been painted a beautiful shade of orange, with intricate swirls all over the carved wood.

"This will be your room for the next seven weeks. You'll stay with *me* first." I could hear Cassius's smile in his voice as he spoke, but I was too enthralled by the room around me to give him my attention. "The priestess and lady will help you adjust to your new home at each transition, but they'll only be staying for a week each time."

"I'll be alone? *Here*?" I swallowed nervously.

Then, Dez leaned in toward my ear again, something he seemed inclined to do a lot. "We don't bite," he whispered, almost startling me, "unless you want us to."

Cassius laughed again behind me, but I shivered, moving away from him with a small blush spreading across my cheeks.

"I still don't understand," I admitted, walking toward my new bed. Running my hand over the bright orange silk sheets, it felt like running my hand through water. I turned back around and noticed Dez stalking toward me.

He brushed a small, black curl that had fallen in front of my face back behind my ear. Then, his hand traveled down my neck, to my shoulder and gently moved my hair, revealing my skin. His thumb massaged over my birthmark branded there. It resembled a star. But instead of having five points to it, there were seven.

Seven gods… Seven lords…

"*A maiden would be born with the markings of the true queen,*" he said as if reading it from a book. "That's what we were told—That's what you were *born* with. No one else in the *world* has this mark."

"What if it's just a coincidence?" I dared to ask. "What if I'm not this queen you think I'm supposed to be?" Every part of my skin that he touched itched with a need I didn't quite understand, distracting me.

"I can smell it, in your blood. Power…" His voice fell quieter, like he too had fallen into a trance. With his eyes pointed at my neck, something about his stare made my body warm with curiosity… and *fear*. "You're bleeding," he noted, stepping closer to me.

Pulling me against him with a tender touch, he lowered his lips toward my ear. My eyes instinctively shut on their own and I gasped when I felt his tongue touch my lobe. The nerves on my skin buzzed and a pool of heat sat low in my belly. *This isn't right. This isn't...* My thoughts faded into nothingness as he glided his tongue down to my neck with torturous ease.

Cassius cleared his throat behind him, and Dez pulled back, blinking a few times as if he had woken from a dream. His usual confidence dissolved back into his blue eyes and he smiled at me. "I'll see you in seven weeks." Kissing my cheek once, he let out a soft chuckle as he left the room, and Cassius smiled politely before closing the door, leaving me to my thoughts.

The only positive thing that fluttered into my mind was the fact that I wouldn't have to deal with the priestess ordering me around anymore. I stared at the room, really taking in the cards that I had been dealt. But even with all of the space, the walls seemed to close in a little.

I'm alone... I thought to myself, *Stuck with a man I don't know... In a castle filled with strangers...*

Maybe death *would* have been easier.

Chapter 3

 ith the unexpected sound of my door opening, my eyes
shot open and I could hear light footsteps shuffling
throughout the room.

I jolted up into a seated position, which seemed to startle the three
ladies carrying towels, gowns, and accessories in their hands. Just as I
began to ask what the hell they were doing in my room, a fourth one
entered from a different set of doors. She looked much older than the other
three and seemed completely unfazed by the expression on my face.

"Your bath is being heated, Your Grace. Our lord sent gowns for you
to choose from for your dinner attire." She gestured to the dresses that the
ladies had hung on the wall on full display. All of them contained orange
accents. It was *clearly* a favorite color of his.

"Wait…" Rubbing my eyes, I tried to convince my body to actually wake up enough to get off of the bed. "Dinner attire?"

The younger girls giggled a little but quickly shut their mouths as the older one shot them a warning glare. When she turned back to me, she approached slowly until she stopped beside my bed. Her clothes were similar to the kind of gowns I wore back at home. Simple and conservative, but different shades of ivory and brown, instead of my usual blue. "You've slept the day away, Your Grace."

"Slept the… I slept the entire day?" She nodded in reply, and I exhaled slowly, grounding myself. Maeryn had always instilled in me how important it was for a lady to be up and ready in the morning. Wasting other people's time wouldn't be tolerated in the real world, especially a *lord's* time. Cassius had likely been furious that I spent my day in bed, rather than tending to him. "I'm sorry. The bed was just so… *comfortable*. I didn't mean—"

"You may rest as long as you'd like to, Your Grace. If you choose to retire back to your room after dinner, feel free so do so. Lord Cassius just thought it would be best to get some food in you. We don't want you feeling unwell."

"You can call me Mor," I insisted.

"Your Grace," she replied with hands clasped in front of her. Similar to how I would present myself to the priestess.

It didn't seem to be a battle worth fighting at the moment. So, I stood and made my way toward the gowns. Picking the least flashy one I could find, I showed it to her and she waved at the younger ladies. They took the motion as a command to move the rest of the gowns into a closet beside the large vanity against the wall.

I was then ushered by the older woman into the bathing room where she helped take off the black gown. As realization rushed in, I turned away from her as quickly as I could, hoping she couldn't see. "I've got it," I assured her, though her eyes looked at me in clear suspicion.

Stepping into the warm bath, I had to suppress the small amount of nausea rolling through me. *That's what you get for sleeping the day away,* I could practically hear Maeryn's voice scolding me in my own mind. The hot water soothed that ache as my body sank into the tub, and the aroma of whatever oils they had used filled the air. It smelled of pumpkin with a little bit of spice that complemented it perfectly. Priestess Maeryn would only allow cold baths, lukewarm at best. *"Cold water is best for the skin, Morrigan. We wouldn't want you getting wrinkles now, would we?"*

Without warning me, one of the ladies grabbed my arm and began rubbing a wet, soapy cloth over it. I yanked it back and held my arms over my chest, covering myself. "Thank you, but I think I can scrub myself."

The older woman chuckled and dismissed them, but sat in a chair beside the tub, giving me some distance. "I apologize," she said quietly. "We are not used to a lady staying in these halls, much less a *princess.* They only wish to help."

"*Princess*? I'm not a—"

"But you *are*, Your Grace," she reminded me. "You are to be the first queen that Andonia has seen in centuries." Sensing my discomfort, she stood with a kind smile on her lips. "I'll let you bathe. When you're finished, join us in the room so we can help you dress."

I didn't want to waste their time. So, I washed myself quickly and stepped out of the tub, wrapping my body in the towel she had placed on top of the chair. When I reentered the room, I only saw the older woman standing beside my vanity; the younger girls nowhere in sight.

Noticing my confusion, the older woman smiled at me. "I thought you'd be more comfortable with just me for tonight."

In that, she was correct. I didn't need anyone gawking over me, making me feel like a caged animal they wanted to stare at. This entire situation felt peculiar enough. What I really needed *now* was time to adjust to it all.

Sitting down, the woman pulled my hair over the back of the chair and began squeezing it with a towel, soaking up the water. I had so much hair, I knew it would take hours to actually dry. But she put forth her best effort before beginning to brush through the curls. Thankfully, the water pulled most of my knots free, and I could actually enjoy the gentle massage of the bristles against my scalp. As I leaned into it, I thought of all the times Lady Guinevere had brushed my hair for me as a child. How gentle she had been.

I suddenly caught her staring at me through the mirror and blushed in embarrassment. Straightening myself in my chair, I cleared my throat. "Sorry," I mumbled. "It felt nice."

The smile she gave me in response eased my mind some as she began pinning my curls up. "There," she beamed. "Let's get you dressed."

She escorted me to the dining hall and the sight of it took my breath away.

The hall was *enormous*. A golden chandelier hung from the high ceiling, and beautiful candles were hanging along the walls in sconces, illuminating the room. The walls had grand designs painted all over them, with large windows that displayed the night sky outside. The table that sat in the center of it all could easily fit 20 people, if not more. And on top of the beautiful wood laid a platter of food big enough to feed an army.

I hadn't even noticed Priestess Maeryn and Lady Guinevere until one of them cleared their throat, pulling me from my distraction. I quickly made my way toward them, where the priestess and lady sat across from each other, with Cassius at the head of the table. He seemed to be finishing his plate already, what might have been filled with meats now looked cluttered by fleshless bones. The ladies, however, hadn't even touched the display of fruits and vegetables on their plates yet. I felt bad, realizing that they had likely been waiting on *me*.

When Cassius finally noted my arrival, his face lit up with a wide grin. Standing from his chair, he looked down at the priestess. "Please move a seat down so the princess may sit beside me," he asked her politely.

Though she bowed her head in agreement, I could see the slight tick of her jaw that made her annoyance evident. Nonetheless, she moved down, and Cassius quickly held the chair for me to sit and pushed it in. I had never been so catered to in my life.

Beside me, the priestess scooped up my plate and leaned over to place food on it, when Cassius grunted a noise to get her attention. "The princess isn't a child," he said with a laugh. "I think she can choose what food she'd like to eat." As he spoke, he began piling more food onto his plate, and I couldn't stop my eyes from widening at the portions.

I didn't understand how he kept his physique if he ate like *this* every day. Did his servants eat this well, also? I cringed at the title that I knew they were labeled. It felt like such a negative word, even in my own mind. They *worked* for him. They weren't slaves. They were… *staff.* That sounded much better. If I truly were to become queen, that would be my first official change.

The priestess's glare caught my attention, and I didn't quite know what to do in that moment. With an insincere smile, Priestess Maeryn finally decided to respond. "She adheres to a very strict diet, My Lord. Her small stomach is simply not used to your… vast appetite."

The smile on Cassius's face faltered slightly and he looked my way, ignoring the priestess. "Would you like to try it?" he asked me.

Shooting the priestess a nervous glance, I saw that she had averted my gaze and picked at the food in front of her. Lady Guinevere caught my eyes with a sweet smile of approval and I nodded at Cassius. With a twinkle in his eyes, he stood and leaned over, grabbing my plate and walking around the table as he made his selection. He placed almost one of everything on top of each other. Then, when it could hold no more, he placed it in front of me and sat back down excitedly.

"Then, you can try it all," he said.

"Thank you," I offered quietly before picking up a piece of meat with my fork that seemed unfamiliar to the kind I had eaten before. Unable to resist the hunger twisting in my gut, I took a bite. A low moan escaped me as the rich juices burst across my tongue. It may have been the most delicious piece of meat I had ever tasted before. But that wasn't exactly saying much. Cassius laughed at my reaction and even Lady Guinevere giggled as she ate her own food

"What is this?" I asked him before picking up another piece.

"It's pork, *Princess*," The way the title rolled from his tongue hit differently than how the woman had said it earlier that day. It made a million butterflies spring to life in the pit of my stomach. "What did you eat back at your home?"

I looked at the priestess, expecting her to answer. But before she could open her mouth, Cassius chimed in again.

"You can speak for yourself here. You are royalty now; you do not answer to anyone anymore. Not even me."

I felt her patience had been tested enough and simply replied with, "Nothing as extravagant as this. I'm grateful. Thank you." There was a wariness in Cassius's eyes as he looked between the priestess and me, but it seemed to disappear with a blink as he returned to his food.

We sat in silence for a short while, and I enjoyed every bite, savoring the taste from each item he put on my plate. I hadn't realized I ate every piece of it until my last bite and noticed the empty porcelain sitting in front of me. Cassius broke out in another fit of laughter that seemed to be the very essence of his personality.

"You eat like a king, Princess." Slightly embarrassed, I grabbed the golden chalice next to my plate and took a sip of the water inside of it. "It's a compliment. I promise," he assured me.

Priestess Maeryn still wouldn't look my way, and I hated how much it bothered me. Regardless of how deep my hatred ran for her, this strange part of me yearned for her approval. I only had her and Lady Guinevere as the women in my life, and for too many years I begged for a portion of her love that I had never been worthy of in her eyes... A truth I seemed to be incapable of truly accepting.

Wanting to escape the shame those emotions brought me, I stood from my seat and addressed Cassius. "May I be excused?" I asked him, keeping my head down.

With a sigh, he set down his utensils. "You don't *need* my permission... but yes." I pushed my chair back in and reached for my plate, when he placed his hand on mine. "My servants will collect it." *There's that word again.* Ignoring it, I nodded my gratitude before exiting the hall.

I'm not sure if they had waited for me the entire dinner, but one of the ladies stood at the door to escort me back to my room. A part of me felt disappointed to see that it wasn't the older one. Regardless, upon our return, she helped me dress into a thin, comfortable nightgown, and left me alone for the night. Even without their commentary, I knew that at least one of them had seen what I so desperately tried to hide. I just hoped they wouldn't speak of it to Cassius.

In the absence of anything to keep me busy, I wandered my room with a busy mind, looking for something to tame it. I ran my hands over the gold-plated vanity and stopped in front of the tall mirror that hung next to my closet. With the pins removed from my hair, my curls now hung down my back, spilling over my breasts as well. My white gown's sleeves were a little transparent and stretched down to my wrists, but the front seemed a bit thicker, with lace covering my chest.

You don't deserve this. Any of it.

Nothing could drown out the self-pity that floated endlessly through my mind as I looked at my reflection. So, I abandoned it and continued looking around the room. On the other side of my closet hung a wide portrait, painted with such expert realism that it drew me in. It was a drawing of the lords, *all* of them. Cassius had his usual smile, with his hand grabbing Dez's shoulder, a clear indication of their bond. Eris sat moping in his chair with the same emotionless expression he graced me with in the throne room. I couldn't place the rest of the faces with names, but one stood out the most and could be recognized by anyone.

His black locks were as dark as his eyes, a bottomless void of shadows. An anger radiated from his glare, an anger that seemed to burn hotter than any fire could. He didn't wear an inch of color, and a small, but noticeable, scar crossed over his left eyebrow. Under his shirt, there seemed to be drawings on his skin unlike anything I had ever seen before. And even though I knew it was just a painting, it felt as though he could see me through it. The idea sent a chill straight down my spine and I shook it off, migrating back to my bed.

You don't belong here, I almost whispered out loud before I closed my eyes and begged for sleep to take me.

The priestess greeted me the next morning with a more than sour look on her face.

Her gaze usually held a certain threshold of disdain, but another emotion seemed to peek through her scowl—more *angry* than disappointed. Shoving my dresses around in my closet, she let out a loud huff before selecting a gown for me to wear. She hadn't shared *why* she insisted on helping me, but I knew it couldn't have been out of the kindness that her heart wasn't actually capable of.

With the gown in hand, she looked over it with her lips curled. "He has you dressing like a *whore*," she jeered.

The gowns may not have been as... modest as the dress I typically wore, but they still covered everything. They were vibrant, filled with so many colors that I could barely take the time to name.

"You ate like a slob last night." It wasn't her words that made me pause, but the tone in which she said them. Every syllable clicked with harsh enunciation, clearly intentional. "We are in the presence of a *lord*. Maidens do not eat like *pigs*."

But I wasn't a maiden, was I? I would be Queen one day. I wondered how *queens* ate. The jabs would have hurt more if Cassius's voice hadn't played in the back of my mind. *"You eat like a king."*

As I chuckled at the memory, Priestess Maeryn whirled me around, her fingers digging into my chin. "Do you find disobedience humorous, Morrigan?"

"No," I said, quickly fixing my face.

"No, what?" Her fingers pushed further into my skin, making my jaw hurt.

"No, Priestess Maeryn," I answered through clenched teeth.

I could still feel the soreness in my bone after she released me. "You may be *Queen* one day, but you will still be ruled by your *King*. They will not tolerate your insolence the way that *we* have."

Before I could stop myself, a hateful laugh slipped past my lips and I instantly threw my hands over my mouth. "I'm sorry!" I said, muffled against my fingers.

With absolute composure, she stared at me. And as I watched her chest rise with her breath, it felt like time had slowed for a moment. "I think another lesson is needed." Her back straightened, barely noticeable, but enough to make me almost flinch. "I disregarded your last escape attempt, and it seems that decision may have been a disservice to you." She let out a sigh that made my chest begin to hurt as it tightened. "Hands on the pillar, Morrigan."

"Priestess," I pleaded as I battled the tears that threatened to fall from my eyes. It would only further humiliate me, and in turn, add to her sadistic satisfaction.

"Hands. On. The. *Pillar*." Each word cut like a knife plunging into my chest. As my jaw tensed, I made my way toward the bed. She had me lower my nightgown and I put my head against the pillar as I held it with both hands, waiting.

It had been a couple of weeks since she resorted to this kind of punishment. She *hated* being embarrassed, which Cassius had flawlessly executed. But, deeper than that... she despised me. And that was all the reason she needed to do this.

Digging my nails into the wood, I held my bottom lip between my teeth as she struck. The belt licked my skin with a hard sting and I tried to hold back any sound that might encourage her. A second strike hit me, and I could feel the skin tear a little. Even as my eyes burned, I denied my body the sweet relief of crying. I wouldn't give her the gratification of watching me break. The seventh strike, though… it brought me to my knees. I could no longer chase away the emotions rippling through me and I panted as I turned to look up at her.

When she threw the belt to the floor, a small streak of my own blood glistened against the leather, like it was mocking me. "You're *no one,* Morrigan," she hissed. "You'd do well to remember that."

The moment the door latched behind her, a violent sob brought me the rest of the way to the floor. Seven more cuts… Which meant seven more scars that no man would ever want to gaze upon. Seven more cracks in my already broken soul that no man would want to share. I had been convinced that the gods chose me as a sick and twisted joke. A broken queen for their broken world.

How disgustingly poetic of them.

Chapter 4

stayed in my room that day, praying my absence wouldn't cause further punishment.

Cassius had visited my door several times, asking if I was alright, but he never entered the room. Though I felt grateful for his concern, it didn't change the fact that I couldn't face him with the wounds still fresh on my skin. Out of kindness, he had my meals sent to my room, along with a few books to keep me company. A part that seemed to hurt almost worse than the wounds themselves, was the fact that Lady Guinevere never came to see me. When the priestess would punish me, Lady Guinevere would almost always come to console me afterward. She had been the only comfort I had through the pain.

An unwelcome sense of hatred seemed to wash over me at the thought of it—hatred toward *her* for allowing me to endure the torture my life consisted of.

For not protecting me.

And also, hatred toward my mother for leaving me all those years ago.

The days blurred by as I sat in my room, laying in my new bed, staring at the new walls that held me prisoner just the same. I would allow the staff to come and go, but I refused to let them assist me with a bath. They didn't question me. But I could see the worry in their eyes. A part of me wanted to run back to that little house and hide myself in the attic again. Better an evil you knew than an evil you didn't—a fact that I had grown used to. This new world would sooner drown me, and I could do nothing to stop it.

Sunday seemed to come faster than I expected it to, and I knew the priestess and Lady Guinevere would be leaving. The door to my room opened, and a familiar voice peeked through. The older woman, who seemed to delegate to the younger ladies, stood in my doorway. I had actually been quite pleased to see her, a *somewhat* familiar face. "Your Grace," she greeted me happily.

But when I turned to exit my bed, I accidentally dropped the sheets I had been holding around me. For a split second, my back was exposed and I stood swiftly, turning to face her so she wouldn't see. But, even if her expression didn't show it, something in her eyes did. She had seen them.

"My lord has grown quite worried about you and asked me to convince you to join everyone for breakfast." The tone in her voice held nothing but kindness and sincerity as she approached me. "May I assist you with a bath, Your Grace? It'll just be me this morning, no one else."

Turning my head, I looked at the standing mirror. My curls were tangled and knotted, and I looked as bad as I had felt all week. Returning my gaze to the woman, I nodded. And without another word, she made her way to the bathing room and prepped the water.

We continued in silence as she helped me into the bath. I tried not to flinch away when she brought the cloth to my back and ran a light touch over the tender skin that still seemed to itch. "I will stay quiet if that is what you ask of me, Your Grace," she whispered to me as she began washing my hair, "but Lord Cassius can help you. If you tell him—"

"No. Don't tell him... *Please*." I turned quickly, grabbing her wrist with pleading eyes.

She cleared her throat as she nodded. "Okay," is all that she said, and I let go of her, turning back around.

After the bath, she pinned up my hair but left half of it down. The curls that hung down covered any scars on my skin that would have been visible through the back of my gown. I wanted to cry with gratitude but instead shared a knowing look with her through the mirror.

"Let's get you dressed, sweet girl," she said and placed a comforting kiss on the top of my head.

As she brought my dress to the bed and laid it on top of the sheets, I watched her every movement. Had she worked for Cassius long? Did she have any children of her own? She seemed to spend so much time at the castle. Where was her family? "I never asked your name."

Turning back to me, she placed her hand out as a gesture. "Shae," she answered with her brightening smile.

She looked closer to Lady Guinevere's age and was just as beautiful. Her eyes were a deep, chocolate brown with swirls of honey that danced at the center of them. Her skin was only a few shades lighter than her dark brown hair, which had a few grey streaks at the roots. As I held her hand, she pulled me slowly toward the bed and helped me remove my robe, careful not to touch my back. She had been so gentle with me without requiring an explanation—A kindness I could never repay.

When we were finished, she went an extra mile and escorted me herself to the dining hall, with her hand in mine the entire distance. She didn't follow me inside, so I kept my head down and made my way to my seat, saying nothing as I filled my plate. But I could feel Cassius's stare. Not wanting to allow the tension to ruin my appetite, I kept my head down and began eating my breakfast in silence.

"How *courteous* of you to grace us with your presence this morning," the priestess sneered beside me.

I considered responding, but Cassius interrupted my thoughts with his own voice. "I'm honored to be so worthy of it."

With a fit of courage, I looked at him next to me and he greeted me with a patient smile. One that eased my mind just enough for me to return it. If he had the tolerance to be kind after I ignored him for an entire week, then I had the strength to make it through this breakfast. I allowed his own energy to radiate through me and returned to my meal.

When we were finished, a carriage waited outside for the priestess and Lady Guinevere. Cassius escorted us all to the main hall to give them a proper goodbye. I didn't seem to share his sentiment. I knew that Lady Guinevere's eyes were on me, and when I finally glanced her way, I watched her mouth open, but immediately close. Whatever she had planned to say fell short at the tip of her tongue, or maybe she was too cowardly to do so in front of the priestess.

Just say goodbye to her, I argued with myself. *She's the only mother you've ever known. Just say goodbye.*

"We will return to escort you to your next home. Be on your best behavior… and remember your *lessons*," Priestess Maeryn said, a small smirk tugging at her lips in some form of triumph.

Lady Guinevere approached me. "We'll see you soon," she whispered to me, reaching her hand out to mine and giving it a light squeeze. I hadn't returned the embrace and prepared myself for the guilt that would haunt me later because of it.

The moment the carriage took off, I let out a heavy breath that I hadn't even realized remained lodged in my lungs. Every part of me wanted to retreat back to my room, but when I turned, Cassius gripped my wrist and held me back.

"Hold on," he said quietly. I stared down at the intimidating grip he had on my hand and he quickly released it, straightening his back with an elegance that only a lord could possess. "You've been cooped up in that room for a week. Join me on a ride... *Please*. I can have my servants bring you a dress suitable for the horses and some riding boots."

Though I appreciated the gesture, I was overcome with embarrassment. "A horse?" I asked shyly.

"Of course, what else?"

"I... I don't know how to ride a horse," I admitted.

Eyes widening in surprise, he gaped at me like he didn't understand the words that came out of my mouth. Then, his expression turned into a solemn grin. "You can ride with me, then."

With Shae's assistance, I slipped into a new gown.

This one had longer sleeves, and an open slit below my waist that showcased the pants that she had me put on. "The sleeves and pants are to protect you if you should fall," she explained to me when she noticed me staring in the mirror.

That only made me more nervous. "*Will* I fall?" I asked her, fidgeting with the string at the front of my gown that held it tight against my chest.

Shae seemed to find humor in my genuine concern and chuckled. "I doubt that Lord Cassius would allow it." Her laughter was soft, the way I would imagine a mother sounded as she spoke lovingly to her children. Her presence made me feel so safe—I didn't know how she did it so easily.

Instead of pins, Shae spent extra time braiding a crown over my head, similar to what Lady Guinevere typically wore. Then, I met Cassius at the entrance of the castle. He stood beside a gorgeous brown horse with a long, dark brown mane. While allowing myself to admire him for a moment, my eyes traced the swirls that adorned his deep orange vest. Beneath it, he wore a simple, white shirt with the sleeves rolled to his elbows. The rest of his clothing seemed more casual: black pants and a pair of *dirty* riding boots.

"I'm guessing you do this often?" I said with a smile, looking right at his shoes.

They were covered in dry mud, like they had never been cleaned a day in their life. Priestess Maeryn would have flogged me for leaving any of my items in such an unkempt state.

Looking down, he laughed before returning his gaze to me and reaching out his hand. "Every day, Princess."

Princess.

I accepted his hand but eyed the horse warily. "I trust that means you won't let me fall, then?"

"Not when you're looking as beautiful as *you* do right now."

The blush on my cheeks from his compliment happened instantly, and I looked away in hopes that he didn't see it. Ignoring my trepidation, Cassius mounted the horse first and I tried to follow his motions. Putting my foot into the small handle dangling from the saddle, Cassius gave me a gentle pull and hoisted me up onto the horse. He allowed me a moment to shift around, finding a comfortable position, before grasping the reins in front of me and giving the horse a gentle kick.

Slowly, the horse trotted forward, and I grabbed onto his arms, still scared of falling. "Nervous, Princess?" he teased, pulling me back a little closer to his chest.

"Just focus on the path," I pleaded.

Riding away from the castle, we made our way across the trail that ran through the vast gardens. He had so many trees filled with fruit, and vegetables in rows along the fields around us. I knew then that I would be asking Shae if I could help tend to some of them. Gardening had been the only peace I could find at my old home—a place where I could enjoy my solitude in silence.

Passing the gardens, we entered a beautiful, wooded area with only small streaks of sun passing through the trees that arched over the paved path. I sucked in a breath and savored the aroma of maple and pine around us. The birds chirped, adding a beautiful melody to the morning air. For a moment, I imagined how it would feel to be as free as they were. Envying their ability to fly away to anywhere that called to them.

In the midst of my peace, Cassius leaned against my ear, his breath tickling my skin. "Hold on," he whispered.

Before I could even ask him *why*, he kicked the horse harder and shook the reins, sending us rushing forward. The air from my lungs had been ripped from my lips as the horse galloped into the trees. Images of us slamming into one of them is all that played in my mind as they blurred in my vision. With the help of Cassius's handwork, we somehow managed to dodge them all, but adrenaline coursed through me like a rip current. The wind in my face felt like pins, making it harder to breathe. And my nerves had my heart pounding so hard that I could feel its pulse in my ears.

"Stop," I whispered. The wind roared over my voice and Cassius didn't hear my plea. Against my back, I could feel him laughing, but it didn't settle my fear. *We are going to die. He's going to kill us. This is it.* "Stop!" I yelled, grabbing onto his arms beside me. "Cassius, please!" I begged.

With a burst of light, the trees opened to a large field of flowers. He pulled the reins, slowing the horse down to a full stop, as he breathed out a low and gentle, "Whoa, there."

Shoving his hands off of me, I pushed myself away from him. When I brought my leg over the horse, I hadn't calculated the distance to the ground and fell straight onto my back. Ignoring the pain that shot through me, I began panting, hyperventilating as I tried to catch my breath. Then, Cassius appeared over me, his eyes wide.

"Are you alright?" he asked. He grabbed my hand and pulled me until I sat up straight, chest still heaving.

"I told you to stop. You wouldn't stop."

"I thought…" I watched as his worry turned into guilt in his eyes. "I'm sorry. I took it too far."

Rubbing the ache from my lower back, a single glance at all of the flowers surrounding us helped to ease the shaking in my bones. My breathing slowed as I felt the soft grass against my hands. A dandelion rested beside me, so I plucked it and twirled it between my fingers. As the little seeds broke off, I stared, watching them blow away with the cool breeze that could be heard through the field. Taking a deep breath, I fell back into the grass and soaked in the sun's warmth.

"Princess?" Cassius asked, concerned. He leaned over me, his shadow completely blocking the sun.

I couldn't stop the laugh that came from my mouth. "I've never seen anything like this."

He lowered himself beside me and laid back just as I did. "What do you mean? There were no fields like this near your home?"

"I've never stepped outside of the grounds." I gazed up at the clear sky. There was no cloud in sight. Just a beautiful shade of blue. "Our house was surrounded by a tall wall. We had a garden, but it in no way compared to any of this." I waved a hand at the breathtaking scenery around us. "I could only plant what the priestess brought me."

"How did you not lose your sanity?" he asked me.

I laughed again, not meaning to let my sarcastic tone slip so boldly, and sat up. "Priestess Maeryn kept me busy with chores and studies. I was taught basic things—reading... writing... Most of what I learned had to do with etiquette, though. How a *woman* should act." I said the last part with intended cynicism this time. "So, I would sneak books from our study room in the middle of the night and read until I fell asleep."

He let out a breathy sigh. "I'll bring in a tutor. You should be well versed in every subject." Then, he turned to me with a smile that I graciously returned to him. "Have my servants been kind to you? Shae has been here a long time, so I figured she would be best suited to help as you adjust."

Servants.

"You're scrunching your nose. Why are you scrunching your nose?" His brows pulled together. "Did I say something wrong?"

Covering my face, I scolded myself for how openly I wore my emotions. "I'm so sorry, no. I just..." I shook my head. "I apologize."

Reaching his hand toward mine, my breath hitched as he pried them from my face. "Tell me."

I bit down on my bottom lip, praying I wouldn't be chastised for my opinion. "Every book I've read always makes the term *servants* sound so... *undignified.* I understand there are social classes, and workers wouldn't be

addressed in the same manner that *you* would be as a *lord*, but it just…
rubs me wrong."

He watched me for a moment and didn't speak. That only spiked my
nerves even higher. If I had spoken that way to the priestess, it would have
certainly earned me a lashing. But to speak so boldly to a lord? I couldn't
imagine what kind of punishment a woman's opinion could earn.

"Forgive me, you asked and I—"

"Is there a term you'd be more comfortable with?"

I felt shocked as his facial expression softened before me. But I
couldn't tell if he was taunting me or not. Perhaps he had simply been
enabling me so that I would dig myself further into my own grave.

"Are they paid for their services?" I asked him, nervously.

"They are," he responded, with a small smirk forming on his lips.

"Then would *staff* not be a more… *appropriate* term?"

His smirk stretched into his signature bright smile and he let out a
loud laugh that echoed amongst the trees. Pure embarrassment caused my
cheeks to burn, and I looked away, assuming he only humored my opinion
in an attempt to taunt me.

"You're right," he said at last, his gaze sharp and unblinking.

I am?

"It is an unkind and outdated term that I shall no longer use."
Standing, he reached his hand out to help me and I accepted it as I stared
into his eyes curiously. "Thank you for your honesty. It is rather
refreshing."

He ran a hand through his horse's mane, but I couldn't stop the
overwhelming sense of confusion that left me standing there. "It doesn't
bother you that I don't share your opinion? You're willing to change your
mind? Just like that?"

"I wouldn't be a very good leader if I couldn't utilize valuable counsel from others." He looked back at me. "Would I?"

"They will not tolerate your insolence the way that we *have,"* Priestess Maeryn had warned me. She would have considered my actions an outburst—a tantrum, and likely would have punished me for even *thinking* of disagreeing with her. She had instilled in my head, *daily*, that it was not my place to have an opinion—that my thoughts didn't matter.

I had so much apprehension coming here, expecting to be greeted by Death himself. But all I had encountered thus far was kindness. Perhaps the nightmares that haunted me were not because of the future I so desperately feared, but of the monster who planted the seed to begin with.

Chapter 5

Cassius instructed some of his staff to assist me with learning how to ride a horse.

But I mostly spent that time falling on my ass as much as possible. I didn't actually mind it, though. I yearned to try anything and everything that I hadn't been exposed to before. My favorite moments were when Cassius would attend the lessons with me. He couldn't be there every time, but he would make an effort to take a break from his work and visit with me to see my progress. *I think he just enjoys laughing at my failures.* But truthfully, I didn't mind that either.

Laughter... His *laughter*. His happiness infected everyone around him, and laughing seemed so foreign to me, but I had done it so much these past two weeks. It felt *good*. Being surrounded by so many kind people... his castle had almost begun to feel like a home to me. At least, more of a home than that cabin had ever been.

"Every week, the seven of us usually host a dinner on Saturdays," Cassius mentioned as we trotted along our usual morning path.

We had just passed his vegetable garden filled with workers as they tended to it. Shae looked up and smiled at me, and I waved as we continued forward. Shae had taken it upon herself to assist me most days. There would be occasional mornings where she couldn't make it, and I would have to try my best to hide my... *situation* from the other girls. But Shae instructed them to ask no questions and to say nothing of whatever they might see. However, I had the strange feeling that even if she hadn't implored, those girls would have respected my boundaries.

Every single person here treated me, not only as some royal figure that they wanted to serve, but as a *person*. A person they might actually... like.

"After your first week going... Well... how it *did*... We thought it would be best to give you an extra week to adjust." I had almost forgotten that Cassius was speaking to me. He had said something along the lines of... weekly dinners?

With all... *seven... lords...*

As I wavered slightly on my horse, Cass leaned forward and placed a hand on my elbow, straightening me out with a smirk on his face. "So, a dinner with seven lords and just me? That's not intimidating." I laughed, thin and hollow, but fear threaded itself through every word I spoke.

"It'll be fine. Kaiden likely won't even show. He's been pretty quiet since your arrival. Well, quieter than usual," he said, looking on at the path ahead of us.

Nodding, I tried to ignore the small ache in my chest as my heart stuttered a little, and *not* in a good way. It felt more like when I would wake from my nightmares. I hadn't actually *known* what Kaiden looked like growing up. I only knew from the guards that, out of *all* of them, he was the cruelest. That his castle looked almost abandoned once he let go of most of his staff. They never said *why* he began living in such solitude, but none of them liked to speak about him at all. I never even dared to ask them about him. But now that I *knew* what he looked like? My nightmares were getting worse. *He* stood at the center of them.

With a small shake of my shoulders, I pushed aside the unpleasant thoughts and tried to enjoy the rest of our ride together. We entered the arched pathway of trees that I loved so much, and I watched as some of the leaves fell from above us. They landed onto the trail, creating a beautiful tapestry of red and orange hues, as the leaves were changing with Fall's arrival.

"May I ask you something that might be a little... personal?" My voice held a quiver that said much more than I wanted it to.

Cassius turned his head to me with his brows furrowed, but amusement twinkling in his eyes. "Should I be nervous?" he teased. But then a smile stretched across his face. "Ask me anything, Morrigan. Always."

Taking his offer, I didn't hesitate as I asked, "What happens at the Offering?"

His horse halted so quickly that I had to scramble to stop mine. Clearly surprised by my question, Cassius just sat there with a blank expression on his face. It almost looked like he was looking for a way to explain it, and that didn't give me any reassurance. If it truly was *voluntary,* as Lady Guinevere had described it, then why did he appear so apprehensive?

There were a few moments that he would open his mouth to speak, just to close it again and continue thinking. And just when I considered turning back toward the castle out of pure mortification, Cassius finally said, "I eat food, just as you do. Gods know I eat food... All of us do. But we also require… other forms of sustenance." Running a hand through his hair, he looked away awkwardly for a moment before turning back to me again. "We don't need it often. Typically once a month, unless we're injured. But the villagers volunteer to allow us to… drink from them."

"Drink from them?" I hadn't realized that my fingers were gripping the reins a little harder than necessary until I felt soreness in my knuckles.

"Their blood," he clarified.

Swallowing against the dryness in my throat, I tried to remain impartial to the conversation. I didn't want him to know how uncomfortable the idea actually made me. "Does it hurt?"

"It *can*, yes. But it usually doesn't. We can make it pleasurable for the donor. Though, by doing that, it tends to get a little… intense." As he continued, I could see how nervous he felt saying all of this. I just didn't know *why* it made him feel that way. This was *normal* to them.

"What do you mean?" I asked.

He accompanied his answer with a dry laugh. "When we feed, it can feel… sensual to the person we are drinking from."

"How could that feel *good*?" My voice seemed to rise a little more than I intended it to, and it earned a few stares from some of his staff as they passed us by on foot.

His head fell back with a laugh, and it was clear that he wanted nothing more than for this conversation to be over. "I don't think I can explain that to you."

I rolled my eyes. "Well, what happens to them *after*?" Dropping my voice to an almost whisper, I leaned forward slightly. "Do you *kill* them?"

Clear shock made his eyes go wide. "Gods, no. Is that—Is that why you asked us that at the Unveiling? Did you really think we'd murder our own people like that?"

"That's what the guards said in my old home."

He straightened his back with a flicker of annoyance clouding the shimmering green of his gaze. "We take *only* what we need and pay them for their contribution. They get enough gold to last them a year of living comfortably... For their *entire* family." With a small kick to his horse, he began trotting forward, leaving me in the dust behind him. "We aren't *monsters*, Princess."

When our stroll came to an end, we arrived back at the courtyard and Shae stood at the bottom of the steps.

She offered me a kind smile before turning to Cassius as he dismounted his horse. "Your visitor has arrived, My Lord."

"Perfect!" This seemed to brighten the mood that I had unintentionally soured during our ride, and Cassius rushed toward me to help me down. "Your tutor is here. I'll show you to the room." The excitement in his voice seemed to resonate onto me and I returned his smile as we walked inside together.

His hand held mine as we approached a tall set of doors. And when he opened them, they revealed a large library. It stood two stories high and had more books than I even knew existed. The walls were lined with a beautiful brown wood, and the floors were separated by a luxurious railing with golden spindles. Movement on the stairs grabbed my attention, and I could see a man walking down with a pile of books in his hands.

"I brought your new student!" Cassius yelled beside me, startling him.

The man gasped in surprise and, as he reached the last step, lost his balance and dropped every single book onto the floor, save one still in his hand. "Graceful as always, Cassius," the man chimed. Without thinking, I ran forward and knelt down as he did, picking up the books with him. "Your Grace, you don't have to—"

"Allow me, please." I grabbed all that my hands could hold and looked up, handing the stack to him.

He looked a little older than Shae or Lady Guinevere. He had full, thick hair that was mostly black, but had patches of grey on both sides. His eyes were a bright blue, darker than the sky but with specks of light at the center of them that illuminated his face. While he appeared mortal, something about him felt... different. The wisdom in his gaze had me assuming that he might have been older than he appeared.

He smiled at me as we both stood and placed the books onto a nearby desk. "My name is Harley, and you must be the infamous *chosen one*."

Reaching out his hand for mine, I accepted it and said, "Morrigan. Please, just call me, Morrigan."

With a small chuckle, he shook my hand. "I had a sister with that name once. She had your beauty as well." He turned back to Cassius and his smile turned playful, but his eyes narrowed. "You're dismissed, Cass."

Cass's laugh carried the same casual warmth he shared with Dez, and as he leaned in, his hand found the small of my back. I didn't expect the slight tremble of my skin beneath his touch. "I'll snag you for dinner later." Then, he left through the doors.

Harley pulled out a chair for me and pushed it in as I sat down. "I taught him as a boy."

Knowing that the lords were centuries old, it wasn't exactly hard to do the math. "So... you must be—"

"Old?" he answered with a deep chuckle. "Yes, very. I like to think it makes me rich with wisdom, as well." Leaning against the desk, his eyes softened as he looked down at me. "Cassius explained to me that Priestess Maeryn, the arrogant woman she is, didn't actually *teach* you anything."

"Arrogant?" I asked, trying to mask my true feelings regarding her. No one had ever spoken so brazenly about the priestess before. It almost felt like a test.

He shot me a knowing look. "It's no secret that Maeryn thinks very... highly of herself. And she's almost as old as *I* am. Unfortunately, my immortality had been gifted to me *after* I had already reached this age. So, while she gets to reap the benefits of her youthfulness for a few decades longer, I stay frozen in time."

He began sorting through the piles of books behind him as he continued to speak.

"The idea of the *chosen one* began centuries ago. It wasn't until *you* were born that people actually realized it to be true. It almost became somewhat of a myth." After finding what he seemed to be looking for, he let out a sigh and turned back to me. "Maeryn spent a lot of time with Kaiden. Gods only know why he would associate himself with the likes of her. But I think somewhere, in that cold heart of hers, she may have grown to... love him. In a sense. And when she found out what that birthmark of yours meant—"

"The priestess?" I could feel the knot between my brows as I scrunched them, staring at him in confusion. "But they can't marry. They devote their lives to the service of the gods."

"As history has taught us, you can't always choose the ones you love."

"Why, then?" I asked. "Why would she volunteer to take care of me if she..."

"She was kind once, in her younger years. I don't think she truly knew what it meant for you to be the 'Chosen One,' and once she found out... I can only imagine *that's* when she changed for the worse." A broad, but gentle hand squeezed my shoulder and the tenderness of his touch almost made my eyes sting for some reason. "I'm sure it wasn't the best of lives that you were given. And for that... I'm sorry."

"I was cared for," I replied, sinking into my chair.

"But were you loved?"

Unlike most, I had never—and would never know the love of a mother or father. Lady Guinevere had been the closest thing to a mother, but even then, did she... love me? Gods knew Priestess Maeryn didn't. At least now I knew why. Jealousy is a poison, and she had been sipping from it for so many years. I should have felt sorry for her, but her lessons made it clear that pity wasn't her strong suit either.

"Let's start tomorrow," Harley offered before handing me a book from his pile. "Cassius told me you like to read. Why don't you take this as a gift?" After I accepted the book, I stood to leave, but Harley called out once more. "Morrigan." I turned to face him and enjoyed the warm smile he graced me with. "For what it's worth, you aren't alone anymore. And I hope that brings you some comfort."

Dropping the book off to my room, I realized that I still had plenty of time before supper, so I took the opportunity to roam the castle.

Admiring the paintings on the walls as I walked the halls, I exchanged smiles with the workers that passed me by. Most of the artwork seemed representative to the gods. Some contained portraits of Cassius, as well as a few with him and Dez. I wondered what it must have been like, growing up with a friendship as close as theirs. Perhaps my childhood would have been just a little brighter, but condemning *another* child to such solitude for my own benefit would have been selfish.

Making my way downstairs, I came across a pair of large, golden doors. Two guards stood on either side of them, standing at attention with swords at their side. I began approaching them, if only to ask what the doors led to, but when they spotted my presence, they moved. In unison, they each leaned to the side and opened the doors for me, allowing me entry. I took the opportunity and didn't ask questions as I walked inside.

Cassius could be seen at the far end of the room, on a throne that sat centered on top of a platform. In front of him stood an older man. His clothes looked a bit dirty, and nowhere similar in style to what Cassius wore. I assumed he must have been one of the people that lived within his land. It was clear that they were discussing something, but Cassius looked bored of whatever conversation they were having. The man, however, sounded concerned.

At the sound of my shoes tapping against the marble floor, they both turned and looked at me. "I'm sorry," I blurted out, unable to come up with a good enough excuse as to why I had disturbed them. "I shouldn't have entered without—"

"Princess!" The dreariness in Cassius's face morphed quickly as his smile grew. Waving a hand for me to approach, he suddenly ignored the man standing before him as he addressed me. "Come stand by me. This is good for you to be a part of."

As I moved closer, I noticed the man had his hat grasped between his hands, holding it firmly with what looked like worry. His brows were pushed together, forming hard creases that enhanced the wrinkles already lining his forehead. Truthfully, the man looked frightened. My eyes stayed on him as I stepped onto the platform, until Cassius grabbed my hand, and with that, my attention.

"I hope you enjoyed your time with Harley," he said quietly and kissed my fingers, forcing an unwelcome blush on my cheeks.

"I did."

Still holding my hand, he turned his stare back to the man standing behind me. So, I turned to face him as well. "You may continue," he told him. The playfulness of his tone had quickly disappeared, and I had the first glimpse into his role as a lord—the command in his words.

The man looked tired and nervous as he looked between the both of us before speaking to Cassius again. "As I said, My Lord…" He swallowed and began to stutter through his words. "Th-there was a fire. I-in my field. This is all I have to offer this month." I hadn't noticed there was a basket at his feet. It was filled with a few bundles of vegetables, as well as meat wrapped and tied.

Cassius exhaled a pointed sigh, his thumb moving absently across the back of my hand. "It's nowhere *near* the taxes that you owe. It's unlike you, Wilhelm. I have no choice but to accept it, but you will owe the difference next month," he warned.

My stomach sank a little as I stared at the basket on the floor. Without thinking, I looked at the man and asked, "Do you have enough food for your family this month?"

The movement on my hand ceased, and I could see Cassius staring at me from the corner of my eye. Wilhelm looked between us again, like he didn't know if he should answer my question or not. Then, a practiced smile masked his worried expression, one I knew all too well. "We will get by until our other crops are ready to be harvested next month."

Looking down at Cassius, he seemed to be studying me, like he wanted to see what I would say. To stop myself from speaking too out of turn, I leaned down so only Cassius could hear me. "You can't possibly expect his family to *starve*, can you?"

"Taxes are due. *This* is how things are done, Princess," he said in a low voice. His expression and position were unreadable.

"He can't pay your taxes if he starves to death alongside his family. You can let him pay you back as he can. I sincerely doubt that *you* need the food." The last part slipped out unintentionally. But it was true. The amount of food eaten by *him* alone could feed an entire village. Surely one month wouldn't affect him that badly.

"Princess..." he cautioned.

"You said it yourself. This isn't like him. Please, just... consider it." Pulling back, I allowed my own vulnerability to show in my eyes. "I know what that hunger feels like."

The sharpness of his gaze seemed to instantly soften and I almost felt bad for saying it. He brought my hand up to his lips, leaving a slow, drawn-out kiss on my fingers once more. Then, he looked back at Wilhelm. "If I allow you to bring this home, could you catch up by the winter solstice?"

Widening his eyes, Wilhelm began to nod his head with excitement. "Yes, My Lord. Once I harvest the rest of the crops, we will be fully caught up with our taxes for this season. I swear it."

After rubbing his eyes for a few seconds, Cassius began caressing my hand again as he did before. "Thanks to your future *queen*, I've been given a reminder of how lucky we are and how fruitful our own crops have been this year. It's *she* who you should thank for the extension. Take the food home to your family, Wilhelm. I'll see you next month."

Tears welling in Wilhelm's eyes, he turned to me in earnest. "Thank you, Your Grace." He bowed and looked back up at me. "Our prayers to the gods will be in *your* favor tonight."

"Just make sure your family eats well."

Cassius waited a few seconds after Wilhelm left to stand and face me, still holding my hand. He was in the usual dark orange suit he wore almost daily. His muscles perfectly outlined under the sleeves.

"I'm sorry," I whispered, looking up at him. "I overstepped."

Peering down at me, he proceeded to stare into my eyes. "You were right." He lowered his gaze to the hand that still held mine as he stroked my fingers with his thumb. "We are lucky enough for what we have. What kind of leader would I be if I allowed my people to starve?" When his eyes roamed back up, a smile lit up his face. "Let's eat."

Chapter 6

Sitting beside each other, Cassius at the head of the table, I couldn't help but gape at the large amount of food that went untouched.

"Do we really need a buffet at every meal?" I asked him. The sight of the food alone had started to affect my appetite recently. Seeing Wilhelm only further enhanced that growing ache, making me unable to eat my dinner.

With a patient sigh, Cassius set down his fork and turned to me. "Should I be expecting more lectures now that you've suddenly found your footing?" He had been teasing, but I sensed some truth behind his question.

"What about your staff? What do they eat?" I pushed.

"My serv… my *staff* are free to eat all that remains after we take our leave. As you've seen, the food is plentiful. I do not allow any of the workers to go hungry." Though I appreciated how quickly he adapted to the new title, it still ate away at me that he found any of that to be appropriate.

"So… they eat our… scraps? Don't you find that the slightest bit… degrading? Insulting?" Placing my utensils down, I succumbed to my lack of appetite and knew that I wouldn't be eating any more food that night.

As he placed his elbows on the table, he rubbed his face with his hands. He seemed annoyed, but willing enough to hear what I had to say. Or maybe he just wanted it over with so he could finish his food. "And what would you propose, *Princess*?"

"That plates be made for them *before* the buffet is placed. You wouldn't even see a difference in the food. If anything, you'll have happily fed workers with enough energy to continue their duties before retiring for the night."

He glanced at me through his fingers before sitting up straight and turning to one of the men standing by the table. I followed his gaze and found the man's expression unreadable, as was with most of the staff while they were on duty. But I could have sworn his lip perked up into a barely noticeable smile when our eyes met. Turning back to me, Cassius seemed to have noticed it as well.

"Myren," he instructed. "See to it that the ser—" His eyes flashed to mine that were already narrowed at him, waiting for the correction. A light laugh trickled from his lips with a roll of his eyes as he continued, "Please have the *staff* prepare plates for themselves now. Tell them that they are free to halt their current duties to finish their food and return to their work once they are finished."

With a bow of his head, Myren smiled at Cassius before returning to the kitchen. The rush of exhilaration I felt, knowing I had made the slightest difference in their day, seemed to be enough to return my appetite. And with an amused glance from Cassius, I continued the rest of my meal in peace.

I spent most of the week with Harley during the day, studying various historical textbooks.

"Read me a passage," Harley said, looking down at his own book.

To make sure I hadn't dozed off, he'd usually stop me at random times to read to him. Sometimes though, he almost seemed to enjoy it. Like a father spending quality time with his own child. Harley might have spoken to me as the role they had shoved onto me, but there were moments that he would sound gentle. Gentler than he'd addressed Cassius since I had arrived. The kindness of someone yearning for the same things that *I* always have.

A friend.

"The kingdom of Andonia had once been ruled by the gods. Ryuk, the god of death, ruled as their king alongside Aisha, the goddess of life. Centuries ago, they divided Andonia into seven territories, to be ruled by the seven lords. The lords were granted immortality and godly power to rule in their stead, so that the gods could ascend to Deorum Ínsula, *The Island of the Gods*."

Peering up at Harley, he returned my gaze with a sharp nod, gesturing for me to continue.

"A scorned love created a feud of jealousy between the gods. In an act of revenge, Rosina cursed the lords, inflicting them with the need to feed on their people. This act caused the people of Andonia to rebel against their lords, which began The Great War. To protect both the people of Andonia and their rulers, the gods created priests and priestesses entrusted with the duties of maintaining peace among the land. When she realized her plans were weakening, Rosina unleashed an army of monsters, set to destroy the villages. The lords fought to keep their people safe, and when the war was won, the gods created a prison to cast out these monsters. Rosina was killed for her traitorous acts, but the war caused unease between the territories. The people no longer felt safe against the ones who promised to protect them."

I heard the sound of a book closing before Harley began walking toward me. But I figured he wanted me to finish the passage anyway.

"Before the gods ascended, they promised a queen—a maiden born with the mark of the true throne. This maiden would unite the seven territories, protecting them against all evil, and usher in a new era of peace."

Guilt rose in my stomach remembering how I sounded when speaking of the Offering with Cassius. Priestess Maeryn had never let me read any of these books. If I had, maybe I would have been more understanding of their situation. Maybe I wouldn't have been so frightened to be given to them. Maybe the nightmares wouldn't have haunted me for so many years.

"Harley," I called to him as he retrieved the book from me. "What *evil* am I supposed to protect them against?"

Glancing over the section of material I had referenced, he shrugged. "To be honest, the gods spoke in riddles most days. The only ones who could truly decipher their intentions would be the gods themselves."

Well, that was helpful.

We spent our days this way and, while they weren't filled with much, they *were* peaceful. Before I knew it, the week came to an end, and with it came the first dinner I would have to spend with the other lords. Sitting with Shae, I waited irritably as she braided my hair into a pretty crown. It always amazed me how she could fit all of my hair in so well. Sometimes, I would have a few stubborn curls poke out, but they tended to complement the hairstyle remarkably well.

Amidst the anxiety that seemed to have my stomach flipping intensely, I had also noticed that Shae wasn't speaking as much as she normally would. She'd usually tell stories of her family—memories with her nieces and nephews. She had no children of her own. Shae had learned at an early age that she could not bear any and dedicated her service to Lord Cassius in lieu of that. I sometimes wondered if that had any influence on how quickly she embraced me into her net of loved ones. Whatever the reason was, I could never express my gratitude enough for it.

Staring at her in the mirror, her eyes began to glass over, like she wanted to cry. "Is everything alright?" I asked her.

With a tentative look, she moved suddenly to kneel beside me and placed her hands on mine. Being closer, I could finally see the tears that clung to her waterlines, begging to fall. She had to clear her throat before actually speaking. "Wilhelm is my brother." I didn't know whether to be nervous or relieved by that information. "My nephew has been very sick, and if they had given up that food…He may have died." The tear finally slipped down her cheek and she kissed my hand before looking back up at me. "Thank you."

"Won't the priests or priestesses help him?"

She sighed with a sad purse of her lips. "Only if they're paid enough to do so."

My vision lost its focus as she stood and returned to her position behind me, finishing the pins to keep my braid from falling. From what I had been reading, priests were meant to be a *gift* from the gods. They were blessed with immortality and were tasked with healing the sick and protecting the people of Andonia. Which explains why they had a priestess as one of my caretakers. I never read of them requiring charges for their services.

Trying to shove down the thought of it, I finished getting dressed and continued downstairs to the dining hall. But I made a mental note to speak to Cassius about it the first chance I had.

When I arrived, there were five other men already seated at the table. My seat beside Cassius remained empty, thankfully. I swallowed my nerves and entered the room quietly, almost hoping to remain invisible for the entire dinner. Sitting across from my seat, Dez was the easiest to recognize. The sensation of him *licking* my ear would be a hard one to forget. Eris, the *prick*, for some odd reason chose the seat beside me. The rest of them, however, I couldn't put names to. I *knew* their names, just not the faces to match them. But there were only six total sitting at the table, and I *knew* Kaiden's face. My entire body seemed to sink in relief at his absence.

As I approached my seat, Cassius stood to pull my chair out. I sat down, giving him a warm smile, and winced at the sudden silence that filtered throughout the room. Individual conversations completely died out when each of them noticed my presence. Even the air around us seemed to shy away from the tension until Dez decided to speak first.

"You look like you're eating, finally." He began shoving his own food in his mouth as Cassius stood and placed food on my plate for me.

"Thank you," I said to him, ignoring Dez's comment.

As much as I wanted to be angry at the slight, I hadn't actually realized just how petite I was until coming here. Now that I had been eating full, enriched meals, I could see my body beginning to fill out a little. It looked kind of *nice.*

"You still look like a twig," Eris muttered beside me.

I had a feeling that *this* was the norm for Eris. I felt the need to push myself to impress him. If he had no interest in civility with me, then neither did I with him. So, I rolled my eyes and began eating my food, refusing to humor his vulgarity. In the corner of my eye, I noticed the man next to Dez had also rolled his eyes before leaning forward with his hand outstretched.

"I'm Naaz." His wide smile lit up the room with penetrating dimples on both of his cheeks.

The vest he wore had been tinted a dark shade of purple but still resembled the design of the others'. I accepted his greeting and offered him my hand, watching him lower his head to kiss my knuckles. He had hair as long as Cassius, but it was more of a chestnut color, maybe even chocolate. His rich brown eyes looked like pools of honey as they glanced at me once more before he sat back into his chair and released my hand.

Next to him sat another good-looking man in a blue vest. He had blonde hair that seemed to fall down to the middle of his back, and his eyes matched Naaz's—just a smidge lighter.

"Dormius," he said shyly. "You can just call me 'D'." He looked to be the gentler one of them all. His voice sounded soft and careful. Quiet.

The last one to speak had a seat beside Eris. He leaned back in his chair and smiled, "Cain."

His vest was dark green and matched his eyes. Not the kind of green that Cassius had. But a deep, shattered, emerald green. A color that looked almost unnatural for a person to have. Being a mixture of both blonde and brown, his hair was short like Eris's—aside from a few small strands hanging in front of his brows. His eyes lingered for a second longer before he lowered himself back toward the table and chuckled softly as he began to eat.

With introductions out of the way, they all resumed eating and conversing with each other. I tried my best to tune them out—far too many voices at once for my liking. Cassius and Dez would laugh at everything the other said, and Eris, thankfully, sat quietly beside me.

"How are you enjoying your studies, Morrigan?" I heard Naaz ask.

I looked up at him and smiled. "Harley is lovely. He's patient with me and doesn't push too hard. Though, he loves assigning textbooks for me to spend my nights reading." I shrugged. "It keeps me busy."

"You know, I was top of the class when he taught all of us," he said, straightening his back and puffing out his chest. "In case you ever need a tutor."

With a loud fit of laughter, Dez slammed Naaz's shoulder with his hand. "You'll get your time to gloat when it's *your* turn, Naaz."

Naaz only rolled his eyes but D chuckled lightly next to them. By the time dinner had ended, I was mildly surprised that it went... *well*. I didn't know what I expected to happen, but I felt a lot more at ease with the entire idea of it all as I made my way back to my room.

Not quite ready for sleep, I perched myself onto a chair beside my bed and opened a book that I could lose myself in for a few hours. I had almost begun to doze off when I heard the sound of a door slamming outside of my room. Jumping from the chair, I ran into the hall and could hear Cassius yelling and cursing from his bedroom, diagonal to mine. After setting my book down onto my nightstand, I left to find him.

Through the small crack in his door, I could hear him mumbling to himself. He sounded frantic. "Cassius?" I whispered, pushing slightly on the handle. I didn't want to invade his privacy, but I needed to make sure that he was okay. When the door opened fully, I could see Cassius leaning against his dresser.

My hand clamped over my mouth when I took in the blood dripping from his side.

The source of it came from the arrow piercing his ribs.

"Oh Gods, Cassius!" With no time to waste, I ran to him and knelt down, hands hovering over the injured area, unsure of what to do. "What happened?" I asked, chest heaving from my own panting.

"The guards caught some suspicious activity along one of the posts at my borders. I went with a team to check it out," he explained through clenched teeth. His face writhed in pain and his skin looked paler than normal. "We were ambushed. They got me with one of their... arrows, and normally I'd heal, but..." Gripping the dresser to steady himself, the wood began to chip from how hard his fingers pressed into it. "It's poisoned. I think they used hellebore—" His own scream cut off his words and his knees almost buckled.

"What can I do?" I begged, trying my best to keep him from falling. "Tell me what to do."

"They disappeared into thin air like they were never fucking there!" He screamed through another bout of pain.

The lords were supposed to be immortal... He *couldn't* be dying. But his wound looked like it was festering. Black veins crawled up his skin as it spread throughout his body. He *had* been poisoned.

Taking a deep breath, he wrapped his hand around the arrow before ripping it from his side. The sound that erupted from him sent icy shivers down my back, bringing fearful tears to the surface of my eyes. He immediately fell to his knees, clutching his side as more blood began to spill out with urgency.

"It's getting worse." My chest tightened, scared for his life. So much blood poured from the wound, and his face had almost lost all of its color.

"I need you," he hissed.

"Tell me what to do." Placing a hand on his shoulder, I tried to keep him upright. Someone had to hear his screams and would be coming to help... right? *I could run out to alert someone*, I thought to myself. It would have taken no more than a few seconds before I'd return to Cass's side.

But before I could move, Cassius leaned in toward me. "I'm sorry," is all he said before he grabbed my wrist and bit down, penetrating my skin.

The pain shot through me so quickly that I couldn't even make a sound. My lips were parted in a silent scream that seemed stuck inside of my throat. It felt as though someone had taken fire and poured it into my veins, crawling up my arms and burning the very blood inside of my body. I just stood there, frozen in place as Cassius made slight moaning sounds in front of me.

Then, I had been ripped to the floor, and like a switch had flipped, I found my voice. But just as I began to scream, his large hand covered my mouth and silenced me. Tears were falling from my eyes and his fingers were so close to my nose that I could barely breathe.

I felt every pull from his mouth as he sucked the blood from my wrist, each one more painful than the last. Another couple seconds and my head started to feel lighter, like my body had begun to float. The shapes around me were distorting as my vision blurred and a tingling sensation began in my fingers and the tips of my toes.

It crawled through my limbs, leaving behind a numb feeling in its wake. I couldn't move. My nightmares seemed to flash before my eyes, remembering the feeling of dying night after night.

I'm dying.

Cassius didn't stop, nor did he seem inclined to anytime soon.

Help me, I cried within my own mind, begging for someone to hear.

Just as my eyes began to close, the door burst open. Harley's voice rang across the room, but I couldn't hear it over the pulsing in my ears. The rhythm seemed to be slowing as the seconds passed. Darkness crept into my vision and prepared to swallow me whole before Cassius was shoved away from me. I barely felt it as my arm fell to the floor, my body practically limp now.

With the small strength I could muster, I turned toward my wrist and saw the blood pooling on the floor beneath my skin. The gaping wound that Cassius left on me spilled onto the sandstone-colored rug like rushing water.

"Morrigan, look at me. Are you ok?" a muffled voice asked me.

Warm hands cradled my cheeks and my head felt heavy as it bobbed toward the source. Harley's eyes were wide with fear. I wanted to answer him, but when I moved my lips, no sound would leave them. My throat had dried completely and even the movements of my tongue were like sandpaper in my mouth.

"Cass, get your ass over here and fix this. *Now!*" he yelled beside him.

I had no more energy left.

My eyes closed on their own, and the darkness claimed me as the pulsing in my ears *stopped.*

Chapter 7

pen your eyes, Morrigan, that strange voice seemed to hum in the back of my mind.

Even though the sounds were fuzzy, I could still hear both Harley and Cassius arguing with each other. Then, I felt the pull of being lifted into someone's arms. *I'm going to die...* The urge to cry got lodged inside of my chest as my body grew heavier and somehow lighter at the same time. *No, Morrigan,* that other voice answered. *Not today.*

Someone's skin touched my lips and a warm, wet liquid smeared over my mouth. "Drink." Cass's voice no longer sounded as pained as it had seconds prior.

Before opening my mouth, I could instantly smell the metallic substance that he had been referencing. Nausea crept up my throat and I wanted to shove him away. I even got so close as to moving my head to the side. But he quickly forced the open wound into my mouth and his blood coated my tongue. I expected a bitter, copper taste to overwhelm me, but to my surprise, his blood tasted... sweet.

As the liquid slid down my throat, each passing second made me feel more energized than before. A sensation seemed to take over me and a rush of adrenaline washed over my body, causing my nerves to buzz throughout my limbs. Without thinking, I grabbed his wrist and latched my lips onto his skin, pulling in more. Behind me, a hand reached up and began petting my hair. "I'm so sorry," Cassius whispered. "It shouldn't have happened like this."

"Cassius," Harley said, quietly.

I couldn't pay attention to what either of them were saying. The feel of his hand brushing my hair in such a tender way made my entire body feel hot. Somehow, I sensed his blood pulsing through my veins—like a string that I could follow as I swallowed more and more. Then, a pounding began in my ears that I originally mistook as my heartbeat. It wasn't in sync, though.

Sucking harder, I craved more... *needed* more.

I leaned my body back against Cassius, not wanting him to stop his soothing caress. "She's fine Harley. Go back to sleep." Cassius draped his free arm around me and wrapped a hand around my waist, tugging me closer as he held me. "Go," he ordered Harley.

I need to be closer, I thought to myself. *I need him.* I pressed further into his chest as I heard the door close.

"Alright, Princess, take it easy," he whispered, pulling his wrist away. An anger seemed to manifest itself and an animalistic growl escaped my lips as I tried to lunge for his wrist again. But Cassius held me in place, even as I struggled against him.

Need... I need...

When I looked up, my eyes landed on his lips and my body seemed to twirl itself until my legs straddled him. Before he could protest, my lips pressed into his, the surprise of it sending him onto his back. I had never kissed a man before, but somehow I knew what to do as Cassius's resolve slipped and he kissed me back.

One of his hands slipped into my hair, his fingers clamping down and fisting my curls before sitting up. He didn't move me. Instead, he pulled me tighter against him, causing a friction between my thighs that I had only ever felt by my own hands. It was too good to stop. So, I pushed my hips against him, enhancing that sensation that made my insides want to erupt. That's when a copper taste finally hit my tongue and I realized it was *my* blood, still in his mouth.

"Morrigan," Cassius warned. "You have to snap out of it. I won't be able to stop myself."

I didn't listen. I didn't *want* him to stop. My body craved him more than I had ever craved anything else. Biting his lower lip, the growl that left his mouth had me throbbing between my thighs.

He finally pushed me away, gripping my cheeks with his hands, and before I could even argue, he whispered, "*Lay.*"

A hazy feeling pulled me toward him, and suddenly, all I wanted to do was obey. As our chests touched, that hunger to practically devour him seemed to pass. The only thing I wanted now was for him to hold me. Repositioning us, he scooped me into his arms before standing and laying me onto his bed. A few moments later, he crawled in beside me and pulled my back against him, enveloping me with his arms.

Reaching over, he pulled my wrist up and I turned my body, watching him slowly lick the wound on my skin. The second he pulled away, it began to sew itself back together. Then, he leaned his lips down to my ear and whispered, "*Sleep.*"

The light of the sun woke me, and I quickly realized that I wasn't laying in my own bed.

Looking around, I noticed that the walls were black with orange marbling. The bed resembled mine, but larger. The illumination through the window clearly indicated that it was well past morning. I had most likely missed breakfast already.

Even though I had slept without a single nightmare, my head felt... groggy. Like hands were wrapped around it, pushing against my temples and causing pressure above my brows. The doors to the room opened and Cassius walked in wearing his riding gear. As our eyes met, every memory from the night before came crashing down like a landslide. I stopped breathing out of pure embarrassment, realizing I had basically pounced on him.

I... *kissed* him.

He didn't take his eyes off of me as he crossed the room, removing his vest and leaving his shirt slightly unbuttoned. Peeking through the top of his shirt, small auburn curls spread across his chest. They were glistening with a light sweat that he had likely worked up from riding the trail that morning. "Princess," he greeted with no hint of whatever emotion he felt in regard to what happened last night.

I remembered him biting me—almost *killing* me. But I also remember the poison that had been ravaging his body. I couldn't be angry at him for protecting himself... and he *didn't* kill me. He *saved* me. That much I knew.

He looked down only to remove his boots, and I pulled the blanket to my chest. Just watching him brought that rush of heat back to my body, simmering on my chest. It had to be blistering red and visible for him. As he leaned back into the chair, his head tilted up to the ceiling and he let out a long sigh.

"My wrist is healed," I said, yearning to break the uncomfortable silence between us.

He gave a slight purse to his lips and said, "It is." Another sigh and he lowered his head back down, but kept his eyes to the floor. "I'm... sorry. I shouldn't have..." Leaning forward, he rested his elbows on his knees and clasped his hands behind his head. "Your blood—it's different. What they poisoned me with last night... It could have killed me. Your blood was the only thing that could stop it, and I wasn't thinking straight—"

"It's okay," I promised quietly. "Really, it is. I'm not angry at you, if that's what you think." Scooting my body, I moved closer to the end of the bed where I could see him more clearly. "If anything, *I* should be apologizing. When you gave me your blood... I don't know what came over me. I'm a little ashamed that I couldn't control myself. I swear, I've never even done anything... I'm not like that."

I pulled my bottom lip between my teeth and somehow Cassius seemed to catch it in the corner of his eye. His gaze snapped to my mouth, his own lips parting ever so slightly. "It's what I tried, and failed, to explain to you about the Offering. It's completely normal. I should have ended it faster; it's my fault."

Something about him looked different to me now. I didn't know *what*, but the way his muscles flexed beneath his shirt had my gaze tracing every inch of them. The invitation that sat on his lips... Like they called my name. Like they were *mine*. I could still taste them... Taste him on my tongue... Feel his hands on my hips as I straddled him...

Unknowingly, I brought my fingers to my lips, rubbing them softly, like it would help me hold onto that small thread of a memory. "I… I think I still feel it a little…" *How long would these effects last?* I couldn't help but squeeze my thighs together as the heat redirected there. *You barely know this man*, I reminded myself. So, why did it feel like his own blood had become a part of mine? Why, looking at him now, did his eyes seem so much more familiar to me than they had the day before?

The corner of his lips began to tilt up in a guilty smirk. "Princess… that's not my blood that you're feeling." With a soft expression on his face that smoothed out every line, making him a vision of absolute beauty, he walked over to me. He stopped at the end of the bed and reached a hand out. "Come here."

It only took a few more inches, and I was in front of him, kneeling on the bed. His fingers moved slowly until they landed beneath my chin, lifting my face. As his thumb stroked that tender area, each movement felt like its own bolt of electricity across my skin. Cassius had this power about him that could make any girl melt—a simple fact. The first moment I laid eyes on him, I felt that want… *deep* in my bones. It was a natural reaction. But now, the want had become a *need*.

My eyes fluttered closed as he continued caressing my skin, and my lips parted like they made their own silent invitation. In response, I could feel the static between us as he lowered his face to mine and hovered his mouth just above my own. "May I?" he asked. His breath tickled my lips and it only made the heat between my thighs even more unbearable.

"Yes," I whispered with my next exhale, like it hadn't even been a question.

Sliding his hand to the back of my head, he gripped my hair lightly as he closed the distance between our lips. His other hand now on my lower back, he pulled me against his chest as he kissed me with gentle urgency, like he *too* felt that unrestrained pull between us. He tasted of cinnamon and spice as our tongues clashed together, but he held onto his control. He drank me in like he wanted to savor every second of it.

When he pulled away, my chest panted with breaths that he had stolen from me. I didn't care, though. I craved nothing more than for his lips to be back on mine, bruising them until he left his mark on them. "Trust me," he pleaded.

I didn't know what he meant, but I almost instantly responded with, "Yes."

Tenderly, he pushed me back until I lay against the bed. As he climbed over my body, my heart began to race like painful flutters beneath my chest. "Don't worry," he assured me. "I won't push you to do anything you don't want to do."

Leaning down, he placed a kiss on my chest just beneath my collarbone, and my body shivered against his lips. He kissed again at the spot where my shoulder met my neck and all of it felt like slow torture. As he trailed his mouth up my neck, the urge to grab him had my skin tingling, but I didn't have the slightest idea how to do any of this. *He* did, and I was comfortable enough to let him take the reins for me.

He finally made it to my lips and a small moan escaped as he opened my mouth with his tongue. "You can stop me," he reminded me.

"I know."

I didn't want to. Instead, wrapping my hands around his neck, I pulled him toward me and deepened our kiss. Arching my back into him, I silently begged for his hands to touch me somewhere... *anywhere*. I needed friction—to release the tension that coiled itself so tightly that it felt almost painful.

Sensing my frustration, he smiled against my lips and moved one of his hands to my leg, lifting my knee until his hand slid down my thigh. My breath hitched when he continued to lower it, sliding under the gown to the thin cotton that separated us. Wasting no time, he trailed his finger beneath the small piece of fabric until his warm touch reached my center, and I gasped into his mouth.

In return, he groaned, letting his fingers still for a moment. "Gods, Princess. You're so wet."

"Cassius," I whimpered.

"Shhh…" His fingers then began to move in slow circles, and the intensity of it all made me want to cry out. This felt nothing like it did when I would touch myself. Having his body pressed against me made that coil want to burst almost instantly. "I'll go slow."

"I don't think I can…"

"You'll try," he ordered. "Just hold out for me, Princess."

Sliding his fingers down a little more, I felt the pressure of him sliding into me and I let go of his lips to push my head into his shoulder. My eyes squeezed shut, and though it hurt slightly, the pleasure overpowered that pain. As he moved his finger in and out of me, I let out a whimpered moan and began moving my hips *with* him.

"That's it," he praised. "Let your body take over. Use me."

His thumb returned to that sensitive area and rubbed me as his fingers thrusted faster. "Cassius," I moaned, unable to hold on much longer. "Cassius, please. I can't—"

"I've got you, Princess. Let yourself go."

At the sound of his words, my body unraveled. The energy that coursed through me left my head spinning and my legs shaking from the pure force. Cassius lowered his head and pressed kisses against my neck, continuing to rub me until I had nothing left to give. Small explosions of pleasure poured through me and I could barely catch my breath.

"Look at me, Princess."

I lifted my head, sweat now forming above my brows, and lips parted from panting. He placed the ghost of a kiss just beside my mouth before whispering, "Next time, Princess… It will be my *tongue*."

Chapter 8

t some point after our… encounter, I must have fallen asleep because the sound of banging on the door had me jolting from his bed.

"I'll have you know," Harley's muffled voice called out, "even *royalty* are not granted the courtesy of slacking off."

Scrambling to pull the sheets over myself, in the event that Harley decided to enter, I yelled out, "I'm sorry!"

"Library in ten." The sound of footsteps retreating had my shoulder sagging in temporary relief. Looking to the side, I noticed that Cassius wasn't beside me. I tried to remember that he *did* have duties to attend to.

But at my feet, a simple gown had been placed. It seemed easy enough for me to throw on myself. With a smile, I stood from the bed and began dressing myself. *He picked it out for me.* And somehow the thought alone became the most loving gesture I had ever received. Pressured to not keep Harley waiting, I didn't let my silly emotions stop me from rushing to the library.

Harley, of course, gave me a pointed look before I sat down, quickly shoving even more books in my direction. "What do you know of the four realms?" he asked me before skimming through a book of his own.

I didn't understand how he did that. How he could focus on so many things at once. "Realms?"

After shooting me a quick glance, he placed the book down and pointed to drawings on the page. An image of beautiful clouds among the large crystal palaces had been painted beneath his finger. "There is Deorum Ínsula, the Island of the Gods." He moved a little further down to a picture that depicted a field of vast gardens filled with colorful flowers. "Eden, our place of rest when we pass." And beneath that was a familiar image of our home. "Andonia."

But below the painting of Andonia, nothing remained. The rest of the page had been left empty. Looking up at him confused, I asked, "I thought you said there were *four*?"

He nodded and produced a different book, one that looked a lot older. It had dust clinging to the edges of the pages as if it had been kept away in the darkest parts of the library. Even the leather looked worn with age and neglect. When he opened it, he knew the exact page he wanted to turn to and placed it down in front of me. The entire paper had been painted black, with a fire lit at the center of it. You couldn't see anything, but the darkness that had been sketched around the fire appeared evil. Like it held things our eyes weren't capable of comprehending.

"The Netherworld," he said quietly.

"What's the Netherworld?" Reaching my finger out, I grazed the page where the fire had burned brightest. Something about it felt... strange. A likeness in a way. As I moved my fingers over it, I could almost hear the crackle of the embers beneath the flames.

Harley suddenly turned the page for me and I came face to face with hideous looking creatures. One looked like a beast with fangs sharper than any daggers I had ever seen. Another creature had a distorted face, like its skin had sunken down to the bone and looked too fragile to hold its own weight. The third creature... it was something out of a nightmare...

"The Netherworld is home to the monsters that the god Rosina created," he said as he cleared his throat. With his finger, he pointed to the passage on the next page. "Read this for me."

"During the Great War, the traitor Rosina created monsters with a similar curse to our lords. She thought it would help to tear down the people's trust in their rulers. These monsters were called *Vampyres*."

I didn't know *how* I knew, but the image of the third monster sprung to mind and there was no doubt that *this* name belonged to it.

"What separated Vampyres from the lords who protect us was their bloodthirsty appetites. If they kept their hunger satiated, they would look no different than any other mortal. But when they became ravenous, their faces would morph into monstrous beings with long, vicious fangs that grew from their gums."

When Cassius had fed from me, his teeth felt sharper, but he didn't have fangs like the photo described. It seemed more like his own canines had simply lengthened just enough to pierce my skin more easily, providing an easy pull for him to drink.

"Do Vampyres still exist?" I closed the book, hoping that Harley wouldn't ask me to continue.

Thankfully, he held out his hand to collect it instead. "No. They were all killed during the war. They reside in the Netherworld now. Their souls will never reach Eden." The strangest hint of sadness seemed to hide itself in his voice.

"Why did she do it?" I asked him. Why would anyone want to destroy their home? I knew she loved Ryuk and thought that he betrayed her, but to curse the lords? To kill her own people? Over a man? Something about it just didn't sit right.

Harley didn't answer me. He continued up the stairs to return the books to their sections and I sank into my seat, waiting in silence. At least I had the comfort knowing I would never do something as heinous as she did. The gods created me to protect the people from evil. And in that library, I made a silent promise to myself that, regardless of the cost, I would fulfill that prophecy.

Another week flew by between our early morning rides and studying with Harley.

When Friday came, I realized that I had shamefully forgotten what I needed to speak to Cassius about. So, during my lunch break I left the library to track him down. Entering his study, I watched him sitting at his desk writing something. His face looked deep in thought while he worked. I didn't realize he could appear even more beautiful than he already had. There was something genuine about seeing him in his usual element. But it ended quickly when he noticed my presence and smiled as I leaned against the door.

"You've never visited me here before," he noted. "How'd you find me?" I began to answer, but he placed a hand up to stop me and laughed. "Shae?"

Smiling, I walked over to him and stood next to his chair, peering down at the paper in front of him. "May I ask what you're writing?"

Before answering me, he grabbed my hand and placed a few sweet kisses against my fingers. "I'm just sending a few extra men to my border stations as a safety precaution. Just until we have answers." He sighed like he had failed in some way. "We still haven't found the assailants who poisoned me."

I couldn't prevent the sharp, mental image of him standing in his room, bleeding out onto the floor as he clutched his side. Even if I barely knew him, the thought alone that, if he hadn't used my blood to save himself, he could have *died*... Well, it was a sadness I wouldn't have expected to feel for a stranger. Fiddling with some of his quills to brush away the memory, I pondered how to bring up the lingering question I had originally sought him out for.

"Speaking of Shae..." He looked up at me from his chair, waiting for me to continue. "Her nephew, Wilhelm's son, is sick."

With a nod, he answered. "The priests have been to their home and deemed his illness fatal. The people of Andonia don't have the same gifts that we have been blessed with." He rubbed my hand reassuringly. "There comes a point where some diseases are too far gone for the priests to heal. We cannot control fate, Princess. It's in Minerva's hands now."

I understood that. And I would have left it alone if Shae hadn't mentioned the reason the priest wouldn't help them. "Shae explained that the priest refused to heal him because they couldn't pay."

That made his back perk up as he narrowed his eyes at me. "Priests and priestesses can't accept payments. They receive a share of taxes from each of us. The people *do not* pay them any currency."

I shrugged. "I don't think Shae would lie to me about that."

"Nor do I," he mumbled quietly. Looking down for a moment, he seemed lost in thought before standing and placing both of his hands on either side of me. My breath halted when he leaned in, but only to place a quick, gentle kiss on my lips and pulled back. "I'll look into it. I promise."

"Thank you." I smiled and hopped off of his desk, making my way back to the library to give him some peace.

As I passed the throne room, I saw a man dressed in black entering it. Nothing about him looked familiar at all, and when I called out to him, he didn't so much as turn in my direction. Cassius hadn't mentioned anyone visiting today, and the others only came for dinner on Saturdays. So, letting my curiosity win, I followed after him.

But when I walked through the doors, I found the room empty. The only sound that echoed against the walls was the clacking of my shoes against the marble. "Hello?" I said out loud, hearing the reverberation of my own voice in response.

Walking to Cassius's throne, I turned and searched the room for where the man could have roamed. When I still didn't see any sign of him, I let out a sigh and traced my hand over the grooves of the arm. Maybe I would have one someday. It likely wouldn't be as big as theirs, but it would be *mine*.

Realizing that I had been keeping Harley waiting on me, I looked around once more before walking back down the steps. *"Morrigan,"* a voice whispered behind me.

I spun around, heart racing at the way it made the hair on my arms stand to a point. But still, no one stood there. The air, though… It felt like eyes were on me in every direction. I could feel someone… some*thing* watching me. It violated every bit of empty space in the room. "Who's there?" I asked loudly, trying to mask the shaking in my voice.

But silence mocked my question as a chill washed over me, and I hugged my arms to my chest. Turning on my heel, I walked quickly out of the throne room and tried to convince myself that it was an echo of my own imagination.

Though I likely *should* have, something stopped me from telling Cass about what I had seen in the throne room

I didn't want to sound crazier than I already felt.

Legs tangled together, I woke beside him the next morning, shocked that we both had slept in. Cass's breaths were deep, causing my head to rise with them. His heartbeat thrummed gently beneath my ear.

A sudden dip in the mattress had me spinning to find Dez beside me. With his head propped up onto his fist, he sported a devilish grin across his face. "Good morning, Sunshine."

It took me a moment to fully register the situation. And when the fatigue finally faded, I realized just how visible my skin was beneath the sheer nightgown. At some point in the night, our blankets had been kicked down toward the end of the bed. Which meant that my body was on full display for Dez.

"Dez!" I screeched, quickly yanking up a few sheets to cover myself.

Groaning beside me, Cass pushed up onto his elbows. I gave him a *"Are you going to do something about this?"* glare, but he simply looked at Dez and laughed to himself before shuffling out of bed.

"Is three still a crowd?" Dez teased, only making me angrier in the process. "Don't worry. You'll get there soon enough." He winked and followed after Cass.

Still angry, I reached to the side and snatched Cass's pillow before aiming it at Dez's face and chucking it toward him. Unfortunately for *me*, he caught it just before I could land a satisfying blow.

Then, he turned to Cass. "She's feisty," he said with a tinge of excitement in his voice. "Is this what love feels like?"

Pretending that I wasn't even there, Cassius chuckled at his friend and began ushering him out. "The only one you *love* is *yourself*." But before he left, he made his way to my side as he threw on one of his white shirts and leaned down to kiss me. "I'll send Shae in to help you dress. I have to speak with Dez, but I'll be back before dinner."

I pressed my lips against his, ignoring Dez's presence entirely and smiled to myself as I pulled away. "I'll see you soon," I whispered.

Then, clearly unable to accept not being the center of attention in a room, Dez stepped beside Cass. "No kiss for me?" he asked.

Fuming, I made to grab another pillow but heard the both of them laughing as they made a run for it. By the time I turned to the door, it was already shut.

Just a few, short minutes later, Shae came in with a beaming smile on her face. She always seemed happy in the morning, but this smile shone far too bright to be her usual giddiness.

As she began brushing my hair, she started to hum. Shae had never hummed before. "Shae?" I asked cautiously. "Is it rude of me to ask if you're alright? You're awfully..." I struggled to find the words, hoping I wouldn't offend her. "You're very energetic this morning."

Waving her hands at me, she giggled and brought me toward the bed to step into my gown. "I'm just happy today," she said sweetly. "A new priest arrived early this morning. He came to heal my nephew."

I couldn't hide the shocked look on my face as she pulled the dress up and began securing it in the back. I knew Cass had promised to look into it. I just didn't expect him to resolve it so fast.

"He's *already* breathing better. The priest said he should be up and about in a matter of days!" When she finished helping me, she turned my body toward her and squeezed my cheeks with her hands. "I believe we have *you* to thank for this."

Though I was excited for them, anger seemed to burrow a way through my chest at the fact that he had been healed—which meant that the disease didn't *need* to be fatal. But a priest had been willing to let the boy die over money he was never owed to begin with.

"There wouldn't have been any thanks necessary if that priest had done his…"

Clamping her hand over my mouth to stop me, I realized she had done me a favor. Priests and priestesses were held in such high regard. They were the closest beings to our gods, save for the lords. "*You* fixed this, Your Grace. Let us be thankful that the boy will live."

Letting go of my lips, she pulled me into a tight embrace that I couldn't help but return. The warmth of her hugs were enough to make me melt. I cherished them. "I'm happy for you and your family," I told her.

"You are going to do great things, sweet girl," she whispered before releasing me to escort me downstairs. "I can't wait to see you grow."

My cheeks were a bright shade of red as we reached the doors and said our goodbyes for the night. With a bright smile, I made my way to my seat where Cassius had already prepared a plate for me. "Thank you," I whispered to him as I sat down. "Shae told me. She's very grateful."

"To you," he clarified. "If you hadn't told me then I never would have known."

"I feel as if I'm missing something," Naaz chimed in, setting down his wine.

"One of my staff's nephews had been ill." Cassius turned his attention to Naaz as he explained. "The priest that assisted them refused treatment, claiming it was fatal. However, the staff member confided in Morrigan that they requested payment from the family. They only refused treatment when the family said they couldn't pay."

"They aren't allowed to receive payments," Dez said, almost skeptically.

"I sent a message to the palace reminding them of that law." Then, Cassius returned to his meal. "It must have jogged their memory." I could see a small smirk tugging at the corner of his lips, and I wondered if the "message" he had sent was more of a *warning*.

"You call your servants *staff*?" Cain laughed. "When did that begin?"

Sparing a glance my way, he chuckled when I rolled my eyes. "I'll let you figure that one out when she comes to stay with *you*."

As I began eating my own food, Dez spoke again. "That kindness?" he said. "They won't forget that." When I looked up at him, he stared at me with admiration in his eyes. It made my heart flutter a little in my chest.

"Anyone would have done it," I murmured, trying to contain the blush in my cheeks as I stared back down at my food.

"No," Eris answered quietly with a hint of emotion in his normally monotonous voice. "They wouldn't have."

Chapter 9

ass hovered over me the next morning with a wild grin on his lips.

"I have a surprise," he gushed. "Put on your riding gear and meet me outside." He leaned down and kissed my head, but I had still been rubbing my eyes by the time he left, leaving me with no room to respond or protest.

Soon after, Shae arrived as if it had been planned and said not a word as she ushered me to the vanity to begin working on my hair. "Should I be worried?" I asked her, only teasing.

With a laugh, she answered, "When it comes to Lord Cass, maybe it's best to be."

I managed to get dressed quickly enough and rushed downstairs to meet Cass in the courtyard. Shae gave me a simple braid that fell down my back, and it whipped through the wind behind me as I ran down the steps to where Cass had been grooming his own horse.

"You wake me up from a very peaceful sleep and tell me you have a surprise for me. Then, you bolt from the room before I can even speak!" I could see Cass's shoulders bouncing with laughter before I actually heard it. So, I continued to tease him. "I have half a mind to be concerned."

With a swift turn, he wrapped his arms around me and pulled me against his chest, almost taking my breath with it. Aside from the small kisses we would share intermittently, he hadn't touched me again since that morning. At least, not like *that*. But I didn't take offense to it. Sometimes he looked as if he, too, had no clue how to manage any of this, or even what to feel. It made him more *human* in my eyes. And every time he grabbed me like this, it reminded me that he did want me... In what way? Well, that was for him to decide.

"Do you not trust me, *Your Grace*?" His emphasis on the last two words were an intentional mockery. He knew how much I cringed at that title when I would hear it in passing throughout the castle. Before I could respond, he lifted me, placing me onto my horse. "No concern necessary. At least not *today*. I'm taking you to the market. I want you to pick out a few things."

"And do *what* with them?" The sheer terror in my voice seemed to almost make him laugh harder. I had never cooked a day in my life. So, if he expected me to—

"I would like to cook for you," he said with a smile.

Thank the gods.

I watched him mount his horse with such grace that it had my lips parting as I gawked. How could the gods make a beautiful creature such as him? It was almost unfair. How do you compete with... *that*?

Trotting along the path that I knew led toward the castle gate, I stared out at the gardens blooming with vegetables ready to harvest. "Where do you get the meat from?" I asked.

"We raise animals on the castle grounds," he answered proudly. "I could take you to the farms we keep them on, if you'd like to see."

Gulping down the thought of actually seeing whatever he slapped onto my plate later, I shook my head in dismissal. "While I may enjoy the taste of meat, I'd rather not put a face to my meal today."

Laughing back, he tossed over his shoulder. "Duly noted."

I enjoyed the peaceful ride through the beautifully sunlit trail.

The trees were full of so many colors. The petals of their flowers had begun falling with the autumn air, floating down gracefully with the wind. Occasionally, I'd steal a glance Cass's way and noted the small petals stuck in his curls. He looked like one of his paintings that hung on the walls of the castle.

Had the gods looked this beautiful? Were they just as kind too? I wondered if that had been one of the reasons they chose him to be a lord in the first place. While Wilhelm was evidence that his people held *some* fear for him, Shae was proof of the love and loyalty they had for their leader as well. He had been so willing to change his behavior toward them and took my criticism with a smile on his face. He cared for his people, that much could be seen by anyone. He surely had the characteristics of a king that Andonia would be worthy of having.

Within an hour, sound began to reach us. The air filled with laughter and music and I assumed that we had arrived at the market. Riding toward a woman who waited for the two of us, I noticed she smiled at Cassius as we dismounted. "I'll take your…" When she turned to me, her words seemed to fade into silence. "You're the… Your Gra—"

"I'm Morrigan," I introduced myself. Stretching out my hand, I waited for her to take it, but she just gaped at me. "It's nice to meet you." With a little more enthusiasm than before, I pushed my hand toward her again.

But instead of returning the gesture, she dropped to her knees with both of our reins in her hands. "Your Grace," she panted. "Gods Blessed…"

Uncomfortable, and a little embarrassed, I tried to lean down and convince her to stand. "You can just call me—"

"Come," Cassius called, pulling me back as the woman continued to bow. Before we moved on, Cassius pulled a cloak around my shoulders and lifted the hood over my head. Then, I watched him do the same to himself. "So we can enjoy your time today," he explained. He turned his gaze down to the woman, still kneeling. "Please tie our horses. We will be here for a few hours."

She refused to meet my eyes again as she nodded, pulling the horses with her toward an area that looked like stables. Once we entered the bustling town, it all came to life before my eyes. A young man at the center of a large opening played a fiddle… or maybe it was a violin. Truthfully, I didn't know the difference between the two. But he danced with his fingers and kicked his feet as people surrounded him—women and children laughing as they twirled together. I watched men swinging their ladies around, smiles as bright as the sun and filled with love I had never experienced before.

Nothing could have compared to this. The joy, the music… This was *life*. This was *living*. I could have… I could have had… *this*… Before I had the chance to upset myself, Cass walked up beside me and I startled when his hand touched my lower back. Leaning in, he whispered in my ear, "Do you want to dance?"

As I tilted my head, watching the girls with cheeks as red as apples dancing with their partners, I shook my head. "No, thank you," I lied. I would have loved to be in his arms, twirling as passionately as they were. I just didn't know how.

Sensing some tension, Cassius escorted me past the musician and into an area lined with carts along the walls of buildings around us. They seemed to be selling all different types of foods and spices. Beside me, Cass pushed a basket into my hands. "Pick anything you want."

"Anything?" I challenged, with a teasing smirk.

His eyes trailed down from mine, stopping at my lips. And somehow the action alone pulled a gasp from my lungs. Though it was quiet, Cass heard it just as my mouth went dry. And with a chuckle, he brought his gaze back up. "Anything, *Your Grace*."

We walked around to the varying carts, and I took the opportunity to smell and taste anything that Cass allowed me to—which happened to be *everything*. If he saw me eyeing something on display, he'd purchase it instantly for me to try. And, by no surprise, there hadn't been a single thing I ate that didn't taste like pure divinity.

Though we wore our hoods, I didn't miss the occasional, weary glances our way. We weren't the only ones dressed in warm clothing now that fall had returned, but with Cass's large stature, we seemed to stand out more than most. Doing my best to ignore the stares, I filled our basket in no time and felt more than ready to burn off the excess food I had filled my stomach with on the ride back home. But as we passed the musician, Cass slipped his hand into mine and, without warning, twirled me around until I faced him.

When he pulled me against his chest, he leaned down and whispered beside the fabric covering my ear, "One dance."

"Cass... I don't know—"

He moved anyway, stepping in ways that I had no clue how to follow. Looking down, I eyed his feet and tried to mirror his movements, hoping to not stumble over my feet and embarrass myself in front of the entire town. But Gods, his laughter filled the air louder than the music and I could barely think anymore.

Willing to risk it, I stole a glance at what became the most beautiful sight I had ever seen. The smile on his face stretched wide and, even beneath the hood, the wind wisped through his hair. "There you go!" he cheered. Then, he winced a little and I realized I had stepped on his foot. My face stung with blistering heat, and I made to pull away but he stopped me. "What's a dance if you don't trip over a few steps? Loosen up."

I couldn't stop the laughter that lightened the weight in my chest and allowed him to spin me again. As the world around me blurred into a smeared painting of reds and yellows, I closed my eyes and embraced the freedom of it all. I let the sound of the music filter through my ears, washing away my anxiety and fears if only just for the day. I tried to imagine a life that I could have lived this way. Where I rode my horse from *my* home, maybe even traveled with *friends*. We would have eaten food until we were too sick to travel home, and then we'd stay in one of the inns just because we could. Because *I* could.

Cass spun me again and again, and my laughter was loud now, almost as loud as his. The musician strummed and strummed and... I stumbled. I stepped too far away from Cass and almost fell back, but he grabbed my hand and yanked me forward, the wind ripping the hood straight from my head. At some point while dancing, his hood seemed to fall as well, just enough for his bright red curls to peek through. And the moment the musician spotted him, he paused on his strings, bringing the beautiful sounds to a halt.

Everyone stood deathly still, searching for the cause of the disturbance, and Cassius swallowed before looking at me apologetically and lowering his hood the rest of the way. I wanted to scream at him to stop, to yank it back onto his head, but a villager nearby spoke before I could.

"Lord Cassius! It is an honor—" Turning to look at him, the man nearby seemed to choke on his words, watching me with his mouth open. "We... We were told of the girl with raven hair... dark as night... and your eyes..." Like the woman at the stables, he dropped to his knees, shoving his clean pants into the dirt without a care in the world. "Your Grace! Gods Blessed!"

"Please," I whispered. "It's alright don't—" But it was too late. The crowd around us stared in both confusion and awe as they all pinned their eyes on me. The whispers were deafening to my ears.

"She's here..."

"The chosen one... "

"It's her..."

I didn't know if I was supposed to say anything to them. Did I bow? Did I curtsey? What do you *do* in that situation? Cassius laced his fingers with mine but spoke to the people instead of me. "Please continue. We just came for some music and food. The princess is in need of rest now."

Even as he pulled me away, the whispers grew louder. They drowned out every thought inside of my head. What if they were looking down on me? Could they see through the façade that Cassius had dressed me in?

Could they see the damage? The pain? What if they thought I wasn't worthy? I *wasn't*—

My dress had been snagged by a pair of little fingers, making me stop in my tracks. Looking down, a little girl stood there, eyes wide and filled with absolute wonder. In her other hand she held a small bundle of orange lilies and her cheeks were painted the perfect shade of pink as she stared up at me. "My mommy says you healed my friend Alas..." she said quietly.

"Oh, no... I didn't—"

"I love lilies. Do you like lilies?" She shoved the flowers toward my chest, pleading with her eyes for me to accept them.

"I do." Letting go of Cass's hand, I knelt down before the girl as I smiled at her. "They're beautiful."

"You're beautiful," she whispered, almost giggling. "You can have them." She nodded her head and pushed them forward again, insisting now.

So, I took them from her hand, twirling the stems between my fingers. But the girl still stood there in front of me. She looked almost as nervous as I felt. Without thinking, I took one of the lilies and reached out to her hair, sliding the stem over her ear until it pinned itself there.

"You're beautiful too," I said to her.

Before she could respond again, she covered her mouth and hid her grin as she ran toward a group of little girls who all began to enclose her in their own circle. At some point, Cass reached down, offering me his hand and I stood with him. I didn't want to take my eyes off of the girls, but Cass pulled me along, waving at the villagers for me as we made our way back to the horses.

When we arrived back at the castle, Cass grabbed our bags and led me inside.

In the kitchen, he threw the bags onto the large table at the center and began emptying them out. "Let's see what we're working with," he called out.

Nerves fluttered in my stomach as I watched him and only quickened as he placed his hands on his hips, examining it all. Leaning against the table beside him, I dared to look up at his face that appeared colder than stone as he focused. "I picked horribly, didn't I?"

Though his laughter didn't sound very confident, he flashed me a cocky smile that seemed to lighten the room. "I can work with this," he assured me before rummaging through the produce, picking them out one by one. "Lena!"

When I turned, a small, older woman with hair as white as snow walked in quickly. She had to have been waiting nearby to answer him so fast. "My Lord," she said with a raspy, but sweet voice. Then her gaze turned to me and her cloudy eyes seemed to soften with the slightest flicker of blue glassing over them. "Your Grace."

"The staff is welcome to whatever the cooks make tonight. I'll be preparing food for Morrigan and me."

Without missing a beat, she responded with, "Thank you, My Lord."

Just as she turned to leave, he called out once more, "Would you start a fire beneath the grill for me?"

Offering him a quick nod, she walked to the corner where an iron rack hung above a pile of wood. The area had been covered by three brick walls, leaving just the small opening in front for cooking. Once the flames were lit, she left the kitchen and Cass finished organizing the food in front of us.

Knife in hand, he began cutting up the vegetables like it was an art to him. His fingers moved quickly, paying no mind to the knife in his hand, but cut with grace and precision. A quick memory of my childhood reminded me of when I wanted to surprise the priestess with cooked food before she returned from one of her weekly trips. I had picked the vegetables and even some flowers as a centerpiece for the table.

Lady Guinevere had been upstairs resting, and I didn't want to wake her. So, I grabbed one of the knives and began cutting zucchini, barely able to see over the counter myself. I yelped when I felt a quick, sharp sting slice through my finger and the priestess happened to arrive home at that exact moment. She rushed into the kitchen and noticed me holding my finger that now dripped with blood. My cheeks were wet from my own tears and I couldn't stop my lip from quivering.

But it wasn't because of the pain.

No empathy shone in her eyes, only rage, as she marched toward me and picked up the vegetable from the table, shoving it into my face. Brandishing the blood that had stained the produce, she hissed, "Look what you've done." She threw it onto the floor in a fit of anger and pointed to the kitchen door. "If you have no respect for the precious food that we provide you, then you can eat nothing! Go to your room!"

I had gone to bed hungry that night, and it wasn't the first time either. But, a part of me had been grateful that it was hunger and not another strike on my back.

Shaking away the rising emotions, I moved toward Cassius. "Could I?" I asked, pointing to the knife. *No better time to learn than now*, I convinced myself.

A large grin made dimples appear on his cheeks as he took a step back. "Be my guest." When I stepped in front of him, my grip on the knife couldn't have made my inexperience any more obvious. Cassius must have realized it himself because he leaned over, placing his own hand above mine as a guide. Grabbing a carrot, he placed it in front of the both of us while his chest pressed against my back. "I'll show you first."

His voice carried no judgement—only patience and kindness. While it was the hardest thing I had ever done, I tried to ignore the feel of his breath against my neck and follow his lead.

"The blade will do its job," he whispered. Placing pressure on my hand, the knife sliced through the carrot with ease and Cass's fingers wrapped tighter around mine as we moved. Each precise cut felt easier than the last, but all I could think about were his muscles enclosing my body against the table. He had me wrapped into him, closed off in his own little box and it had me shifting on my feet, not knowing what to do.

Turning my head, I *had* to sneak a glance at him… At the lips I had kissed before. I couldn't stop thinking about how they bruised my own, dominating me like he had been deprived of nourishment. My body became hyper aware of how his skin felt against my hand… How his breath made my hairs prickle on my neck.

"Pay attention," Cass ordered teasingly, and my cheeks flushed red as I turned back to the task at hand.

"I'm sorry…" But as I bit my bottom lip in an attempt to redirect myself, the knife slipped just a little and nicked my index finger. "Gods…" I hissed and yanked my hand away.

"I did tell you to pay attention." Cass brought my finger to his mouth and licked the blood away. The small act alone sent a thrilling heat between my thighs.

I should kiss him, I thought to myself. *I should lean forward and close the distance. Show him what I want.*

And when his eyes locked onto mine, I was convinced that I might actually do it. The hazel sharpened into a scorching desire that seemed to light up as they pierced into me. And the urge to feel his tongue in other places felt debilitating, but… my nerves got the best of me. Clearing my throat, it broke the trance between us and I watched the intense heat instantly cool as he took a step away toward the fire.

He grabbed a black pan and set it on top of the metal grate. That's when my rambling began, trying to shake the embarrassment of the past five minutes away. "Did your mother teach you how to cook?"

"I've never met my mother." Grabbing the vegetables, he placed them into the pan, a loud sizzle crackled from the heat of it searing the produce.

"What do you mean?"

He walked back over to me and, without warning, moved a single curl that had fallen over my brow. "We were orphans, all seven of us. We lived in the Holy Palace before there were *seven* of them. We were surrounded by other orphaned children and assisted as servants to the priests and priestesses. I still don't know why the gods chose *us*. They never gave a reason for their decision."

His finger moved to my chin and he ran his thumb over my skin tenderly with a soft look in his eyes that made my head spin. "Did you ever try to find them? Your parents?"

Pressing his lips together in a thin line, something that resembled pain seemed to crack through his face. "I did. We *all* did. We didn't find them, though. And it's been centuries now. The oldest recorded Andonian died at age 270. Whoever they are, they're long dead, Princess."

"I'm sorry," I whispered. "I would have given anything to at least know who my parents were."

Placing a gentle kiss on my head, he lingered for a moment and I closed my eyes at his touch. When he finally let go, he moved the food onto some plates and placed them in front of us, smiling. "Let's eat."

Chapter 10

The food Cassius had cooked us tasted like nothing I had ever eaten before.

Who would have known a lord such as him could cook such elaborate meals, especially being stuck with the mediocre food selection that I provided us with. When we both finished our meals, Cassius grabbed my wrist and raised my hand to his lips. One by one he licked the tips of my fingers, cleaning them off of any food that still lingered. I didn't know such an act could make my body yearn so badly. But as I watched him, I found myself staring only at his lips.

"I'm sorry for that night," he said quietly. Tangling his fingers with mine, he kept my hand close to his chest but stared into my eyes expectantly. "I'm sorry I lost control and scared you like that. I can't stop thinking about it."

After swallowing down every amount of inhibition I had, I finally gathered the courage to ask what I had been wondering for too long. "Is that why you haven't touched me again?" He looked taken aback by my question and brought his brows together. But before he could respond, I spoke again. "You *did* scare me. I thought I was going to die."

Seeing his jaw tense so hard, I could tell that my words caused some pain. "I won't forgive myself for that—"

"I do," I answered quickly. Even though the fluttering in my chest made my heart feel like it would explode, my mouth hadn't seemed to catch up. Because the moment his eyes lowered to my lips, I kissed him.

He let out a deep groan, not bothering to hold anything back as he pushed his tongue inside of my mouth. Pulling me into his chest, he deepened the kiss and fisted the fabric against my lower back. In response, I grabbed at his shirt, wanting to be as close to him as possible. I needed to touch him. I needed his skin on mine, his lips burning a brand into every part of my body. Without thinking, I bit his bottom lip and pulled away to look at him.

But the gentle eyes that had been there before were gone. They were dark now, filled with a primal desire that had my body shaking. "Lay back," he whispered. But it came out as more of a growl.

I wasn't sure what he planned to do to me, but Gods if I didn't want to find out. I pulled myself onto the table and lowered myself until my head touched the wood.

"Do you remember what I told you?" he asked.

His hands began tracing my thighs as light as a feather, slowly pushing my dress down to my hips with my knees raised. "Remember what?" My voice sounded breathless because I *was*. The way he stared at my body had my lungs forgetting how to work and my heart threatening to fall into my stomach.

Before he answered, he let out a deep chuckle that I could feel in my own bones. "You're about to find out." Offering no more explanation, he leaned down and placed a kiss along my inner thigh, stealing my breath.

That's when I remembered his words. *"Next time, Princess… It will be my tongue."* Almost panting already, I propped myself onto my elbows to look down at him. His kisses trailed slowly down my thigh, closer to my center. And just before he reached it, his lashes raised and I could see the hazel mocking me as a grin spread across his face.

"My Queen must be pleased. And I am *nothing*, if not a man of my word." Then one of his hands pressed against my waist, pushing until I lowered myself again. "Now, lay back down. I seem to have worked up another appetite."

Unable to look away, I trembled beneath him as he closed in, barely brushing his lips against my center. But I could feel his breath tickling me, and it made goosebumps rise on every part of my skin. He lingered there as I closed my eyes, deciphering if my desire to run outweighed the absolute need my body had for him in that moment.

"Cass…" Before I could say another word, his tongue darted out and licked me, putting pressure against my clit and forcing me to suck in a sharp breath. The only sound I could make came from my jagged breathing that I could scarcely control.

Then, he did it again. His movements were slow and intentional, making them all the more torturous. I didn't know my body could get so hot, but with his tongue moving the way that it was, I could very well have been on fire. "You taste so sweet," he groaned.

Placing his hands on my thighs, he spread them wider and I let out a whimper when he began sucking at the sensitive spot that now felt like it was throbbing.

"Like fucking *nectar*." Now his own voice sounded strangled, like he struggled finding a way to pace himself. "Do you want to come, Princess?"

"Yes!" I hadn't meant to yell, but my body physically burned with the coil wound so tight. I didn't want it; I *needed* it. "Yes, please!"

As he shoved his fingers inside of me, his lips moved to my thighs, and I almost whimpered from the loss of his tongue. But when I looked down at him, his eyes bore into mine with such intensity, it made me want to faint. "Do you trust me?" he asked, barely above a whisper.

"*Yes.*"

A second later, he curled his fingers again and the knot broke just as I felt the slight sting of his teeth sinking into my skin. It was nothing like it had been *before*. That night, he teeth were like jagged razors ripping apart my wrist and feeding boiling poison into my blood. This time? The sting was somehow pleasant, and it pushed my body into such a euphoric state that I thought I would actually pass out from my orgasm. My back arched as my head floated, light and dizzy, while my body tightened and convulsed around his finger. Each pull he took of my blood caused another spasm through my body, filling me with absolute bliss.

My moans were loud, but I didn't care. It felt so amazing. His teeth bit down harder, like he wanted to devour every bit of pleasure from me, and I screamed out his name finally before I fell back onto the table, barely able to keep my eyes open. I hadn't even noticed him releasing my thigh and crawling on top of me until his shadow loomed above my body. A slight prickle on my nose alerted me to how close he hovered above my face.

He kissed my cheek. "Are you alright?" Still trying to come down from whatever dimension that had just sent me to, I nodded. "Wrap your arms around my neck."

When I did, he lifted me from the table and held me, letting me cradle against his body, as he carried me back to his room.

CASSIUS

She had all but passed out in my arms, and I almost feared that I might have taken too much from her.

But the sound of her heartbeat fluttered strong in her chest—her breaths making her chest rise slow and deep as she sank further into her dreaming state. She didn't even stir when I laid her down on my bed, which had somehow become *our* bed as of late. Though, I didn't mind. I would have changed her into something more comfortable, but she looked so peaceful that I couldn't bring myself to wake her.

The black braid that Shae had placed in her hair now looked completely disheveled, curls hanging and knotting all over her face and pillow. I had no doubt that Shae would have a few choice words for me in the morning once she tried her hand at brushing through the mess I created. I had never seen a color so dark before on a mortal's body. It made her skin look as fair as porcelain in comparison, and the blush on her cheeks even deeper.

I almost flinched as she turned over, pulling the blanket with her and faced away from me. Gods… she might have been the most beautiful creature I had ever seen in my life. And she looked at me like *I* was a god.

She looked at me like all she wanted to do was please me, but her lips alone could bring me to my knees without even trying.

I shouldn't have bit her, but… *fuck.* I wanted to hear her crying in pleasure from it. I wanted to show her how different it could feel so she wouldn't have to fear what I had done that night, even if she claimed that she forgave me. I needed my own peace of mind.

Still, it was a selfish thing to do.

Placing the softest kiss on her head, I stood quietly before leaving the room. Harley happened to pass by with a book in his hands, just as I shut the door. "Is she sleeping?" he asked me.

Nodding, my hand lingered on the door for a moment longer, contemplating just going straight to bed with her.

"You've done well with her. She's happy, and she's safe. Which is more than I can say about the conditions she had been in before." A grimace of displeasure seemed to shine through his usually cool tone. "Walk with me."

I reluctantly let go of the door and followed after him. "How is she doing with her studies?"

With a hearty laugh, Harley tipped his head back and smiled. "She may be the smartest person I've ever encountered, especially for her age. She learns quickly, *too* quickly." He gave me a scornful look. "Maybe having me teach her wasn't the smartest idea you boys have come up with."

I shook my head in disagreement. "She deserves *that* much at least."

All of this had been so selfish. This game of playing house… enjoying her company as much as I did. In the beginning, I didn't mind it, but now? Morrigan was this ray of sunshine wherever she went. Every room she entered shone brighter than it did before. Every person she spoke to fell in love with her; they couldn't stop it if they wanted to. Pretending like everything was fine seemed to be getting harder and harder as each day passed.

Sensing my unease, Harley simply nodded and continued with me down the stairs where we parted ways. He walked toward the library and I made my way to the courtyard, sitting down on the steps. The sun would be setting soon and I stared out at the orange hues in the sky covered with deep grey and purple clouds. The mountains in the distance were beginning to look like nothing more than shadows as the darkness of night crept in, chasing away the light.

I could hear soft footsteps approaching and turned to see Shae as she stopped at the base of the stairs. Smiling up at me, she held out a basket of flowers and looked down at them. "She loves the scent of lavender."

Her words were those of a mother. Whether she intended to or not, that was the role Shae had now taken on with Morrigan. She loved her so deeply that she had reserved sections of the garden just for Morrigan to tend to when she had the time. Sometimes it seemed that *she* knew things about Morrigan before *Morrigan* even had the chance to learn them.

She looked back up at me, her smile glistening as white as pearls. "I've been placing it in her baths. It helps her sleep."

Morrigan… This perfect, beautiful girl.

Staring at the flowers, I thought of the child we had seen earlier that day. The way that Morrigan knelt down with no hesitation to give the girl her full attention… The way Morrigan's eyes lit up when the child complimented her, something she didn't seem used to. And Gods, if it didn't pull at my own heart to watch her place that flower in the girl's hair.

She didn't see it, but everyone around us had basically stopped breathing as they watched the interaction. I could see the light in everyone's eyes as they gazed at her, sparks of wonder seemed to fall through the crowd in waves.

Dangerous waves.

"She's lucky to have you," I told her. And another wave of guilt began to spoil the food in my stomach.

"No, My Lord." Her bright smile fell into a tender, soft one. "I believe *we...* are the lucky ones."

Chapter 11

MORRIGAN

Tuesday morning, the sound of Cass rummaging through the room woke me well before the sunrise did.

Groaning, I rubbed my eyes as I sat up. He had thrown on his riding gear in an unusual hurry. "Can't we skip? Just this once?" I asked with a yawn. Not that I didn't absolutely love our morning rides, but the bed happened to be calling my name. And extra sleep sounded like an absolute delight.

Turning around, the hard lines that seemed to stress his face instantly softened when his gaze met mine. He walked over to my side of the bed and sat down next to me. The area beneath his eyes looked a little darker than normal. "A guard went missing from his post at the border." He sighed and moved my hair from my face. "I'm going to be gone until

Thursday at the earliest. I'm sorry. But I can't risk your safety or anyone else's. I've increased the number of guards at the castle in my absence."

Leaning down, he pulled me in slowly for a kiss, and I did my best to hide my own disappointment. I knew he had no choice, but the time I spent with him would soon be coming to an end, and I wanted to savor every second of it.

"Promise me you'll stay within the castle grounds while I'm gone," he pleaded against my lips.

Nodding, but not wanting to pull away, I whispered, "I promise."

We relished a few more seconds until reality reeled him back and he pulled away. I watched every one of his steps as he left, feeling the distance as it grew. Thankfully, my own exhaustion made its way to ease me and when I laid back onto my pillow, my eyes gave me sweet, temporary relief.

The sleep didn't last long, of course. Because with Cass gone, Harley took the opportunity to make the rest of the week a studious one. He thought it would be a good distraction and a better excuse for me to brush up on some of the things we had already discussed together.

We got through it a lot faster than he expected us to and ultimately sent me away early for the day. With nothing to do, I had considered taking a walk through the gardens. But it began raining the moment I stepped out of the library. I decided to cut my losses and asked Shae if she could bring some hot tea to my room. Curling up in a ball beside my window, I let the sound of the rain tapping against the glass soothe me as I sipped from my cup and pulled out the book Harley had given me a while back.

The Diary of Daisies and Hellebores.

The pages themselves were written as an actual diary, even listing the day of the week at the top of the entries. It was a unique format that I hadn't actually read before, and when I turned the book over to find the author's name, it didn't contain one. The book had been bound in leather and felt incredibly stiff, as if it hadn't been read before. That wouldn't surprise me, though. Cass had thousands of books, and I had never actually seen Cass even hold one in his hands. This had likely been left on one of those shelves for centuries.

As the grey clouds looked overhead, casting a shadow over the fields of gardens in my view, I leaned against the cool glass and lost myself in reading.

I had lived twenty-one years of my life sleeping by myself, but my bed had never felt emptier with Cass gone.

Trying my best to stay distracted, I asked Shae to accompany me on a morning ride. She had been thrilled and even sat down with me afterward to eat a small breakfast. With Lady Guinevere relatively out of my life now, Shae seemed to task herself with that role. Almost every day I would annoy her with my gratitude, and each time she'd shush me and explain that my thanks weren't necessary.

But they were.

She saved me, in a way.

That week, when I had practically isolated myself from the world, she cared enough to push. She didn't judge me and she didn't take advantage of the knowledge she learned. Shae had to be one of the most genuine women this world had to offer—the kindest too. And I'd remind her every chance I could.

When my session with Harley ended early again, I decided to assist her with some gardening now that the sun was out and shining brightly. As I leaned down and smelled the lavender in front of me, I felt Shae place her basket down next to mine.

"May I ask you something?" Her voice sounded a little distant, like she felt unsure if she should speak at all.

"Of course," I responded brightly, hoping to reassure her in some way.

When I turned to her, she nibbled nervously on her bottom lip. "I've tried not to speak about them, but I was curious if it would be too forward to ask who gave them to you."

She didn't need to explain any further. She was talking about my scars.

"It's just… I don't understand. You're our future Queen. Who would allow anyone to—"

"I was a bit of a troubled child," I interrupted her. Tilting her head, she looked at me like she didn't understand what I meant. "I gave the priestess a *very* hard time growing up. I would yell back, play too loudly, break things… She called them *lessons*. She felt that, without them, I would lose my sense of discipline. And if I couldn't get my act together, I would disappoint the *lords*."

While her expression didn't move an inch, she cleared her throat before picking a few stems of lavender, placing them into my basket. "You were a child, sweet girl. Gods blessed…"

She rested her hands on her knees as she knelt against the ground, looking as though she needed to breathe for a moment. Even though her eyes were closed, I could see the dampness that clung her lashes together. But she blinked the tears away and turned to me with a smile.

"Why don't we draw up a nice, warm bath for you?"

Just as eager to move on from the conversation as she seemed to be, I answered, "I would like that very much."

My saving grace from the tension slowly building in the castle was waking the next day to a kiss from Cassius. He leaned over me as I opened my eyes, grinning ear to ear. "Did you find the guard?" I asked sleepily.

Nodding, he leaned down to kiss my neck and whispered, "He had injured himself somehow, though he had no memory of the incident. But he is home safe now, recovering at the palace." The feel of his breath against my skin made my body shudder. Planting more kisses along my collarbone, he grabbed my leg and wrapped it around his hip. "I missed you," he groaned.

"I missed you, too."

And just as I thought he would go lower, he made his way back up, placing a kiss on my lips. "I have work to catch up on." He pried himself away, leaving me a steaming hot mess, and called over his shoulder, "I'll see you at dinner!"

Tease.

With Cassius busying himself trying to catch up, Saturday arrived sooner than I wanted it to.

I dressed myself for dinner but asked Shae to assist me with my hair. Truthfully, I had way too much of it to do on my own, and I preferred that it didn't remain a bird's nest on the top of my head. If I wanted it to actually look presentable, I knew Shae was my only option. So, she pinned it up the way she normally would when it wasn't in a braid, and, for the first time, I made it to the hall before any of the guys arrived.

Relishing in the temporary silence, I made my way to my seat, letting my hands drift over the top of the chairs that the lords would soon sit in. Their seats almost felt assigned now. On the opposite side it would be D... then, Naaz... then, Dez... My finger grazed the seats and I counted off the next few names in my head. *Cain... Eris...* Once I got to my own, I smiled at the head of the table where Cass would sit.

Then, a sudden blush crept in, making my cheeks almost cramp as the memory of Cass laying me back on the kitchen table played out in my mind. His hands on my thighs... Biting me... His tongue in my—

"Why is your face so red, Princess?" Dez startled me from the side, causing me to jump. Even my heart felt like it had almost burst from my chest.

With my hand soothing the fluttering between my breasts, I tried to hide the redness that now bloomed there as I shook away the imagery. "Wouldn't you like to know?" I teased him.

Eyes twinkling in amusement, and somewhat of a challenge, he pulled his seat out and watched me as he lowered into it. "Oh... I *would*."

Each time I saw Dez, he somehow looked more beautiful than the last. I didn't know how that was possible, but something about his eyes was so mesmerizing—the way the blue danced and shimmered in the light. Sometimes they almost looked like they were actually glowing... And his lips... They were practically begging to be kissed. When a small smirk tugged at them, I realized that I had been staring at him.

"Well, it's none of your business," I said quickly, dropping down into my seat and praying for the gods to take away the embarrassment that shone clear across my face.

Gods... I thought to myself. *These men are corrupting me.*

The others began filtering through, and I eased when I felt Cass's hand touch the back of my neck as he approached. "You're an early bird today." He laughed and sat down beside me.

I opened my mouth to reply, but the doors opened with a loud bang and a deep, dark laughter seemed to rip the air right out of the room. "A bird. I rather like the sound of that."

I knew I would regret it... and I *did*. The moment I turned toward the entrance, my heartbeat seemed to cease altogether. Standing before me was the man who had been placed at the center of my nightmares. Wearing all black, he looked like night itself in the worst form. His black hair barely hung over the front of his face, cut short above his ears. The darkness that filled the hall behind him seemed to cling to his tan skin—like he *was* that darkness and could bend it to his own will.

His black eyes, devoid of any emotion or color, met my own and we stared at each other. "It suits you, does it not? *Little bird?*" He walked toward Naaz, refusing to remove his gaze, and claimed his seat before Naaz could sit down. "Drifting from cage to cage... You're like a sad, black dove." Then, something in his eyes seemed to glisten within the shadows. But whatever the thought was, he kept it to himself as he swiped a grape from the platter in front of him and popped it into his mouth.

"You didn't tell us you were coming, Kaiden." I felt Cass's hand touch my thigh, giving it a gentle, reassuring squeeze. As if he wanted to convey, *"I'm here, don't worry."*

"I wasn't aware I had to, *Cassius*," Kaiden spit his name out like it disgusted him. But then, he turned back to me again, and his penetrating stare felt like an animal stalking its prey before it attacked. "So many aviaries to choose from now, *little dove*. Seven in fact. How lucky you must feel."

I had to physically pry my eyes away from him and look at Cassius, begging for some form of relief from the tightening that began in my chest. But Cass had his eyes pinned on Kaiden, fury lighting the brown specs close to his pupil.

"Don't ruin our appetites, Kaiden," Dez said amongst the silence. "Let us eat and be done with this."

Any joy that our dinners typically consisted of had now crumbled amidst the unspoken anger that seemed to loom above us like a cloud. I didn't even know whose anger it was. But it bounced off of the walls in echoes, leaving me at the center of tangled webs that I couldn't decipher.

Unable to form a verbal response, I tried to scoot back into my seat and relax with Cass beside me. I had a feeling that he wouldn't let Kaiden hurt me, even if everything in his eyes told me that's *exactly* what he wanted to do. Thankfully, Cass began loading food onto my plate as he sensed my own unease, and Kaiden let out a loud, crude scoff diagonal to me.

"Does he hand feed you too?" he asked. His tone sounded condescending enough that I felt two times smaller than I had before—like my body was literally shrinking. Trying to avoid his eyes, I could feel them like knives, striking the side of my face.

To my surprise, Eris leaned in near my shoulder. "Ignore him, Morrigan. It's been so long that *Kaiden* has forgotten how to act in the presence of a *lady*." Eris's voice dripped with hatred, and I then realized he had never spoken to me like that. But he continued as he sat up straight again. "He's surrounded himself with too many *whores*, it seems."

"A *lady*," Kaiden mocked, ignoring the jab that Eris made toward him. "I highly doubt *anything* that's happened within these castle walls would be considered ladylike... Now *would* it, little dove?"

Something about the nickname he chose for me made my body shiver. It felt like a bad omen. I couldn't help myself as I raised my eyes to meet his again, my limbs instantly cold from the ice in his stare.

Leaning forward with his elbows on the table, he sneered and pulled his lips back in disgust. "I can practically smell him on you, My *Lady*. Did you let him fuck you too—"

"Kaiden!" Cass stood, slamming his hands on the table, and I could almost feel the earth shake beneath us in response.

Kaiden glared at Cassius with a raging fury that seemed deeper than whatever *this* was. It had nothing to do with me, that much could be seen by anyone with eyes. But what really caught my attention was the change in *his* stare. His black eyes had the faintest, silver shimmer to them and I could have sworn shadows danced along his skin, crawling around on the markings beneath his shirt.

"She behaves with more grace than *you* do," D said quietly from his chair at the end of the table. "And you're hundreds of years older than her."

Everyone seemed a little shocked at his interjection, and Dez smiled to himself across from me. After a few seconds of Kaiden not responding, I released the tension that had me gripping my fork enough to turn my knuckles white.

I jabbed it into the piece of meat on my plate and stopped midair when Kaiden spoke again, more quietly this time. "I guess Maeryn *did* teach you something, after all."

Don't let him get to you, I begged myself. *Eat your food and ignore him.* So, I pushed the food into my mouth as a reason not to respond.

"She misses you, little dove. She looks forward to seeing you soon."

As I tried my best to chew my food, one by one the scars on my back lit up like flames under my skin. Just the thought of her felt like five more lashes had torn into me. Nausea began to roll in my stomach, realizing that I would have to see her again. As the food in front of me blurred, tears seemed to gloss over my eyes. I didn't even mind the sting; it was nothing compared to the fire sizzling along my back.

"There's the frightened little bird she told me about." He sounded so amused, like he was proud of himself for destroying every ounce of confidence I had built since arriving here—breaking the backbone that took *weeks* for me to develop. "Do you know what I think, little dove? I think your leash is too long." I could feel him leaning closer, and his words somehow reached my ear in a painful whisper. "I'll be sure to shorten it when it's my turn."

Before anyone else could react, I shoved my chair away and stood from the table. I didn't even say anything as I walked out of the hall, rushing to find privacy before they all bore witness to me falling apart. I somehow managed to make it to the courtyard before bending over the side railing and puking into the grass below.

You let him get to you, I scolded myself. *You've dealt with his kind for twenty-one years, and you let him get to you in a single night.*

I almost yelled when a hand touched my shoulder, but I turned to see Shae standing behind me with a worried look on her face. "Sweet girl, are you alright?" She tried rubbing my back, but the tears were on the cusp of falling.

"I'm fine, Shae," I lied. Shrugging her off, I quickly recoiled from the railing and ran down the stairs. "I just need a walk."

"Let me accompany you, dear."

Putting a hand up, I didn't bother turning around as I called over my shoulder. "No, really, I just need some air. I'd rather be alone right now, thank you!"

As I walked past the garden, I followed a path that trailed into the woods. I didn't know where it led, but I didn't care. I just needed to *go.* Eventually the paved ground turned to grass and dirt, and even with alarm bells ringing in my ears, I continued on through the trees.

"You're like a sad black dove." Black doves represented mourning, grief… anguish. He and Maeryn really did deserve each other.

Branches and briars pulled at the hem of my dress until one snagged the fabric, causing me to stumble over onto my hands. I let out a loud curse as I quickly brushed the twigs and pebbles from my palm before pulling at my gown. It had lodged itself through vines of a broken tree trunk that didn't want to let go.

"Little dove..." The name rang through my ears in the perfect cadence of his own voice, only infuriating me more. "Let." I pulled at the dress. "Me." I yanked it again, growling my words through my teeth. "Go!" On the third try, the end of the fabric tore apart and I fell onto my back with my chest heaving.

I can't do this. Why would they choose me *for this?!* Self-pitying tears burned in my eyes as I looked up at the sky that had now fallen dark. My glare shot to the gods that put me in this compromising position in the first place. "Why are you doing this to me?!"

That's when the tears began to fall. I couldn't stop them even if I tried. They fell like rain down my cheeks, soaking the leaves tangled in my hair on the back of my head. I wasn't a queen. I wasn't a lady. I was *no one.*

A loud snap of a twig had me gasping, and I sat up quick enough to make my head spin. Looking around, I could barely see more than a foot in front of me with the sun now gone. I did the first thing I could think to do, and that was to grab a large branch from the ground and stand, holding it out in front of me.

"Who's there?!" I yelled.

No one replied. I only heard the sound of more leaves crunching, like someone had begun circling me, *stalking* me. I was sure my heartbeat could be heard for miles as it pounded in my chest. The branch grew heavy in my trembling hands. Cass had said that there were attacks recently, but his castle was heavily guarded. They couldn't be here. They *wouldn't* be here.

"Come out, now!" I demanded, though the shrill pitch of my voice didn't exactly give off *menacing and dangerous.*

A deep laugh from behind startled me, and I swung the branch in its direction, but my body collided with a chest as hard as stone. *Cassius.* "Are you alright?" he asked, his voice shaking with concern.

"Was that you?"

Looking down, he noticed the branch in my hand and cocked his head a little, clearly stifling a slight grin on his lips. "What were you going to do with a *branch*?"

"I heard something... in the shadows... and I..." When I realized that Cassius was, in fact, mocking me, my fear simmered into a slight irritation. "It was better than nothing!" Throwing the branch to the ground, I pushed past him and searched for the trail back home.

"Princess! I'm sorry!" he called out behind me, but I ignored him even as he stepped beside me. *Curse his long legs.* "You ran off upset, understandably so, but then Shae burst through the doors concerned about you. She said you stormed into the woods and she didn't know what to do."

When I refused to turn and face him, he pulled my arm to stop me from walking any further. Then, he twisted me until his hands cupped my face and he forced me to look into his eyes.

"I'm sorry. I sent everyone home. It's just you and me."

Knowing they were gone, I let out a disgruntled sigh and pushed my head into his chest. "I thought you said that Kaiden wouldn't attend the dinners," I said, sniffling away the remaining tears.

Pulling me tighter, I could feel the worry in his embrace. I really *had* scared him, and Shae... I owed her an apology. "He didn't tell anyone he would be coming. If I had known, I would have... I'm sorry."

I thought *Eris* was bad. But the emptiness in Kaiden's eyes and the hatred behind every word he spat at me weighed me down like bricks. Not that I expected each of them to like me, but he spoke like I disgusted him in every way a person could. He looked at me like I was no better than a rabid pest that he wished to exterminate from his presence. And Maeryn? She would only fuel the fire within him, adding to whatever cause he had to despise me.

Cassius pulled back and kissed my head. "Come, Princess. Let's lay down."

As we walked back to the castle, my mind continued to race through every possible outcome this year could have. I had grown to feel so safe with Cassius, with Harley... Shae...

Kaiden? He planned to ruin me, and I had a gut-wrenching intuition that it would only end in death. The only question that remained was...

"*Whose?*"

The Diary of Daisies and Hellebores

I saw him today. I tried to keep myself from blushing every time our eyes met, but it was near impossible. He is so beautiful. Beautiful and forbidden. I understand why we cannot be together—the consequences of it—but they do not make me want him any less. He does not notice me, though. It is likely for the best. I can only truly remain content in my dreams. So, for now, that's where I will wait for him.

Chapter 12

Monday morning felt solemn because it marked my sixth week
with Cass.

Two more… That's all I had. Yes, I would still see him
every week at dinners, but I would be expected to share my time with
another man. A man who would likely be putting equal, if not more, effort
into courting me the way that Cass had. I knew that was my purpose, but it
didn't stop the feeling of being a "used-up toy" from making me second-
guess everything Cass and I had done thus far. Which, in turn, made it
relatively impossible for me to focus as Harley sat across from me,
quizzing me on new things I had learned recently.

Harley pulled out textbooks the week prior on *"the gifted"* that lived
among the mortals in Andonia. He stressed the absolute importance of me

knowing and understanding the different abilities these people possess that vaguely mirrored the lords' own powers.

When it was clear to him that I hadn't a lick of memory on the subject—due to my mind dwelling on my looming future that involved a certain black-eyed monster—he handed me the textbook to read on my own. In his own way, I could see that it was an attempt to give me space, while also holding me accountable. Either way, I hoped he sensed my gratitude as I rushed back to Cass's room.

He must have mentioned something to Shae, because she arrived moments later with a hot cup of tea. Smiling as I took a sip, I shrugged to myself and made my way to the window, basking in the sun's warmth, and opened the textbook.

While the gods were not allowed to bear children *together*, they made no law stating gods could not bear a child with a *mortal*. These encounters resulted in gifted individuals, born with an ounce of their parental god's blood inside of them. With their mortal blood diluting most of the power transferred to them, it caused the gods little concern. In truth, these gifts came to be of great use to the kingdom, and the war that came to be.

- **There were those born with elemental gifts, the ability to manipulate our earth and the energy that nature provides us with: earth, water, fire, and air. While fire is usually considered unpredictable and dangerous, these wielders contributed fiercely to the war and became the right hands of the lords in the aftermath. Their gift is considered rarer than the other elements, and far deadlier.**
- **Shadow walkers are known to manipulate darkness to travel. They could slip into a single shadow and arrive thousands of**

miles away in the blink of an eye. Of course, the walker must have an image of the location derived from their own memory for it to work. They became essential to the lords, as they could transport others with them, as well.

♦ Seers live out their days in the palaces with the priests and priestesses. They are blessed with visions of our past, present, and ever-changing future. Andonians consider them the keepers of our tales, making our very history immortal in their eyes. What makes their gift especially unique, is their inability to see visions pertaining to the gods.

The lords share in some of these gifts, as they have been personally blessed by the gods themselves to protect our kingdom. They can manipulate elements but also contain special abilities that are exclusive to each of them.

While there are many fascinating realities of the powers that have come to be, there is also tragedy. There are gifts that are so dark, so deadly, that the people of Andonia will not even mention them by name. These gifts are known as—

The doors to my room were kicked open. Whipping my head around, I saw Cass standing in the empty space, panting frantically. "Cass?" I asked, but his eyes seemed to be in a daze of sorts as he stared at me. Then, he blinked, and I could barely register it as he ran across the room with one hand balled into a fist.

Grabbing me, he forced me against his chest and buried his face into my neck. His breathing was so hard it sounded like his lungs were wheezing. Tangling one hand in my hair, he inhaled a shaky breath as he crushed my body with his.

"Are you okay?" I asked, wrapping my arms around him in return.

"I had to make sure you were safe." I had never heard his voice sound so pained. Whatever he had seen... *heard*... Cass was *scared*.

His arms constricted further, almost hurting me. "Cass," I exhaled. "You're holding me too tight."

Immediately releasing me, he dropped into the chair that I had been sitting on without saying another word. He then lowered his head, staring at the floor in deep thought, so I knelt down in front of him.

"What's going on?" I asked him. The front of his hair appeared slick and drenched in sweat. Even his cheeks had flushed a deep red.

I reached out to touch his face, but he stopped me with his hand, lowering my wrist back down. If he clenched his teeth any harder they would have shattered into pieces. "Dez is coming tomorrow to take you back with him."

I couldn't help but feel shocked. Falling back onto the heels of my feet, I looked up at him. "Did I do something?" I whispered. "I still have the rest of this week *and* next week with you. Do you... Do you *want* me to leave?"

It was only then that I really looked at his other hand, which still sat balled into a fist in his lap. He had refused to meet my gaze since he arrived to the room so abruptly, but the moment that he did... his eyes melted in an instant and he brought his free hand to my cheek.

"I don't," he answered quietly. Then, sighing, he pressed his forehead against mine and I could feel his own heat radiating from his body. "There was another attack." Opening his hand, I looked down to see a piece of fabric hidden in his palm. Not just *any* fabric, though. It was from *my* dress. The same dress that tore in the woods outside of his courtyard. "While my guards were searching for them, they found *this* lodged into a tree with an arrow penetrating it."

"My gown..." My voice barely fell above a whisper as I gaped at it.

"I thought…" He cleared his throat and when I looked back up at him, the rim of his eyes were red. "I thought they had taken you."

"Who is doing this?" I asked.

Closing his eyes, he stood sharply and I almost fell back from the wave of air that rushed at me. His eyes were closed and he began pacing the room. "I don't know." He let out a curse under his breath and retreated back into the daze he had been in when he arrived. "They just fucking *disappear. How* are they disappearing?!"

"Cass?"

When he turned to me, the expression on his face looked desperate. "Your safety comes first. Whoever they are, they've been here. At *my* castle. The best option is to move you and find them before they realize you're even gone. Dez is prepping his staff and investigating anyone that seems even the slightest bit suspicious. You'll be moved quietly."

I stood, approaching him cautiously. "But…"

"No, Morrigan!" The cutthroat tone in his voice made me flinch, but I knew he didn't mean it. *He isn't her. You're okay,* I told myself. Cassius seemed unfazed by my reaction and continued to yell. "I will *not* risk your safety! Even for my own selfish desires."

Before I had a chance to respond, he grabbed my face and kissed me fiercely. I didn't even have time to think. Just the taste of him was enough to send me into a trance of my own, now savoring every second I had left with him.

These… *people* were looking for me. *What if they had been in the woods with me that night? Was the laughter I heard from Cass, or someone else waiting in the dark to snatch me? What would have happened if Cass hadn't shown up when he did?* No one knew who these people were, or what they wanted. But they pierced cloth from *my* dress into that tree as a warning.

Pulling me onto his bed, Cass cradled my body against his, and neither of us were willing to leave the room for the rest of the day. This would be my last night with him. Tomorrow, everything would change… *again*.

My chest tightened a little as I noticed that Cassius wasn't beside me when I woke the next morning.

Sluggishly, I threw on a robe and made my way downstairs for breakfast. I knew that Dez would be coming, I just didn't care to make a show of myself to anyone. No one had warned me that this would be difficult. Growing up alone most of my life, I never actually had the opportunity to understand the feeling of loss. There were no friends to play with as a child, no boys to fawn over. But now, it was a feeling I would have to grow accustomed to over the next year. Though, I had a sense that gratitude is the only thing I would feel if I made it out of *Kaiden's* castle in one piece.

When I arrived at the hall, the food hadn't even been served yet—and Cass was still nowhere to be found. Letting my fingers trace the wood of the table, I slowly made my way to my seat as if my steps could slow time itself. I didn't know when, or *if*, I would be here again.

My first home away from home.

Sitting silently, I waited in my chair for everyone to arrive. Rain began to fall, like the clouds felt my own anguish and wept tears for me—droplets slithered down the glass, leaving a trail of water behind them. At least I could feel some form of relief knowing that it was Dez that would be retrieving me. Aside from Cass, Dez had spoken to me the most out of the lords so far. He seemed approachable, maybe even likable. That was, when he didn't act absolutely infuriating with his overinflated ego and persistence. Still… my situation could have been worse… by a lot.

Just then, the doors to the hall opened. Dez and Cass's laughter filled the empty silence, making the room a smidge lighter than it had been before. Their friendship seemed to be the most genuine relationship I had experienced thus far. Every joke to them seemed to be a secret that only *they* shared, and I almost envied it.

Noticing my stare, Dez caught my eyes and smiled. "My *princess!*" he announced loudly. "I've come to steal you at last." As they walked to their seats, he seemed to take in my choice of clothes. His smile twitched a little, showing the smallest crack in his cool demeanor. "It's decided. Only the thinnest of robes will be allowed in your wardrobe."

Rolling my eyes, I pulled the clothing closer to my chest, covering myself completely. "Perv," I whispered.

"Don't flatter me, Princess." He winked and made his way to his seat.

Behind me, I felt Cass's hand touch my chair and my grief turned to anger, knowing that it was his decision for me to leave him so soon. Yes, he wanted to protect me, but I had absolutely no say in the matter. And for that, I was furious. I moved my body away from his touch, an obvious snub that he noticed immediately and retreated his hand because of it. "Let's just hurry. I missed dinner last night and I'm *starving.*"

"I find that hard to believe," a voice called from the doors—the very *last* voice that I wanted to hear—even if I knew that she was coming. "You look so…" Her voice trailed off and the sound of her heels clacking against the marble crammed the empty space between us. "*Healthy.*"

Ignoring her remark, I stared down at the table and waited as the staff brought in plates instead of a full buffet of food. Shae placed mine in front of me and put a gentle hand on my shoulder, smiling sadly. I had so many words to say to her, but I knew that if I spoke now, Maeryn would find a reason to be angry. It was better for all of us if I remained as silent as possible while we ate. So, I offered her a small smile in return and watched her leave the hall, disappearing into the kitchen.

Regardless, my interaction had somehow irritated the priestess, and she let out a scoff beside me. Finally turning to look at her, I realized that Guinevere was nowhere in attendance. "Where is the Lady?" I asked Maeryn.

She didn't look up at me as she answered, "Preoccupied at the moment." Her lips curved upward at the corners, barely enough to notice. "It will be just you and I this week."

That was enough to ruin my entire appetite. It meant no respite from Maeryn's words or *lessons*. Perhaps Lady Guinevere didn't want to come. I wouldn't even tell her goodbye the last time we saw each other. Cass's hand slid onto my knee, and I could feel the hesitation in his touch. But I didn't move away. I didn't want to. Instead, I kept my mouth shut and began eating my food, praying the gods would send a divine miracle to intervene with this day.

When our meals were finished, the priestess clapped her hands together once, loud enough to make my entire body jump. "Let's get dressed!" she exclaimed. The happiness in her voice had to be laced with some kind of venom. She was *never* happy.

"I'm not a child anymore, Priestess. I can dress myself." Looking around the room, I hoped to see Shae's face somewhere. I could have used her as an escape to avoid being alone with Maeryn.

"She's a little spitfire now," Dez laughed, pushing his plate away from him. "What did you *do* to her, Cassius?"

"She seems to have developed a knack for putting people in their place," he said, looking up at me with amusement. I lost myself in his eyes for a moment, hoping to remember every speck of color in them. "She sure puts me in mine most days."

The men chuckled together, but I could feel the heat radiating from the priestess. "Until your coronation, you are still under my care," she reminded me. "*I* will assist you."

Twisting in my stomach, the food quickly turned sour. But I kept my emotions in check as I stood from the table. Giving Cass a stiff smile, I turned to leave and my heart beat in rhythm with her heels behind me. She didn't waste any time. The second the doors to the hall closed, she wrapped her bony little fingers around my arm, digging them into my skin. *Don't flinch,* I thought to myself. *Don't even react.*

"You've grown some nerve," she hissed into my ear, walking me up the stairs.

It took every ounce of courage I had to answer her. "You can't speak to me like that."

Her laughter almost did the job, but I kept my body still, refusing to let her win.

We finally arrived at my room—*my* room, not the room that I had actually been sleeping in for gods knew how long. Maeryn would have likely had a coronary attack if she knew. *There's an idea*, I chuckled to myself.

But the humorous depiction of Maeryn being the one struggling on the floor died out as I heard my bedroom door slam behind me. I turned to her, a snarky remark hanging from the tip of my tongue, when her hand cracked across my face so strong it sent me straight to the floor. As I knelt there, gasping for breath at the utter shock of it, her feet came to view in front of me.

"You are no *queen* yet. You are *Morrigan. No one.*" She spat her words at me with deeper disgust than she had ever shown before. *Maybe Kaiden had said something to her about our encounter.* "You may have been gone for a couple of weeks, *girl*. But I will remind you how to address your *priestess*."

A newfound anger bubbled in my chest and, holding my cheek that now pulsed with pain, I tilted my head up to her. "I know about Kaiden," I sneered. Blinking a few times, she took a small step back. "Is that why you're so cruel to me? He doesn't *love* you Maeryn. I don't think he even has the capability of loving someone."

Though her face showed no change, her eyes simmered with profound anger. The blue turned to piercing ice and her movements were slow as she reached toward my vanity and grabbed a leather belt sitting on top of it. It almost felt planted there, like this had been her plan since she arrived.

You know *it was.*

With a faint, angry blush creeping across her cheeks, she whispered, "Hands on the pillar, Morrigan." Then, her lips curled back as her eyes raked down my body. "And take off that robe… You look like a *whore*."

"No," I refused. It took a copious amount of effort to try to settle the trembling in my hands. But Maeryn wasn't backing down… she wouldn't.

"Don't drag this out longer than it needs to be. Pillars."

Just call for someone. Call for Shae, for Cassius… even Dez.

I don't know why I didn't. Maybe it was the familiarity of it all. What would they even *do*? Lords didn't have the power to govern priests or priestesses. They were their own people—made their own rules and laws. I learned that quickly in the textbooks Harley gave me. The lords couldn't intervene in their affairs. The only ones with the power to do so were the gods themselves.

So, I stood slowly, averting my eyes to the floor to avoid her glare. Pulling the strings to my robe, I allowed it to fall down to my feet and reluctantly leaned into the pillar, wrapping my hands around it. I closed my eyes and did my best to relax my body as much as possible; it always hurt worse if I tensed.

"If you yell, I'll hit harder," she warned, hissing like a poisonous snake. "Keep your mouth shut."

Strike.

The first hit took the breath from my lungs. It had been so long that my body no longer took it in stride. The crack of the leather burned into my skin, and I had to bite down on my lip to muffle the sound now stuck in my throat.

Strike.

Don't be weak, Morrigan. My thoughts were the only assurance I had. *She wants you weak. Don't be* weak.

Strike.

Each hit felt harder. Harder than any *lesson* in the past. I couldn't even think over the tears that were pouring from my eyes. Their droplets splashed against my toes on the wooden floor, soaking the robe beneath me. All I could do was cover my mouth, keeping my cries silent so no one would hear. But the feel of my skin tearing on my back made me want to scream.

Four more strikes came before I fell to the floor, unable to hold my own weight. Bringing my knees to my chest, I started to sob. My cries were overpowering, making my entire body shiver and convulse. *"You are no one,"* played in my head on repeat, a broken echo that circled through my ears. *She's going to tell Kaiden of this.* It was undoubtedly his idea in the first place—a message for me... a glimpse through the curtains of what my life would be like soon, once he got his hands on me.

As she placed the belt back on the vanity, it made a small *clank* sound when the metal touched the wood. Then, she moved to my bed, laying out a familiar, blue gown. "Clean yourself up and get dressed so we can leave," she said with no emotion lingering in her menacing voice. When she left, the rest of my body fell to the floor, curling into a ball.

I lay there, crying… alone. I was always *alone*. I always *would be* alone. I would have to find a way to hide the fresh wounds from yet another person, and I wouldn't have Shae this time to cover for me. Sniffling, I began to sit up when a quiet knock on my door put my body on high alert.

"Princess?" Dez whispered through the crack that Maeryn coincidentally left open. Moving quickly, I grabbed a blanket from the bed and covered my chest before wiping the tears from my cheeks.

"I'm not decent!" I called to him, though it likely wouldn't have stopped him from entering. If anything I had probably given him an incentive to barge in. "I'll… I'll be out in a moment!"

Correct on my assumption, Dez ignored me and walked into the room. "I could hear you crying, love. I know you're upset about leaving, but I swear…" he stopped short when he saw me on the floor. Pulling the blanket tighter against me, I tried to make sure he couldn't see any evidence of the wounds that stung as I pressed my back against the bed. After assessing me, his eyes lowered to the floor and his usual baby blues appeared to swirl with storm clouds brewing within them. "Are you hurt?"

Looking down, I saw clearly what he was referring to. Directly beside me were a few drops of blood, perhaps that's what I had felt soaking my robe. Thankfully, it remained hidden beneath the blanket covering me.

I let out an insincere laugh, hoping it fooled him enough to redirect his impression. "Just a little wardrobe malfunction. You know how fussy those dresses can be."

As I cleared my throat, his eyes lifted back up to mine, but the hollowness that filled them showed me that he didn't believe a word I had just told him.

"Just let me get dressed and we can leave… Please."

The *"please"* seemed to soften his features enough for him to nod in agreement. But he said nothing as he closed the door behind him.

Chapter 13

It took a few extra minutes of composing myself to get dressed before making my way to the foyer.

Cassius and Dez stood huddled together as they whispered. But when they noticed me approaching, they both stopped talking. Dez offered me a smile that didn't quite meet his eyes, and walked outside, leaving me alone with Cass. I didn't know what to say to him, not after what happened.

Thankfully, he broke the silence first. "You were crying."

Thanks, Dez.

"I'm fine," I lied, hoping to convince myself as well.

His hand reached up and gently wrapped around my arm. "What happened?"

The door to the courtyard remained open and I turned to see the priestess standing at the bottom of the stairs. To any outsider, she looked as though she was admiring the garden, but I knew better. She was thinking of every way she could kill it. Plastering a smile on my face, I turned back to him.

"I'm just going to miss you. That's all." It wasn't a lie. I *would* miss him… every night.

Without letting it show if he believed me or not, he let go of my arm and cradled my face with his hands before kissing me tenderly. I opened my mouth, treasuring the taste of him, and melted into his body, letting him hold the weight of my whole world in his hands for once.

But when he released me, it came crashing down again. "I'll see you Saturday," he promised, and turned, walking back toward the dining hall without a second parting glance.

I waited until he completely disappeared before gathering my strength and stepping outside. Beside the priestess stood Dez and a short, dark-skinned man. He had long, brown hair with thick braids that were tied back, keeping them out of his face.

When I reached the bottom step, they all turned to me. The man smiled and bowed, but Dez spoke for him. "This is Faelar," he said with a smile. "He is my shadow walker."

When Faelar straightened, he extended a hand to mine and I accepted it. "It's a pleasure to meet you, Your Grace." Then, he lifted my fingers to his lips and kissed my knuckles.

I returned his warm smile, but as Dez's hand touched my lower back, I winced slightly from pain. "Are you alright, Morrigan?" Maeryn asked, an obvious show to every one of my discomfort.

I nodded and kept my smile stitched into my face. "Are we ready to go?"

When Faelar reached his arm out, I placed my hand on it and noticed Dez pulling me a little closer to his body, almost defensively. As the darkness consumed us, I pretended, for a moment, like he could protect me—like he would *want* to.

I had always been afraid of the dark as a child.

It's not that I actually believed that there were monsters lurking in the shadows, waiting to kill me. But, in the darkness... I felt *alone*. There was no light to guide you, to soothe you, to remind you that you were indeed alive. The other half of that fear is something I had never admitted to anyone before. But sometimes, I swore I could... *hear* things in the darkness. Like something, or someone, called to me.

As always, when Maeryn learned of this fear, she used it to her advantage.

One night, I had successfully managed to sneak out of the house without waking anyone. I tried to be quiet as I snuck past the remaining guards crowding around the garden. I spent weeks *studying their rounds and plotting the perfect time to dodge them, but this night they seemed keen on carrying on their conversation.*

Tiptoeing around the side of the house, I crept into the grass and toward the side wall. Just before I reached it, the sound of leaves crunching behind me made my body freeze. That, and the sharp edge of a dagger that had been placed against my throat with cold metal pressing into my back. Turning my eyes as much as I could to the side, I saw the sleeves of a guard's uniform, the armor reflecting my own face back at me.

"Sneaking off, little one?" the man whispered in my ear. Traces of alcohol seeped from his mouth and made its way to my nose. I almost wanted to gag.

I shook my head, and he laughed at my blatant lie. "I just wanted some fresh air. I swear."

His lips pressed closer to my ear and I wanted to squirm away, but the dagger scratched my skin any time I tried to move. "I'd bet the priestess wouldn't be too happy to see you out here this late at night." One of his hands lowered to the hem of my nightgown, and I could feel him fiddling with it as my pulse spiked in fear. "Wouldn't want you earning any more lessons with her, now would we?"

As a single tear began to fall down my cheek, my body shivered beneath him. I couldn't overpower a guard. I was at his complete mercy. "Please," I begged. "Just let me go back inside." His fingers lightly brushed my thigh beneath the gown, rising slowly until they reached my hip and I inhaled a sharp, daunting breath.

But then, footsteps sounded behind us, and the guard dropped the blade from my neck, removing his fingers, and twisted me around with his hand on my shoulder. In front of me stood Priestess Maeryn, gaping with what looked like shock. "Morrigan," she gasped. "Do you know how late it is?"

"I found her sneaking through the garden, Priestess," he said to her, conveniently leaving out the part of his wandering hand on my thigh and the dagger he had pressed into my throat.

I took a step toward the priestess, praying to the gods that she had seen it. "Priestess, he—"

"These guards are here to protect *you, and you're* whoring *yourself out to them?! Did you think he'd help you escape?" I would have preferred*

*being stabbed with the dagger than to have to hear her accusations.
"You're 16; compose yourself as a lady."*

*Stuttering in disbelief, I couldn't stop blinking at her. How could she
actually believe that I was... Before I could argue again, she grabbed my
wrist and pulled me back toward the house. "P-Priestess, please! Y-You
have to believe me. I wasn't—"*

*"Shut your mouth," she snapped. "I'm tired of your ungrateful
attitude. You are fed, clothed, and protected. Yet, you act like an entitled
brat waiting for every possible moment to escape what others would kill to
have."*

*Opening the door to our basement, she dragged me down the dimly lit
steps and brought me to the back of the room. I knew where she planned to
take me, and I was willing to claw my way out of her grip if it meant
evading my punishment. "No! Priestess, please!" I begged, pulling my arm
as hard as I could to break free of her hold.*

*Her fingers only dug in deeper. "If you can't appreciate the luxuries
that you clearly don't deserve, then maybe some alone time will remind you
of just how lucky you are."*

*Panicking, I kicked against the floor trying to stop her in any way that
I could. But she dragged me until we reached the back room and opened
the door, throwing me inside. Turning quickly, I planned to make a break
for it and shove past her, but she slammed the door in my face and
enclosed me in absolute darkness.*

*"PRIESTESS!" I screamed at the top of my lungs, so much so that it
burned my throat. "PRIESTESS, LET ME OUT! PLEASE!"*

*I patted the door, searching for the knob, but as I pulled at it, I knew it
would be locked. I had heard the sound of the key turning when she closed
it. Still, I yanked, and pushed, and punched... hoping to break out.*

"Priestess, please don't leave me in here!" I cried.

The tears were stinging my eyes. Not that I needed them anyway. No light filtered into this room. It made you completely blind to your surroundings. There was no way to even know the size of the space. To do that, I would have had to step away from the door, and I never dared to even think of doing so. The door was the only thing that grounded me when she would throw me in there.

"PLEASE!" Banging helplessly on the door, all hopes of someone coming to let me out began to dwindle. They never did. Lady Guinevere would never interfere with orders from the priestess, and the guards didn't care. Not unless I had something to offer them in return.

Accepting my fate, I sank down to the floor with my back against the door and my hand still on the knob. Even though I couldn't see anything in front of me, the shadows felt like they were alive. The walls seemed to groan, shrinking and expanding around me as they tried to suffocate the last of the breath I had reserved in my lungs. That's when the whispers began. Through the deafening silence, I could hear them. There were no words that made their way through, just sounds... so many of them.

Sometimes they'd laugh, other times they'd weep. I would feel surrounded by people and things that I couldn't actually see, but I knew weren't there.

Bringing my knees to my chest, I let go of the knob and covered my ears with my hands, crying and begging for them to stop. Over and over again, it felt like the shadows were trying to pull me. It usually started as a tickling sensation in my feet. Like the darkness wanted to lure me in. Then it would creep up my legs, my waist, my arms, and after endless torture... with any luck... I would finally fall asleep.

A hand touched my shoulder and Dez's voice filled the silence as he whispered, "We're here."

I wasn't sure when I had closed my eyes, but as I opened them, nausea swirled in my stomach. Placing my hand against my waist, another hand slipped beneath it and sent a soothing heat to my abdomen. Cass had done the same thing for me when we traveled to his castle.

Grateful, I turned to face Dez. "Thank you," I sighed as the nausea subsided quickly.

With a smile, he linked my arm with his as we walked toward the steps of the castle. It looked so different from Cass's. The pathway in the courtyard had been lined with red and white roses, and along the castle walls were vines tracing every corner—like the earth had wound itself into the very stone that held it together. A large fountain stood at the center of the yard, with water pouring from the top of it in a beautiful stream. It looked like something out of a dream.

The priestess stepped toward us with her hand outstretched for me to take. "I will escort Morrigan to her room."

As I moved to take it, Dez placed his body between us. "About that..." After he snapped his fingers, I heard light footsteps rushing down the stairs and took in the petite young lady, close to my age, walking hastily toward us.

Her brown hair had been braided across her head and looked like honey in the sunlight. Two small strands dangled and bounced in front of her face as she stopped beside us. Her gown was blue, with laces that tied in the front and thick white sleeves that stretched down her arms. It was similar attire to what Cass's staff wore, but this dress seemed slightly more elegant than the ones I had seen before.

"Eowyn has been officially appointed as Morrigan's handmaiden. She will assist Morrigan with gowns, bathing, anything that the princess requires." Her bright, blue eyes peeked up at me and she blushed when she noticed my stare. "She will *also* be with Morrigan at *all* times, unless specifically instructed otherwise by the princess herself. And *you*... will be leaving."

Staring at him in shock, the priestess had her lips parted like she didn't know what to say. "You... You can't just..."

Dez took a step forward and the rays beaming down from the sun seemed to follow him. The amount of power he held in a single movement could move mountains. "This is *my* castle, *Priestess*. You may think you have influence with other people, but beyond your palace walls, on *my* land, you answer to *me*."

Losing her composure, I could see Maeryn fidgeting with her hands as she realized the lack of control she had in that moment. I thought Dez would be done with it, but he took another step, practically shaking the ground beneath us.

"Run back to your lord, *little Priestess*. You can tell him *I* sent you there."

With a huff, she turned on her heel to face Faelar and looked expectantly at him. Exchanging a glance with Dez, he took a step back, away from the priestess, and her eyes widened even further.

"Faelar is within *my* employ," he reminded her. Then, a sly smile spread across his lips in triumph. "You can have a horse."

Maeryn didn't say another word as she stormed off. And Gods... did I want to wrap my arms around Dez's body and thank him. I should have expected nothing less from the man that Cass held in such high regard.

Once Maeryn was gone, Dez leaned into me, placing a soft hand on my arm. "I have to speak with my men about reinforcing the wards, but Eowyn will show you to your room. Your wardrobe has been filled. If there are any alterations required, it will be done at your command." Without warning, he placed a small peck on my cheek. "I'll be back before dinner is finished," he promised. Then, with a wink, he trailed off with Faelar and a guard dressed in a black and red uniform.

As I watched Dez walk away, I wished I could have saved a portrait of Maeryn's face when he spoke to her like that. It was truly one for the ages. Eowyn stepped forward, nervously looking up at me through her lashes. "Would you like to go to your room?" she asked quietly.

Offering her a genuine smile, I nodded. "I think I'd like that."

Chapter 14

My room closely resembled the one before.

There were a few minor differences, of course. Instead of orange-colored accents, there were hues of reds and pinks all over the walls, painted as roses and daisies. Red satin sheets were fitted tightly against my mattress, with black ones covering my pillows. Making my way to the closet, I peered in with a curious eye and was in no way surprised by the selection I had found.

Hanging gracefully were gowns covered in lace, cut so low they would barely hide the skin on my chest. They were flashy and eccentric, and a clear joke put here by Dez himself. He knew by now that I had no interest in wearing any of these, but it was a game. A *test*. He wanted to see what I would do with the selection he provided, and most importantly, if I would lay down and take it like the pet they all see me to be.

Plucking the most modest dress I could find, hidden in the far back, I asked Eowyn if she could draw me a bath and excuse herself, in the most polite way I could manage. I didn't really want to explain myself quite yet. Positive that she had left, I began pulling my dress down and off of my body, hissing in pain as it tugged on the scabbed wounds on my back. I must have bled even more, and the fabric clung to my skin as it dried.

Great… This is just great.

I had already known the bath wouldn't be a pleasant one and instantly regretted failing to ask Eowyn to keep it cool. Because the moment I stepped into the water and felt the warmth prickling my skin, I knew it would be a painful experience. Nonetheless, these cuts needed to be cleaned before I *really* had to explain myself.

Keeping my head high, I took in a breath and sunk down until I was seated in the tub. Even the water seemed to hiss as it touched the slices all over my skin. *Yeah… Thanks. I get it*, I spat in response. Once the burning turned to a bearable sting, I grabbed the cloth that Eowyn left out for me and got to work on cleaning any remaining evidence still on my skin.

Dressed and ready, I followed Eowyn, who was eager to take me on a tour of the castle.

She showed me where her room was, should I ever need to find her. She gave me a quick glance into a library that looked vaguely similar to Cass's. As we walked the gardens, it surprised me to see a large patch of lavender isolated on its own. When Eowyn noticed me staring, she let out a small giggle that almost made me want to smile.

"What is it?" I asked her.

Gesturing her head at the purple flowers, she said, "Lord Cassius told him you were fond of lavender. The very next day, Lord Dez planted these and ordered them not to be touched by any of the ser—" Her eyes widened and she bit back a smile. "He ordered the *staff* to leave them on their own. And that *you* were the only person with the authority to touch them."

Note to self, Cass and Dez talk... a lot.

"I'll be sure not to share any secrets with either of them." I hadn't meant to say it out loud and didn't actually realize that I had until Eowyn let out a loud fit of laughter.

"That's probably wise, Your Grace."

After exploring together for a few hours, Eowyn and I let the day get the best of us and soon it was time for dinner. She escorted me to the dining hall, and I expected to be the first one to arrive. Dez had explained that he might be late after all.

It was *huge*. The walls were decorated with grand, red drapes that covered the windows, making the room darker. Multiple large chandeliers hung from the ceiling, filled with lit candles that didn't seem to be actually melting. It had to be some kind of magic causing them to burn that way.

The table, made of a deep brown wood, stretched out across the room, topped with pink and red cloths. Even the chairs had a dark maroon cushion built into them. With Eowyn following behind me, I sat in the seat beside the head of the table and heard her retreat to where I assumed was the kitchen. Moments later, she returned with a plate in her hand and set it down in front of me.

The utensils were made of a shiny, sterling silver, bright enough that I could almost see my face in them. "Thank you, Eowyn," I said quietly, and began to eat in silence.

I had actually enjoyed the peace. It was the first true alone time I had been granted since leaving my home. Eowyn stood somewhere behind me, and I wanted to invite her to sit with me, but I didn't want to insult Dez in some way. So, I tried to pretend she wasn't there as I ate the delicately made steak on my plate. The flavored juices burst in my mouth, making me moan as I took another bite.

And in that moment, Dez decided to walk through the doors, loudly making his presence known. "For the love of the gods, Princess," he exclaimed. "Please, make that sound again."

Perv... I thought, and smiled to myself as I stopped myself from saying it out loud... *again.* "Is everything alright?" I asked him, keeping my focus on the food in front of me.

When he sat down, he let out a small grunt and placed a hand on top of mine. I paused chewing to stare at it, then at him. "*No one* will be coming in *or out* without my knowledge."

Forcing the bite down with a hard swallow, I smiled and gently removed my hand from beneath his. "That's good."

I had just had his best friend's tongue shoved down my throat that morning. I didn't think that holding his hand would be a very appropriate way to end my day. Ignoring the strange tension that I caused, Dez leaned over excitedly. "I have a surprise for you this week."

When I met his gaze, his smile looked wicked. It was the kind of smile that showed that he had been up to no good and I should have likely been terrified of whatever it was. I tried to laugh it off. "I'm not sure I can handle any more surprises."

I meant it.

Narrowing his eyes, he sat back in his seat with an over-confident glint to them. "I think you'll like this one."

Dez had been all but preoccupied for most of the week.

He attended dinners with me, but claimed he wanted to get ahead on some of his duties so that he could give me his full attention on Saturday. With nothing to do, and no one I truly knew, it left me with more free time than I was comfortable with. Sitting by my window became a new routine of mine, letting the remaining warmth of the sun keep me company as winter made its slow approach.

Eowyn would perch herself in one of the chairs beside me, staring out at the vast distance between us and the mountains. The view from my bedroom in this castle had an unearthly glow to it in the evenings. If I caught it at just the right time, beams of purple and pink would illuminate the clouds as the sun descended behind the mountains. The image alone seemed to paint the pathway to Eden itself.

"Eowyn," I mused, leaning my head against the glass.

"Yes, Your Grace?" She seemed to perk up in response.

Rolling my eyes, I turned my head toward her. "I asked you to call me *Morrigan*."

Her eyes widened and she blushed a little. "Right... Sorry, Your Gra—Morrigan." Although the stumbling of her words made her appear nervous, the small smile that curved the corner of her lips put me at ease. "Did you need anything?"

"Do you know where Dez's study is?" I asked. It had been two days of him cooping himself up in there. Maybe it was rude of me to want to pry, but without anything to do, I feared I might have gone mad.

Eowyn's eyes showed slight trepidation, and it made me all the more curious. "I believe Lord Dez is busy at the moment..."

"Am I not allowed to see him?" The question seemed to slip from my tongue harsher than I intended it to. But Cassius always welcomed me to visit him. That was the entire point of me being here, was it not? I needed to get to know each of them, spend time with them. And if they truly intended to make me... *queen*... I should have permission to visit them as they work.

Though, Cass never required me to ask for it.

As Eowyn struggled with a thought that seemed to dance in her head, her eyes met mine and looked defeated by the end of it. "Of course you are." Standing, she smoothed her dress and nodded. "I'll escort you."

Walking through the halls, Eowyn kept her head down. She had been relatively quiet for the past two days, but she looked especially tense as she fumbled with her fingers in front of her. I realized quickly that the source of her hesitation was now exiting the door of what I assumed to be Dez's study.

A woman.

Her long blonde hair had perfectly styled waves that fell down her back and hugged the same curves that her red dress cinched to. I hadn't seen her since arriving, nor had Dez even mentioned her. Turning as the door latched, she paused when she saw me. But, without missing a beat, a slow, sultry smile spread across her face, and her head made a mocking bow toward me.

"*Your Grace*," she said, but spending as many years as I had with the priestess, I recognized a *snake* when I saw one. Even her footsteps seemed to slither toward us with the bite of a viper.

I didn't respond. And as she passed the two of us, she made no acknowledgement to Eowyn, who looked ready to hide herself from my gaze. I wasn't sure why Eowyn had been nervous for me to see the mystery woman. I understood that Dez was a grown man. He had his own needs, needs that *Cassius* took care of for *me*, so why would I be angry at him?

I *wasn't* angry.

Once the blonde had disappeared behind us, I leaned in toward Eowyn with a polite hand on her arm. "Thank you," I whispered to her.

The breath of relief she exhaled resonated through my fingertips and she smiled up at me. "I'll wait for you back in your room." And with that, she turned on her heel before retreating down the hall.

Placing a fist up to the door, it took me a few extra seconds to work up the courage to knock. But once I did, Dez called out, "Come in."

I made my way inside, taking in the stacks of books and papers on every surface. His study was a lot less organized than Cass's, and *that* was saying something. Neither of them seemed to be capable of tidying up their work. When Dez noticed who stood before him, I watched his smile fall in a swift blink and he pushed his chair out to stand so quickly that he almost tumbled.

"Princess... I..." His eyes glanced at the door and back to me, and I knew that he was wondering if I had seen what I now knew to be a secret of his. He didn't want us to meet, and I kept that noted in the back of my mind.

"I didn't mean to interrupt," I told him, though by the looks of his disheveled shirt, he had *clearly* already finished.

As if on cue, he reached up and buttoned the top of it and returned an uncertain smile. "Not at all. Please," he gestured to his desk, "join me."

More papers were sprawled out on his desk, and he quickly tried to organize them as best he could. With the shameful blush on his cheeks and his hair frantically falling across his brows, I had never seen him appear so... *human*. Something I knew he wasn't. "The woman..." I started, carefully. His jaw ticked a little, but he continued shifting the items around on the surface in front of him. "Is she..."

"No one," he answered quickly. Then, he turned to me with a smile, but I could see his chest rising and falling unsteadily, far from his usual demeanor. "She's no one."

"Right…" Lowering my head a little, I gave him a pointed glare. "You don't have to pretend. It's okay if you have someone that you… I just mean… I know I'm young and I haven't lived as long as the rest of you, but…"

Cass's smile flashed in my mind as I watched Dez's smile falter.

"I'm not holding some kind of expectation toward you," I explained.

That's when his expression turned to one of guilt, which I truly hadn't meant to cause. With a sudden quickness, he grabbed my hand and pulled me toward him. "No one," he repeated. "She is no one."

I almost felt sorry for the woman, but Dez's eyes were always so… *distracting*. They'd pull you in and make you want to believe every word that fell from his lips. And the shimmer they had in the rarest moments… It made the blue shine brighter than the sun reflecting off of waves in the ocean.

"I'm sorry I haven't been around much this week." Bringing my hand to his lips, he kissed my fingers and held them there. "I just want tomorrow to be perfect."

That's when I smelled it. The lingering scent of a floral perfume that singed my nostrils as I inhaled. Every ounce of heat that began to build from his touch faded quickly with every breath. Stepping back, I cleared my throat and pulled my hand away. I wasn't angry at him. I certainly wasn't *jealous* of a woman I had never met before—touching a man I had only met just over a month ago.

Stop fixating, Morrigan, I chastised myself.

"No chance you'll tell me what the surprise is yet?"

Chuckling, Dez shook his head. "Not until tomorrow, Princess."

Hoping to rid myself of the uncomfortable position that I threw myself into by coming here uninvited, I let out a theatrical sigh and walked around the desk. "I guess I'll leave you to your *duties* then…" I wanted to leave and crawl back into my spot at my bedroom window. With any luck, I could forget the strange feeling that left a hollow point in my chest.

He owed nothing to me. *None* of them did.

But his hand grabbed mine once more and stopped me from taking another step. When I turned back around, he had a chair pulled out, motioning for me to sit. "Stay for a little. Sit with me."

"I don't want to intrude..." *Especially if there's a chance that a certain blonde guest might turn back around.*

"You're not intruding."

"What if..." Glancing toward the door, I couldn't stop my cheeks from stinging slightly. "I wouldn't want to keep any visitors waiting."

Clear discomfort showed on his face, and maybe a hint of regret. He took a deep breath and motioned once more for me to sit. "No one else," he assured me. "Just you. Stay... *please.*"

Against my better judgment, I sat down in the chair and watched him lower himself slowly into his. An unwelcome thought invaded my mind as I watched him return to his work. Did Cass have his own blonde seductress? Maybe she had red curls... like he did. Perhaps he went to her the moment Dez took me back to his castle...

The idea made my stomach twist, and I wanted to stand to leave just so I could escape to my own solitude. But as if Dez could sense the tension building within me, he placed the gentlest hand on my knee, giving it a light squeeze. And somehow, the gesture seemed to quiet every bad thought in my mind.

It reminded me that all of *this*... still outweighed every second of my life wasted back at home.

I recalled the words he had said to the priestess, and the silent vow he made to me by forcing her to leave.

He hadn't asked me any questions regarding what happened in that room, but the look on my face had been enough for him. He acted on instinct, and his instinct was to protect me.

So, scooting my chair the slightest bit closer, I searched for a book worthy of reading, and leaned back into my seat as I opened it. As Dez immersed himself back into his work, we both remained silent and I busied my mind with literature.

Learn to enjoy the little things, I reminded myself. *You never know when they might end.*

Chapter 15

ater that evening, Dez wasn't in attendance at dinner.

He hadn't missed one before, and after the encounter earlier, it left me with a sour taste in my mouth that maybe *she* had spent it with him—that the moment I left, he had invited her back.

Not that it mattered.

It *shouldn't* have mattered.

Gods… what is happening to me? Why do I even care?

Eowyn had been plucking the pins from my hair that she meticulously put in that morning—she was blessed with the same skills that Shae had when it came to taming my hair. As I stared through the mirror at her reflection, I couldn't help but wonder what a girl her age was doing working in the castle as much as she did. She had spent the entire week at my beck and call. She had to have a family… Maybe someone she loved…

"How long have you worked for Dez?" I asked her.

Without looking up to answer me, she said, "I'm the same age as you, Your—" Her eyes peeked up and she bit back a smile. "Forgive me… *Morrigan*…"

I tried to keep my chuckle silent as she returned to my hair. At least she made an effort into calling me by my name. The rest of the staff looked at me like I had three eyes when I would ask them to—like the question alone would cause the gods to smite them where they stood.

"I'm actually the youngest of the serv—" she let out a huff of frustration at the second word she almost slipped up on. "*I'm sorry.* Lord Dez told us that you weren't fond of that word. And we appreciate the change… It just takes some getting used to."

"At least I won't feel like such a child anymore," I laughed, trying to help her change the subject. In the short amount of time that I had known Eowyn, it was clear to me that she strived for perfection.

Between styling my hair and assisting me with gowns, everything had to look seamless. If a single curl fell out of place, she would fix it quicker than I had time to notice. It got so bad during dinner that she swore she would be carrying around spare pins from now on. I wanted more than anything to laugh when she said that to me, but then I realized she hadn't meant to say it out loud and looked utterly embarrassed by it. There seemed to be a lot of similarities between the two of us. The priestess would have hated her.

Maybe that's why I liked her so much.

When my hair gently fell down my back as the last pin came out, I almost let out a sigh of relief. It felt like a weight lifted from my neck, letting the curls run free over my shoulders. "Did you want to read with me for a little before heading to bed?" I asked her, standing to change into my nightgown.

"I would love to," she answered with a smile. "But Lord Dez has requested that you see him in the drawing room after dinner."

This late? I gave her a skeptical look. "Should I be worried?"

Shaking her head, a light smile formed on her lips. "He adores grand gestures. Now that you're here? He'll likely be using every card up his sleeve to impress you. He hasn't stopped speaking of you since your Unveiling."

That's funny, because he had someone else's *perfume clinging to his clothes hours earlier.*

Shoving the bitterness down, I nodded. "Well then… lead the way, I suppose."

When she brought me to the drawing room, Dez stood beside a man holding layers of fabric in all shades of red.

As both Eowyn and the man excused themselves, I noticed a display of jewels lying across the desk beside them, and Dez waved me over when he saw me enter. "Princess!" He jogged, meeting me halfway across the room before scooping my hand into his. "I have something for you." The excitement on his face lit up the room. And when I realized that the scent of perfume no longer lingered, I was able to relax enough to follow him to the desk.

"What is all of this?" I asked him.

"The very heart of my land." He pulled me closer, wrapping a hand around my lower back as he pointed with his other one. "These are red diamonds."

His fingers brushed over a black felt surface that displayed jewelry with beautiful red diamonds. Taking a closer look, it appeared as though there were mixtures of red and black glass, shattered within them. The way the light reflected off of it made it shine, changing the shade of the red from a deep blood colored garnet to a bright, shimmering crimson.

"These are jaspers…" The next case held rounded gems that were a beautiful shade of cherry. Inside of them it looked like someone had taken a paintbrush and stroked in every intricate line, showcasing different shades of red and pink.

Lastly, he pointed to a box filled with the most beautiful orange gemstones. They were nowhere similar in color to the other two but instead lit up like flames within the sparkling stone. The deep orange had been complimented with streaks of iridescent light that seemed to come to life as we moved closer to it, changing the way the light poured through it with our movements. It resembled…

"Fire opal," Dez whispered. *Fire…* It looked like *fire.* "I want you to pick one."

Shooting him a disconcerted glare, I looked at him as though he had gone mad. "I couldn't. These all look far too expensive."

Refusing my rejection, his voice lowered a little. "You can, and you *will.* Pick one."

I simply rolled my eyes at him. The move might have worked on his little blonde friend, but the mask he wore didn't fool me any. The man didn't have an intimidating bone in his body.

When I refused to answer him, he plucked one of the necklaces from the box with fire opals and smiled. "This one, then." It happened to be the most extravagant of all of the necklaces I had seen displayed. *Go figure.*

Walking me to the standing mirror nearby with his hand still on my back, he moved behind me and brought the necklace to my collar bone.

Plated with pure, thick gold, it held three large gems with two, smaller ones below it and one at the very bottom, giving it a beautiful, triangular shape. The necklace felt cool as it touched my chest, making me inhale a little. Then, as he clasped it behind my neck, his fingers lingered there for a moment.

I hadn't noticed that his lips lowered to my ear until he whispered, "Beautiful." And the way his breath kissed my skin sent a strange shiver down my spine.

There was no way I would let a man who had been in the arms of another make me feel this way, especially in the same day. It wasn't happening. "I can't wear this," I told him, and made to take a step forward, but his hands fell to my shoulders, making me freeze in place.

"Morrigan." Though it came out as a kind of warning, it sounded like more of a plea.

When I looked at him through the mirror again, his baby blue eyes were staring back at me in the way they always did... the yearning that swirled within them... *trapping* me. *He isn't Cass,* one side of me tried to remind myself. *Don't prove the priestess right.*

But the issue with your conscience is that there always seems to be two sides... doesn't there? Because, while one very reasonable side told me I needed to step away from him and go back to my room, the other side had me holding my breath when his hands drifted down to my hips, unable to look away from his penetrating gaze. It took weeks to grow this kind of comfortability with Cass... But Dez? He had this way of breaking down a person's inhibitions somehow, igniting fires within that shouldn't be fueled. The skin on my neck where he had touched felt like lightning, still zapping within my blood in the wake of its absence now.

"Do you know what *my* unique ability is, Princess?" he asked, referring to the gifts that the gods had blessed them with. Each of the lords had their own, special power that separated them from the others.

When I shook my head, his thumbs began to caress my sides where he still held my waist. The battle between my consciences was raging a war inside of my head. And all I wanted was to turn them both off at this point.

"I can feel the emotions of others…" Lowering his head, he placed the lightest of kisses against my shoulder. "I can feel their happiness… their grief…" Nerves made my skin physically itch in anticipation as I realized where his words were leading to. "Do you know what I'm feeling from you, Princess?"

You don't want to know, one side told me.

You want to know.

I, myself alone, would be the death of me. "What do you feel?" I asked him.

His chuckle sounded dark and filled with more desire than I thought could be possible. "So… much… *need*." He couldn't possibly have felt that. He couldn't… could he?

Swallowing, I discovered my throat had suddenly gone dry. "I don't know what you mean…"

"Want to know what else I can do?" The challenge in his voice didn't help the slow growing ache in the pit of my stomach.

Walk away.

Stay.

I nodded. *Traitor.*

Watching his reflection, his irises began to glow until the blue resembled a bright ring of light. "I can… *enhance* them."

I wasn't prepared for the ache to turn to a blistering heat that shot its way straight to my center. Gasping, I almost fell back, but his chest caught me and he inhaled deeply against my skin. "Dez." The word slipped from my mouth in a manner I wasn't proud of, and I could hear him groan behind me.

"I can't wait to dance with you tomorrow night." He placed another kiss just below my ear, and I almost thought that I hadn't heard him correctly.

"Dance?" I whispered, letting my eyes flutter down until they closed completely.

His teeth grazed my skin without actually biting down, and I was ready to throw away any hesitation and shove him into the chair beside us. Until he said, "I'm throwing you a ball."

No amount of influence could have stopped me from standing up straight, pulling away from whatever magic he had wrapped around my mind as I gaped at him. "A ball?" My eyes were almost wide in horror.

Laughing at my reaction, he reached for me again, but I stepped back. "What's wrong with that? It's just dancing and drinking. You'll have a blast, Princess."

I shook my head and began fidgeting with my fingers nervously. "No, I... I don't..." Now I felt downright embarrassed. I made enough of a fool of myself when Cassius took me to the market, stepping on his toes every few seconds. The last thing I needed to do was embarrass myself at an actual ball.

As Dez gazed at me, his eyes softened in a sudden understanding. Then, he held out his hand to me, gesturing for me to take it. "I'd like to show you something."

We entered a large ballroom where some of his staff were busy decorating and hanging red curtains from the ceiling.

The walls around us were covered in gold-lined marble with rose engravings along the pillars that stood in rows on each side of the room. Above us was a breathtaking painting of the night sky. Stars seemed to flicker against the dark colors that covered the ceiling. I had never seen a more beautiful sight. It felt like the gods themselves were looking down at us as we stood on an empty dance floor.

At the end of the room stood a large throne, but beside it was a smaller one—both made of gold, with thick red cushions built in. I felt Dez lean in beside me. "I had that made for you the second I saw your face…" he whispered to me. "A queen deserves her throne."

Unable to form any words, I turned to the other side of us and could hear the faint sound of the musicians tuning and practicing with their instruments quietly. On the platform was a harp, a violin and a cello, but directly in front of them stood a black grand piano. The material shined so brightly that the stars painted above reflected along its surface.

When Dez left my side, I watched as he approached them, asking them a question. They all nodded with smiles on their faces, and he ran back over to me, reaching out a hand before bowing. "What are you doing?" I whispered.

The musicians began playing a soft tune that slowly filled the hall and echoed against the walls. The acoustics of the ballroom made the music loud, resonating and trapping its beautiful sounds within the tall ceiling above us. "I'm asking you to dance," Dez said. "I'm going to teach you."

Chapter 16

Staring nervously at the onlookers surrounding us, I hesitated in accepting his offer.

But before I could make a run for it in the opposite direction, Dez snatched my hand and yanked it fast enough to give me whiplash. As he spun me, everything blurred until I landed directly against his chest with a loud thud… Or maybe that was my heart beating loudly in my chest.

He took my breath away with his movements as he began gliding the both of us across the dance floor. "Dez," I pleaded, staring down at our feet in the hopes that I wouldn't ruin his perfectly polished black shoes.

Pinching my chin, he forced my gaze upward until our eyes met. "Eyes on me, Princess, not the floor." His hand dropped from my face and pressed into my lower back while the other one entwined our fingers together. "I won't let you fall," he promised.

Holding his stare, I did as he commanded. Somehow, as I lost myself in the oceans piercing me, I managed to follow his steps—as if our bodies were two magnets, pushing and pulling in unison as the music swept away our feet. Being so close to each other, I could barely even think... So, I let him do *that* for me too.

In perfect rhythm to the melody that seemed to fill the room, I would have never guessed that my body could move the way Dez had me floating. I couldn't even feel my own feet as Dez twirled me and pulled me in, dancing faster as the piano finally joined in with the rest of the instruments. With a power of its own, the music seemed to place me under a spell, leaving Dez the only thing left that I could see in the room. A cool breeze flushed over my face, chilling my warm cheeks as I became aware of just how low his hand was on my back.

"Do you understand what it means for you to be *chosen*, Princess?" he asked me.

Dizzy from the spinning, I could barely hold my own weight as we danced. Thankfully, it was yet another thing that he did for me. "What do you mean?"

Pulling me closer to him, we began slowing down as the melody drew itself out. I held my breath with his face inches away from mine. "You were made for us, Morrigan. Each of us." His hand slid further down, stopping just above my ass. "You don't have to deny what you're feeling."

Swallowing, I felt embarrassed that he was even pointing it out to me. Even if what he said was true, this wasn't *normal*. Going from Cass being the center of my world, to now... being unable to keep my eyes from drifting down to Dez's lips.

"Cassius knows it… I know it… You don't have to be afraid of what you're feeling," he assured me.

"Do you…" I paused for a moment, unsure if I should finish my sentence. *Finish it.* "Do you feel it too?"

"Princess," he groaned. "When I look at you, I can barely breathe. Your beauty alone steals the air from my lungs." Lowering his face, his lips stopped inches away from mine. "Having you so close to me is the sweetest torture I've ever had to endure."

"This is all so new to me," I said through an exhale.

A beat of silence passed between us. Then, Dez tickled my lips as he whispered, "Then let me *lead*."

My body required no more convincing. Without thinking, I closed the distance, and when his lips touched mine, I felt like I was falling. The intoxicating taste of him had me leaning into his kiss, letting his tongue explore my mouth as it twirled with mine. I hadn't realized that we stopped dancing until he began moving us, forcing me to walk backwards until my back hit one of the pillars behind me. As I gasped, he stole my breath away, taking it back for himself. And once his hands dropped to my hips, he reached down and pulled my leg up until it wrapped around him.

"Dez," I whispered into his mouth. "Dez, they'll see."

I had forgotten that we weren't alone. Not only were the musicians here, but so were the workers setting up for the festivities the next day. Dez huffed in defiance, ravaging my lips until they were swollen. I wanted nothing more than to let him have me—to feel his hands on my skin and taste every part of him.

But just as my body began to accept it, my brain decided to remind me that I wasn't the *only* girl he had kissed today. And the thought made the food in my stomach feel like poison before I let go of his lips and used my hand to push against his chest.

"Prophecy or not," I said, panting as I tried to catch my breath, "I'm not someone's second choice, Dez."

It took him a moment to realize what I meant, and I watched the lust in his eyes fade to shame. "No…" he agreed, stepping back and allowing me to fix myself. "No… You're not."

Reaching behind my neck, I removed the necklace he had placed on me, before shoving it into his hand. "I'll see you tomorrow," I whispered.

I didn't look back as I moved past him, ashamed that I had even allowed it to go as far as it did.

I told you.

You shouldn't have said anything.

I wanted to tell my subconscious to shut its mouth, but I realized it was just *me* arguing with myself.

Behind me, I could hear Dez call out, "Princess!"

But I knew that if I turned around, I wouldn't have the strength to step out of this ballroom without throwing my arms around him and letting him do whatever he wanted to me.

And I wasn't *no one*.

Not anymore.

Sinking into my bath, I tried to ignore the thoughts that kept circling my mind.

Everything felt so… *confusing* here. And Dez didn't make it any better. For a reason beyond my knowledge, every time he stood nearby, my body felt completely on edge. The idea of touching another man after Cassius no longer felt as foreign with each day that I spent with Dez. And I felt horrible for it. But, if what Dez had said was true…

Gods dammit.

Why did it have to be *me*?

My skin heated for reasons other than the water that had swallowed me. As I remembered the feel of his lips on mine, I sank down further. *His hand on my upper thigh... His hips pressing into mine...* The only thing that reeled me back was the feel of my fingers sliding down my waist.

I let out a huff of annoyance and shot back up from the bath. *Get your shit together, Morrigan.*

After our encounter, I had tossed and turned all night, getting little to no sleep. My body had betrayed me in the worst way imaginable. I should have been disgusted with Dez for even entertaining another woman before having the *audacity* to take a crack at me. But... Kissing him felt electric. Maybe he had been right. Maybe whatever this... *prophecy* was, tied me to them in some way.

If the way my body lit up from just the touch of his lips meant anything, then I was in for a world of pain if I had to deal with the rest of them as well.

Rising from the bath, I grabbed my towel and stepped out of the tub. After scrubbing my face dry, I wrapped it around my body, hugging myself, when I felt a sudden chill in the room. My teeth chattered against each other at the strong wisp of air that seemed to slide down my spine.

Then, like a breath had fluttered against the back of my neck, I heard someone whisper, *"Morrigan..."*

Turning around with a yelp, I expected Dez to be behind me, screwing with me. Not that he would have been able to get in without me noticing, but who knew what other secret gifts the lords could be hiding? Realizing that I was, in fact, alone in the room, I jumped once more when Eowyn scrambled in through the door with wide eyes.

"Morrigan, what's wrong?"

"I…" I had to take a couple of breaths to shake the feeling left in my chest. "Nothing… Sorry. I didn't sleep well last night."

She seemed to accept the lie, letting her body rest against the frame. But that voice… It sounded oddly familiar, but almost… filtered, in a sense. Thinking back to a memory from Cass's throne room, I realized it sounded eerily similar to the distorted voice I had heard there— immediately after following a man into the room, only for him to disappear the moment I entered.

Am I going crazy…?

"You scared the living daylights out of me." She placed her hand over her chest as if to slow her own heartbeat. Then, she waved her hand at me. "Come, let's get you dressed. Your dress is here."

On top of my bed, Eowyn had laid out a beautiful red gown covered in black lace. The sleeves were long, with a slit that seemed to slide up from the wrist all the way to the elbow. The material was thin, but at least it looked like it would cover all of the… *important* bits that I preferred to remain hidden. Beside the gown lay a red mask. It had the same black lace covering the silk fabric, but on the corner of one of the eyes, two red roses had been sewn in.

Curiously, I turned my head toward Eowyn, keeping my eyes on the mask in front of me. "What's that for?" I asked her.

"It's a masquerade ball!" The enthusiasm in her voice almost enthralled me. "Everyone will be wearing masks. It's a tradition for us, in a sense." Eowyn began helping me into my dress—thankfully it required no lacing on the back. "We have them once a year. All of the villagers look forward to it. Some have even traveled from other parts of Andonia to experience it for themselves."

"But… it's just a *ball*."

The flash of her eyes, and the worried glint that tried to hide itself, shifted me to an unsettling feeling. "He really hasn't told you anything about it?"

"No," I answered, shaking my head.

"Well…" Standing up straight, she moved to the chair and offered for me to sit. "I'm sure you'll enjoy it, nonetheless."

"Should I be scared?" I asked her nervously.

But she ignored my question and instead, pulled out a small, golden tube and lifted its top to reveal a deep, maroon stick. "Lipstick," she explained. Then, Eowyn laughed as she reached down and began applying it to my lips. "He *does* love his reds."

In an obvious attempt to prevent any further questioning, she rushed me out of the room and insisted that Dez would be waiting for me at the stairs. Loud music radiated from the ballroom and filled the halls. I could hear laughter and conversations nearby, everything seeming to be perfectly normal. And when I noticed Dez, he almost took my breath away.

He wore dark, wine-colored pants with a white shirt, and a vest that matched my dress. In the pocket of his shirt, pinned into the fabric, was a red rose. He looked like something out of a fairytale. And the mask on his face was made of pure, black fabric with tiny roses stitched into it. The moment he noticed me, his eyes widened beneath the mask, and his blue eyes shone through the dimness of the lights around us.

"I've changed my mind," he breathed, quickly making his way to my side where his eyes roamed every inch of me. "I'll have to kill any man that even looks at you tonight. Let's just go back to my room." A wicked smile pulled his lips apart and I shoved him playfully.

"You don't get to make all this fuss and not let *me* have my fun." With slight hesitation, I looked over the railing to the small crowd that I could see through the open doors. *Maybe this is a bad idea.* Perhaps Dez's offer would have been better. "What if I'm not what they thought I would be?" I asked him.

The only other time I had truly been in public was with Cassius at the market. The little girl may have been kind to me, but most of the other villagers just stared. They looked at me like I wasn't human—like I wasn't one of them. Even the way the man and woman bowed made me feel like they were somehow afraid of me.

Afraid of *me*.

I had no strength, no courage.

What if *these* people saw right through that? How long before someone realized that they got the shit end of the stick with *me* as their queen? Gods knew I wouldn't be able to hide these scars forever, I had barely gotten by with hiding them from Eowyn. The look in her eyes every morning that she assisted with my gowns told me that she knew something was off.

These people would as well.

They'd see the broken girl, who had been practically raised in an attic most of her life. They'd see shame, weakness, desperation—

Dez's hand slid into mine and wrapped it in his arm. I had unfortunately forgotten that part of his gift. Looking up at him, I could see the glow in his eyes and suddenly, all of that anxiety began to ease at his touch. When the glow disappeared, I realized that it was a physical manifestation of his abilities. He had used that power to calm me.

Leaning down, his lips brushed my ear. "You are the most breathtaking creature that has ever stepped foot on this earth, Princess," he whispered. "Let the world see it."

Unable to argue, let alone form any real words with his body as close as it was, I nodded and clung to his arm a little tighter.

"If it brings you any comfort, no one knows you are here. You could keep the mask on and none of them would know who you are... *what* you are." That did ease some of the anxiety that had my stomach doing acrobatic flips. "Are you ready?" he asked, the sincerity in his voice showing me that, if I had said "*no,*" he would have respected my decision.

But, as stubborn as I was, I didn't spend almost fifteen years trying to escape a prison to become a quitter now.

"As I'll ever be," I said, letting out a long breath until my lungs completely deflated.

Placing his hand on mine, we began to walk down the stairs.

Chapter 17

Beneath the anonymity of my mask, no one seemed to bat an eye as I entered the ballroom with Dez.

The guests didn't seem to care much that their lord had entered, but as Eowyn had told me, this was a normal event for them. They recognized him easily, nodding and bowing as he passed them by, but they all continued their activities as if he were one of them.

The ballroom had been transformed entirely since Dez and I had danced in it the night before. With no sunlight to brighten the room through the large, arched windows, the only illumination came from the dim light of the candles. It gave an awfully intimate feel to the entire atmosphere.

Looking up, I quickly realized what the red drapes had been for. Girls dressed in what I would barely call *clothing* were twirling in them. With parts of the drape wrapped around their legs and arms, they continued pointing their feet and doing impossible poses while displayed for everyone mid-air. I watched carefully as they moved with grace, in a beautifully practiced manner.

But then, my heart dropped when one of them began twirling and fell down the drape. I gripped Dez's arm and gasped, a scream building in my throat, but she jerked to a stop right before her body could hit the ground, her lips pursed like she was blowing air. Beside me, Dez noticed my reaction and started to laugh.

"Relax, Princess," he whispered quietly so no one around us could hear. "They're wind wielders—very well trained in what they do. They aren't going to hurt themselves."

Beside the dance floor, chairs and couches with red velvety cushions had been placed against the walls. Men sat there, with women on their laps, dancing and swaying their hips. While some of them were clothed, I quickly realized that some of them were... *not*. Their tops had been removed and the men's hands were groping every part of their skin for everyone to watch.

I understood it now, the look that Eowyn had given me when she asked if Dez told me anything about the ball. I wanted to scold her for not telling me herself, but she *conveniently* couldn't be seen anywhere in attendance.

As Dez pulled me along, I realized that he was dragging us to his throne. The throne that had *mine* directly next to it. *"Dez!"* I whisper-yelled at him. When he didn't respond, I tugged on his arm.

Turning his head toward me with a quizzical look, he leaned down for me to speak.

"I thought we weren't... I thought I didn't have to be... *me*."

"You don't," he reminded me.

"But the throne…"

"Oh," he chuckled. "You're not sitting on *that*, Princess."

Not understanding his implication, I allowed him to tug me along until we reached the platform. My feet paused at the steps, and Dez let go of me, making his way to his throne. Then, he sat down, facing me with a large, devilish smile. The contrasting shadows on his face made it look sinister in the best possible way. A challenge hid inside of those dimples, and it didn't take me long to decipher just *what* that challenge was.

Dez's hand slid to his lap as he gave it a gentle, condescending pat. "Well?" He waited for a response.

"You *seriously* expect me to sit on your *lap*, Dez!" I tried keeping my voice to a minimal level so those around us couldn't hear.

He shrugged and leaned back into his throne. "You could always remove the mask, then… Take a seat in *your* throne."

Groaning to myself, I mulled over the odds of me doing that. Sitting on his lap would make me look like one of his *whores*—which I was sure he had plenty. But… people didn't seem to blink an eye at that here. At least not at this *ball*. If I removed my mask, or even sat in the throne, I'd be telling everyone who I was. The entire atmosphere could change, and possibly not for the better. I didn't want the eyes on me again, not tonight.

So, with a sigh, I crept my way up the steps to Dez. Without giving me a chance to change my mind, he tugged my hand and dropped me down onto his legs. His smile only grew as he wrapped his arms around me, pulling me closer and breathing in my scent with his nose pressed into my neck.

"I should order a perfume to be made that smells like you," he whispered.

I almost wanted to laugh at the suggestion. "That smells like what? Fear and crippling anxiety?"

Taking another slow inhale, he shook his head at my response and placed a soft kiss on my shoulder. "Like everything a man could need for the rest of his existence."

I had to gulp at his words—they would likely be the death of me, now. If he continued to speak to me the way that he had for the past day and a half, all of my resolve would crumble to ash. Thank the gods the mask hid the upper part of my cheeks, because they had to be molten red by this point. And, of course, Dez likely knew that already. *What a stupid gift,* I thought to myself. I couldn't hide anything from him even if I tried.

"Flattery will get you nowhere," I whispered.

Lifting his head, he gazed at me with his deep blue eyes illuminated by the candlelight surrounding the ballroom. "Are you sure about that, Princess?"

One of his hands slid to my thigh, then down my leg, as he teased the hem of my dress. "Dez," I warned.

"Why do you insist on lying to me about what you want?" When his hand touched my ankle, it sent a jolt of lightning into my body. I *did* want him, but I didn't want to be *her*. I didn't want to be anyone's *her*.

As his hand slid up my calf, leaving a trail of heat in its wake, I sucked in a breath. "I don't... I'm not..."

"No one," he answered. His lips pressed against my collarbone, and my breath disappeared. "You aren't."

"Then what am I?" I asked him.

"*Everything.*"

I could barely get my own lungs to work as his hand moved further up, now touching my thigh. The heart in my chest beat so violently that it would likely explode at any moment. The beat of my pulse made it to my head, throbbing with the same intensity as the one between my thighs.

Just as his fingers almost slid their way to my center, I instinctively tightened my thighs together. "Water," I gasped. "I need water."

Chuckling with a knowing look, he peered up from his lashes and removed his hand, gently smacking my thigh. "Why don't you go explore a little? Get some fresh air. I'll grab a drink and find you."

"Wait…" Dez ignored me as he basically shoved my body off of him. "No, wait, I can't just—"

Disappearing into the crowd, Dez didn't even look back to see me squabbling to find the will to move my feet. *I can do this. This is totally fine*, I failed at assuring myself. *Just go outside and… mingle? Pretend to be a guest?*

You could have been making out with the hottest guy here if you weren't such a wuss.

Nope. Wasn't arguing with myself again. With that, I found the courage to walk down the platform and scoured the room for an exit.

If I thought that *inside* of the ballroom had been bad, nothing could have prepared me for the events taking place *outside*.

Dez likely should have prepared me for the first time I would see *true magic*. While, yes, I had read about it in books that Harley gave me— *nothing…* no books nor scrolls could have helped me wrap my brain around the actual sight of it.

In one spot on the grass, a girl in a pretty, green gown—that seemed to be made of flowers itself—had her hands pressed into the soil. Small vines crept through her fingers, growing on their own as spectators gasped around her. She twisted and morphed the vines, turning them into flower crowns, and placed them on some of the ladies' heads.

Somewhere nearby there was a fountain. I had only seen it once or twice during my walks with Eowyn. Beside it stood a man in a deep blue outfit. Across the distance, I could see the glow of his eyes as he stared into the water, his hands dancing in the air. Walking closer to get a better look, my eyes widened when I saw just what he was doing. Along the fountain, he had been creating tiny ice sculptures, the carvings of them were perfectly drawn, and they shone beneath the moonlight.

But what really caught my attention happened after a loud, excited yell of a crowd nearby caused me to almost fall over. When I turned my head, there were large O-shaped rings lit on fire. They were connected to metal poles, allowing the rings to float in the air as men and women hung from them. They touched the fire with no fear or hesitation, and the flames seemed to lick at their skin as if it were birthed from their own flesh.... Because it *was*. They were *fire wielders*.

Something about their ability always fascinated me more than the rest. It looked beautiful. Dangerous, yes, but to step into the blistering rage with no way of being burned, it looked invigorating. I took a few steps, disappearing into the cluster of guests around me to get a better look, when a hand wrapped around my wrist and tugged.

Frightened, I swatted at it and yanked my arm free, only to find a girl, who wore the same outfit as the rest of the fire wielders, standing in front of me and laughing. "Can I help you?" I asked her, keeping my hands close to my chest.

Still giggling, she answered, "You're new here." *Great. Thanks, Dez for the misplaced assurance that people wouldn't bat an eye in my direction.*

"I..." I didn't know what exactly to tell her. I barely knew anything about the land that Dez ruled. I didn't know the towns, the people... What if she asked me for my name? "It's my first time."

Something in the way she cocked her head at me made me feel like she was searching for lies. She wore a black mask, made completely of lace. And while the other female fire wielders seemed to have a bit of skin showing, her attire mostly covered her. What it *didn't* hide was her overly toned arms and muscular legs that somehow made her both frightening and breathtakingly beautiful at the same time.

She took another step toward me, and I had half a mind to back up. But we were surrounded by too many people, and I'd likely slam into someone, causing even more of a disturbance. "What's your name?"

Fuck.

Consequences of your own actions.

"Lizbeth," I blurted out. *Lizbeth?! I had never even heard of that name, let alone met someone actually called that.*

The strange female chuckled like she could see through my lie but held out her hand toward me with an unexpected warmth. "Okay, *Lizbeth*." Even the word on her lips sounded completely made-up. "Would you like to see?"

I knew that Dez would be looking for me by now, but with the mask on, it wouldn't hurt to have some fun. And, though I didn't know her, the female gave off such a welcoming essence, it made it impossible to say no. "Alright," I whispered, and placed my hand into hers.

Pulling me along, she stopped at an empty ring that hadn't been lit. I wondered if it had been the one that *she* was using, and my thoughts were confirmed when she reached out to touch it. The moment her finger grazed the cool metal, it lit up into beautiful yellow and orange flames. The heat of it singed the hairs on my arms, but I didn't care. I couldn't stop my eyes from gaping at the beauty of the fire that danced along the structure.

My gaze tore from the orange light to the female who slinked her body onto the ring and maneuvered her legs until she sat inside of the "O," smiling as she looked down at me. That's when I noticed the glow in her eyes that looked like honey shimmering against sunlight. "I have to say," she pumped her legs out and in and made the ring begin to sway, "I find it *strange*. You look as if you've never seen a fire wielder before."

Pushing my brows together, I stepped closer to speak quietly, but not too close for the fire to actually burn me. "As I said, it's my first time…"

"Right." She laughed and continued swinging. "Didn't your textbooks teach you anything, *Lizbeth*?"

"What are you talking about?"

"Fire Wielding is not a very common gift to be born with. And when we *do* show our faces, a vast majority of us are selected into the Lord's Guard."

The Lord's Guard…

Well, shit.

She then hopped off and flaunted each step of hers until she stopped directly in front of me. I wanted to run back inside and find Dez. I was almost positive that she would have outed me for who I was and the entire anonymity of the night would have been ruined.

But instead, she held out her hand, this time for me to shake it. "I've wondered about you; we all have. I know you may *think* that mask conceals you, but," not waiting for me to offer it, she swiped my hand and pulled me closer until her lips were at my ear, "there isn't a soul alive with raven hair and blue eyes that shine the way that *yours* do."

Still unsure of why she was telling me all of this, I pulled back enough to see her face. The glow in her eyes simmered now that the fire behind her had been doused. "I wasn't ready for… I didn't mean to *lie*."

The smile she returned looked completely genuine as she said, "I won't tell if *you* won't." Then, our hands finally shook. "My name's Lyra."

Chapter 18

At some point, Lyra had dragged me back inside and found a couch for the two of us to sit on.

Thankfully she found a non-occupied one, and I didn't have to deal with the awkwardness of basically watching two people have *sex* beside us. I wasn't judging. It had just been so *new* to me. Gods knew I felt nervous enough letting Dez kiss me the way he did in the ballroom the day before. I envied their confidence, truthfully.

"Would you like some wine?" Lyra asked. In her hand was a large decanter, full of a rich colored red wine. She must have snagged the glasses from a nearby tray as we reentered the room, before sitting down.

"Sure." I hadn't drank wine very often. I would occasionally have it at meals with Cassius, but I knew how quickly it could influence one's actions. So, I tried to keep my distance from it for the most part.

After she poured my glass, she handed it to me with a smile and leaned back against the cushions, allowing her eyes to roam over me freely. I almost wanted to blush beneath her stare. "What's your name?" Her question took me a little by surprise.

"Morrigan." Taking a sip of my wine, I tried relaxing into the couch. "If you're a part of Dez's guard, wouldn't you have known that already?"

She laughed, and it echoed in me. It had a lightness to it that made me want to join in. And the deep dimples that appeared on her tanned skin only made her more beautiful. "I did," she admitted. "But I thought you might feel better if *you* told me."

She wasn't wrong. I probably would have given her a double take if she had outright said my name in the middle of our conversation. My eyes trailed off to the crowd in front of us, watching them dance in ways I had never seen before. Their hands groped at each other like they were starving for touch. They kissed, and licked and...

"It's okay to feel nervous, you know?" Lyra reassured me. I had to pry my eyes from the dance floor to look back at her, and her expression had softened. "While this might be normal for *us*, it *is* a first for *you*. You don't have to feel pressured, or ashamed..." She nodded her head to something behind me. "Lord Dez sure isn't."

Turning around, I realized that Dez had returned to his throne.

Accompanied by the *snake* herself.

I'm not sure what I had expected—especially after learning what this masquerade was *really* about. Though, I couldn't lie to myself and pretend it didn't sting to have another girl on his lap moments after *I* had been there.

As the woman clung to him, pulling at his shirt and smearing her own lipstick on his skin, Dez's eyes seemed to search for something amongst the heads in the crowd. The moment our eyes met, I realized he had been looking for me. A taunting smirk played on the corners of his lips, and I knew that this was a game to him.

An *insulting* one, and a challenge I didn't quite feel like matching.

I didn't need to *beg* for Cass's attention. And, no matter how badly my body craved Dez, not a single man here would make me crawl on my knees for them.

I startled slightly when Lyra's hand squeezed my knee, bringing my attention back to her. "You know…" she whispered, then, leaning in, she brought her lips beside my ear. "He just wants a reaction from you, Princess."

Trying to ignore the tension that her fingers left on my skin, I said quietly, "If I give him one, he *wins*. Doesn't he?"

The breath of her chuckle grazed the side of my neck. "I can think of a couple instances in which *you* win." That's when her hand began to move upward, ever so slowly.

Swallowing nervously, it took every ounce of courage to keep my resolve. "I can't use you as a pawn to get back at him. That isn't right."

But her lips didn't move from their position. Instead, her body shifted closer, letting her own leg push against mine. "On the contrary, *Your Grace*…" Her mouth dropped to my shoulder before she placed a kiss against it, barely allowing her lips to press down. "It would be an *honor* to be used by you."

Turning back to Dez, I noticed his eyes had now narrowed at us. Even with his hands gripping the woman's thighs, the playful glint that had shone in his eyes moments before had turned dark. He didn't like Lyra touching me, almost as much as *I* didn't like that woman sitting on top of him. But... This is what the ball was for, right?

"Are you sure?" I whispered to Lyra as her fingers slid into the slits of my dress and they touched my inner thigh.

"Would you like me to beg, Princess?"

Gods... "Okay," I breathed, not allowing my mind to change.

Nothing had been going as I expected it to go tonight, but the most surprising part was the shiver that slid down my spine when she finally kissed my neck. Using her hand on my leg, she pulled it until her knee moved beneath it, causing a gap between my thighs for her. I inhaled a sharp breath when her fingers stopped barely an inch away from my center, nerves bubbling within my stomach.

Her lips made their way up to my ear, and she nipped lightly against my skin with her teeth. "What a fool he was to let you walk around alone like that."

The moment the tips of her fingers brushed against the thin cloth that separated us, I no longer cared about Dez seeing. My eyes fluttered closed, unable to think or move—and I thanked the *gods* for the back of the couch as my body slumped into the cushion.

"I bet you taste as sweet as you look, don't you, Princess?"

I didn't mean for a whimper to fall from my lips, but her fingers continued to tease me, barely pushing any further. They made my body physically ache, along with the sweet words she continued whispering in my ear.

When she laughed, I could feel it in her chest. I didn't dare open my eyes, not with the heat that had my cheeks blazing. "Do you want me to touch you?" she asked.

Biting my lip, I groaned as my hands fisted the fabric we were sitting on. So many people danced around us—so many eyes could see. It should have deterred this sensation that continued to build as she baited me, but it only added to the need. It wasn't like they weren't doing the same exact thing. Some of them doing it on the *dance floor*. I nodded, praying it would be enough.

"You'll need to use your words here, Princess."

I let out a huff, and pried open my eyes, staring directly into the swirls of brown staring back at me. They danced with fire and adrenaline, her own cheeks flushing with what looked like desire. "I... I want you to touch me."

Smiling wide, she closed the distance between us and kissed me. Her lips stole my breath, claiming mine with an intense need that I couldn't help but return to her. Something about Lyra... I didn't know her, which made this completely wild, but Gods... I... *wanted* her. I wanted her confidence, her fearlessness, her strength. I wanted her to give it all to *me*—to taste her tongue as it pushed against my own.

Her fingers slid under the fabric, and I moaned once they touched my center. It had been throbbing for her touch, and she began soothing that ache. Matching her rhythm, I couldn't help but thrust my hips against her, begging for them to move faster. Dez could have the snake tonight, I wanted *Lyra*. I wanted her to be my unravelling. In response, my hands reached out to her, placing one against her chest to push her back into the couch.

She stared at me with wide eyes once our lips detached from one another. But the smile that stretched across my face felt like another person entirely as I threw my leg over her lap and climbed on top of her. She looked like she wanted to say something, but I didn't give her a chance before claiming her lips again.

Gripping my hips, her fingers dug into my skin, pressing into my gown as our bodies fought for control. Tongues clashed, our lips bruised each other's, and I suddenly felt like I was riding on a high. She wasted no time in sliding her hand beneath me again and bringing her fingers to my center.

"Please," I begged her. "I need you to touch me."

Smiling against my mouth, she pulled away just long enough to say, "As you wish, *Your Grace.*"

I felt two of her fingers slide into me and almost cried out in pleasure. But she captured my lips, swallowing my sound as she moved them in and out. Even though her fingers were smaller than Cass's, Lyra knew things that even *I* didn't know about pleasure. The way she curled them, pulling and pushing against every sensitive spot inside of me, I felt like I would explode at any moment. But I didn't want to, I wanted to stay like this for as long as possible.

I wanted to touch her. I wanted to make *her* feel as good as she was making *me* feel.

"Fuck," Lyra rasped. "You put on quite a show, Princess."

Leaving her lips, I kissed her cheek, then her jaw, making my way down to her neck. "It's not a show," I moaned against her ear.

The climax I needed built rapidly inside of me, and when she began to massage her thumb against my center, I let out a cry into her shoulder. So close... I was *so... close...*

Just before I could finish, a hand slid into my hair, fisting it and yanking me back. When I opened my eyes, Dez stood above me, causing me to go still. A deep rage simmered in his eyes, making the blue look like storming seas beneath his mask. Panting, I could still feel Lyra's fingers inside of me, but I didn't move. They had me stuck in the middle of both of them, Lyra's other hand still gripping my hip.

"Did I tell you to stop?" he asked, his voice sounding positively feral. Even his jaw tensed, muscles ticking under his skin.

I didn't know what took over me, but my eyes remained on him as I began moving on Lyra. Grinding against her, I took over and moaned as her thumb began to move again. My eyes threatened to close from the pleasure returning, but he pulled my hair a little tighter.

"Oh no, Princess..." Lowering his head, he stopped inches from my mouth. "I want you to look at me while she touches you." Lyra's body shifted beneath me, and then her own lips touched my chest, just above my breasts. Dez appeared practically drunk with lust, staring into my eyes. "Does it feel good?" he asked, bringing his hand to my throat and caressing it before wrapping it around my jaw.

"Yes," I whined, as his thumb brushed over my bottom lip.

Lyra bit the top of my dress, teasing the fabric as she pulled it down slightly.

"Do you want to come, Princess?"

Tears were beginning to well in my eyes—my body *ached* for the release. "Yes..." I panted. "Please, yes."

With another impulsive thought, I dropped my lip and pulled his thumb into my mouth. I licked at it and sucked, watching his eyes soften in desperation.

"Leave us, Lyra," he ordered through clenched teeth. If it had been a game that we were playing, the look in his eyes would have been a clear indication that *I* had won.

"Yes, sir," Lyra whispered against my skin before sliding her fingers out of me.

Dez gently pulled until he forced my legs to move, standing me in front of him as Lyra made a quick exit. I wanted to groan and protest. Dez had interrupted us, as if he hadn't already been preoccupied with the *blonde*. I had come so close to finishing, and he stopped her right before my body could release. I knew he had done it on purpose.

One hand still in my hair, and the other now wrapped like a necklace around my throat, he leaned down until our lips were a breath away. "You'll let *her* touch you, but not me?"

"You seemed to have enough hands on you already." *Gods... Way to not sound jealous, Morrigan.*

Sliding his fingers along my neck, he trailed them down to my chest. "I don't want anyone else's hands, Princess."

He moved again, drifting over the top of my gown and brushing across my breasts. I had already known my nipples were hard, and the thin lining of the gown did nothing to stop me from feeling him pass over them. Their sensitivity flared from his touch, and I tried my best not to show my body's reaction to it.

The moment he brought his mouth to my neck, I whimpered. "Dez..." he kissed and sucked my skin like he was starving. "Dez, I don't want to be one of your—"

"I'll never touch her again, Morrigan," he panted. "I swear to the gods, these hands will be yours."

The hand that had gripped my hair dropped, pressing onto my lower back as he slowly pushed against my body. I arched my back as he lowered his lips to just above my breasts, and he held me so I wouldn't fall.

"These lips will never kiss another soul," he whispered. Then he bit down on my skin, just enough to sting a little. "I need you more than I need air to breathe, Princess. I'm begging you."

Swallowing the last of my pride, I had a feeling that I would regret it, but still I said, "Yes."

Chapter 19

With his hand clutching mine like a lifeline, he dragged me across the dance floor and out into the hall.

I bit my lip to refrain from smiling, but the thrill of excitement that coursed through me could barely stay contained. I cared deeply for Cass, but… Dez? Something had always felt so *right* about him. Like this part of me called to him and he *felt* it.

We didn't make it up the stairs. Instead, he pulled me into the drawing room and within seconds, had spun me around until his hands clasped my face. Before I could breathe, his lips found mine in a hungry, suffocating kiss. He kissed me like he would have *died* without tasting me, and I returned every part of it. Fisting the sides of his shirt, I pulled him closer, no longer willing to remain even an inch apart from him.

I hadn't noticed that I was moving back until I felt myself hit a desk. Dropping from my face, Dez's hands lowered to lift me, and he placed me on top of the wood. That's when the realization had my breath pausing, suddenly stuck in my lungs. "Dez..."

His mouth latched onto my neck, kissing and nipping at my skin. In one swift motion, his hands slid under my gown, pulling it up to give him full access.

"Dez... I haven't..." I could barely speak through the moans that were rippling through me from every part of my skin that he touched. My body had already been blazing with need after he denied me my release.

But Dez paused after he seemed to mull over my words. Our bodies still tangled together, he pulled back enough to look me in the eyes. "You can say no," he reminded me. "We don't have to..."

"I want to." I didn't allow him to finish his sentence. *Gods* I wanted to. That wasn't even a question in my mind. "Just..." My cheeks heated from the blush that crawled over them. "Just go *easy*... please."

The next kiss that Dez gave me had a gentle tenderness to it. He pushed his tongue inside of my mouth—tasting like sweet desire and wine. Carefully, he pushed me down until my back laid against the desk, but he didn't stop kissing me. As our lips clashed, his hand slid beneath my gown again until his fingers reached my center. And, without warning, they brushed over what was already swollen and sensitive with need. I gasped when I felt him rubbing me, my hands flying to his hair to hang onto it.

"Dez," I moaned into his mouth.

But he said nothing as he moved his fingers, rubbing them in circles until my body began to shake. The climax he had taken from me now sat on a cliff, ready to dive at any second—it had been there, waiting desperately for *him* to touch me.

"Oh, Gods... Dez," I cried.

"Give me everything, Princess. I need it." His whispers were muffled against my own lips.

And then, the string broke, and I almost yelled out in pleasure from the intensity of my orgasm—having held onto it once he forced Lyra to leave, which only made it a thousand times stronger. Dez continued to rub me, more slowly, as my body trembled under him, emptying every bit of my desire.

When my body finally decided to stop shaking, Dez pulled back again to look at me. "Are you sure?" he asked.

Nodding my head, I let go of his hair and placed a hand on his chest. "Just go slow."

He wasted no time in pulling the fabric from my hips and down my legs. Fluttering rapidly, I could hear my pulse in my ears as I watched him move his pants down. That's when the fear kicked in. I saw *him*, his *size*, and I knew this would be painful. When he noticed my stare, he almost smirked. "You'll be fine, Princess. I promise you." He grabbed my legs, making me bend my knees, and pulled me down until my ass almost hung over the ledge. "We'll take it easy... *This time.*"

That's when I felt him, teasing at my entrance. I closed my eyes, tensing my entire body as I waited for the inevitable sting. But Dez leaned down and pressed his forehead against mine.

"Don't," he whispered. "Just look at me."

As my eyelids peeled open, I could see the soft blue eyes staring down at me. Just as they began to glow, a sudden wave of calm rushed through my body. The storming waves had returned to a beautiful sky blue, and I wrapped my arms around his neck for support. *Beautiful*, I thought to myself. *He's so beautiful.*

As he pushed in, I almost tensed once more as I felt him enter me, but Dez closed the distance and kissed me again. Every inch was met with his own lips, claiming mine in a way that made me unable to think of anything else. I could feel the pain of him stretching me, but as one of his hands found my waist, all I wanted was to feel *every* part of him.

"Breathe, Princess," he reminded me. I hadn't even realized that I wasn't breathing. I let out the breath that had been lodged inside of my lungs, and Dez pushed in the rest of the way, ripping a cry from my lips. "Fuck…" he groaned. "Gods, you feel so fucking good."

It took a few seconds of inhaling through the pain before it began to subside, and once Dez felt comfortable with continuing, he pulled his hips back and began thrusting slowly. I could see the restraint in his eyes as they closed, like he needed every ounce of it to hold himself back. It took a little longer than I wanted it to, but eventually the feeling of him pushing inside of me sent a new wave of pleasure through my body.

Every time his hips would shove forward, he would hit a spot that made my back want to arch up. "Dez," I exhaled. I could feel another coil of release building slowly.

When he lowered his head, I expected him to kiss me, but his lips moved to my neck instead. "Do you trust me?" he asked, softly.

It took no convincing for me to nod my head, and then his teeth seemed to sharpen against my skin. That tension that had been rising burst like a damn when he sunk them into my neck, breaking the skin and shooting currents of blissful fire into my veins. "Dez!" I yelled, unable to keep my voice any lower than a scream.

He thrusted harder, sucking as he shoved himself inside of me, and I could feel his own groans deep within my chest. When he let go, my body still shook from the second orgasm, and I watched him take a small knife on top of the desk to his own neck. He made a minor cut, and somehow my body knew exactly what to do—it wasn't like I hadn't done it before.

But this time, my body *craved* it. I wasn't thinking as I wrapped my arms around his shoulders and pulled him down to me. My lips clamped over the wound and he tasted almost as sweet as his words were. "You're so beautiful, Princess," he whispered. "I want to keep you."

As his blood coated my tongue, another moan left when he picked up speed. A kind of… warmth rose in my chest, one I remembered feeling with Cass. My own, rapid pulse seemed to follow it, pounding in my ears as my veins thrummed with his own blood. It only took a few more thrusts and Dez stilled inside of me, holding back his own yell. Pulling his neck away from me, I didn't fight him. All I wanted was to be enveloped in his arms. Even after, as he lowered his chest down to mine to catch his breath, it felt as though his own heart beat with mine. *Right*, I thought to myself, *he feels so* right.

"Hey, Dez?" I asked quietly.

He had no energy to speak and simply nodded his head in response.

"Touch her again and I'll cut off your hands."

I waited for him to push himself up and scold me for giving him an order. But after a few beats of silence, his entire body shook as he erupted in laughter. "Princess… I can promise that, without a doubt, you have *officially* ruined the idea of anyone else for me."

I didn't know how long we stayed that way, wrapped together like vines on top of the desk.

But my exhaustion quickly kicked in, and I couldn't help but yawn. "Not that I'm *not* enjoying this," I said, letting my fingers play with his blonde locks. "But I'm not sure I can keep my eyes open much longer."

At those words, Dez finally sprang up. "I didn't even think about that. Sorry," he mumbled. Pulling himself away, I could feel him lean down with a cloth, wiping me. Then, he extended a hand to help me sit up.

"Thank you," I had begun to say, but my fatigue flushed through my head, causing me to grip his arms for support. "Sorry… I didn't know I was *this* tired."

Wrapping his arms around me, Dez twisted until he could lift me, cradling my body against his chest. "I'll carry you, Princess."

I hadn't expected my night to end this way, being whisked away in Dez's arms. I would be lying if I said that Cass didn't cross my mind then, and guilt twined itself with the lasting pleasure I still felt from it all. But I tried to remind myself that I was only human.

He walked out of the drawing room and made his way toward the stairs, my body swaying with each of his steps. Unfortunately, just as he reached the first one, a vaguely familiar voice called out. "Dez!" My stomach twisted into a little knot and I didn't bother moving my head from his shirt to look at her. "Are you going to come back?"

What enraged me more was the fact that Dez had been holding *me*, and she had the audacity to expect him to return to *her* after. I wanted to throw something at the snake's face. But before I could even ponder what I knew would be an irrational response, Dez spoke instead. "Enjoy your night, Gwenyth. I'll be retiring for the evening."

A sweet sense of victory had me smiling as we made it to my room. It was the validation that I had wanted, knowing I didn't have to share.

He was *mine*.

Lowering me to the floor, he whispered, "I'm just going to help you change first."

I hummed in response, not willing to fully release his body as I leaned against it. He smelled divine. Scents of flowers and wine were practically soaked into his clothing. I wanted it to be a part of me. First, he removed my mask, then his own. And as he began to twist my body away from him, I felt his fingers tug on the sleeve hanging over my shoulder. A quick burst of energy had my eyes widening in fear and I barely turned in time as my dress fell to the floor. "No!" I yelled.

Staring at me in shock and confusion, he kept his hands in front of him. "What's wrong? Did I do something?"

"No! I…" What were my options? If I asked him to let me dress myself after an outburst like that, he would *know* that I was hiding something. But, if I turned around, he'd *see* them. And I didn't want him to look at me differently.

The way he gazed at me in the drawing room had given me so much power, so much confidence. The yearning in his eyes made me feel important and valued. Once he saw my scars, he'd realize the damaged goods that had been thrown at him. He'd see the cracked portrait of a girl who's known nothing but pain and loneliness, and none of the strength that his kiss convinced me I might have had.

I could already feel the sting of tears in my eyes as I realized how long I had gone without responding. That's when Dez's eyes suddenly softened, and my fear turned into petrifying terror. "The blood…" Hearing his realization made my chest feel like it had physically cracked in half. "You were on the floor…"

He looked down, his eyes wandering to the same position beside my bed that he had found me in on my last day with Cass. Then, his eyes widened before he rushed toward me.

"I should have *known*," he hissed in my ear, holding my entire body hostage against his. "I should have killed the bitch instead of letting her go."

When I felt his shirt suddenly soaked against my cheek, I knew that I had been sobbing. "I'm sorry," I cried. "I tried so hard to hide them. I didn't want any of you to think—"

"Sorry? *You're* sorry?" Pulling back, he cupped my face in his hands firmly, but the expression on his face showed nothing but kindness. He took in a long, slow breath before continuing. "Morrigan... If she so much as lays another *finger* on you, I will *kill* her."

"You... you can't. You're not allowed to interfere—"

"I will *kill* her, Princess," he repeated, a threatening firmness to his voice. "Do you understand me?"

As I nodded, he wiped both cheeks with his thumb, clearing away the fallen tears. Then, he helped me into a nightgown and brought me to my bed. I hadn't expected him to crawl in beside me, pulling me onto his chest. But as he stroked my hair, it eased my heart, allowing its fluttering to slow down.

"I won't let anything happen to you, Princess," he promised quietly. "You're *mine* now."

The Diary of Daisies and Hellebores

Though we have spoken many times in the past, today felt different. I was tending to my garden when he approached me with a flower. A daisy. How did he know that those are my favorite? We walked together through the garden and he asked me if he could visit again. I had never seen him smile before today. It was breathtaking.

Chapter 20

The dream began with fields of roses, every color imaginable.

It had been quite peaceful, a vast difference from the dreams I grew so accustomed to throughout my life. Running my fingers through the flowers, I walked the field and basked in the warmth of the sun above me. There was no sound, not even the whistle of a breeze nearby, but something about the silence made me feel content.

After a few moments, I noticed the flowers begin to change. There were blooms of dandelions now at the end of their lifespan, their seeds beginning to part as my hands touched them. Without the presence of wind, their feathered petals fell to the ground, and, for some odd reason, I felt... sad for them.

The dandelion field didn't last as I ended up in a patch of daisies. They were in full bloom, and I had the sudden urge to kneel down and pluck one. But the moment the stem left the earth, a sudden chill rushed through me, ripping my hair over my shoulders and sucking the breath from my lungs. A dark shadow crept above the sky, crawling like webs until it covered the sun, leaving me in total darkness.

I tried to call out for help, but my voice was lost. I could move my lips but no sound would leave them. That's when I heard the crunching of dead grass like footsteps behind me. Too scared to turn, I stayed in place, clutching the daisy in my fingers.

When the footsteps halted, I could feel the stranger's presence, making the hairs on my neck prickle. A single breath against my skin is all I felt before I heard a familiar, distorted *voice whisper,* "Morrigan."

I woke with a startle, a slight sweat beading above my brows.

It hadn't quite been a *nightmare...* Truthfully, I didn't know *what* that was.

A soft knock on my door pulled my attention away and I heard a small, feminine voice call through. "Your Grace, it's Eowyn."

Rubbing my hands over my face, I then turned to the side and realized that Dez had left at some point. It would have been nice to wake up with him after what happened... but I couldn't expect him to drop everything for me. I tossed my legs over the side of the bed and said over my shoulder, "You can come in, Eowyn."

As I yawned, I moved to the vanity and paused by the standing mirror, taking in my appearance. That's when Eowyn opened the door and also stopped short. The pins in my hair were tangled and knotted all throughout my curls. I looked like a rabid animal. Turning to Eowyn, I could see her eyes widen.

"Say nothing," I begged. Gods. Had Dez seen this when he woke up? "Please fix me."

Laughing, Eowyn walked toward the doors to the bathing room and opened them. "Let's get you cleaned up."

After my bath, I dressed myself and sat in the chair of my vanity as Eowyn approached me with a small bottle.

I took it from her hand and lifted the top off, bringing my nose down to sniff it. It had no odor and almost looked like plain water. "What is this?" I asked her.

"An… elixir, Your Grace." Her cheeks reddened instantly. "It's to protect you from any… surprises from last night. Lord Dez asked that I give it to you."

"Surprises?" It took me longer than I wanted to admit for me to realize what she meant. "Oh… Thank you."

I threw back the liquid, swallowing it quickly. It surely didn't *taste* like water. It tasted of dirt and earth and sour fruit. If this was what I would have to do every time, I began considering celibacy as a legitimate option in the near future.

Shaking off the taste that still lingered on my tongue, a hard knock had both Eowyn and I turning to the door. But as I heard the voice that called from the other side, a large smile made my cheeks burn. "I hope you enjoyed your week off! Because now you'll have to study on a *Saturday!"*

Jumping from my chair, I ran to the door and opened it. Harley stood with a grin on his face, leaning against the wall. "Harley," I said cheerfully.

He nodded his head to the side. "Let's go." Then, his eyes peeked over my shoulder to where Eowyn likely stood now. "Your handmaiden may join us if she'd like." He said nothing more as he turned to leave.

Looking back at Eowyn, I shot her a pleading glance. "Would you?"

She seemed surprised by the offer. "I… I would love to, Your Grace."

With that, I linked my arm with hers and pulled her along, walking behind Harley as we headed toward the library.

Eowyn quickly took to the books, barely willing to listen to Harley's instructions. She said it was the first time she had ever been invited into the library and looked fascinated as she scanned the titles along the shelves. Harley and I shared a secret smile, leaving her to browse as we sat together at one of the desks.

Flipping through the pages of one of the books Harley had handed me, I paused as I read the word "hellebore" in one of the passages. "Harley?" I asked over my shoulder, still staring at the inked text in front of me.

"Yes?"

"The attacks… Who do you think is behind them?"

Letting out a long sigh, the pages fluttered as he closed his book. He traded his chair behind me for one closer, on the other side of my desk, and leaned back. "I don't have the slightest idea, unfortunately. Their attacks aren't consistent, and there haven't been many. But each time, they disappear as if they hadn't been there at all."

"Cass said…" I took a breath, remembering how scared he had been when he found the torn fabric of my gown. "He said that they were after *me*. What could they possibly want with me?"

Harley shrugged. "Leverage? You were hand-picked by the gods. Perhaps they seek to control you." But then, something in his eyes darkened a little, causing my own body to chill. "There's power in your blood, Morrigan. Maybe not power like the *lords* wield… but your blood alone can heal the poison of hellebore. It should have *killed* Cassius." Slowly, his blue eyes turned until they locked with mine. "Who knows what else it can do?"

Just then, the doors to the library opened abruptly, slamming against the walls with force. "Princess!" a familiar voice called.

A buzz of excitement had me turning to the entrance, igniting a smile when I saw Cass standing with his arms crossed over his chest. "Cass!" I yelled and left my conversation behind as I ran to him.

When he pulled me against his chest, wrapping his arms around me, I savored every scent I could capture as I breathed it in. As if he yearned for the same, he buried his face into my hair. "I've missed you," he whispered quietly.

"I must insist that you stop distracting my star pupil from her studies," Harley teased from somewhere behind me.

"Say the word and I'll sneak you away from here," Cass baited low enough for only me to hear. Then, his hands dropped slightly on my back as he pulled me in tighter, making me gasp. "I'm positively *starving*, Princess."

"I've had her for a week, and you're already plotting to steal her back?" Dez had walked in and Cass let me go just in time to see the theatrical pout on his friend's face. "That doesn't seem fair."

Something about having both of them standing before me *should* have been terrifying. I should have felt some shred of embarrassment, having spent the night tangled next to Dez after... *well*... That was beside the point. But as I searched for any guilt that lingered in the back of my mind, the only emotion that had my skin practically buzzing came from *happiness* as I stared at the both of them.

That had to be wrong... right?

"Are they all here?" Cass asked him, to which Dez nodded.

With a sigh, Cass wrapped an arm around my back again and pulled me close enough for him to bend down, pressing his lips against my cheek. "Another time, then," he seemed to promise.

Giving me a quick kiss, he released me and left the library, leaving me with Dez, who had one eyebrow raised at me. "So…" Taking slow steps toward me, he began reaching out to my arms, placing a gentle touch on my skin. "Is three still a crowd?"

"*Dez!*" I shoved him away and tried to hide my own amusement as he laughed. "I will hit you if you don't leave."

With a dramatic sigh, Dez turned and waved himself off. "I'll see you at dinner, my love!"

My brain had been thoroughly overworked by the time the day came to an end.

I knew the guys were likely waiting for me to join them. But as I stared at Eowyn, I felt guilty at the thought of her needing to stand behind me again, waiting for me to finish. "Eowyn?" I called to her. "Will you join me tonight? For dinner?"

Blinking a few times as if she didn't understand what I had asked her, she then cocked her head to the side. "I think you forget that I'm still just… *staff*, Your Grace. We don't eat with the lords, let alone a *princess* such as yourself."

"You're my friend, Eowyn. At least… I think you are." I had suddenly grown a little self-conscious at the idea that she might not have shared that feeling. "Do you want to be my friend?" I asked shyly.

Eowyn stared at me with wide eyes for a moment, making my own insecurities grow. Then, her expression softened with a sweet smile that lit up her blue eyes. "I would like that very much, Your Gra—"

"*Morrigan*," I pleaded. "If we are *friends* now… I would like for you to call me '*Morrigan*'."

She nodded in agreement. "I don't know if Lord Dez will approve, though."

Linking my arm in hers, I smiled mischievously. "Well then, it's a good thing he has no say in the matter."

We both laughed as we left the library, making our way to the dining hall.

As I had already assumed, the guys were seated by the time we arrived. And to accommodate Eowyn, I took a seat at the end where she could sit beside me. Eowyn gave me a worried look, but I pulled her down beside me anyway. Even as they all stared in shock, a simple glance at Dez showed me he had no issues with my decision. That was all the permission I needed.

Someone laughed at the table, breaking the silence, and I looked up to see Cain scratching his chin with his thumb. His smirk remained hidden under his fingers. "Wow, Dez. I knew you all had become very... *inclusive* as of late, but to have the help eating with you as well?"

Eowyn tried to stand from her chair, but I placed a hand on her thigh, sitting her back down. She was *my* guest, and I wouldn't tolerate anyone allowing her to feel unwelcome. "You know, Cain..." I began. "I read today that in Kaiden's land, unsolicited advice like that could very well get your tongue cut out." He all but dropped his jaw as he gaped at me. "Eowyn is *my* guest tonight. And I didn't ask, nor do I need, your opinion on the matter." I then offered him my most practiced smile, courtesy of Maeryn's twenty-one years of teaching.

As the guys all began laughing at my obvious insult, Cain leaned forward, clearly prepared with a rebuttal. "You little—"

"My, my," a chilling voice called from the doorway. My lips pulled themselves together in a thin line, knowing that any hope for an enjoyable evening had now crumbled with his presence. "What a *mouth* you have, little dove."

I decided to turn my gaze to him, seeing him leaning against the frame. "Kaiden," I responded curtly.

Watching the sly smile spread across his face lit a fire in my belly that made me want to slap it off of him. He may have succeeded in getting to me the last time we saw each other. But this time, he would not.

"Do you plan on ruining *every* dinner, Kaiden?" Dez sighed from the head of the table.

Not answering Dez, Kaiden kept his eyes on me in a silent challenge as he made his way to the seat across from mine. He wanted me to falter— to look away first. Unfortunately, Maeryn hadn't briefed him on just how stubborn I could actually be.

"A certain *priestess* informed me that she wasn't allowed to assist you in your first week here, dove." Kaiden leaned back in his seat, unbothered by the fact that not a single person wanted him there. "She thinks you're being *corrupted...* I think 'whore' is the phrase she used, actually." Then, he took a long, slow inhale. "And I might be inclined to agree."

I remembered him saying he could smell Cass on me last time. And Cass and I hadn't even... *Gods. What an invasion of privacy.*

Dez, the savior, intervened with laughter from the other end. "What do you think, Princess? Are we corrupting you?" he asked playfully.

Not willing to let Kaiden win this round, I let out a long sigh and nodded my head, turning my eyes to Dez and Cass. "I'd be thoughtless not to agree. Maybe you should send me back to that lovely cottage." I returned my gaze to Kaiden with a fake smile. "You can all just take turns visiting my bed now that I've turned into such a *harlot*." My words were spilling with venom as I said the last part, and the same anger reflected back at me in Kaiden's black eyes.

For two people that knew nothing of each other, Kaiden and I were now linked with a poisonous hatred that I didn't even feel for *Maeryn*. Just seeing his face made me want to bite someone's head off. From the other end of the table, I could hear someone spit out their drink, followed by Cass's boastful laughter. Kaiden, however, didn't stray an inch from the mask so obviously stitched onto his face.

Even the storm brewing in his glare didn't falter when he finally replied, "You should learn to hold your tongue, *little dove*."

I could have sworn that I saw my own breath from the ice in his words. The kitchen doors opened then, staff filtering in and carefully placing our plates in front of us. Some of them paused when they saw Eowyn beside me, something I had almost forgotten in the midst of Kaiden's arrival. But, I watched as one of them closest to the kitchen ran in, grabbing an extra plate.

"That's quite enough, Kaiden," Eris said stiffly. "Let's just enjoy the rest of our meal, please."

"I'm quite enjoying this," Cain snickered nearby.

But D seemed less than amused as he let out a long, disappointed sigh. "Yes, well, some of us *aren't*."

"I forgot to ask, dove." Kaiden's voice rose slightly, almost in a mocking fashion. "How is your *back*?"

I had stopped breathing entirely, as did everyone else at the table, which led me to believe that Dez had shared that information with them. But I didn't believe for a second that he shared it with *Kaiden*.

"Kaiden," Dez said, his voice low and filled with a controlled anger. "I'm warning you."

Ignoring him, Kaiden leaned forward, realizing his words finally had an effect on me. "I was informed of a... wardrobe issue the day you left for

Dez's castle." Even his lips twitched upward into a menacing smirk. "I sure hope it's healed well."

And just like that, it was as if he had opened every wound on my back and laid me bare in front of everyone. I could feel their eyes on me, waiting for a response. Not even Dez cared to speak for me in that moment—not that he had to. It was *my* burden to bear, not theirs. Though, I couldn't stop the small stinging in my eyes at the minor tears teetering along my waterlines.

"Poor, broken little dove."

I had half a mind to grab the knife beside my plate and jam it straight into his throat. It wouldn't have killed him, but it might have felt damn good for *me*. Before I could allow my impulsive thoughts to take over, Eowyn placed her hand on top of mine that still laid on her knee, now clinging to her dress.

"Her Grace hasn't been feeling well today," she offered sweetly. "If you'll excuse us, I'd like to make her some tea to help her relax."

Kaiden's smirk only inched deeper at her words, but I knew she was giving me an out. When Dez agreed, we stood together, her arm in mine, and walked out of the dining hall, leaving my anger behind with them. "I'm sorry," I whispered to her the moment we were out of earshot.

"That was all him," she sneered, the first time I had ever seen her actually angry at something. "You didn't deserve that—*no one* deserves that. He's always been a cruel bastard."

Scoffing, I turned to Eowyn with wide eyes. "When did *you* learn such crass language?" I teased her.

She laughed as she shoved her shoulder against me. "I guess we're *all* corruptible, aren't we?" Then, she nodded her head toward the stairs to the rooms. "You go get comfortable. I'll grab us some tea and food to eat while we read."

As she made her way back to the kitchen, I began my slow ascent up the stairs, clutching the railing a little harder than necessary. I hated what he called me. That stupid pet name. Gods, how could someone be as cruel and uncaring as him? Had he never known kindness? The answer to my question had already been answered. No person with an ounce of kindness could be with the likes of *Maeryn*. Maybe they truly did deserve each other.

As I turned down the hall, I heard the soft sound of a footstep behind me and had no time to block myself before someone shoved me against the wall, knocking the breath from my lungs. Raising my eyes, I saw black ones staring back at me as Kaiden's forearm pushed hard into my chest, keeping my back pinned.

"Leave me alone," I hissed at him, having to clench my teeth through the pain of his hold.

Teeth bared, his lips curled back in what looked like disgust.

"I have *centuries* on you, little girl." Once again, I noticed a strange darkness that seemed to cloud the markings on his neck—like tiny flecks of shadows kissing his skin. "Yet, you walk around these castles like you have the freedom to do so."

As his forearm dug into my flesh, I kept my lips pressed together in a tight line, trying to ignore the pain it shot into my chest.

"You're no *savior*, little dove. You have no gifts. No power," he sneered. "You're *no one*."

"You think you scare me, Kaiden?" I asked through teeth clenched so hard I thought they would surely shatter. "Quite frankly, you *bore* me. I lived through *years* of Maeryn's daily abuse." Pushing my head forward, I strained my neck until our noses were but an inch apart. "Why don't you run back to your *whore*. I'm sure she'd love to hear you spewing the bullshit that comes out of your—"

His forearm moved from my chest and a hand wrapped around my throat, cutting off my airway just enough to leave the smallest room for slight gasps. "I could *kill* you," he warned. "You're so tiny and breakable, little dove. I could snap your neck and end this senseless parade they've all put on for you."

"K... Kaid..." I clawed at his hand, trying to remove it, but I could barely form a full word.

"You think you're special because of a simple birthmark on your shoulder?" He laughed and shook his head. "I've got plenty of those, sweetheart, and they're far deadlier than yours."

The strange mist on his markings began to thicken, pouring down his body and seeping from the collar of his shirt. They *were* shadows. Shadows that he somehow controlled.

Loosening his grip slightly, a small smirk played on the corner of his lips. "She would complain to me of your nightmares—how they terrorized you. She'd show up exhausted from hearing your screams all night."

I scoffed, still holding onto his hand around my throat. "Did she... tell you that... while you were *fucking* her?"

My lungs screamed, begging for a larger breath that I couldn't take yet. But Kaiden's eyes twinkled with amusement as he leaned down, brushing his lips against my ear, and I could almost feel his shadows reaching for my skin. My hair prickled in anticipation, waiting for the pain to come.

"Would you like to know, little dove?" The moment his other hand touched my waist, tears began to form in my eyes.

He wouldn't.

Wouldn't he?

"Should I *show* you how she likes it?"

The tears finally toppled over, and as if he could taste the growing fear, he began to laugh. A shiver ran down my spine at the feel of his breath against my neck.

Finally letting go, my body dropped to the floor the moment he stepped away and I grabbed my neck to soothe my aching skin. I couldn't stop the tears, though. "I hate you," I cried, staring into his soulless eyes.

Looking down at me, he showed no emotion as he said, "I'll get you soon. And we'll see how much you sing when you're in *my* cage, little dove." And then, darkness consumed him, leaving me stranded in the empty hallway.

Chapter 21

I hadn't bothered telling Dez about my encounter with Kaiden. Kaiden likely expected me to run straight to him, but I meant what I said. He didn't scare me. The worst that he could do was kill me, and he didn't know how many times I *begged* for my life to end throughout the years. I *was,* however, surprised by the fact that Eowyn never once commented on what Kaiden had said at the table. She still hadn't seen my scars yet, which I knew wouldn't last much longer. They couldn't stay hidden forever. But she respected my privacy, returned to the room with hot tea and a book for herself, and proceeded to sit with me by the window.

"Did you hear me, Princess?" Dez asked, sitting beside me at the dining table.

I snapped out of my thoughts and turned to him with an apologetic smile. "I'm sorry, what did you say?"

"It's tax season, which means I'll be spending a day in each of my villages as I collect their dues," he repeated for me. "I wanted to know if you'd like to join me this week."

Peeking up at him from my chair, my mood lifted instantly at the idea of getting out of the castle grounds and seeing his land. "I would love to." It didn't take me longer than a second to add, "Can Eowyn come with us?"

Laughing, Dez looked beside me at Eowyn, seated and eating her food. She had paused with her fork in her mouth the moment I asked him. "Would you like to accompany Morrigan and me this week? She'll need someone to keep her company while I'm busy with the tenants."

I watched her swallow her food and slowly sit up straight. "I—of course, My Lord."

Dez didn't comment on Eowyn joining us for breakfast the day before, nor did he seem bothered by it at dinner. I had felt as though I owed Eowyn a "redo" after the performance Kaiden *and* Cain displayed that Saturday night. But now, with the others gone, it actually felt quite peaceful having her beside me. It was a lot better than having her standing *behind* me as I ate my food. "We leave tomorrow," Dez said, pushing his finished plate away from him and making his way to stand. "Pack whatever you ladies need for the week; we will be gone until Friday."

As Dez exited the dining hall, Eowyn nudged me with her shoulder. "You have a funny habit of volunteering me for things."

I couldn't help but laugh. "I'm sorry. I would say I promise to stop, but I don't know if it's a promise I'll be able to keep."

We finished our breakfast quickly and went back to my room to pack. It took up most of our day. Thankfully, Harley hadn't retrieved us to join him in the library. I assumed he had his own things to tend to in his free time.

Eowyn had insisted on me bringing different types of dresses. According to her, I needed comfortable gowns to walk in, nightgowns— but I *had* to bring robes in case it got too cold—*and* some fancier gowns to eat in with Dez. When I looked at the several cases of clothing that *I* had compared to the *one* case she had packed, I argued that she needed more. But all she had responded with was a snarky smirk and said, *"The luxuries of royalty aren't my burden."*

Rude.

My eyes were closed, but… they didn't feel *like my own.*

I stood on something hard and uneven. It felt like rocks, maybe. I had no shoes on and the ground beneath me didn't feel very wide. On the edges of my feet, I could almost feel a dip where it came to an end—perhaps it was a thin bridge of some sort. I remained where I was, my breaths steady and deep as the surrounding air radiated a quiet heat. The kind that normally poured down in rays from the sun but intensified to a level that could almost singe the hairs on your arms.

After what felt like hours, *I opened my eyes slowly and the first thing I could see was a blazing orange and red light illuminating the area in front of me. I* had *been standing on a bridge, one made of some kind of stone, and it could barely fit my own two feet. Before I had any time to fear the potential of falling off of the bridge, I could smell the source of the light. Fire.*

Not just a small fire, either. The flames seemed to surround me. But even in their glow, the rest of the world appeared swallowed by the shadows. Wherever I was, it looked as if it stretched for miles in complete darkness with an unseen path that could lead anywhere.

As I tried to survey the area, searching for any kind of hint at where *I was, my feet began to move. Looking down, I realized that they weren't* my *feet at all. This wasn't* my *body.*

So whose was it?

I began to walk along the bridge, passing through clouds of smoke and dark fog like it was second nature to me. My lungs didn't appear bothered by any of it. Well... their *lungs. It took a moment for sound to actually trickle in. It started with the crackling of embers rising from the fire, but beneath the flames called a different kind of sound.*

It started far away, but slowly drifted up, growing louder as it approached. They were screams. Screams of hundreds, maybe thousands of people. They sounded painful. Screams of pure agony floated through the sky. But whomever's feet I walked in didn't falter at the sound, they ignored it—like they were familiar with this place.

We moved forward, wading through air as dense as fog. To any other person, it would have been suffocating. Just breathing in the thick smoke that clouded our surroundings would be enough to kill a man. So I couldn't understand why it wasn't affecting us.

Soon enough, a structure began to form from the darkness before us, and as we approached it, it morphed into a large, iron gate. The walls holding it were made of the same stone that designed this bridge—dark enough to be considered black, but when the light of the flames licked it, you could see undertones of red within their cracks.

Suddenly, my hand lifted as we approached the entrance, reaching toward the gate. But before my fingers could touch it, I paused—a wave of loneliness washing through me that I knew wasn't my own. Still, an emotion I understood all too well. An emotion that had become second nature to me in the solitude of my attic room, much like the darkness of whatever cave we walked in now.

Without warning, this strange awareness seemed to cloud my own mind, and I whipped my head around as anxiety made my arms flex in anticipation. We were looking for something....

"Well, well, well..." a familiar distorted voice called through my mind. "How did you get here?" he asked. I realized then that he was talking to me.

I wanted to answer him to tell him that I didn't even know where here was, but the flames began to dim around me. The darkness that surrounded us started to close in slowly, making its way toward us. Panic crept through my body, and I didn't know what to do. I couldn't move, I couldn't run, and the shadows were threatening to consume me.

"Until next time, Morrigan." His words turned into nothing more than a whisper before everything faded from my eyes and the darkness swallowed me whole.

Heart racing, I jolted up in bed and pressed my hand against my chest.

It had all felt so... *real.* I knew that it was only a dream, but how could I have created something so elaborate? If I told anyone, they would truly think I was insane. I most likely *had* gone insane. Hearing voices, seeing them in my dreams...

My door opened, causing me to jump again and I watched Eowyn enter the room. With a sigh of relief, I dropped my hand back to the bed. "You know, you used to knock."

She responded with a playful smirk and tilted her chin up as she made her way to my vanity. "You know, *you* volunteered me to go," she reminded me. "Now, stop sleeping in and get over here so I can fix that nest of yours. You've already missed breakfast."

"Shit," I exhaled, and hurried out of bed. Once I was seated at the vanity, Eowyn placed a small tray in front of me with a couple pieces of food good enough to hold me over until lunch. I sighed in relief and began eating it as she pulled and tugged at my curls. "What would I do without you?" I asked with a mouth full of food.

"Starve, clearly."

Finally dressed and ready, we made our way downstairs and outside to the courtyard. Dez stood beside Faelar, observing the gardens as they spoke with each other. They both offered a smile as Eowyn and I descended the steps.

"Good morning, Faelar," I said to him with a smile.

"Good morning, Your Grace," he offered with a bow. Then, his eyes rose to Eowyn's and visibly softened under her gaze. "My Lady."

Oh... This is going to be fun.

It took him a few seconds to quench whatever look danced in their eyes before he straightened his back and turned to me again. Dez's hand slid behind my back, pulling me into his side. "I've already transported your belongings to where you'll be staying tonight."

Holding out his arm, Faelar waited for the three of us to accept it. "Are you ready?"

Beside me, Eowyn looked nervous. I realized this may have been the first time she had ever traveled like this. "Will..." She chewed anxiously on her bottom lip. "Will it hurt?" she asked him.

Faelar's smile held a gentle warmth as I watched his eyes trace along the features of her face. Such subtle movements that even *she* didn't seem to notice him doing. "I'll be gentle," he promised her.

My lips pressed together, trying to stop my smile as I watched her blush in response before reaching out and placing her hand on his arm. Then, for the second time today, darkness called to me, and I had no choice but to succumb.

Chapter 22

With Dez busy during the day, Eowyn and I spent our time walking among the towns we visited.

Roses seemed to be a pretty big thing here, and I wondered how they all stayed in bloom with winter making its approach. Though fall lingered nearby, the chilled air seemed to rush away the remaining warmth of summer. Back at the cottage, my roses would have withered by now. But here, the petals still remained as vibrant as ever.

When I asked Eowyn about it, she explained that Dez had enchanted the flowers, being that they were his favorite. He made it possible for them to grow and prosper all year round.

Unfortunately, I wouldn't be seeing much of them on our last day. As I sat on the windowsill to our inn, I stared at the droplets of rain against the glass with microscopic bubbles of the villagers walking through caked mud. And with Dez so busy, I would have to wait until dinner to see him. He'd eat with the both of us and usually join me in bed. But he would typically pass right out by the time his head hit the pillow. He probably could have done this on his own, but I suspected that, after the ball, he no longer wanted me out of his sight.

Eowyn sat beside me with her nose deep into a book, completely unbothered by our solitude, and it only made me even more frustrated. "It's just a little rain," I argued.

"What if your hood gets soaked? You would need to remove it," she so willingly reminded me. "*You* insisted on keeping your identity a secret still."

With a heavy sigh, I slouched further against the frame. A small leak had allowed a droplet of water to seep through the wood, and it dripped slowly against the glass. "What if we took a short walk?"

Now Eowyn let out her own sigh, quickly remembering just how stubborn I could be. "*Fine, fine…*" Standing from her chair, she smoothed the bottom of her dress and set her book down, marking the page she stopped at. Then, she pointed a finger at me. "But don't say I didn't warn you."

Smiling, I jumped down from the window and grabbed my cloak, throwing it over my shoulder and binding it tightly around my neck.

I didn't care that my shoes were getting ruined as we walked together. If I had it my way, they would have been off completely. I loved rainy days as a child. Not *storms*, but when I could, I would stand beneath a perfect gloom of contempt as the clouds encompassed the sun and the rain would fall like silver threads, stitching the earth to the sky. The priestess would get so angry at me for running around outside and tracking mud in the house at the end of the day. I didn't really understand why she cared so much when *I* was the one who had to clean it anyway.

Just the sound of the droplets lightly padding along the wooden walls could lull me to sleep. That was, until the slitted roof of the attic began allowing water to seep through. Sometimes, I would wake with my mattress completely soaked, leaving a mildew scent in the air until I had the energy to drag my bed outside, allowing it to dry.

As Eowyn and I continued down the wet trail, we eventually stumbled upon a large lake near the edge of town. Even in the rain, families were fishing together on the pier. Some were even stepping into the water with large nets, teaching their young ones how to use it. As we watched them, I hadn't even noticed an older man step beside us until he spoke up.

"Have you ever fished?" he asked. Turning a little, but making sure to keep my hood down, I could see him holding a pole in his hand. He had shoulder-length, white hair and a short beard that covered the bottom half of his face.

"No," I answered quietly.

"Would you like to learn?" He sounded kind, but I knew that spending any time with him meant the risk of being exposed. I didn't want another fit of stares.

Eowyn, my savior, stepped between us with a smile. "We were just out for a short walk, but we really must return. We wouldn't want to get sick—"

"Is that who I think it is?" I recognized the voice instantly and squeezed my eyes shut, whispering a curse to myself.

Of course she would know that you're here. She's on his guard, you idiot.

Eowyn stilled, not knowing what to do, but I turned and faced her as she walked up to us with a large smile on her face. She seemed entirely different than the last time I had seen her—more clothed too. Wearing a brown, short-sleeved top and dark, oak pants, she bore much more of a resemblance to a warrior now than before.

"Still hiding, I see." She almost sounded disappointed as she lifted her hand to the bottom of my hood and toyed with the fabric. I couldn't help but blush a little at the fingers that had also been *inside* of me.

I glanced nervously at the man beside us who looked confused and leaned into Lyra so I could whisper without him hearing. "I just wanted a peaceful week without… *prying eyes*."

Noting the man behind me, Lyra then let out a loud laugh before wrapping an arm around my shoulder and turned me to face him. "Uncle Hagen," she addressed him. "This is… *Lizbeth*." I could feel her chest bounce with another chuckle from the name.

Looking between the both of us, it took him a moment or two, but eventually his eyes widened. "Liz… Oh… Your—"

He began to bow, but Lyra let go of me and placed a hand on his shoulder, shaking her head at him. "Not here."

Through the surface of his confusion, an understanding peeked its way through and he nodded. *Uncle. Of course it would be her uncle.* Reaching out my hand, I offered it to him, shaking it when he accepted. "It's a pleasure to meet you, Hagen."

Gods… please tell me he doesn't know how *we met.*

"Well…" Letting go of my hand, I watched him lean down to pick up a basket filled with fish he had likely caught himself. "I'm going to prep these for dinner. You're more than welcome to join us, Your…. *Lizbeth*."

You are such an idiot.

I turned to Eowyn, who offered a smile, encouraging me to accept. "Lord Dez won't mind," Lyra continued. "He's preoccupied tonight."

"Oh…" Work must have been taken longer than usual. So… If Eowyn didn't mind, and Dez wouldn't be attending dinner… "Then, yes. I would love to join you."

"Let's get you changed first," Eowyn insisted.

I had forgotten that my dress was likely caked in mud by now. "Right. Let's do that. I'll see you both—"

"I'll walk with you," Lyra offered.

I had to physically swallow down my nerves at being so close to her again. She had a frustratingly intoxicating aura to her that seemed to scramble every coherent thought in my mind. But before I could reject, she slipped my arm into hers and began walking, dragging me with her.

Leaning into her side, I whispered, "You really don't have to—"

"I *want* to." The smile she gave me made it hard to form a proper argument.

Walking a few steps behind us, Eowyn kept quiet as we made our way through the homes and shops, looking for the inn. Everyone around us seemed so quiet and peaceful—I wondered where Dez had been conducting his work with the rain making it impossible to stay outside for too long.

Lyra began talking, filling in the silence that had stretched for far too long. She told me of the boar she had been hunting in the woods before it evaded her. She had used the last of her arrows on it and returned to purchase more, dead set on finding the animal again, when she saw me on the pier. I couldn't stop my fidgeting beside her, memories of the ball replaying in my mind against my own will.

Noticing my behavior, Lyra leaned in and lowered her voice. "Do I make you *nervous*, Your Grace?"

I opened my mouth to respond with a lazy excuse, but a flash of red caught my attention. A familiar, thin blonde stepped into our path causing us to stop. It was the same blonde that had been sitting on Dez's lap, and the same one that visited his study.

A smug smile pinned her face as she looked at us, and I knew that *she* knew exactly who I was. The moment she took in my carefully draped hood, her grin widened. "Your Grace!" she exclaimed loudly. Then, in a blatant form of mockery, she bowed but kept her eyes pinned on mine. "How gracious of you to *bless* us with your presence."

Immediately, the people walking around us stopped. I didn't dare turn to look at them, but their stares could sink me into the ground like weighted bricks.

"Gwenyth," Lyra warned.

"What?" Gwenyth placed a hand on her chest as she rose. "Is... the princess... *embarrassed* to be seen with her people?"

The lingering gazes turned to wary whispers and I knew that I had no choice but to accept the position that Gwenyth had thrown me into. Pinching the fabric between my fingers, I pulled the hood down and heard collective gasps as they realized who I was. At this point, I would have needed to cut my hair in order to remain hidden.

"I don't think Lord Dez would appreciate you patronizing the future queen," Lyra hissed.

She pouted in response, and the lack of remorse in her face made my stomach turn. "Would you like me to retrieve him for you?" she asked innocently. "Actually... I was just on my way to see him." Her lips curled into a vicious smile as she aimed her venomous stare at me once more. "He asked me to join him for dinner. But I'm sure you already knew that, *Your Grace.*"

She's lying. He promised.

Even with the sting her words left in my chest, I tilted my chin up and gave her a small quirk of my lips. "I hope you enjoy yourselves tonight."

And without another word, I pulled Lyra alongside me and continued toward the inn.

When we returned to Hagen's house, he answered the door with a large smile on his face.

"Your Grace..." He lowered his head slightly. "Please, come in."

Stepping aside, I allowed Lyra to enter first and walked in behind her. "You don't ever answer the door like that for *me*," she teased him.

He let out a hearty laugh. "That's because you usually bring trouble with you each time."

With a look of shock, Lyra placed a theatrical hand over her heart. "Me? I would *never*—"

"Aye!" he yelled at her, snapping his fingers. "Take your shoes off before you ruin the floors!"

"Sorry! Sorry!" Lyra kicked off her boots and plopped into a chair by the table.

Though their home appeared small, the weight of its wealth in love could be felt in every corner of the house. The heart of it seemed to pulse in the very wood that held the foundations. He had a quaint little kitchen next to the front door, with a square wooden table beside it hosting four simple chairs. Past that, a living area had been decorated with beautiful, classic drapes along the windows and a simple, but elegant settee at the center. With the drapes pulled back, you could see the lake. I tried imagining how beautiful the sunset would look from that spot. What really caught my eye, though, were the small drawings I could see on the wall, at the level of my hands.

I approached them and knelt down, examining the stick figures and hearts colored all over the wood. "That was my Lyra," Hagen said softly.

"I couldn't bring myself to remove them. She loved to draw as a child. Her mother was—"

Lyra cleared her throat behind us. "Let's eat. I'm sure Dez will want her back soon."

As we ate, Hagen shared stories of Lyra as a child—the rambunctious fire starter that had them chasing her every step of the way. In every story, he spoke of him and his late wife, but none of them consisted of Lyra's parents. My curious mind pushed at me to ask, but it wasn't my business in the first place. I figured, if and when Lyra felt ready to, she would tell me.

It felt bittersweet as the sun set and dinner came to an end, but I knew I would need to be heading back eventually. *I just don't want to have to face Dez after my encounter with Gwenyth.* Lyra offered to walk me back, and as we said our goodbyes, Hagen stopped us on the way out. "It's been a long time since I've had a new face at that table," he admitted. "Lyra usually joins me for dinner every Friday. If you ever feel so inclined, you are always welcome."

It took me no more than a second to answer him with, "Yes." Just the idea of sitting with a family, eating small, homecooked meals, had my heart fluttering.

As Lyra and I walked back to the inn, she had been relatively quiet. We walked side by side with her hands in her pockets, staring down at the ground. I had almost spoken to break the silence, but she beat me to it, pausing our walk as she stood, facing me. "They died," she said with no other context.

They died... Oh... "Your parents?" I asked.

She nodded. "It was... There was an accident. Hagen is my father's brother, and he took me in. He and Mira, my aunt, raised me after that."

I couldn't help but reach a hand to her, placing it on her shoulder. "You don't have to explain yourself to me..."

"I do." When she looked at me, even the brown in her eyes glowed without the presence of sunlight. Her beauty surpassed anyone I had ever met before. "I can feel it in you. That emptiness that nothing ever seems to fill. Dez told me how they raised you…"

She stepped in closer and pushed a fallen strand of hair behind my ear.

"Our home will *always* be open to you," she whispered. "I just want you to know that."

"Am I interrupting something?" Dez's voice sounded from behind us, and Lyra took a step away.

"Just returning her to you, My Lord."

When I turned, Dez had a smirk on his face that I truthfully wanted to slap off of him. I said goodbye to Lyra and made my way to the doors of the inn, stopping as I stared at Dez blocking the way. "Did you have a good evening—"

"I'm tired," I interrupted him. "I'm sure you're *exhausted* from dinner, and I'd like to return to my room now."

As he reached a hand to me, I kept my chin up, disregarding it.

"*Alone*," I added.

And with that, I pushed past him through the door and stomped my way up the stairs.

Chapter 23

hadn't spoken to Dez at all the day we returned to the castle.
Eowyn didn't mention it as she'd been there when
Gwenyth approached me. She *did* however beg me to not force
her appearance at dinner that night. It seemed that I wasn't the only person
affected by how Kaiden acted. But she promised to wait for me in my room
after. I wouldn't make her sit through another evening with him. Kaiden
was an absolute bastard that could likely scare even the strongest soldiers. I
prayed all morning for him to stay home.

Arriving at the dining hall before everyone else, I took my usual seat
beside Dez. Even if I was annoyed with him, I didn't need an excuse for
Kaiden to sit near me again. Dez had been the lesser of the two evils.

As they all filtered in, I greeted everyone but Dez and could see the frustration in his blue eyes. I hoped it would stew there a little longer.

"Good afternoon, *Princess*," he said quietly, sitting down.

"*Dez.*"

He leaned in beside me, lowering his voice so that only I could hear. "What is wrong? You've ignored me for almost two days now."

"I think you've received plenty of attention from those you want it from."

"What are you talking about—"

"How was your dinner with Gwyneth?" My voice came out in more of a hiss, and louder than I intended it to.

When I turned, most of the guys were staring at us. "Trouble in paradise?" Cain teased from the end of the table.

"There isn't *trouble* in *anything*." Stabbing my fork into my food, I shoved it into my mouth to end the conversation.

"It's a simple misunderstanding," Dez insisted.

Right. And I'm sure you just happened to fall inside of her that night too.

"Are you alright?" Cass asked me.

I just wasn't in the mood. I nodded and answered, "*Peachy*," before shoving more food in.

When dinner finally came to an end, I was eternally grateful that Kaiden had stayed away. I happily excused myself from the table and hurried back to the stairs, returning to my room. But as I approached it, barely two doors away, I felt something nearby. Not in a literal sense, but almost this tickle inside of my mind. There were large pockets of shadows that hid along the walls near my room, and it felt as if they were telling me something.

I didn't have time to decipher what it was before someone twisted me and pushed my chest against the wall, causing me to grunt in pain. "Kaiden," I seethed through clenched teeth. I should have known better.

"Miss me, little dove?" His whispers were beside my ear with his hand on my back. He barely held me against the wall; he didn't need much. With his strength, I wouldn't be able to move away from him. "Were you disappointed when I wasn't at dinner?"

I tried shoving against him, pushing myself back, but I barely moved an inch. "No. I was rather relieved to actually enjoy my food for once."

"If you were smarter you'd keep your mouth shut around me, little bird. Most people who mouth off to me, the way that *you* do, wind up dead."

"Didn't Maeryn tell you?" I asked, still struggling to slide my hands between me and the wall. "I never know when to quit."

It was a small window, but I found enough leverage to slip from his hold, dropping down before grabbing the knife I had swiped from the table. Kaiden clearly hadn't expected it. He had no time to react before I stood and turned, aiming the sharp end at his throat.

"I'm a fast learner," I said to him. I could have sworn I saw the corners of his mouth twitch upward.

"That wouldn't kill me. You *know* that."

I shrugged. "No... But I guarantee I can make it hurt enough to be worth it."

An actual laugh left his chest and it distracted me enough to not notice the shadows before they swallowed him up. A quick blur of movement swept behind me and before I could turn, something grabbed my wrist, yanking it up to my own throat. When I looked down, I noticed more markings on Kaiden's arm as he held my wrist, placing the knife to my neck.

"Not fast *enough* it seems," he taunted.

As I wriggled against him, I could feel it cutting against my skin. "If you don't let go of me, Kaiden, I'll—"

"Don't make threats you can't follow through on, little dove." He let the knife press in harder, just enough to draw blood on my neck, making me squeeze my eyes from the sting. "You're trembling."

He could kill me right now. He wants *to kill me.*

What did you think would happen?

"Are you scared yet?" he asked.

Though my heartbeat thundered under his grasp, I knew the true answer to that question. "I haven't feared death in a long time, Kaiden. So, if you really want to kill me, why don't you do us both a favor and do it now?"

The pressure on the knife stilled. Then I felt a puff of air from his lips as he let out a deep laugh. "They were wrong about you."

"Who was wrong about—" Before I could finish, the knife left my throat and I felt a shove on my back, pushing me forward. When I turned, Kaiden was gone.

I ran hard, the short bursts of breath burning my lungs.

"I can smell *you, little dove." Terror filled my body at every turn through the dark hallway. I didn't know where I was, but the ground felt hard and uneven and the light offered by the torches on the walls didn't illuminate enough to see my surroundings. "You can't hide from me!"*

Tears streamed down my cheeks, soaking my skin as I looked for a room to hide in. But there weren't any doors. The only thing that greeted me were more empty halls with walls that looked as if they were painted black. Behind me, he began whistling. The melody was the same tune that

Lady Guinevere would hum to me at night, lulling me back to sleep after one of my nightmares.

"It'll be quick, little dove. I swear it." His laughter echoed throughout the halls like he was somehow all around me at once. "I can make it feel good too. I thought you liked that? When Cass sunk his teeth into your thigh..."

Nausea crept into my throat just as a room appeared before me. Wasting no time, I pushed through the door before slamming it shut. There wasn't any light around me, so I had to slide my hand along the frame to find the handle, locking it as quickly as I could.

Pressing my ear against the wood, I slowed my breathing to listen for him. His footsteps were loud and heavy against the ground, kicking pebbles as they moved. They grew closer, and I clasped my hand over my mouth to silence any noise that could alert him. But I knew he'd find me.

Clicking his tongue, I watched as the small light beneath the door disappeared by the shadow of two large feet. "All this time they spent teaching you, and you're still just a foolish little girl." I knew I had only minutes before he would break his way through the door. The handle rattled and shook violently as he yanked at it. "Come on out, little dove," he growled. "I've been dying to hear you sing."

I jumped back when he began to pound with his fist. It seemed to shake the entire room. Walking backward into the darkness, the only light I saw came from the illuminated edges of the door frame. I had no choice but to try and hide in the darkness behind me. But as I moved, the pounding grew louder the further away I got from the door. With my heart beating rapidly in my chest, I kept both trembling hands over my mouth, praying to the gods that he would walk away.

"You're making this harder than it needs to be." His hiss seeped through the door into the air around me. "I'll get you eventually. And when

I do? You're mine.*" That's when he began to laugh again, maniacally.*
Time was running out and I was going to die.

"Morrigan," *I recognized that voice. I only ever heard it in my dreams.*
"Morrigan, wake up. It's just a nightmare. This isn't real."

"Let me in, little dove!" I ignored the screams from behind the door
and tried to focus my mind solely on his *voice.*

"Close your eyes, Morrigan. Just follow my voice."

I did as he asked and let my feet guide me. It was likely my
subconscious giving me a voice of guidance that I had craved for so many
years. But regardless of its source, his voice was home.

As the sounds of his pounding began to fade in the distance, I could
feel them again... the shadows. They licked at my skin like a cool mist,
encompassing me until the darkness swallowed my body. And the last thing
I heard was a different voice calling my name.

I woke to my door being slammed open.

In the empty space stood Dez, panting as his shoulders heaved. He
hadn't even bothered dressing before coming to my room. "Are you
alright?"

I pinched my brows together, not understanding why he was even here
to begin with.

"You were *screaming*, Morrigan."

My lips parted as guilt sunk in. "I'm sorry." I pulled myself up,
leaning against the headboard. Bringing my palm to my head, I could feel
the sweat that slicked the skin above my brows. "It was a nightmare. I'm
alright."

He seemed to visibly relax as he inhaled deeply. I expected him to leave then, and return to his room, but he stood in the doorway for a moment. It had been four days now that I kept him at a distance.

"Princess…" Dez let out a long sigh and leaned against the frame. "I never touched her. I wouldn't have even dared to."

With a scoff, I threw the blankets off of me, getting out of bed. "Don't patronize me, Dez." I needed cold water on my face before I could even attempt to go back to sleep now. "I *know* you met with her that night," I called over my shoulder, making my way to the bathing room.

Before I could reach the door, Dez's hand wrapped around my wrist and stopped me in my tracks. "Yes! I saw her at dinner," he admitted. "But only to explain things to her."

Tilting my chin up at him, I pressed my lips together. "And what exactly is there to understand?" I took a step toward him, having to crank back my neck to keep our eyes locked. "You had no problem enjoying her the week you brought me here. What changed your mind, Dez?"

"You did!" Without leaving me time to react, both of his hands grasped my face and Dez pushed forward until my back hit the door behind me. "Don't you see? The moment I tasted your lips, I knew that nothing else would ever be enough. Your ocean-deep eyes stalk my dreams, relentlessly. Even *this*—this simple brush of your touch—fills a hollow part of my soul that I never knew existed."

"Dez…"

"Gods dammit, Morrigan. I couldn't even touch another woman if I wanted to. You have had me captivated from the second I saw you. But the moment you gave yourself to me, you tied a cord around my heart that would bring me to my knees for you. Is that what you want?" he asked, a pleading look to his baby blue eyes. "Do you want me to get down and beg for you to touch me again? Because I will. I'll *beg* you, Princess."

"I…" Raising my hands, I wrapped them around his wrist, but I didn't push them away. "I'm sorry… I'm sorry for assuming. I shouldn't have—"

"Just let me back in," he pleaded. "I only *just* got you. Don't let me go yet… *please*."

Nodding, I pushed up on my toes, bringing my lips to his. It wasn't a passionate kiss, but a tender one—another apology as he gave his own to me. His hands remained on my face, holding on to me for dear life. Then, when we both let go, he kept his forehead pressed against mine.

"Stay with me?" I asked him. Regretting the fact that I had allowed myself to waste four days of our time together.

"I'll stay with you forever if you let me, Princess."

Chapter 24

By the time Friday arrived, Eowyn insisted on putting my hair up before leaving to see her own family for the night.

With Lyra being a highly appointed guard, we collectively decided that I wouldn't need any extra hands while visiting Hagen. Eowyn more than deserved to spend time with her own loved ones instead of following me around all day.

"Don't you have better things to do than stick pins in my hair?" I groaned, feeling the ends of the heavy-duty metal poking into my skull.

"Who else is going to do it?" she teased. "If you had it your way, it would sit in a pile of knots. Your own fingers would cramp up if you even tried braiding this."

Rolling my eyes, I accepted defeat as I sunk back into my chair. But I wouldn't give up the last word *that* easily, not even for Eowyn. "If you're quick enough, you might even catch Faelar before we leave."

I earned a well-deserved pull on the strand that she had been pinning up. "Oops," she squeaked.

All week, the pair had been exchanging nervous glances toward each other. But neither of them would say an actual word in their presence. It drove me insane. Their affection could be seen by anyone with eyes but was so clearly denied by them both. I didn't push her, though. I kept my mouth shut after my last comment and eventually made my way downstairs to meet Faelar in the courtyard.

Shadow walking had become so easy now, almost normal. The darkness no longer scared me in the way that it used to. Instead, I welcomed it as I touched Faelar's arm and felt like I was walking through shadows of thick clouds, instead of falling. When we arrived at the town, Lyra had been waiting for me.

"I'll remain at the inn until you're ready to return home, if that's okay with you, Your Grace."

"Of course," I answered him before turning to see a grinning Lyra approaching us.

"I'll take it from here!" she called out, and when I turned, Faelar had already disappeared. "You need to change." Lyra tugged at the side of my gown with her nose scrunched.

Looking down, I examined it for any imperfections, but it looked perfect. "What's wrong with my dress?"

"It's not practical for what I have planned for you today."

Planned for me? Lyra pulled at my arm, dragging me back toward Hagen's home without any other explanation. "What exactly are we doing that would require me to change?"

Lyra's laughter felt almost cynical as she turned back to me, eyes glistening with mischief. "You'll be catching our dinner tonight."

After changing into one of Lyra's brown shirts and pants, I followed her into the forest, not far from Hagen's home.

Lyra scoped out the area, surveying it for animals before selecting a spot by a tree, perfectly hidden by a large bush. It was fascinating to watch her focus. The way her pupils dilated as she listened for every sound around us looked almost predatorial. She had tied her brown hair back in a tight, high pony tail. And with it out of the way, I noticed just how perfectly sculpted every part of her face had been. Her cheek bones were visible and beautiful in such a feminine way, but every part of her screamed dominance.

As we waited, Lyra eventually leaned back onto her heels, relaxing a little. "Can I ask you something?" she whispered, barely loud enough for me to hear.

"Of course."

Clearing her throat, I watched her pull the bow from her back and set it between us. "The day after the ball, Dez informed his guard that Priestess Maeryn was no longer welcome in his land. He even sent word to the Palaces, informing them that if she trespassed without a formal invitation, she would be executed."

I owed Dez my gratitude. I knew he wanted to do much more than he actually had, but he would never understand how much peace he brought me by making her leave. And to know that—within his walls at least—I had been truly safe... It was a gift that I could never repay him. But Lyra hadn't told me this for no reason, she wanted to know *why*.

"I have... scars. On my back." Hesitantly, I pulled at my shoulder until the fabric revealed a small part of the tattered skin. Lyra turned slowly, like she wasn't sure if she actually wanted to see them. But when she did, nothing in her expression faltered. "Dez saw them the night of the ball." I didn't go into further detail. I knew that Lyra was smart enough to fit the pieces together without my help.

Lips pursed, she gave me a curt nod and turned her eyes back to the clearing in front of her. The brown turned to a deep whiskey as her face hardened just a little. "That woman is evil," she hissed under her breath. "She should pray to the Gods that our paths never cross."

Perched into a stiff position, Lyra lifted her bow slowly, placing an arrow against the string. She pulled until it looked almost ready to snap and aimed at something I couldn't even see from where we stood.

"I can promise you this much, Your Grace." With one swift release, the arrow flew through the air, a burst of wind blowing against my face. "I never miss." In the clearing, a bird fell from a tree nearby, her arrow piercing its chest. "Come." She gestured for me to stand, offering a hand to help. "We need to find a new spot."

"Take this," she whispered beside me.

Her eyes were trained on a spot ahead of us where a rabbit peeked up from the grass. "Lyra!" I looked nervously at the bow in her hand as she shoved it into mine. "I don't know how to use this!"

Rolling her eyes, she pulled an arrow from the quiver beside her and moved herself behind me. "Do you really think I'm not going to help you?" Hesitantly, I held the bow in my hand and tried to mimic what Lyra had done before. "Good. Now..." Thrusting the arrow into my hand, she guided my fingers to the bow, placing it carefully until the end of it pushed against the string. "Pull," she whispered in my ear.

I kept the arrow aligned as I added tension to the string, pulling until I couldn't expand it any more. "It's pinching my fingers," I complained.

"You'll get over that eventually." While one of her hands guided me, her other laid against my side, holding my waist to keep me steady. The rush of heat it sent across my skin was hard to ignore. "Hold it," she ordered.

The rabbit had been moving, peeking up and dipping back down. I tried to focus on the creature, but even her breath along my neck sent shivers across my body.

"Keep holding."

Her thumb on my side moved, massaging my skin through the shirt she had given me, and I could barely hang onto the arrow any longer. "Lyra," I whined.

"Release it!"

The moment the words left her lips, my fingers slid from the string. The ends of the arrow lightly scraped my cheek as it shot through the air, aiming straight at the rabbit. It took only seconds for the arrow to pierce the animal between its eye and ear, and I watched its limp body fall forward.

Jumping up, I let out an excited gasp. "I... I got it!"

I dropped the bow and ran to it, falling down to my knees as I gaped at the creature before me. "That was a good shot, Your Grace."

"I... I probably shouldn't be this excited over killing something."

Lyra laughed and knelt beside me. "It's the adrenaline." Pinching my chin, she turned my face to examine my cheek. "Just a small cut. You held it too close to your face." With her thumb, she wiped my skin, leaving behind a small sting from the pressure. "How do you feel?"

She hadn't removed her hand, and all I wanted to do was stare into her eyes. With the last of the sunlight shining down, the whiskey turned to smooth honey that glistened in its reflection. "Amazing," I said with an exhale.

The silence between us stretched the longer she held my face. As my cheeks blushed, I remembered how it felt kissing her at the masquerade. Lyra's eyes flicked down to my lips as if she had the same memory playing through her mind. Then, she blinked and pulled her hand away, swiping the rabbit from the ground and throwing it over her shoulder.

"Right..." Standing up, she helped me with her and offered me a tight, reserved smile. "Let's go grab the bird and head back."

I hadn't known whether to be embarrassed or grateful for Lyra interrupting whatever... *moment* we had shared. But I knew it was wrong to feel anything toward her. Our lives had only crossed by pure chance. I knew that I had been... *created* for the lords. In a few weeks, I would have to leave, and Lyra would stay behind. All of these relationships were temporary, and it was just a fact I needed to adjust to.

When we returned to the cabin, Hagen furrowed brows as he took in my dirt covered clothes. "Lyra... tell me you didn't have our future queen *hunting*."

"Damn straight I did," she laughed, as she handed him the rabbit and bird. Then, turning back toward me, she grabbed my hand and led me inside. "Let's get you cleaned up."

Thankfully my dress had remained clean and I was able to change back into it before dinner. The food tasted just as delicious as the first time I had met Hagen, and I savored every bite. Hagen continued telling stories of Lyra, and Lyra rolled her eyes at every one of them. It must have been nice having someone to brag about every little thing that you do in life. It may have annoyed her, but I would have given anything to have someone to annoy *me* that way.

"If you're on Dez's guard, why don't I see you at the castle?" I asked as I helped Lyra clean up once we had all finished eating.

"Only his self-appointed guards remain in the castle. The rest of us have quarters we stay in near the castle grounds." Handing me a dish to dry, she turned to me with a smirk. "Why do you ask, Your Grace? Have you found yourself missing me?"

She had been teasing, but I never would have had the courage to tell her how right her accusation had been. Something about Lyra drew me to her. It was a feeling that both scared and excited me all at the same time. I knew the guys wouldn't appreciate it. Which is why I kept it to myself.

By the time we finished cleaning, Faelar returned and took me home.

I found Dez in my bed when I returned to the castle.

He resembled a portrait, sprawled out on the mattress with the red satin sheets barely covering his body. He ran so warm that he never really needed to wear much clothing to sleep. I sure didn't mind. The only thing I loved more than reveling in how beautiful he looked, was to feel his heat against my body as he held me.

After I had forgiven him—over something that didn't need forgiveness to begin with—Dez barely wanted to leave my side all week. He spent each night in my room, sleeping with his arms wrapped around me, like he was scared I would slip away without them. Now, he laid there peacefully, eyes closed and fluttering with whatever dreams his mind had immersed him into.

I slipped out of my gown, tiptoeing across the floor, careful not to wake him. Crawling into bed, I slid under the sheets and snuck into his side, wrapping my arm over his waist. I wanted to wake him and tell him how exciting my night had been. I wondered if he would have been proud of what I did. But as I stared at his features, so soft and relaxed, I couldn't bring myself to ruin it. Instead, I snuggled into his radiating warmth and laid my head onto his chest.

When he stirred slightly, his arm covered me, pulling me in closer, and a sweet sigh fell from his lips. I didn't know what was happening—what these feelings meant. But I did know one thing: Dez had a heart that none of the others seemed to come close to, and he gave it to *me*. Whether it had been designed by the gods themselves, or a pure act of fate, Dez had somehow burrowed himself into my soul.

But would I truly be able to choose between them? Could I go back to Cass after all of this was said and done? Could I leave Dez behind? If I had been *made* for them... Could I not just have them... *all*?

Chapter 25

Grabbing two apples from the kitchen, I made my way down to the library.

I knew I would find Harley there, and Eowyn had yet to return from her visit, so I thought I would spend some time reading with him. When I arrived, he had been leaning against his desk, a book propped open in his hand. I laughed silently to myself at the image alone, wondering if he ever spent time without his nose stuck to a piece of paper.

"Don't you have any hobbies?" I teased him. Once he looked up from the page, I tossed an apple to him.

He smiled as he bit into it, turning his head back down. "Don't you?"

"Pestering you is the *only one* I have as of right now." I took a seat beside him and propped my feet onto the desk, waiting for a side glance from him. He hated when I did that. "I *did* kill a rabbit yesterday, though." I had to tell someone, and Dez had been gone by the time I woke up.

Harley laughed and set his book down, finally giving me his attention. "Shall I sleep with one eye open now, my young assassin?"

Nodding, I took another bite of my apple. "It might be for the best." That earned a genuine laugh from him before he pushed off of the desk and walked toward the shelves. "Think about that the next time you give me extra textbooks to read on the weekend!" I called to him, making him laugh even louder.

"You're the one pestering *me!*" he yelled back, grabbing a handful of books before bringing the stack to the desk.

We lost ourselves in peaceful silence as we both read together. We even shared a quiet lunch before taking a walk through the gardens. I loved spending time with Harley. With the guys, he had a firmness to him—he spoke to them with a disciplined tone and always offered them guidance. But when we were alone, he laughed the way that Hagen would laugh with Lyra. He had so much love that seemed to be locked away, and I never wasted a moment to bring it out of him.

Truthfully, he reminded me of Lady Guinevere some days... I hoped that she was happy. Regardless of the resentment I held for what she watched me go through... she had been a light in my life where all I had known was darkness. They would have enjoyed each other's company— that much I had been sure of.

When dinner time came, I braced myself. I knew Kaiden would make an appearance. Whether it would be during dinner or after, I was ready. The guys were all seated when Harley dropped me off at the dining hall, and Dez pulled my chair out for me as I walked in.

"I heard you killed a ferocious beast yesterday," Eris teased beside me. "Shall I watch for you in the shadows now?"

"Only if you fear them." Rolling my eyes, I refused to allow *his* voice to affect me. Thankfully, *he* took the seat beside D at the end of the table, but even he seemed to grimace in *his* presence. "Are *you* scared of the dark, little dove?"

Looking up, I gifted him with my best smile. *"Kaiden,"* I greeted him. "Do you torture everyone in your life, or am I just truly blessed to be the only one?"

Amusement melted from his face, annoyance taking its place. "You think you're so brave."

"Could I please eat in peace tonight?" I snapped. "Insult me all you want, but can you at least do it after I've enjoyed my food? I'd rather not lose my appetite tonight."

Everyone at the table had gone silent, staring at the two of us. But Kaiden paid them no mind, he kept his eyes on mine, calculating what he wanted to say. To my surprise, he nodded, leaned back in his chair, and began eating his own food.

"Looks like she's got *you* in a cage now, Kaiden," Cain chided across from him.

"Don't goad him," D hissed in his direction.

Kaiden only smiled, not sparing a single glance his way. But I could feel the change in the air before it happened. A slight tingle on my skin made my hairs stand straight, and the shadows of his shirt seemed to darken. Then, Cain's chair skidded as it tilted back, sending him flying to the floor.

"Gods dammit, Kaiden! You son of a—"

"Shhh," he shushed him. "I'm trying to enjoy my dinner."

The others chuckled lightly, unsure of whether to help Cain or go along with the first joke I had *ever* heard Kaiden make. I could have sworn I saw black swirls clearing from the whites in his eyes.

Cain, clearly mortified by his own embarrassment, sneered in Kaiden's direction as he stood from the floor. But he said nothing while he yanked his chair back up and sat down.

To my surprise, Kaiden remained relatively silent for most of the dinner. It should have made the night more pleasant, but for me it just felt… odd. He would occasionally smirk in response to one of the many conversations happening around him, sometimes even allowing a scoff to come through. Though, it had been evident that his reactions were at the guys' expense. The regard he had for the guys seemed extremely low. I yearned for whatever history they shared that birthed the hatred he bore for each of them.

Kaiden had been the first to leave when dinner ended, but I knew better. As I walked back to my room, I slowed my breathing to listen for any sign of him in the shadows. Swiping the knife last time had been foolish. I knew it wouldn't actually do anything, but I thought that if I showed him that I wasn't helpless, maybe he would leave me alone. Showing up tonight proved just how wrong that assumption was.

The halls were silent, even the sound of my footsteps seemed to echo within them, reverberating against the walls. But even without hearing him, some part of me knew that he was there. The darkness that clung to the walls, evading the light of the torches hung on them, felt heavier than normal. The shadows seemed to stretch further than they usually would.

And as I reached my hand toward the door handle to my room, I finally heard it—the small slide of a foot against the slick wood beneath us… A quiet exhale, barely audible, but enough that I knew to move. So, before he could grab me, I twisted just as I felt the prickling of his hand behind me and used all of my force to shove him into the wall.

"You've become predictable, *My Lord*."

I no longer expected him to actually hurt me. Even if he wouldn't say it, this was becoming a game between us—a battle of wits, waiting for the other to grow tired of playing. But as much hate that Kaiden spewed at me, if he truly wanted to hurt me, he would have done so already. I may not have known his true intentions, but any fear I once had of him dissolved these past few weeks.

Laughing, Kaiden kept his back against the wall and gleamed at me. It wasn't a friendly look, but one that a guard might have given a soldier in training. "Should I start surprising you, then?" he asked, with challenge in his voice. "I'm not sure if I enjoy this shift in dynamic, little dove."

"Have you truly grown so bored of your own home that you feel the need to terrorize mine?"

He narrowed his eyes in response, pushing off the wall, and took a step toward me. "This isn't your *home*," he spat. "Are you truly so naïve to not see through the glamourous façade that's been painted for you?"

"I'm tired of this, Kaiden." I refused to look away, even as I yielded ground with each of his steps toward me. "Can you not wait until it's *your* turn? Let me enjoy what little time I have—"

"*My* turn?!" He laughed and pushed until my back hit the opposing wall. But, refusing to cower, I kept my chin up to him. "What on earth would have you believe that I want any part in this?"

I could feel the pinch between my brows as they furrowed in confusion. "Don't you want to be—"

"I want *nothing* from you, little dove." I flinched as both of his hands slammed against the wall on either side of my face. "You are but a mouse in a den of *lions*. You think I'm bad?" As he chuckled, he leaned his head down, closer to mine and caused a sense of panic to rise in my chest. "You know *nothing* of this world... of the *real* monsters that lurk in the shadows... Shall I introduce you to them?"

I puffed out my own huff of frustration. "Kaiden, I'm done with your games. If you want someone to play with, you have a perfectly receptive whore back at home."

The moment the words left my mouth, all playful intimidation left his eyes. They turned to steel as they bore into me, pinning me in place. I may not have feared Kaiden, but there was a darkness that hid in his eyes that could make my body tremble…

"Their little lamb," he said with disgust. "They've trained you so well, haven't they?"

Matching his own expression, I curled my lips back and pushed off of the wall, letting my chest hit his. "Any training I have is thanks to *her*. Make sure to advise her of my *gratitude*."

Without another word, he evaporated into the air, becoming darkness himself. I wanted to yell in frustration at the riddles he constantly left me with. Any rational person would have run to Dez and told him of this nonsense, but I couldn't just allow Kaiden to win like that.

Instead of allowing my anger to take hold of me, I stormed into my room, slamming the door behind me.

"Are you sure I can't convince you to stay a little longer?" Lyra asked as we cleaned up from dinner.

Stifling a giggle in my throat, I tried concealing the obvious blush on my cheeks. "Maybe another time."

Before Lyra took me hunting again, she set up a target on a nearby tree and had me practice my form. With it being only my second time using a bow, I surprised myself with how much easier it felt. My fingers seemed to recognize the string and relaxed faster than the last time. Even the strain on the tips didn't hurt as bad. Hagen called my quick learning a burst of luck, but Lyra insisted that the skill I exhibited had been hidden somewhere already.

Every time she looked at me with wide, proud eyes, it warmed a part of my heart that I didn't know yearned for praise.

Releasing a dramatic sigh, Lyra threw the rag back onto the counter. "*Fine.*" But before we could leave, she ran to a room in the back. "Hold on! I almost forgot!" she called over her shoulder.

When she returned, there was a different bow in her hand and a strap hanging over her shoulder. The bow had a dark, brown wood, with stencils of roses carved into it. "What is this?" I asked.

"Hagen and I…" Clearing her throat, I watched the vulnerable expression fade from Lyra's eyes as she masked it with her usual, cool tone. "It's nothing, really. We just thought you might like to practice when you're not around."

Reaching out, I grasped the bow in my hand, appreciating the weight of it on my palm. It felt heavier than the one Lyra had me use these past two weeks. "You didn't have to—"

"We *wanted* to," Hagen insisted, placing a gentle, but firm hand on my shoulder.

Lyra must have seen the tears swelling in my eyes, because she stepped between Hagen and me, grabbing my hand. "Alright, let's go. No need to make this a thing."

After meeting Faelar at the inn, I couldn't wait to get back to the castle.

All I wanted to do was race to Dez and show him the bow. But as I reached the steps in the courtyard, I heard the faint sound of a whisper behind me. It could almost be dismissed as whistles from the wind whipping through the air. Trying to ignore it, I took another step, but then I heard them again.

I turned around, expecting Faelar to be behind me. But the only thing I could see was the empty courtyard and fountain at the center of it. "Hello?" I asked. In response, the whispers began again and I clutched my cloak tighter to my chest, not knowing if my shivers were from the chill in the air, or fear. "Who's there—"

"Ecce..." It sounded like multiple voices at once coming from all around me. I spun, searching for its source, but there was no one nearby. When I opened my mouth to speak, the voice grew louder. *"ECCE!"*

A strong gust of wind blew through me, taking my breath with it, and my body stood frozen on the stairs. When I tried to move my lips, they remained still—frozen together. While I could *feel* my body, I no longer felt like it was my own. Almost like the dream I had on that bridge. My mind held its consciousness, but my feet... they began to move without my consent. I wanted to scream for Dez... for Faelar. But not even the guards were stationed at the courtyard tonight.

Before I knew it, an invisible force took me toward the woods, into the darkness, and fear for my life kicked in with no ability to stop it.

Chapter 26

My feet dredged through the grassy trail, between the slight opening of the trees.

The path hadn't been marked, but by the way the branches seemed to part, it looked like it had been used in the past. Still, as I tried to pull myself from whatever trance had full control over me, my body wouldn't stop moving. *"Ecce,"* the voices continued to whisper. And as I moved through the woods, they only grew louder in my head. Chanting over, and over again…pulling me as if they held the end to a string that had wrapped around my mind.

Eventually, the smooth surface beneath my feet turned uneven, causing my legs to wobble. When I looked down, I noticed that the grass transitioned to rocks. That's when a clearing in the trees revealed a large beach. As I stepped forward—away from the woods—the voices came to a halt. Every bit of fuzziness that clouded my mind disappeared and I stumbled over my own feet as I regained control.

"What…" Turning around, I tried to make sense of what had happened, but… I was just as alone as I had been before.

You were brought here for a reason, whatever it may be, I tried convincing myself.

Maybe it wants to eat you.

I thought back to the comment that Kaiden made—of the monsters that lurked in the shadows.

In front of me stood a long pier, much larger than the one near Hagen's home. It sat atop the glistening water that reflected the stars above like a perfect, still mirror. I knew I had two options. One, I could return to the forest and pray that I would make it back to Dez before… *whatever* it was took over again. Or…

I'm going to regret this.

I took a step… then another… until my feet paused at the base of the wooden pier. Sucking in a deep breath, I let the cold air fill my lungs before advancing further.

Nothing strange stood out as I walked to the edge, letting my hand graze the soft, sanded railing. At the very end of the pier, it opened up, allowing me to sit and stretch my legs over, dangling my feet into the water.

I felt every bit insane as I looked around, waiting for something to creep from the darkness behind me. "Well… I'm *here*!" I called out, though no one responded.

This is ridiculous.

With a change of heart, I moved to stand, but a single voice came through, different than before. It sounded like a distant hum, and the air around me seemed to still. Frozen in place, I carefully surveyed the beach, scared to move an inch. Then, I noticed little ripples in the previously still water. And the source of it hadn't been from my own feet. As the humming increased, I followed the tiny waves until I saw something that made the terror in my body spike.

Two, bright blue eyes were staring back at me. They didn't resemble human eyes. No… they looked far too predatorial. I wanted to push away from the water, to turn and run back to the castle. But as the song invaded the distance between us, every bit of my will faded into the mist that hid below the pier. The song called to me, pulling me just as much as the invisible string had.

"Ecce," the voice whispered again, beneath the beautiful, luring song.

The eyes that started off as two small dots were now moving closer. Their glow brighter than the moon above them. "Please," I whispered. But before I had the chance to mutter another plea, something wet and clammy wrapped around my ankle.

With a strong jerk, I yelped as the back of my head hit the edge of the pier before I was pulled beneath the water. My fingers reached out frantically, scrambling to grab part of the wood and haul myself back up. But by the time the thought had even occurred, I watched the pier fade away and blur as my body sank down.

The shadows hid the creature from my sight, but I used every ounce of strength that I had to kick at it. And though its hold on my ankle was strong, I flailed my body in every way that I could, yanking and shoving my legs. Finally, my free foot seemed to hit something hard, and I heard a *hiss* as the creature released me. Air escaped my lips in relief, and I used my arms to claw my way to the surface. There were no lakes or rivers near my cottage, so I never needed to learn how to swim. But I understood the basics and tried to push my way through the water.

As I approached the shimmering surface, I jerked up and sucked in a painful breath before screaming, "DEZ!"

It was the only word I got out before being ripped back under, this time faster. The moonlight quickly disappeared, and the hold around my ankle felt bruising. *I'm going to die*, I thought to myself. Every bit of fight that I had remaining began to dwindle as the pressure made my ears pop. I wanted to cry, but the water kept my tears lodged in my eyes. *I'm going to die... I don't want to die.*

As my lungs tightened, pleading for air, the creature finally let go of my leg. Without the strength —or skill—I floated in the water, feeling my head growing lighter. That's when I saw the eyes again.

I wanted to scream, to thrash my arms out and stop them from hurting me, but my limbs felt heavy beneath the weight of the sea. They approached slowly—five ruthless and dangerous-looking pairs of eyes. And as they neared, the light from their glowing gaze illuminated the rest of their bodies. They looked... human... *almost*.

Their skin had a deep tint of grey and blue—the color hard to decipher without enough moonlight shining through. Every part of their body seemed to be imbued with coral and shells, sunken deep in their skin as if they had become a part of the ocean itself. And where legs should have been, they were together in a fish-like tail. Harley hadn't taught me about these kinds of creatures. But my lack of knowledge didn't matter. My eyelids drooped, and the weight of my chest grew unbearable—the water coaxing me to inhale as my lungs ached for relief.

Then, multiple hands grabbed at me, and I waited for the pain to come. But with blurry vision, I watched as the creature in the center closed its distance. Bubbles rose from the gills on the side of its neck as it seemed to take in its own breath... and blew. To my surprise, my lungs seemed to inhale air that wasn't my own. It hurt like something fierce, but as it continued breathing for me, my struggle ceased. None of it made any sense.

"Ecce," the four others whispered around me.

Before I could truly decipher the meaning, they all let out a loud screech, and the breath was captured from my lungs again. I gaped in horror as parts of the sand morphed into ropes, ripping the creatures away from me, and a set of arms wrapped around my waist. Turning my head, I could see two, glowing, blue eyes staring down at me with fear. *Dez.*

Holding onto me, he hauled the both of us up, and I couldn't help but stare back down at the creatures as they reached their hands toward us. *Ecce…. Ecce…* I heard them calling in my head. When we broke the surface again, I must have swallowed some water, because I couldn't stop coughing. It rubbed my throat raw.

Dez slung me over the pier and I grasped onto the wooden railing, hunched onto my knees as I struggled to regain control of my breathing. "Princess," he rasped, running over to me. "Oh Gods… I had been outside, looking for you, and I… I heard you scream… I thought…" Placing a hand on my chest, he forced my back straight and the light in his eyes illuminated the space around us. "Let me help you."

It started as a pull in my chest. Then, for only a few seconds, I couldn't breathe at all. I began clawing at his hand in fear. But eventually, I felt the rising of liquid in my throat, and as it touched my tongue, I was able to cough out the last of the water with Dez's help. "What…" Talking physically hurt, and I had to hold onto Dez or risk the chance of falling back over. "What were…"

"Water wraiths," Dez answered. He settled down in a seated position and pulled me into his chest. "How did you even find this place? That trail had been closed off years ago."

"I heard…" *Do I tell him what I heard? Do I also tell him the other insane things that are happening to me?* "I'm sorry. They started humming and I couldn't stop myself."

"Their song lures people to these waters. I'll need to place up extra precautions if their reach is spreading that far. We had… *issues* in the past."

He didn't need to explain. I felt the pull of their tune. I could only imagine who else they had trapped there before me. But it didn't help to make sense of *why* they didn't kill me. "Where… Where did they come from?"

With a sigh, Dez leaned back and lifted my legs over his lap so that he cradled me in his arms. "They were thought to have been handmaidens of Rosina… cursed for following her when… when the war began."

"Why don't you just kill them?" I asked.

I could hear the strain in his voice as he said, "I-I can't bring myself to do that—even after they began slaughtering people who came to visit the beach… Maybe it makes me weak. But I feel responsible for them."

"It couldn't possibly be *your* fault that this happened."

A beat of silence stretched between us, like he actually believed that it *was* his fault. Dez. The man who wore his heart on his sleeve and had more love than the world knew what to do with.

"Regardless of what they say of Rosina she… she had always been kind to me. She built the castle I live in, and if these women lived there with her… Well… then they're *my* people as well." Sighing, he stretched an arm under my knees and lifted me as he stood. "Let's get you cleaned up."

But as my neck grazed his arm beneath me, I felt a sharp sting. Reaching around with my hand, I pressed into my hair and I could hear the squelch of blood. "Dez…" I whispered wearily.

"What's wro—" His words were cut off when his eyes trailed down to the crimson coating my fingertips. "Oh Gods, Morrigan. You need blood. I need to give you my—"

Before he could finish his sentence, my eyes fell closed and everything faded away.

Waking up, my eyelids weighed heavily as I tried to open them.

The last thing I remembered was the feeling of being carried, floating and bouncing in Dez's arms, unable to lift my own. As my eyelashes fluttered in another attempt to open them, I reached my hand behind my head where a light throbbing radiated. When the wraith had pulled me into the water, my head hit the wooden pier. There had been blood... I felt it with my hand before losing consciousness. Though the area still felt tender as my fingers pressed against it, there didn't seem to be an open wound anymore.

"Oh Gods, Morrigan," Eowyn exclaimed loudly, causing my ears to ring. "My Lord! She's awake!"

I threw my hand out toward her voice, willing my blurry eyes to adjust. "Eowyn... Too loud..."

"Oh!" she whispered. "I'm so sorry. You've been asleep all day. We were all so worried..."

"What... What happened?" I could see her now, thankfully. She had a chair pulled up to the side of my bed so that she could lean against the sheets.

"When Dez brought you back to the castle, he ordered Faelar to retrieve a priest. Dez did what he could, but you had bled so much that his... The priest worked on you for hours. He claimed his magic was meeting some kind of... resistance. No one understood why it took so long."

"Princess!" Dez yelled, and a groan escaped my lips as I covered my ears.

Eowyn lifted her finger, shushing him for me. "It's her head," she explained to him. "You'll have to lower your voice, My Lord." Then, she turned back to me again. "When the priest left, he wasn't sure when you would wake. You slept through almost the entire day."

"Are you alright?" Dez asked quietly as he took a seat beside Eowyn.

Nodding my head, I rose slowly until I sat with my back against the headboard, pressing my fingers into my temples to ease the tension. "I think so... It's just a small headache."

"I'll get you some tea." When Eowyn left, Dez sat in her seat and reached out, taking one of my hands into his own.

"I was so worried..." Dez's face looked white with concern. Even the pinks that usually flushed his cheeks seemed to pale.

"I'm alright," I assured him with a gentle squeeze.

When Eowyn returned, she placed the tea in my other hand and I sipped from it slowly. Even through the pain, I couldn't get the image of them out of my head. I couldn't stop the words they had chanted from repeating in my mind. They weren't trying to hurt me. They *had* hurt others but... they could have let me drown. They could have pulled me down with them and—

"You'll need to eat," Eowyn said softly. "An injury like that... You need to replenish yourself."

"Maybe we can cancel the dinner tonight." Dez brought my attention back to him with a pull of my hand. "I can tell them to leave. Just say the word."

I furrowed my brows in response. "Leave? They're here already?"

"They've *been* here," Eowyn whispered.

"I told them the moment I called the priest." Dez offered an apologetic smile. "They were all worried. They've been here since this morning."

Scoffing, I took another sip of the tea. "I'm sure Kaiden will be highly disappointed in my recovery."

But when Dez cleared his throat, he looked almost… *uncomfortable* as he said, "Kaiden was the first to arrive."

The Diary of Daisies and Hellebores

He's visited several times now.

Each time he comes, he smiles and laughs a little more than before. He always brings me daisies. I have now taken it upon myself to discover what his favorite flower is so I can plant it in my garden… He called me beautiful today. He brushed my hair from my face and his fingers grazed my cheek. I thought I was going to faint.

Chapter 27

After everyone meticulously assessed me, confirming I was indeed okay, Kaiden spent the entirety of the dinner *staring*.

He hadn't asked how I was feeling, like the others had, though I never actually expected him to. He just ate his food, staring in my direction, examining me like a bird... in a cage. *How fitting.*

It wasn't until everyone had finished their meals and began chatting that he leaned onto his elbows and narrowed his eyes. "You look like shit today."

I nearly choked on my water as I slammed the cup down beside my plate. "How studious of you to take note, Kaiden. Thank you for your insight."

"She's fine," Dez assured him. "The priest gave a very thorough examination before leaving."

"I'm failing to understand why it took him so long in the first place. If you would have allowed me to—"

"My priests are just as good as yours, Kaiden," Dez quickly interrupted. "He believed that whatever linked her to the prophecy was rooted in deep magic that likely imbedded itself into her blood. He had to work through it in order to heal her."

"You could have at least allowed me to see her—"

"Why do you care?" I sneered at him. When his eyes returned to mine, his brows pulled together with a deep crease between them. "You've made it very clear that you—"

"You know *nothing* of what you speak—"

"You were probably wishing that I would have—"

"Always rambling with your damned mouth without any knowledge of—"

"Get a bloody room!" Cain yelled over us. We both turned to him, now redirecting our anger. Slamming his napkin down in frustration, he stood from his seat and shook his head. "I'm glad to know our precious cargo is still alive. Now, some of us have actual duties to attend to." Shooting us a glare, he dipped his head. "If you'll excuse the rest of us."

A pulsating pain in my temples began to brew from my annoyance with Kaiden, and I pinched my lips together as I released the napkin in my hand. "I'm going to rest some more," I whispered to Dez.

Reaching his hand out, he placed it on top of mine. "Do you want me to come with you?"

As much as I enjoyed sleeping beside him, my body blistered with heat and my mind felt scrambled. Shaking my head, I leaned down and placed a kiss beside his lips. "I'll see you in the morning."

Cass stood and kissed my cheek as I made my way out, saying my goodbyes to the rest of them—all but *Kaiden*. Rubbing my fingers against my temples, I had been overcome with surprise when I made it to my bedroom uninterrupted. With Eowyn gone for the night with her family, I was ready to soak in a nice, hot bath.

It didn't take long for me to fall asleep shortly after. But with the night came dreams of darkness lit by a large fire somewhere on the horizon. The embers rose, resembling stars in the sky and at my feet were daisies. As the dream came to an end, the flowers were slowly consumed by black webs, killing them. And within the crackling of the flames, a faint whisper of my name carried with the wind.

My days were blurring together, and Kaiden's absence from our dinners seemed to only go noticed by me.

When I wasn't studying with Harley and Eowyn, I spent a lot of free time practicing my archery. Lyra made it a point for me to have to kill our meal each week during our visits with Hagen. I enjoyed the proud look she'd give me as she watched my skills improve. Sometimes she would sneak by during the week to train with me.

Before I knew it, my seventh week arrived and I had to wrap my head around the fact that I would be leaving soon. As I laid beside Dez, I traced circles over his chest with my finger. He was still deep in sleep, breathing heavily as my body rose with it. *First, Cass… Now, Dez… How do they expect me to make a choice?* Each of these men continued stealing a piece of me that I would never get back.

Cass had taught me courage and how to laugh again, but Dez… He opened up a part of my heart that I didn't even know existed. He made me feel things, *want* things… I felt much more connected to him than I had with Cass—like our hearts would beat in unison whenever we held each other at night. Just touching him lit my body on fire in a way I had never felt before.

And Lyra…

Eowyn…

I would have to lose them just as I had lost Shae.

Trailing my finger up his chest, I looked at his face before touching his cheek. That's when he let out a sweet sigh as his lashes fluttered. "Good morning, Princess."

"It's our last week." Pushing myself further onto his body, I planted gentle kisses along his collarbone. "I don't want to leave you."

With a deep groan that reverberated in his chest, one of his hands went into my hair. "I don't want you to leave either."

I made my way up to his neck, and then below his ear. "Let's just stay in bed for the rest of the week."

As he chuckled, I reached his lips and straddled his hips with my legs. "You strike a hard bargain, Princess."

Then, he pulled me in for a kiss and I relished in every part of his taste. Our tongues danced and the heat at my core grew as he moved his hips between my thighs. "I need you, Dez," I whispered in between kisses.

He wasted no time in lifting me until he adjusted his length at my entrance. And as I lowered back down, I gasped in his mouth when he entered me. Being on top always pushed him in deeper, and he would hit a part of me that sent my nerves into a shock of pleasure.

"How are you so wet already?" His hands gripped my waist and I moved against him.

I didn't want to tell him that my body craved his touch every second of the day—that I could spend every bit of my free time wrapped in this bed with him, savoring this feeling of having him fill me. "I always want you," I moaned against his lips.

As our thrusts met each other, I sat up straight and placed my hands against his chest, letting my head fall back. Each time he pushed inside, sparks set off in my body. I didn't want to lose him. I wanted this every day for the rest of my life.

"Princess," he groaned. "Gods, I can't last when you're on me like this."

"Don't hold out," I begged. He didn't need to know that I was already halfway there myself. "I want to feel you."

"Fuck," he cursed under his breath. I couldn't look down at him. My eyes remained closed as he took over and moved my body faster on top of his. Then, his finger made its way to my center and I wanted to cry out in bliss.

He pressed against the sensitive area, moving fast as my orgasm approached rapidly. "Don't stop," I begged. "Please... I'm close..."

"Come with me, Princess." All of my senses were shot as he rubbed me faster, pushing against the dam that craved breaking.

"I'm going to... Dez..." My words were cries. I teetered the precipice and needed to fall more than I needed to breathe.

"You're so fucking beautiful," he grunted. "Gods, Morrigan. Look at you... I think I..."

Before he could finish his words, he pinched the sensitive spot and I yelled his name as the orgasm rippled through—stronger than it ever had before. My lungs could barely catch any breath and my nails dug into his skin as I tried to ground myself.

Pushing through my shaking body, Dez made one final thrust and I could feel the warmth filling me inside. *Mine. He's mine.*

As my body collapsed onto his chest, he wrapped his arms around me and pulled me close, reeling down from his own release. "Perfect..." he panted. "You are *perfect*."

Neither of us had the will to move, and I didn't mind it. I would have kept him trapped in that bed if he had allowed me to. Nuzzling into the crook of his neck, I watched his pulse pushing against his skin and thoughts of Cass made their way into my mind.

"Can I ask you something?"

He shifted us so that we could look at each other. "Anything, Princess."

"Cass used to..." *Gods, this was embarrassing.* But I only felt comfortable asking because of how close their relationship had been. "He used to incorporate... *biting* a lot when we would be... intimate."

Dez's body stiffened slightly beneath me, but his expression never changed. *Maybe I shouldn't have said that.* "Is that something you... want?"

"I... I don't know. I just assumed, with how much you enjoy these things, that *you* would want to."

Dez placed a hand on my cheek and massaged my skin with his thumb, looking down at me curiously. Before he responded, he smiled softly and placed a kiss on my forehead. "I only want whatever you're willing to give me, Princess. Even if that meant *nothing*. The aphrodisiac that is released with blood play can be exhilarating..." Then, he brought his lips to mine and kissed me deeply before pulling back. "But a simple kiss from you could bring me to my knees."

My cheeks stung from the blush he caused and I couldn't help but smile. "You really have a way with words, don't you?" I teased him.

"In truth," he whispered. "I always seem to run out of them when I'm with you, Princess."

Placing my head back onto his chest, I snuggled as close as I could. "I don't deserve how well you treat me."

"You've got it all wrong," he replied, holding me tighter. "You deserve a lot better."

Chapter 28

ithin the doors of the dining hall, I could hear loud arguing coming from multiple men.

One of them sounded like Kaiden.

Taking a few, tentative steps toward where the guards were standing, I tried to listen in to whatever had him in such a foul mood. *Am I going with him next? Is that why he's here?*

Before I could get close enough, the doors tore open. Every shadow in the room shrunk down, like they too needed to retreat from the path of his wrath. When he noticed me standing in front of him, he let out an angry puff of air and shoved passed me. "Enjoy your cage, little dove," he hissed, and when I turned around to argue, he was gone.

Shoving off the strange feeling it left me with, I entered the dining hall and noticed both Eris and Dez sitting together as they ate their food. "Why was Kaiden here?" I asked as I approached.

With a scoff, Eris wiped his lip with the napkin beside his plate. "He wanted his *turn* with you."

The way he said those words made my skin crawl. His *turn*. "And what did you say?"

"No, obviously." Dez stood and pulled out my chair for me. "We had already decided the order in which you'd visit our homes. He will have to wait."

"He shouldn't even get the *chance*," Eris mumbled under his breath.

Alright. Eris I could deal with. Yes, half of the things that left his mouth were rooted in arrogance and condescension. But he had at least taken the time to speak to me for the past few weeks. "When do we leave?" I sat down and began eating my own food.

"Right after breakfast." The doors to the hall opened again and Eris stood to greet the guest. "Here's the priestess now."

The priestess... No... Dez promised.

"Priestess Marceline," Eris announced.

In the doorway stood a petite young woman with dark brown hair, braided into a familiar crown. She had golden leaves sewn into her head and wore the same gown that Maeryn did. As she approached the table, her head remained low and she stopped just as she reached the chair across from mine.

Bowing, she kept her hands clasped in front of her, the same way that Maeryn would make me address *her*. "Your Grace," she greeted me. "I have been assigned to escort you due to Priestess Maeryn's... relocation."

"Priestess Marceline is from *my* palace," Eris assured me. "There, they understand the importance of structure and class. And they hold themselves to the highest standards of etiquette and respect."

Eris spoke proudly of them, a smile growing on his face.

"It's nice to meet you, Priestess Marceline. Please," I gestured to the seat, offering for her to sit. "The staff here make the most delicious food. Enjoy."

As she sat down, I looked toward the doors again, waiting.

I waited… and waited… and as the guards closed them, I turned to Dez in confusion. "Lady Guinevere isn't here." I knew that Maeryn claimed she had been preoccupied last time, but I was almost positive that she would be here for this one. Turning to the young priestess, I questioned her next. "Where is Lady Guinevere?"

As she lifted her fork, she paused, glancing nervously at Dez.

"Why are you looking at him like that?" I asked her.

The sound of metal clinking turned my head toward Dez as he set his fork down. With a sigh, he met my stare. "Lady Guinevere is being questioned at the Holy Palace in *Kaiden's* land."

"Questioned for what?!" Raising my voice, I faced the priestess once again, now with eyes filled with fury. "What is she being questioned for?!"

"Princess," Dez whispered, placing a hand on mine. But I ripped it from him as I glared at her. He knew. He *knew* and he didn't tell me.

"There have been… accusations." The priestess looked anxious, like she had already said too much.

"And what are these *accusations*?" As my volume grew, so did my anger.

"Morrigan," Dez warned. "I am looking into it, I swear. But they live by their own laws. You cannot demand things like this—"

"Can't she?" Turning to Eris, I watched as he calmly continued his meal. "The woman raised her. She has every right to at least know *why* she is being questioned."

Thank you, Eris. "I'm inclined to agree," I spat toward Dez.

"Princess, we will make inquiries."

"Then *inquire* of *her*."

"Princess, I cannot just force an answer from a—"

"But I —"

"Morrigan," Eris's voice was deep, almost intimidating.

Closing my eyes, I tried to take a breath to calm myself. Maeryn had put too foul a taste in my mouth for the likes of Priestess Marceline, and it wasn't her fault that I harbored so much rage. When my nerves no longer felt like they buzzed in my palms, I looked back at Dez. "You swear you'll look into it?"

"Yes," he promised. In the blink of an eye, his demeanor changed with the shift of subject. "Eris and I have discussed something that I think will ease your mind a little. I'll show you after we eat."

When the plates were cleared, the four of us made our way to the courtyard where Eowyn met me at the doors. In her hands she held a large bag that Eris quickly took from her. "What's that for?" I asked.

With a bright, excited smile, she whispered, "I'm coming with you."

"What?!" I turned back to Dez, who nodded in confirmation, and I yanked Eowyn into a tight hug. "How..." Pulling back, I held her arms with my hands. "But your family..."

"Lord Dez and Lord Eris agreed to allow me weekly visits with them every Saturday."

I pulled her in for another embrace, this time even tighter than before. "Thank the Gods."

"That's not all." I looked back at Dez as he began walking outside and followed behind him, arms linked with Eowyn.

Standing near the gardens, was a man wearing a uniform similar to what Faelar wore. I assumed that it had been Eris's shadow walker. Beside him stood a tall, familiar, brown-haired beauty, dressed in a guard's uniform. "Lyra!" Running down the steps, I let go of Eowyn and wrapped my arms around her. I didn't think I would have a chance to say goodbye.

"We have officially appointed the first member of your own royal guard," Dez exclaimed.

Royal... I looked up at Lyra and saw her smiling down at me. "You're coming too?"

Nodding, she stepped back a little and readjusted her uniform. "Better safe than sorry. The attacks may have stopped for now, but we wouldn't want to risk your safety." I wrapped my arm around hers and leaned my head against her shoulder as we waited for Eris to finish speaking with his shadow walker. "We will still be allowed to visit my uncle every Friday... If you'd like to."

"I would love that," I whispered, smiling to myself as Eowyn stood on my other side.

Once Eris seemed ready to leave, Dez pulled me from Lyra and cupped my face with his hands. "I'm going to miss you, Princess," he said quietly, bringing my lips to his.

But before he could kiss me, Eris let out a sharp whistle. "I'm running late as it is. Let's get going."

With a laugh, Dez placed a kiss on my forehead and released me, walking quickly toward the stairs to the castle. My heart ached as the doors closed, and behind me, the shadow walker approached. When I turned to face him, he bowed with a soft smile on his face.

"My name is Newt, Your Grace."

Wiping a stray tear that had fallen from my eye, I nodded and forced my own smile. "It's nice to meet you, Newt."

Once everyone looked situated, Newt reached out his arm for us, and Lyra shifted uncomfortably on her feet. "Scared, Lyra?" I teased her.

"Oh, shut it." Her cheeks looked flushed with nerves.

Pulling her to my side, I laughed as I relinked our arms. "Don't worry, I'll keep you safe."

Before she could argue, shadows swirled and swallowed us, sending us into pitch-black darkness.

When I landed, I fell over into the grass, barely able to catch myself.

I had never arrived so roughly with Faelar when we traveled. Sitting up, I massaged my wrists that now felt sore from breaking my fall. "Well... That was..."

When I looked up, I realized that I was... *alone.*

"Lyra?" I called out.

I heard nothing other than the sound of the breeze sifting through the trees. I wasn't anywhere near a castle. I couldn't see any sign of Eowyn, Eris or Newt nearby.

"Eris!" I yelled. "If this is some kind of joke I swear—"

The sudden sound of leaves crunching behind me caused my body to still. When I turned, I watched a man step through the shadows of the forest and into the light. His dark, inky hair covered his forehead, and on his cheeks were scars that covered most of his skin. Stalking toward me, a slow grin spread along his cracked and scabbed lips.

"Your Grace." He gave a theatrical bow but kept his eyes on me, and every single alarm rang out within my mind. "How the Gods bless the worthy."

Swallowing, I slowly rose and took a step back. Everything about him screamed danger. "Who are you?" I asked. *How did I even get here?*

Unfazed by my question, he continued approaching me with careful steps. "This is such a pleasant surprise, Your Grace. He'll be *very* happy that I found you."

I realized in that moment just how devious his intentions were. I had somehow walked directly into a lion's den. "He *who*?"

Could it be Kaiden? Did he send someone to take me from Eris?

My back stopped against a wide tree, and before I could move away, the man stood before me. Using his arms, he trapped both sides of my body and pinned me against it.

"Your beauty truly *is* unrivaled, Your Grace." He licked his lips as his disgusting eyes raked down my body. "I could make you forget. He'd never know I even touched you."

"Please," I whispered. My breathing picked up and I dug my nails into the bark behind me. We were alone in the woods. No one could help me. "I'm sure that Eris would be willing to—"

"*You will not scream, you will not fight.*" His eyes had the same glow that Dez's did when he used his gifts. I wanted to do the exact opposite, but as I stared at him, my body no longer felt like my own. I couldn't make a sound anymore. "*You will come with me... quietly.*"

His words captured my mind and I couldn't deny them. Nodding, I tried to force down the lump in my throat as I followed him. With my hand in his, he led me toward the trees and my chest continued to tighten as I fought back painful tears. This man wanted to hurt me. He *would* hurt me, and I had no way of fighting him, no way of defending myself.

With a quick gasp from the man in front of me, I felt a strong gust of wind beside us. He spun me until my back pressed against his chest. In a quick move, he pulled his dagger out and placed it just beneath my chin.

In front of us stood Eris, Lyra, Cain and Newt. *Thank the Gods.* I wanted to scream for them, but it felt like my lips were sewn shut. *"You will not scream,"* he had said to me. *How is he doing this?* I hadn't read of any of the gifted inheriting the lords' compulsion.

Lyra's eyes were wide and scared, but I could see the fire sparking at her fingertips.

"My, Lord! I…" The man seemed to stumble over his own words. His grip on the blade's handle trembled. Then, I felt the dagger press further into my skin, scraping my neck. "If you come any closer, I'll slit her throat."

The sparks lit up as bright flames along Lyra's palm as the brown in her eyes glowed a fearsome orange hue. "Lower your dagger," she warned.

"I'll do it!" I'll—"

Eris stepped in front of Lyra, eyes a bright, shining blue. *"Lower. Your. Dagger."*

Without any hesitation, the man behind me lowered the blade. Compulsion was truly terrifying to watch, even more so to experience.

"Step back from the princess."

The moment he stepped away, I ran into Lyra's arms, sobbing as I looked at Eris beside us. His eyes were still glowing as he stared at the man standing in the clearing.

"Princess," Cain whispered from somewhere behind me. "Are you alright? Did he hurt you?"

I shook my head, still unable to make a sound.

"Who sent you?" Eris asked him. There was a slight eeriness to his voice that made my arms tremble.

"I…" The man blinked a few times as if trying to remember but couldn't seem to form the words. "I… He… I don't know, My Lord."

"Perhaps his mind has been tampered with, Eris," Cain suggested.

After a moment, Eris nodded in response. "Then he is of no use to us." Straightening his back, he kept his eyes on the stranger. "Lyra, turn her away." Unable to argue, Lyra twisted me until my back faced Eris as a final command left his lips. "*Slit your throat.*"

My breath caught in my lungs and my heart seemed to still until I heard the sound of a body falling to the ground. Seconds later, like a lock clinked open, I let out a cry and clutched Lyra's uniform to keep from dropping.

"Lyra," I gasped. She held me, soothing me as my body shook close to convulsing. "I-I couldn't speak. I couldn't f-fight him."

"Shhh," she whispered, smoothing over my hair. "I've got you."

"He was a Mind Renderer, Morrigan." Looking up at Eris through blurry eyes, I noticed the glow had dissipated. "Gifts like his are forbidden... He shouldn't have even been alive."

Turning to Cain, the lord nodded in agreement. "I'll look into it—see if anyone has any information as to who he was."

With hesitation, I turned until I could see the man's lifeless body sprawled out on the ground. Blood pooled beneath him, soaking the dead grass and turning it a dark crimson. Lyra's warm hand touched my cheek with a gentle ease. "Did he hurt you?" she asked.

I shook my head. "No... You... You came just in time." Then, I looked around for Eowyn. "Where is—"

"She is at the castle," Eris interrupted. But when he returned my gaze, he looked almost furious. "What did you do?"

"What did *I* do?!" I yelled back. "Where were *you*?!"

"*You're* the only one who wasn't there. You're lucky Cain smelled your blood the moment you arrived and retrieved me immediately."

"You think I did this?" I marched in front of him and shoved him back. "You think I wanted my life threatened like that?" I screamed in his face.

"Okay, let's all just take a breath," Cain insisted as he tried to defuse the situation. "She's safe… The man is dead. Let's get her back to the castle and get her cleaned up."

"I could compel an answer out of you," Eris threatened.

"You wouldn't dare."

"Eris," Cain called. "I have better things to do than listen to the two of you bicker on my land."

Composing himself, Eris stepped back and turned to Newt. "Take us home." He nodded and reached his arm out.

Huffing, I rolled my eyes and moved to stand as far away from Eris as possible. *I hate this place already*, I hissed in my mind before darkness consumed us once more.

The Diary of Daisies and Hellebores

He kissed me...

He actually kissed me!

He begged me not to tell the others, and I agreed.

If they found out, this would all come to an end.

And I... I think I might love him. I know I

shouldn't, but I think I do. Could he love me as

well? Could we keep our secret and find a way

to live in peace? I could be his happiness, and

he could be mine...

We can find a way.

Chapter 29

Eris's castle looked exactly as I expected it to.

With diamonds and jewels decorating the furniture and walls, it screamed everything I knew about his personality. Even the paintings had real gold embossing.

After the disturbing encounter in the woods, Lyra insisted on accompanying me at every meal and refused to sit at the table when asked to. She didn't trust anyone—not even Eris. On occasion, I would catch her glaring at him, a bitter taste of distrust evident on her face. I tried not to pay it any mind. She had every right to form her own opinion of him.

I still had zero inclination on how I got onto Cain's land. The only assumption I had derived was the idea that whoever wanted me messed with our travel and pulled me from Newt's grasp. But nothing that I had studied with Harley hinted at that even being a possibility.

My conversations with Eris went much like they did every week at dinner. We would greet each other, give a small fact about some part in our day, and eat our meals in silence. We weren't close in any way, but I really didn't mind it too much. At least he didn't pretend to like me for the sake of impressions. Besides, I had my girls to keep me company. Eowyn and I spent the entire first week walking the gardens that were almost wilted now with winter's arrival. I wasn't sure why Eris didn't feel the need to place the same enchantments on them as Dez liked to.

Flowers made the place look more alive.

By the end of the week, Harley had arrived and we dove into our studies again—keeping me busy.

During dinner on Thursday, Eris had his eyes glued to a few papers in front of him on the table. After pulling my chair out for me, Lyra continued staring at Eris as she moved back into her place behind me. I couldn't convince Eowyn to attend any dinners. She felt intimidated by Eris, and I couldn't fault her for that.

"I've been struggling with some of my current studies with Harley," I said, hoping to ignite some form of communication between us.

Without acknowledging me, he continued sipping his wine and reading the parchment in his hand.

"I could use some help, if I'm being honest," I continued.

Sighing, he set down his glass. "Isn't that the entire reason we have Harley to begin with?"

"I can't expect him to spend every waking moment with me," I argued. Though, Harley likely wouldn't have minded. He usually enjoyed our weekend readings in the library when I had nothing better to do.

"Well, I'd rather not waste any more money on yet *another* tutor for you."

Rolling my eyes, I picked up my own glass. "That's not what I was suggesting."

I hadn't drank much wine with Dez. But Eris seemed to love it. His tasted rich, with undertones of both bitter and sweet berries. Everything that came from Eris's kitchen tasted like bliss. He had the best wine, best cooked meals and the most expensive looking gowns. I'm fairly certain my dresses had been hand sewn by the gods themselves. He had even left an entire drawer of jewels in my vanity for me to wear and… I can admit… I may have indulged in some of them.

"Then what *were* you suggesting?" he asked with a clipped tone.

"Are you avoiding me, Eris?"

"I'm sorry?" He still didn't bother looking up from the paper in his hands as he answered me. It enraged me how easy it was for him to be rude like that.

"I've been here for four days and the most conversation we've had was the day I arrived." Crossing my arms over my chest, I leered at him as I leaned back in my chair. "I'm supposed to be getting to know you, and you spend the entirety of your time in your study."

"Dez spent much of his time working as well, did he not?" I glared harder, hoping he could feel my piercing stare—willing for his paper to burst into flames. Finally, with a sigh, he placed the papers down and ran a tired hand over his face. "Morrigan, have you not been getting to know me these past couple of months?"

"I saw you once a week!" I argued. "That doesn't count, and you know that."

Leaning back in his chair, his tense smile twisted into a sarcastic smirk. "Do you want to see me more? Should I arrange scheduled visits? Walks in my garden?"

I pushed my chair out, letting it scrape across his marble floor, and prayed that it left scratches. "I've lost my appetite." But when I began to stand, his hand wrapped around my wrist, pulling it down against the table.

"If you want something from me, then *tell* me. I won't grovel on my knees for you like Dez or Cass." Rising from his chair, he kept his hand against mine on the wood and leaned toward me. In the corner of my eye, Lyra took a slight step in our direction. "In this castle, you'll need to use your *words*. Can you do that?"

Appalled, I yanked my hand from beneath his and rolled my eyes. "Goodnight, Eris." I didn't turn back as I stormed from the dining hall.

"He's such a dick," Lyra whispered as we walked up the stairs.

"Sometimes he's less of a dick," I admitted. "He *can* be enjoyable. But he cares only for himself."

Eowyn sat on a chair in the corner of my room reading when Lyra dropped me off. Due to the incident in the woods, Lyra insisted on remaining outside of my door during her watches. When she needed to sleep, she would instruct one of Eris's guards to temporarily take over.

But only after vetting every single one of them the entire first week here.

"What are you reading about?" I asked Eowyn, unraveling the string behind my dress.

Without looking up from her book, she answered, "Did you know there used to be a species of hellebores that were extremely deadly? They were banned from the entire kingdom centuries ago. I guess the gods had learned that the species was poisonous even to the lords. It's the only thing that can *actually* kill them."

"I learned about them when I lived with Cass…" I tried to block the image of him bleeding onto the floor away from my mind. "You know, I have a book called, *The Diary of Daisies and Hellebores.* I think you'd enjoy it."

"You have what?" Suddenly, she looked up from the book and gaped at me.

"It's a… diary…" I said warily. "I don't know who it was written by, but it's a great read."

Still staring, she remained quiet for a moment before closing her book loudly and changing the topic. "How was dinner?"

I narrowed my eyes at her, but I couldn't contain my annoyance with Eris any longer and needed to let it out. I huffed in frustration, plopping down to my vanity chair. "He's *incorrigible*… and just plain rude, Eowyn. But I have this incessant need to continue." I looked back at her through the mirror as she approached. "I hate this stupid connection I have with all of them."

"You're complaining that you have seven men tied to *you* and *only* you?" she teased.

"Six… *maybe*," I corrected.

"What?"

"Kaiden hates me. Like, literally hates my guts. There isn't a world in which that man would want me and I have to admit, I share his sentiment."

Laughing, she shook her head and removed the remaining pins in my hair. "Maybe you should do the same thing that Eris is doing to *you*," she suggested. "Ignore him. Give him the peace he claims that he so desperately needs and see how *he* feels being the one to beg for *your* attention."

So, the next night, after dinner with Hagen and Lyra, I did just that.

As I passed Eris in the hall, I didn't offer him any acknowledgement. I kept my chin tilted up and could feel him turn back to look at me, but he said nothing. And neither did I. I walked straight to my room, changed, and crawled into bed to sleep.

The next morning, breakfast had been quiet. Maybe my actions were childish, but I didn't care. I ate my food—not even greeting Eris—and I could feel his looming stare over his papers as I pulled out one of my books to read.

"No questions to pester me with this morning?" he asked.

"Nope."

He laughed and I heard the clink of his glass as he set it down. "Are you throwing a tantrum, Morrigan?"

"You're awfully talkative this morning." I glared at him and watched his amused eyes turn irritated. "Can I not enjoy a peaceful, silent breakfast?"

"You didn't speak to me yesterday either," he noted.

"And you're interrupting my reading."

"So this *is* a tantrum." Leaning forward, he rested his chin onto his fists.

I sighed and closed my book, accepting defeat. But I didn't humor him with any more words. Finishing what was left on my plate, I then placed the utensils on top for the staff to collect before grabbing my book and leaving.

When dinner arrived, I made it a point to sit between Dez and Cass, who both stared at Eris as I took my seat. Eris gave an amused glance and I ignored it as Kaiden let out a whistle from the end of the table.

"Is something wrong, little dove?" I shot him daggers as well and he only laughed in response. Gods knew why he even still attended these dinners. Why couldn't he just stay away? Why couldn't he accept that *no one* wanted him here?

"The princess is throwing a hissy fit," Eris told him, still staring at me. "It will pass."

"Will it?" I challenged.

Anger brewed in his blue eyes and all it did was fuel the fire I had begun.

"Have you gained any news about the man from the woods?" I asked Cain in an effort to piss Eris off with the change of subject.

Eyeing Kaiden, Cain looked nervous as he turned back to me. "I have not. I promise to tell you as soon as I do."

"Man in the woods?" Kaiden looked confused. It was actually the first time I had ever seen him look that way.

"It's none of your business," I sneered at him.

"Every breath that you *breathe* is my business, *little dove*." Before we could begin arguing again, Eris explained what had happened and I could see the anger in Kaiden's face. "She was almost *taken* and you're still allowing her to visit some peasant's home every week?!"

Slamming my fork on the table, I stood from my seat and faced him. "Would you rather him lock me inside? I'm not a prisoner, Kaiden!"

"If it were me, you'd be lucky to even see the light of day."

"Kaiden," Eris interrupted. "If you can't agree to a single, peaceful evening, you're more than welcome to leave."

Gritting my teeth, I sat down slowly and returned to my meal. *Stop letting him get to you. He wants you to react. Don't give him the satisfaction.*

When dinner ended, I ignored the rest of them as I stormed off to my room but stopped short when I heard Eris behind me. "That was a complete embarrassment, Morrigan."

Rolling my eyes, I turned to face him as he walked up and stopped in front of me. "I've embarrassed you at every one of those dinners," I reminded him.

"This is my home, Princess. It's a little different now."

"I think you're just upset that I've been ignoring *you* now. Wanting something you can't have, Eris?" I lifted my head at him, reminding him how little he intimidated me.

"Are you so sure?" Heat and rage flashed in eyes, shining under the light of the candles in the hall.

"You've ignored me all week, Eris. I have tried time and time again to talk to you and you've done nothing but embarrass me each time. So please, forgive me if *I* embarrassed *you*."

"I think you're spoiled. This is *my* home, and you *will* respect me in it. You may have had free rein to do whatever you pleased with Dez and Cass, but I won't stand for insolence."

"I think you're a coward."

"Don't push me," he warned, taking another step toward me until my back hit the wall.

"Bite me, Eris."

Finally, our feet touched and he leaned his head down beside my face with a hand next to my head. "Is that an invitation, Princess?"

A confusing sensation of flutters had my stomach spiraling. *It most certainly is* not.

Are you sure about that?

Oh, fuck off.

Quickly, I turned the handle on my door. "Goodnight, Eris." Sinking into my room, I closed the door behind me and let out a shaky breath.

"You know this door can't protect you, Princess," he laughed.

"Go away, Eris!"

Our words were like tug of war. We had spent weeks going back and forth.

Normally, I had the reassurance of the other guys always being around when I would instigate him, but now it was just us... alone.

I heard a chuckle from him as he walked away and released another breath I didn't know I'd been holding. As a tiny smirk formed on my lips, I leaned my back against the door, looking into my room filled with gold and jewels. These next six weeks would be long. This little game of cat and mouse that we were playing would eventually come to an end. One of us would win.

I just wasn't sure which role I wanted to play.

The cat.

Or the mouse.

Chapter 30

The priestess left the next day, unbeknownst to me.

Truthfully, I had forgotten that she was ever here to begin with. She remained quiet the entire week, eating her meals in her room. I had wondered if my attitude toward her on the first day caused her isolation, but any apology would be too late now.

I did, however, contemplate giving Eris one for my behavior the night before. But in the end, I decided that he had deserved every second of it. So, for the next few days, I continued to ignore him. At each meal, I could feel his temper rising more and more when I failed to answer his questions or respond to a simple greeting in the hall.

Eowyn bit her tongue, holding in laughter every time I pretended he wasn't present. I had a feeling Lyra reveled in the exclusion. When

Wednesday finally came around, I decided I would put my pride aside and speak to him again. But before I could mutter a word, Eris spoke up.

"Maybe I've been... *difficult* to live with."

Raising my eyebrows, I looked at him and leaned back in my chair, giving him my full attention. "Maybe?" I asked, with a twinge of sass in my voice. I truly couldn't help myself.

Shifting in his seat, he rolled his eyes at my rebuttal. "The idea of sharing doesn't come easy to me, Morrigan," he admitted. "You becoming Queen means I'd have to do just that. I will have to share my wealth, share my lands, share my... *myself*. This isn't only strange for you, *Princess*."

I smiled softly at the rare glance of vulnerability he had offered me. "I didn't think about how it must be for you all. Maybe I *have* been a little spoiled..." He scoffed in response and I had to bite my tongue to not slip into an immature response. "But that doesn't excuse the way that you act. You can't not speak to me when the entire point of me being here is to get to know you."

Leaning back in his chair, he took a long, slow sip of his wine and set it down. "You're right. I'll... I'll do better at that."

I wanted to chuckle at the clear display of discomfort we both were likely showing from the conversation. "Thank you," is all I chose to say as we returned to our meal.

"You know..." he began, staring at his plate like he needed to contemplate what he wanted to say. "You speak so freely with all of us... even *Kaiden*. I just don't understand..."

"Don't understand what?" I asked, picking at the fruit on my plate.

"Why you never stood up to the priestess in the same way."

I dropped my fork with a loud *clank* as I stared at my plate. "*Speaking* and *acting* are two very different things," I reminded him.

"Right. No, I understand that. I just…" When I turned, his eyes were on me, curiously. "I look at you and I see a strength that hadn't been there at the Unveiling. And I just wonder what she could have done to suppress that for so long."

That brought a bitter laugh from my lips. "I can *show* you if you'd like."

As he sighed, I could feel the weight of it from my seat. "Twenty-one years…" he whispered. "Had she truly treated you that way your entire life? How did you *survive* it?"

The truth was, she *hadn't*.

Laying in the grass, I stretched my legs behind me and kicked my feet as I continued drawing.

The sun felt warm against my skin. I loved laying in the grass during the summer. I would watch Lady Guinevere garden as I colored more pictures to hang around the house. She always looked so pretty… The braids in her hair made her look like a goddess, and I would always ask her to braid mine. But with my unruly curls, it always took much longer than her own.

Priestess Maeryn used to tease me that her fingers were going to fall off when she would attempt it herself.

Looking down at my paper, I finished the drawing and smiled to myself. It was the three of us, standing in the flowers that Lady Guinevere let me help plant, just last year. Behind us stood the house, with the sun shining directly above us. I even drew the guards standing by the wall, the ones who kept us safe every day. I couldn't wait to show the priestess.

Two pretty shoes stopped beside my arm. And when I looked up, I saw Lady Guinevere smiling down at me. "It looks beautiful, flower," she said sweetly.

"Do you think she'll like it?" I beamed at her.

Reaching her hand down, she helped me stand and I picked up the paper with me. "I think she'll love *it. Let's get you cleaned up before dinner."*

Running inside of the house, I could already smell the food from the kitchen. I knew the priestess had been cooking and I wanted to give her my drawing before taking a bath. So, I ran toward the smell. The moment I saw her, I ran and hugged her, wrapping my arms around her legs.

Laughing, she returned the embrace. "You'll dirty my robes!" she yelped.

"But I made you something!" Looking up at her, I passed the paper into her hand and watched as her smile grew.

"It's beautiful, Mor..." Her eyes traced along the drawing, looking at every section of it.

"It's you, me, and Lady Guinevere!" I told her proudly.

Laying a gentle hand on my cheek, she leaned down and placed a kiss on the other side. "Thank you," she said. "I'll be sure to add it to the wall in our study room."

I felt giddy with excitement. I always loved when she added my artwork to the walls. It gave me a sense of pride and accomplishment.

"Would you like to help me with the stew?"

...

A few days later, I had been sitting in my room, looking through my window at the rain falling down. Priestess Maeryn had been gone for a day or two, receiving our supplies. I had heard the door open and the priestess's voice calling from downstairs. As I ran through the hall to greet her, Lady Guinevere stopped me just as she exited her room.

"Mor!" she whispered loudly. "You need to—"

I quickly slipped past her hold and made it to the stairs. "Too slow!" I yelled back at her and skipped steps in-between rushing down.

When I saw the priestess leave the kitchen, I ran toward her, but she took a step back and avoided my hug. Not understanding, I looked up at her with my brows pulled together. I knew I had completed my chores that day and *turned in all of my writing. So, I didn't know why she would be upset with me.*

I walked toward her again and she stopped me, holding me in place with her arms stretched out. "Stop," she ordered in a cold, unusual voice.

My eyes stung from tears beginning to form. "Did… Did I do something wrong?" I asked.

Standing up straight, she turned away from me. "Go to your room, Morrigan."

She had never *called me by my full name before. "But I—"*

"Now!" she yelled.

I jumped at the cruelness in her voice. Running to the stairs, I raced to my room before the tears could slip and fell into my bed. A few moments later, Lady Guinevere arrived and pulled me into her lap.

"She's mad at me," I cried. She had never been mad at me before.

Shushing me, she began humming her lullaby in my ear. "You did nothing, my flower… Not by choice."

Soon after, the priestess refused to even speak to me. Eventually, with no explanation, my room had been moved to the attic above. All of the paintings that had once hung in our classroom, now hung on my own, cracked walls. She didn't want them anymore. I spent most nights crying myself to sleep and the priestess no longer allowed me to color in the garden. Instead, my days were filled with more chores and duties, making sure I had no free time other than to eat or to sleep.

"How did you survive it?" he had asked me.

Pushing my plate away, I wiped my lips and stood. "Some days," I said quietly, "I'm not even sure that I have."

"Did you grab your gloves?" Lyra asked me, waiting in the courtyard beside Newt.

Pressing my lips together, I gave her a tight smile. She knew I hadn't.

"It's a good thing that *one* of us is responsible," she teased, tossing me a pair of white gloves.

Once we disappeared with Newt, I could actually feel my lungs constricting as I waited the quick, three seconds for us to land back on the ground. Naturally, I reached out, grabbing onto Lyra's arm to confirm that she was still there.

"I'm here," she whispered under her breath, knowingly. "You're here. I'm here."

Once Newt vanished away, back to Eris's castle, we made our way to Hagen's home where he greeted us with a warm hug. He had been fishing that day, giving me a break from our weekly hunts. But Lyra jabbed her elbow into my ribs with a wide grin. "You can help me skin them."

"*Lyra*," Hagen scolded. "Queens don't even cook their own food, let alone skin it."

With a dismissive laugh, Lyra wrapped an arm around my shoulders and yanked me into her side. "This one does!"

I couldn't stop my smile as I leaned into her embrace and followed her to the kitchen. Everything seemed rather easy. I mimicked her every move as we worked alongside each other. When I finished mine, she looked it over and nodded with approval before handing me the third to try on my own while she prepped the rest of the food.

"What about the bones?" I asked her as I finished skinning the last fish.

"We'll handle them after they are cooked. They're softer and easier to remove then."

Once she finished cooking, we sat together at the table. It brought back the memory of what Cass had told me, about how they grew up in the Holy Palace. Looking at Lyra and Hagen, I wondered if they ever had dinners like this together. Perhaps that's why they still did it every Saturday.

Had anyone loved them the way that Hagen loved Lyra? Even if she wasn't his own? Maybe that was why Eris acted the way he did.

"Are you alright, Your Grace?" Hagen asked, still refusing to use my name like I had asked him to.

"Apologies," I smiled, "just a little distracted is all."

"With as many years as mine comes wisdom, Your Grace. I would be honored to share some of it, should you need any."

I thought about it before speaking, finally. "Do you know much of Eris?"

Taking a deep breath, he leaned back in his chair, causing a slight creak in the wood. "I know his people aren't the fondest of him."

"Why?"

"He's not *cruel*… But he's not been known to be *kind* either," he answered carefully. "While most of the lords have fairly equal levels of society, fair trade amongst the villagers, Eris does not."

Leaning in, I pressed my elbows into the table. "What do you mean?"

"Eris encourages the divide between his people. Those who can make more, earn more. It isn't unfair, but it causes tension between the villagers who may lack the resources to thrive. This creates different levels of society. The *rich* and the *poor*."

"He would consider us the latter," Lyra mumbled.

Hagen swatted her head and she yelped in response, massaging the spot he had hit. "He is *still* one of the Seven. And whether you like it or not, you will respect him."

Even Lyra seemed surprised by his sudden shift in demeanor.

"Do you understand the *blessing* they have provided you with, allowing you to watch over our queen?" he asked. "They can take that away, at any given moment."

Rolling her eyes, Lyra returned to her meal with her head lowered. "I'm just saying... maybe if he gave back to the community every once in a while... Gods... even just *visited* them—they'd see him in a different light."

Like a sudden spark, an idea popped into my head that I couldn't ignore. Eris would absolutely loathe it, which meant that it was the right thing to do.

Chapter 31

had been pleasantly surprised to see Naaz at breakfast the next morning, in spite of Eris having some work to complete in his study.

"Are you still on a talking strike, then?" he asked me, smirking from across the table.

"It seems I am not as resilient as I thought," I sighed.

As he laughed, his dimples deepened, giving him an ethereal youth to his face. How in the gods were they all so stunning? "He wasn't much better as a child, if that provides any relief to your efforts."

As he spoke, a young man on Eris's staff walked by, retrieving my plate. I smiled at him while he cleaned off the table and watched his cheeks blush as he returned the affection. Then, another woman brought me a cup filled with warm tea. Thanking them both, I sipped on it with closed eyes, enjoying the sweet, earthy taste.

"He certainly wasn't as liked as you are," Naaz noted.

Looking up from my tea cup, I could see him gazing at me. "It costs nothing to be kind." He almost seemed surprised by my response.

With a *humph,* he went back to his food.

"Why *are* you here?" I asked.

"Eris said you needed some help with your studies." His words were muffled as he shoved the rest of his food into his mouth. "I happen to be the smartest out of the seven."

Naaz never missed a chance to boast about himself. "That's awfully kind of you."

Smiling, he downed the rest of his cup before slamming it back onto the table. "And it cost me nothing. How about that."

As we entered the library together, Naaz found some textbooks and pulled up a seat beside me as we began studying. Minutes turned to hours, and my own head throbbed from the information it was attempting to absorb.

When I leaned my face onto the table in defeat, Naaz chuckled. "You'll get the hang of it," he promised. "You're smarter than you know."

Groaning, I lifted my head onto my hands. "Don't flatter me, Naaz. This is impossible." Then, I frowned. "It also feels like nonsense. We have scholars that live in the Holy Palaces. Why do I need to learn something that will never be of use to me?"

"You never know what you need until you need it, Princess." Collecting our books, he began returning them to the shelves and I rolled my eyes.

"Why me?" I asked.

Naaz turned, narrowing his eyes. "What do you mean?"

"Why choose *me*?" Sighing, I fiddled with the pencils sprawled out on the desk.

"Why *any* of us?" Naaz countered.

"Did they ever tell you why they chose you all?"

Shaking his head, his brows pulled together. "We assumed that it was random—that we just happened to be seven boys all together at the time that they needed us to be."

"I wasn't even born yet, and still my fate was chosen for me somehow." I looked down at my shoulder where my dress hid the scar on my skin. "Kaiden wasn't far off. I'm a little bird, flying from cage to cage. My life isn't even my own. It never was."

When I looked back up, Naaz watched me with sympathy in his eyes. "I wish I could tell you that you have a choice. I wish I could tell you that *we* did, that we *do*."

Nodding in understanding, I stood and cleaned up the rest of the papers, making sure the library looked as it did when we entered. And as we left, Naaz grabbed my hand, pulling me to look at him. "You deserve more," he said. "Regardless of any of this... the past... the future... know that you're worth more than all of this..."

His honesty warmed my heart a little. "Thank you, Naaz."

"Don't," he said quickly before I could turn back around. "Don't thank me." Then, he let go of my hand and began walking away.

Kaiden, in his usual, unreliable fashion decided not to attend dinner.

I drowned out most of the conversation throughout the night. And when it was over, Naaz, D, and Cain left while Dez and Cass stayed back with Eris—finishing their wine together. As I stared at Cass, I noticed that the usual flush in his skin seemed to be fading.

"The Offerings," I remembered. Shifting uncomfortably, I realized he would have needed to feed by now. And when the jealousy swirled in my stomach, it made my food turn sour.

Cass and Dez exchanged a look. *Dez would have to feed on someone soon, too…*

When Cass recognized the panic in my face, he reached forward and placed a hand on top of mine. "I haven't needed to yet," he assured me.

"I don't understand. I thought that they were once a month."

"Your blood is different… like Dez had told you when you first arrived. You're made for us. It's held me over longer than normal blood would."

"What happens when you need to feed, or you, Dez?" I asked, realizing my feelings toward it were a bit more obvious than I intended them to be. "I don't want you… I sound so selfish."

Shoving my face into my hands, I tried to hide how embarrassed I felt. "It will be arranged," Eris said beside me. "It's been almost two months for you, Cass. Maybe it's best that we do it today. We're still unsure how her blood affects us and it's best to be safe."

My head snapped up to him with red cheeks. He wanted Cass to feed… from me… *here…*

"We'll find a day for you to come by as well, Dez. After the encounter in the woods… I think it's best to eliminate any vulnerability." Eris stood as Dez followed. "I'll walk you out, Dez."

It took everything in me not to cringe at the bluntness of the situation. Did he not know how feeding would affect me? He *had* to know. As Cass moved to stand beside me, my entire body felt flustered. I could see his hand in the corner of my eye.

"Come here," he whispered. Accepting his help, I stood and kept my head down. "Hey… Why do you look so ashamed?"

My fingers fidgeted together nervously. "I feel more embarrassed than anything." Letting out a long breath, I forced my eyes to look up at him. "It feels a little hypocritical of me to expect you both to not... I don't know. I don't have the right to be so territorial. I'm over here switching between the seven of you... well *six*... I can't just expect you to—"

Before I could finish, he lifted me until I sat on the table and wrapped my legs around his waist. "That *is* the expectation, Princess." Gently, he grabbed my face and cradled it with his hands. "I *belong* to you, Morrigan. Even if you don't choose me."

"That doesn't seem fair," I said quietly as my breath hitched from being so close to him again.

"Don't think like that." Leaning in, he pressed his forehead against mine. "I *want* no one else, Princess. Even after you make your decision, I am *yours*."

I missed these moments with him. I missed his skin against mine. Underneath his own sweet scent, I could still smell his blood somehow. I could practically taste it on my tongue.

"I don't want your lips on anyone else, Cassius. Just the thought of it might drive me mad," I admitted.

Pressing his body forward, I gasped as it pushed between my thighs. "Only you," he whispered, and dropped a hand to my back as he lowered his lips toward my neck.

Only me. Letting my head fall, I flinched slightly at the light pinch on my skin as he bit down, but it quickly morphed into warmth. It spread down my back, straight to my core as I felt him pull from me. I had to grab at his waist to keep my body steady. I wanted to moan, to pull him further into my center, but I didn't want to disrespect Eris in his home like that. The blissful sensation only lasted for a minute or two before he pulled away.

Instinctively, my eyes shot straight to his neck, involuntarily remembering how we would share. "Do you want something, Princess?" he asked quietly.

Slowly, he picked up a knife beside us and wrapped my fingers around the handle. "I couldn't," I whispered.

Bringing my hand up to his collarbone, he pressed his lips against my ear. "If you want it... You *take* it."

With adrenaline coursing through my body, I pushed against his skin until I saw small beads of red forming beneath the knife. *This is so wrong*, I thought to myself. But I couldn't stop my hand. I pressed and pulled until a small cut had been made and hesitated for a moment, sharing a glance with Cass.

"Take it," he insisted.

Leaning in, I licked the blood that had begun to drip down his skin. As I felt a rush of pleasure through my veins, my eyes rolled back a little. Cass's hand reached up into my hair and held it tightly, letting out a small groan as I drank more. The moment I felt my body grind against him, I pulled back to stop myself.

"Princess," he moaned, tilting my chin up as a drop of blood began to trickle down my lip. "I've missed you."

Holding his restraint by a thin thread, Cass leaned down and licked up my chin until he reached my lips, kissing me softly.

"We'll see you next week," Eris called from the entry. I jumped away from Cass, scrambling to untangle myself from his hold.

But Cass just smiled and kissed my forehead. "Until next time," he whispered and left me sitting on the table.

Before Eris could make his escape, I jumped off and ran to him. "I have a question!" I yelled just as he turned on his heel.

Groaning, he paused and angled his head toward me.

"It's actually a favor…" I admitted.

"Why do I have the feeling I won't like this favor?"

Smiling, I bit my lip. "Because you won't."

The Diary of Daisies and Hellebores

I think the others are getting suspicious. They've been looking at me differently. We spoke of it today during our walk and decided that we must be careful. Together, we came up with a solution for us to see each other in private. A place where only we can go, a place no one knows of. We hid the entrance and it only reveals itself to the two of us.

A perfect escape.

Chapter 32

The look on Eris's face as we stood beside Newt was enough to make the entire thing worth it.

"This is *ridiculous*," he complained.

"It is *not*." I tightened my cloak around me, shivering from the cold air when Lyra popped up beside me.

She had a lifted eyebrow as she stared down at my hands and shoved gloves into them. "Incorrigible," she muttered under her breath.

"We won't be needing you today, Lyra," Eris said blankly, adjusting the cuffs on his wrists.

"I'm the princess's guard, My Lord," Lyra insisted. "I think it would be best for me to—"

"You aren't... *needed*." Giving her a warning glance, I could see the annoyance radiating from his glare.

To prevent an altercation, I placed a hand on Lyra's arm and smiled. "I'll be fine, Lyra. You stay here and take care of Eowyn."

Lyra's lips curled back a little. "Eowyn's going to make me sit and read... for *hours*."

I laughed. "Consider it a day off."

"But I don't want a—"

"Let's go," Eris called, interrupting her.

We arrived at the entrance to town, a mixture of conversation and laughter emanating from beyond the homes around us. "Would you like me to stay here, My Lord?" Newt asked Eris.

"No. We might be a few hours. Feel free to roam. I'll find you when we are ready to return home."

Newt bowed first to Eris, then to me. "My Lord... Your Grace."

The moment Newt left, Eris extended an arm to me and I took it graciously. "Thank you for doing this," I whispered to him.

"A single visit isn't going to make people like me more. And frankly, I don't *care* if they like me," he huffed.

But as I looked in his eyes, I realized that I didn't believe a word he had said. I think he did care if people liked him. And he had just spent too many years alone to realize it.

Making our way through town, the voices grew louder as we approached the town square. The sound of a harp played nearby as children danced in circles, reminding me of the time I visited town with Cass.

Crowds were laughing and socializing together with large smiles. That was, until our presence had been noticed. The silence we received felt louder than anything I had ever heard. I assumed that everyone had been staring at me, looking as if they had seen a ghost. But I quickly realized that they were looking at *Eris*.

He truly never came to visit his people, and it was evident. No one knew how to act or what to do as they gaped at him. Shifting anxiously next to me, I could feel Eris's hold on my arm tighten.

When a young woman began approaching, he took a small step back. "Your Grace..." she greeted me, bowing. Then, she looked up at Eris. "My... My Lord..."

Beside her, a young man shuffled to her side with a small barrel and bowed as well. "Wine, Your Grace," he offered. "Our family has made it for centuries. Please... We would be honored if you accepted it as a gift."

Looking at Eris, I offered him a nod of approval, encouraging him to accept. And when he stepped forward, pride blossomed in my chest. "Thank you," he said to them. "The princess and I will be here for some time. I will have my men retrieve it when we leave."

With that ice breaker, the talking picked back up and the villagers seemed content to continue their day in our presence.

"It just comes so easily to you," he commented, looking down at me in what appeared to be admiration.

"What does?" I asked.

"Kindness." His eyes softened at the words, and I thought for a moment I would get another glimpse at the vulnerability he so rarely showed. But he quickly shook it off, motioning for us to walk.

We explored together, paying our respects to those around us. Some of the men and women wore clothing that was clearly more extravagant than others. Even the way they walked, it's like they floated on clouds. I also noticed the difference in Eris's tone when speaking to those villagers, compared to the others.

Stopping at a small cart on the side of the pathway, Eris turned back toward me with a flower in his hand. "Daffodil," he said. Blushing, I pulled it from his fingers. "They represent new beginnings."

The flower had an orange center and faded out to white. Bringing it to my nose, I inhaled the sweet scent of honey and vanilla. "Thank you." I leaned up, placing a kiss on his cheek.

We were quickly interrupted by the sound of a loud crash which was followed by a man screaming. Eris wrapped a protective arm around me and I turned toward the sound. A man lay on the ground next to a broken cart, gripping his thigh where blood spilled profusely. Pushing out of Eris's arms, I ran toward the man as villagers began surrounding him. I dropped the flower and knelt on the ground, placing a hand on his shoulder.

Harley had taught me very little on first aid, but enough to know that his leg needed to be tied to slow the bleeding. I told a man beside me to put pressure on his wound and looked around frantically for a long piece of cloth to tie around his leg. With how fast he was bleeding, I knew time was of the essence. So, I pulled my gown from under my knees and ripped the end of it.

Wrapping the cloth around his leg, I tied it tight above the wound and waited for the bleeding to slow. The minutes felt like hours, and it wasn't slowing down. "He was trying to fix the top of the cart and it broke. A piece of wood impaled his leg and when he pulled it out it started gushing," said a young woman beside him. "He's bleeding too much. We'll never make it to the palace in time." Her hand covered her mouth but her eyes screamed with terror.

Looking down, I could see the puddle of blood had reached my dress, soaking the fabric beneath me. I turned to Eris who had been watching the incident but wasn't intervening. "We have to do something. There has to be a priest somewhere. Please, Eris," I pleaded.

"He'll be dead before a priest can get here." His words held no emotion, no compassion.

"We can't just let him die!" I yelled. The villagers grew silent as the woman beside the man began to sob.

Staring at me with an unreadable expression, Eris waited for a moment. Then, he leaned down and picked up the flower that I had dropped before twirling it in his fingers.

"Eris!" I screamed, holding the man's wound with my own hands now.

Kneeling beside me, Eris continued gazing at the daffodil. "Did you know that plants have life?" He placed his other hand on the man's leg, below the wound. "Though you can't see it… it's there. A living organism."

I almost began to yell at him again but when I looked up, I saw the flower begin to wilt. The color drained from it as Eris's eyes glowed brightly. Gasps sounded from all around us. Looking back down, the man on the ground started breathing steadily again. The color that had been fading from his face now flushed pink against his skin. And his wound… It was *closing* itself. The skin stitched together and the lesion all but disappeared.

When I turned back to Eris, I couldn't hide the amazement in my face when I saw the flower had turned to dust, falling from his fingers like ash. Brushing the remaining dirt from his hand, he stood and looked down at me, almost bored—like he hadn't just saved a man's life. "Your dress is ruined," he said coolly. "And you need a bath."

With furrowed brows, I sat there watching him, unable to understand how he could remain so indifferent. Beside me, the woman who had been sobbing now laid against the man, showering him in kisses. "Thank you!" she cried to Eris. "Thank you!"

I went searching for Eris later that day and found him holed up in his study.

I barely knew what to say to him after the incident in town. He handled it in a way that left me completely speechless. When he noticed me standing in the doorway, he looked up with tired eyes. "Can I help you?" he asked.

"Was that your gift?" I nodded my head toward his hand. "The healing?"

When he leaned back in his chair, I took it as an invitation to join him. "It's not healing, exactly. I'm able to drain energy from any living thing, and *with* that, I can then transfer that energy to someone else. So... by draining the life force from the flower, I was able to redirect it to the wound, giving the body enough strength to heal itself."

"You saved his life," I said, almost breathless. Replaying the memory, my chest warmed in a way I wouldn't have expected with him.

As he stood, he smirked. "You'd have had my head if I hadn't."

"That's not why you did it."

I didn't realize that I had been walking toward him until we stood toe to toe beside his desk. "Don't set unrealistic expectations of me, Morrigan," he pleaded. Reaching up, he tugged on a curl hanging over my shoulder. "I'm selfish. I don't do things out of the goodness of my heart like you do."

"You could have let him die," I argued.

But as his fingers brushed my chin, tilting it up to him, nerves flickered beneath my skin. "But then you wouldn't be looking at me like this... would you?" Leaning down, his nose brushed my cheek, the action making my breath shake slightly. "You have this effect on people, Morrigan. They *crave* your affection. I thought I had been immune to it."

"Eris," I warned.

"But just seeing that proud look in your eyes... I..."

Just as his lips grazed mine, the door to his study opened with a loud bang. "My Lord!" a guard yelled, causing Eris to shove me behind him. "There's been a breach!"

My mind quickly reverted back to the attacks and the man in the woods. *Have they come? Will this be the day they finally take me?* Looking up at Eris, I could see the wheels turning in his own eyes as he likely thought the same. When he turned to me, his brows formed a worried crease between them.

"Go to your room with Lyra and Eowyn. You will remain there until I come to your door, do you understand?"

I nodded. "Yes."

"Go. Now."

Without a second thought, I raced from the study and ran through the hall. I just needed to make it to the stairs and I knew that Lyra would be close. *I don't want to die. I don't want to die.* That's all I could think as I moved my feet. The castle had never felt larger than it did in that moment—like each hall began to stretch longer than they actually were.

I wanted to feel relief when I saw the stairs, but a hand tugged mine, twirling me until my back hit a wall, and my heart stopped.

"Morrigan!" a female whispered loudly.

After blinking a couple of times in complete disbelief, I looked up at the brown eyes staring back at me, her hair no longer braided as it normally was. "Lady... Lady Guinevere?"

What is she doing here?

"There's no time to explain," she rushed. "You need to come with me."

"Go with you? Go with you *where*?"

"Anywhere! I need to get you out of here. I'll find a place for us to hide. We can come up with a plan—"

"What are you even doing here?" I asked her. "They said you were on trial. How did you…" Based on the frantic movements of her eyes as she surveyed the halls around us, I realized quickly that *she* was the breach. "What have you done?"

"Morrigan, there's no time. I need you to trust me."

"Trust you?! You left me! You never came back!"

"I tried to—"

"If it hadn't been for Dez, who knows what Maeryn would have—"

"You can't trust them, Morrigan."

I scoffed at her oblivious accusation. "I can't trust *them*?"

"Don't you see?" Placing her hands on my arms, the lines on her face softened along with her eyes. "Morrigan… There's… There are things you don't know. Things *I* didn't know. Please… I'll tell you everything if you just come with me."

"Step back!" I instantly recognized Lyra's voice and looked over Guinevere's shoulder to see her standing with her sword pointed at us. "Step. Back. *Now*."

"I will not." I couldn't hold my surprise at the sudden switch in Guinevere's voice. "I won't let them have her." Guinevere slowly lifted a dagger from her side and aimed it at Lyra. "I won't let them turn her into some—"

Seeing my chance, I quickly sprung my hand out for the handle, taking the Lady by surprise. She had gone insane if she thought I would let her threaten Lyra in any way. Just as I distracted her, Lyra used it as an opportunity to attack from the side. Struggling against my hold, Guinevere yanked the knife from my hand, slicing it down my palm just as Lyra wrapped the sword around her front and held her back.

"How many more are there?" she hissed in Guinevere's ear.

But the lady had begun to cry now, staring at me in a way I couldn't quite understand. Why would she come here? She had to know that Eris wouldn't just let her take me. Why would I have wanted to leave? None of it made any sense.

"I'm sorry," she sobbed, dropping her knife to the floor. "I'm so sorry, Morrigan. I should have protected you. I should have...."

"How many more are there?!" Lyra pressed on.

The sound of heavy feet running came from beside us, and I turned to see Eris marching over with fury. He looked first at Guinevere, confused and angry, but when he turned to me, his eyes widened slightly when he looked down at my hand. Following his gaze, I realized that it had been dripping blood onto the floor.

"Take her away," Eris commanded Lyra. "I will question her after."

I watched Lyra drag away the Lady as she cried and pleaded, making my head reel with confusion. How had she even gotten into the castle?

"You're hurt," Eris whispered as he stopped at my side.

"I don't understand..."

"We will figure it all out. But first..." Lifting my hand to his lips, I watched his tongue slide along the palm of my hand and could feel the skin slowly stitching itself together again. But whatever blood I lost had me feeling dizzy already. I swayed a little, and Eris wrapped an arm around me to steady my legs. "Let me help you."

With a quick bite, he created a small wound in his wrist and brought it to my mouth. I didn't think twice as I drank it in, not focusing on just how good it tasted on my tongue. Guinevere's face was all I could see. As the warmth of his blood ran through my veins, a strong pull tethered around my chest. All thoughts of what had happened faded from my mind and I sucked harder, a natural instinct taking over.

"Take what you need," Eris whispered.

I took that and more. That was, until that tether recoiled and I felt an uncomfortable snap somewhere in my own mind. Scrambling back, I let go of his wrist and my head began spinning once more.

"Morrigan?" he asked, concerned.

"I don't... I don't feel..."

A wetness pooled above my lip, and I reached up to wipe it only to discover it was blood dripping from my nose.

"Morrigan?" That strange voice said. I hadn't heard it in so long, I thought I had rid myself of the hallucination. *"Morrigan."*

My head started to pound like drums in my ears, and before I could say another word, my body fell to the floor.

Chapter 33

I stood in a hallway made of the darkest stone I had ever
seen.

The only light emanated from the dimly lit torches
carefully perched along the wall. Between them were thick pockets of
darkness that gave the impression of eyes lurking within them, watching my
every move.

Reaching out, I brushed the tips of my fingers along the hard stone,
walking and allowing my arm to trace the wall with each step. I didn't
know where I was. I remembered fainting beside Eris after Lady Guinevere
had cornered me in the hallway. But nothing around me looked the
slightest bit familiar.

Looking down, my feet were bare. But the dress that I was wearing certainly didn't come from my closet. The black fabric hung loosely down my legs, almost touching the floor. It didn't have any designs on it, but it covered most of my arms as well. That's when I noticed the chill in the air. I could almost hear the whistle of the wind through the darkness in front of me, lightly brushing my hair back over my shoulders.

Something about this place felt cold, but not only in the literal sense. It ran deep into my soul, giving me a hollow loneliness... abandonment—like all of my happiness had been drained and only the worst parts of myself were left behind. But underneath it all was a... familiarity.

When the hallway came to an end, I entered a large room with much more light illuminating the empty space. At the far back sat a large throne. The room had vague similarities to the throne room of my Unveiling. But there was something different about this one.

Approaching it with caution, I noticed that the arms were a dirty off-white, and there were almost hundreds of the same type of material structuring the rest of the chair. It wasn't until I stood before it that I realized they were bones. The throne had been formed by bones.

"What are you doing here?" I recognized the voice instantly and turned, facing the source of my hallucinations.

"I must be dreaming," I whispered.

Standing in the center of the room was a man as tall as Kaiden. His shirt and pants were a darker black than my dress, and a mask, also carved of bone, covered the top half of his face. A dark shadow was cast over his eyes, concealing them completely.

He took a step toward me, and I couldn't help but retreat with one of my own. "How are you doing this?" he asked.

I didn't understand his questions. It wasn't like I had control over my own dreams. This place wasn't real and neither was he. "*I want to wake up. How do I wake up?*"

Even beneath the mask, I could almost see his face contorting in confusion. When he took another step, the back of my ankle hit the leg of the throne, causing me to stand still. "You don't know how many times I've dreamed of seeing you like this."

Dream? How could he dream? "*I don't understand. Who are you?*"

As he stepped onto the platform, I felt too scared to move aside. No... I wasn't scared... But I should *have been. "You've known me for a long time, Morrigan." The usual distortion disappeared and when I recognized his voice, it felt like the room had suffocated every bit of oxygen that remained in my lungs.*

My dreams... That was the same voice from my dreams... Had it been my own subconscious the entire time? Had I created this... being *as a way to protect myself? "I've never* seen *you, though. Why am I seeing you? You aren't* real.*"*

Lifting his hand, I gasped when I felt his cold skin touch my cheek. "Do I not *feel real?" he whispered.*

Nothing in my dreams had ever felt so... solid. *But it couldn't be possible. He was merely a hallucination that my mind had created from whatever was wrong with me. My nose had been bleeding when I passed out. Something had likely happened and Eris would be with a priest, healing me as this transpired.*

"Something is different about you," he said quietly, letting his hand trail down to a curl hanging over my chest. "Your skin is hot..."

I felt silly as I laughed at him. "Why is that weird?" If I was *dreaming, there had been no point in fighting it. I would wake soon, in my bed, with Lyra or Eowyn at my side.*

"What are they doing to you?" As the question left his lips, a sharp, icy sensation crawled its way to my chest. It felt eerily similar to my encounter with Guinevere.

"I'd like to wake up now…" Stepping to the side, I removed myself from his grasp and made my way down the platform, but he grabbed my wrist, turning me toward him again.

"Don't you see?" he asked.

"Please…" I pleaded silently. "Just let me go. I want to wake up."

With a sigh, he nodded and reached into his breast pocket, before pulling out a flower. A daisy. Placing it into my palm, he closed my fingers over it and wrapped my fist tightly. Then, his palm touched the side of my head, covering my temple.

"See for yourself," he whispered.

Darkness swirled around me, blurring the images and contorting them into mist as my vision went black. But through the shadows, I could hear the remnants of a whisper in the air.

"I'll be waiting for you."

"She's waking up!" I heard as I willed my eyes to open.

Someone shuffled around quickly, stopping beside me, and I woke to see Dez leaning over my bed. "Are you okay?" he asked breathlessly.

Narrowing my eyes, I tried pulling myself from the fog of the dream I had, trying to understand why Dez was here to begin with. "I'm fine," I grunted, pushing myself up to sit.

I lifted my hand to my nose, feeling for where the blood had fallen, but it was clean now. "All of us came as soon as we heard. By the time the priest arrived, you were already healed from Eris's blood still in your system." Dez's lips pressed together quickly as his face fell.

"What happened? Where is Lady Guinevere?"

"They brought her back to the palace..." he answered carefully. "Princess... she..."

A rush of nerves hit me and I shoved the blankets away, making my way to stand, but Dez tried to stop me. "I need to see her," I insisted.

"Rest first... *Please*." Dez looked up at me with his soft, blue eyes. "Morrigan, you were convulsing. Eris said he could barely keep control of your body with how violently it shook. It lasted for thirty straight minutes before you finally stopped."

I didn't know what that meant, but I knew it wasn't good. Politely pulling him off of me, I shook my head and walked toward the bathroom. "I *need* to see her."

Next, I walked to my closet and snatched a simple gown before returning to my bed. "You need to sleep, Morrigan," Dez continued.

"I will sleep after I speak to Lady Guinevere."

Something about my interaction with her left me with an unsettling feeling in my gut. And then that dream...

"You're not going anywhere."

The tone in his voice had me pausing where I stood. Turning my head slowly in his direction, I glared at him with a newfound irritation that I wasn't used to feeling around him. "What are you going to do, Dez?" I asked him quietly. "*Compel* me?"

He visibly flinched at the question and relaxed his shoulders, in a clear display of surrender. "We can go see her, but not *now*." Taking the dress from my hand, he laid it out across the bed. "Eat first... *please*. There will be a... trial... of sorts tonight. Only then can you see her."

"A trial?" I scoffed. "A trial for what?"

They were acting as if she had kidnapped me and threatened my life. The cut on my hand was from my own doing by grabbing that dagger. Yes, she had broken into his palace, but a *trial* for that?

"Morrigan…" Dez whispered. Reaching out, he placed his hand on mine. "Guinevere… She killed a priest when she escaped the palace."

My head reeled. Guinevere… She wouldn't have… "No…"

Stumbling back, my hand hit the pillar of my bed and something fell from my gown. When I looked down, a smushed, vibrant daisy lay on the floor. The exact same daisy that… *he* placed in my palm in my dream. My dream.

It wasn't a dream….

What is happening to me?

Making my way downstairs, I found them all in the dining room.

My feet felt numb as I walked. Nothing felt real. The dream that *was* a dream apparently *wasn't* a dream. And with the way he spoke of them… and then Guinevere… It's like a piece had been missing from the entire story. Even with Dez walking beside me, an uneasiness lingered in the air where there had once been a complete sense of security.

"What are they doing to you?"

What did he mean? Who *was* he? And why have I heard his voice in my dreams for the past ten years or so? The conversation turned into yelling and multiple voices began arguing. Though, I couldn't distinguish between them or make out the words that were being spewed. Everything moved in utter slow motion.

As I entered the room, the yelling ceased and I rolled my eyes. "I'm getting really tired of that," I mumbled, keeping my head down as I walked to my seat.

Before I could sit, Kaiden's large hand wrapped around my arm and stopped me. "Why was your nose bleeding, Morrigan?" he asked in an almost snarl.

Why did it always feel like such an accusation when he spoke to me? I could get stabbed in my chest and Kaiden would ask me why I allowed myself to bleed. Leering at him, I squinted my eyes and pulled at my arm. "How should *I* know that, Kaiden? I'm not a priestess." Attempting to yank again, his fingers dug deeper in response. "Maybe you should have brought your *whore. She* could have looked me over for you."

Anger flashed over his eyes in the form of shadows, swirling in a way I had never seen before. "Watch your tongue," he warned.

I couldn't stop the laughter from leaving my lips with sarcasm tainting every bit of the sound. "I'm sorry. Was that rude? I must have forgotten my manners. Actually…" With my own anger driving my impulsive thoughts, I began tugging at the fabric on my shoulder to push it down. "I have quite a few things I would *love* for her to heal…"

But Kaiden's other hand stopped me from continuing and his eyes looked almost completely black now. Just beneath his shirt hovered a vague depiction of shadows, rising from the markings on his skin.

"You can speak about Maeryn however you'd like," he whispered. "But you will *not* disrespect me and act as if you know *anything* about me." Flicking his eyes to the chair beside me, he let go of my arm and curled his lips. "Now sit and eat."

I wanted to continue to fight him, but my body seemed to comply on its own. Sitting down, my eyes rolled when he lowered himself beside me. I didn't understand what had taken over Kaiden in the months since my arrival. He went from wanting the most distance between us to being the only one still willing to give me commands. It should have angered me, but a part of me needed it. Even if it was rooted in anger, arguing with Kaiden sometimes felt more real than any of the interactions I had with the rest of the lords.

A couple of hours, I thought to myself.

In a couple of hours I had a feeling secrets would be revealed that would change everything for the worse. She killed a *priest*. Killing a priest was an offense answered only with execution.

They were going to kill Guinevere...

But not until I got the answers that I needed, first.

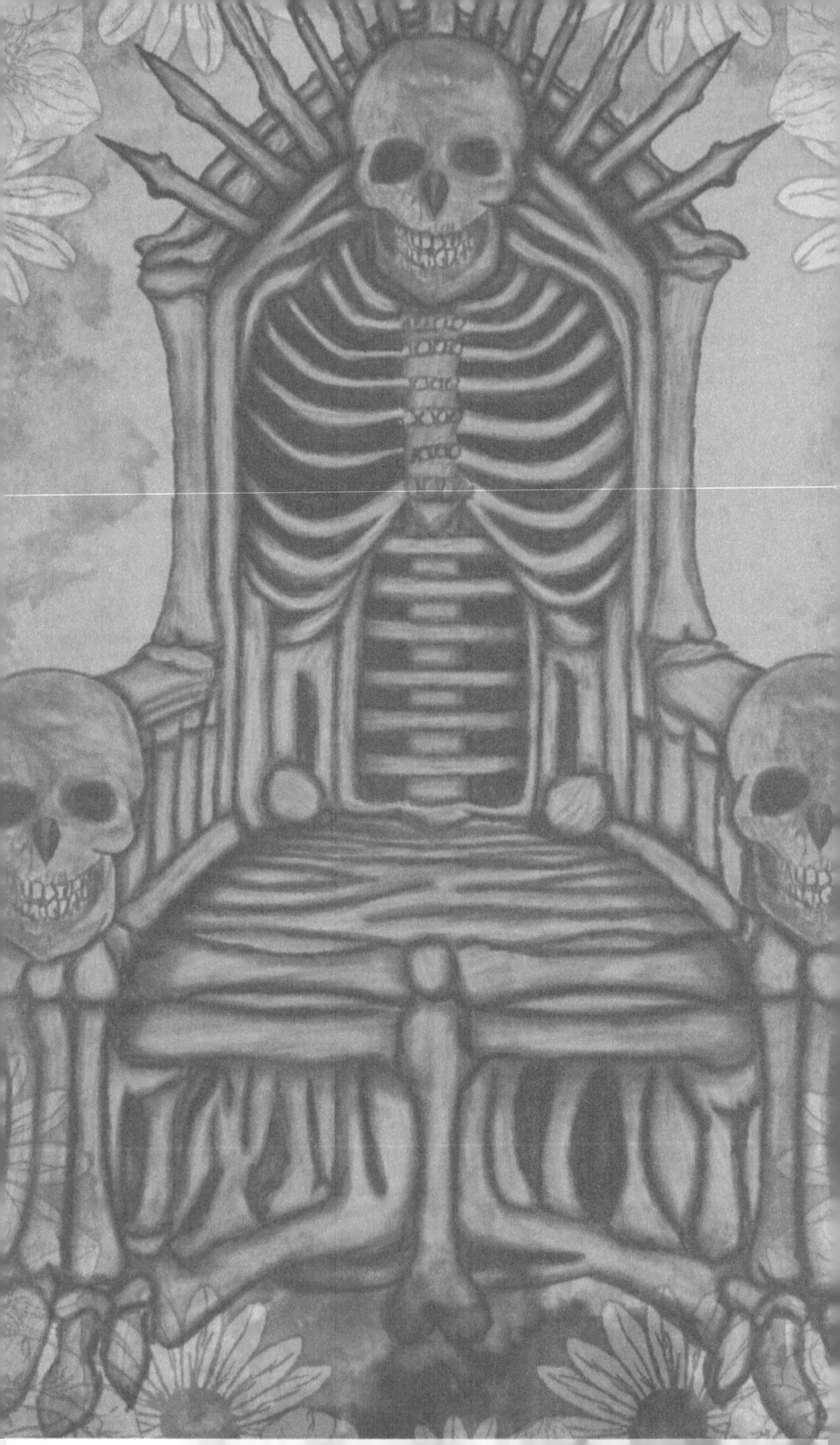

The Diary of Daisies and Hellebores

It has been a couple of months now, and I believe their suspicions have died down. If they haven't, they do not speak of it. He told me that he loved me today, and I said it back. Three words that cannot be rescinded, three dangerous words that could bring the end of us.

He is a different person when he's with me, so kind and gentle.

He's never like that with the others.

Chapter 34

We all made our way to the courtyard, each of the lords standing beside their shadow walkers.

Kaiden stood alone, confirming the theory I had already calculated over my time here—that was *his* unique gift. Bypassing Cass, Dez and Eris, I stopped in front of him, waiting for his attention.

"Can I help you?" he asked.

"Will *she* be there?"

His pupils unfocused before nodding curtly.

Pressing my lips together, I began turning but stopped midway and faced him once more. "Why?"

He looked puzzled as he tilted his head. "She's a priestess, so she's expected to—"

"Why *her*?" I clarified. "I know you hate me and I know you want no part in any of this, but you *know* what she's done. You know *who* she is."

Instead of responding, he simply stared at me—eyes an empty black void like they always had been. They held no emotion or remorse or even an inkling of compassion, and I wasn't sure why I expected them to. This was Kaiden—an open book devoid of any feelings for anyone else but himself.

"Don't you see?"

They both had said that to me. Guinevere and... whoever *he* was.

See what?

Before Kaiden could disappoint me further, I walked to Eris and let Newt take us to the palace.

The guys all insisted that they come with me. Even Kaiden. And as we arrived, I noticed an older priest waiting at the palace doors, clearly expecting our arrival. I let go of Newt, and Lyra stepped beside me, placing a pair of white gloves into my hands, bringing an instant smile to my face.

"What would I do without you, Lyra?"

With a solemn grin, she shoved her shoulder with mine. "Pray to the Gods that you never have to find out."

"I'll meet you all inside," Kaiden mumbled and pushed his way toward the doors, disappearing into the shadows.

Have fun with Maeryn, I hissed in my own mind, praying the wind would drag my words to Kaiden and bite him in the ass.

The palace stood almost as tall as the lords' castles, made of a dull grey stone, stretching up through the clouds. Cracked rocks lined the pathway toward the towering, golden doors engraved with symbols of the gods. "Princess," the old priest called. "We are grateful for your visit."

"I'm not here for you," I blurted without thinking.

Lyra nearly chuckled beside me but the lords all looked tense. With a nod, the priest motioned with his hands for us to enter. "I shall escort you, then."

Walking inside, we were passed by several priests and priestesses as we roamed the halls. There were even young children assisting the staff—orphans, I assumed them to be, just like the guys were. I slowed my steps until I fell into rhythm with Dez.

"How many are there?" I asked him.

"Each palace holds close to fifty priests and priestesses," he answered quietly.

"*That many?*"

He nodded. "They were created during the war. When we realized we were losing more than we were killing, the gods blessed them to help heal the injured. Some even fought alongside us."

"And now?" I asked. They weren't immortal in the same sense that Dez or the other lords were. Their aging was much slower, but they *did* die.

"Now, only the purest souls are chosen to be blessed. The elders of each palace select them, and they devote their lives to serving the gods on Earth."

With no sign of Kaiden still, I buried away my anger toward him. He made his choice. He had always chosen her. He didn't know me and I didn't want to know *him*. So, to fill the silence in my own head, I counted my steps as we walked behind the priest. I just needed to speak to Guinevere. She couldn't have killed anyone. It wasn't in her. Maybe she had been confused. Something *had* to have happened.

Nothing... *None* of this made sense.

At the end of the long hall were two large wooden doors. My pulse quickened as he opened them slowly. The room inside was larger than I expected it to be. Rows and columns of seats trailed up the walls in a circle, making the room feel like it intended to smother us. Seated were hundreds of priests and priestesses from every palace.

This doesn't look good.

At the center of the room sat a large platform with two people standing, waiting. As we approached, I could make out a tall, older priest, and beside him... My feet stumbled beneath me and Dez had to catch my elbow to keep me standing upright. Maeryn stood on the platform, with a large grin on her face... the same one that had haunted me for years.

"She doesn't get that satisfaction, Morrigan," Dez whispered in my ear. "Stand up straight and look her in the eyes as you walk."

Locking my gaze with hers, I continued stepping forward, a deep rage boiling in my stomach as her smirk grew even more sinister. But before we reached the platform, my arm was yanked to the side, removing me from our group. Looking up, I saw Kaiden with an expression that I couldn't quite place. When he finally stopped, I saw the first flicker of emotion in his eyes that I had ever truly seen.

And it almost frightened me.

"We need to talk. Now," he said quietly.

I tried pulling my arm free of him, but he held strong. "Now isn't the time, Kaiden. Let me go."

"Morrigan, I need to tell you something. It can't wait."

"Why is it 'Morrigan' all of a sudden?" I scoffed. "What happened to your impertinent pet names? And where *were* you?" Looking over my shoulder, I found that Maeryn continued smiling at us. "Wow, Kaiden. I must say, I'm impressed with your speed. Are you sure you don't want another round at it—"

He shook me, interrupting what I wanted to say and stepped closer. "You need to *listen* to me," he hissed.

Harley stepped beside us and I couldn't hide my shock at him being here as well. "Kaiden," he warned. "You're making a scene, boy. We can discuss whatever it is when this is over."

"What are you doing here?" I asked Harley.

"I came for you." One of the guys must have told Harley what was happening, and he came to support me. I wanted to hug him out of gratitude, but Kaiden wouldn't let me move an inch.

"Harley," Kaiden swallowed, "you need to take her. Get her out of here."

"I'm not going anywhere! I need to speak with—"

"Morrigan please! Just listen to me this once!"

I finally removed myself from his grasp. "I'm not going anywhere."

"Harley," Kaiden pleaded. I've never known him to beg, and—if I'm being honest—it wasn't his best look. "She can't be here."

"What did she say to you?" Narrowing my eyes at him, I paused when I noticed that his were filled with a sympathy that made my breath feel the slightest bit heavier.

This wasn't Kaiden. A complete stranger stood before me right now.

"We really must proceed now, and the princess is as much a part of this as anyone else," the old man said from beside Maeryn.

I turned away and walked toward Dez and Lyra, moving to stand between them. At the side of the room, Kaiden and Harley continued arguing and I did my best to tune them out.

"Let's begin," the priest announced, causing a hush to crash around in a silent wave.

Two priests walked out from a door on the side, one of them with a rope in his hands. And connected to that rope was Lady Guinevere, tied by her wrists and ankles as they pulled her to the platform. Instinctively, I moved to run toward her, but Dez stopped me.

When she made it to the steps, our eyes met and hers widened in terror. "Don't make her watch this!" she begged. "Please!"

Maeryn ignored her, and I pushed my way to the front, keeping my eyes trained on the Lady as she stood beside the priest at the center. "Lady..." I pleaded quietly. "Tell me it isn't true. Please. You have to tell them who did it."

Slow tears fell from her eyes as she looked down at me. "I... I don't know what happened, Morrigan. I swear. I blacked out and I—"

"What proof do you have that she killed anyone?" I turned my rage to the priest, ignoring Maeryn's penetrating glare.

Smiling with a false sense of apology, he pulled out a familiar looking plant, displaying it for everyone to see. "The priest had been poisoned, and this was found in her belongings as she tried to escape the palace."

Hellebore....

Hellebore no longer grew anywhere in the kingdom. The only people that were known to have it were the... Looking back up, I could barely hide the horror on my face. Was she with them? Did she help poison Cass that night?

"Tell me they're wrong," I begged. "Tell me you weren't behind this... *All* of this."

"Mor, please..." she began to speak, but Maeryn interrupted.

"I think we are leaving out an incredibly important piece of information." My eyes drifted to her, stinging from the tears I had been forcefully holding back. Stepping forward, her smile grew larger as she watched me. "She had one more motive that solidifies our judgment. The entire *reason* she was being held in the first place." Pulling on Guinevere's ropes, the Lady stumbled toward her. "Are you going to tell her, or shall I?"

"Maeryn, I'm begging you. Just let her leave," she cried.

So many emotions filled my chest as I looked between them. I didn't understand what was happening or what it had to do with me. I couldn't wrap my head around what could cause Lady Guinevere to do any of these things, and I still wasn't sure I believed it.

Clicking her tongue, Maeryn shook her head. "You see, Lady Guinevere had been in our service for years. She pledged her life to us. She had even been chosen to be blessed and become a priestess herself." She turned eerily slow toward the Lady. "But you had a secret, didn't you?"

"Ernmas?" Harley suddenly appeared beside me, staring in confusion at the women.

"What?" I asked him.

But Harley's eyes were glued to Lady Guinevere. "I don't understand. What's happening? Who is Guinevere?" he asked her.

My brows furrowed as I watched the both of them, but Lady Guinevere wouldn't look at Harley. Her glassy eyes remained on me.

That's when Maeryn began to laugh hysterically. "Everything is making so much sense now!" she exclaimed. "She hid it well from us. No one knew the entire time. Clearly not even *you*, Harley. We never would have known if she hadn't chosen to write to you one night." Pulling a piece of paper from her robes, she held it out in front of her to read, but she looked at me instead. "Let me start with the forgiveness that I'll never be able to earn… *My daughter.*"

My daughter.

My daughter?

My eyes widened painfully as I gaped at her. At Lady Guinevere. No. That wasn't right. She wasn't… She was…

"Mom?"

The sounds around me were quickly muffled like the room had submerged in water. The only thing filtering through my ears was a ringing that wouldn't stop. Voices around me were stifled, but they were yelling, I knew that much. But everyone sounded so far away as I stared into the eyes of the woman who raised me. The woman who I *thought* had abandoned me. The woman who watched every time Maeryn left a new scar on my back. And the same woman who lulled me to sleep after every nightmare.

My mother.

She was my *mother*.

Hands touched my arms, and I guessed that they were Lyra's. She tried pulling me toward her, but I wouldn't budge.

When I turned toward Harley, I realized that he too was staring at me. His blue eyes looked pale in comparison to the deep sapphire that usually shone. In that moment, something clicked between us, and the shock of it caused me to stumble back into another person's arms. I was going to be sick. Somehow the world stood still but every part of me seemed to fall apart at once.

Harley mouthed something to me, but I couldn't hear him. The only voice that slipped through the madness that had erupted was Maeryn's. "So, which is it? Guinevere or Ernmas?" she laughed.

Turning back toward my mother, I watched as she cried, barely holding herself up with the priests clinging to her arms. *"Don't you see?"*

Oh Gods... I could see it now. I could see our resemblance. I could see our connection. My nose... My cheeks... They were all mirrored back at me in her face. And Harley's eyes... His smile...

"I think we've all seen and *heard* enough," the older priest announced. "Lady Guinevere, you have been accused and found guilty of, not only killing a priest, but committing treason against Andonia by organizing attacks against our lords and conspiring to abduct the future Queen. The punishment for these crimes is death."

"Wait..." I said quietly, moving slowly toward them. I was still trying to sort out the noises happening around me, but I could hear his plain as day.

"May the goddess Minerva seek mercy on your soul and grant you entrance to Eden, in spite of your crimes." Nausea churned in my stomach, but I redirected all of my strength to my feet, which felt heavy with dread.

"Wait!" I yelled.

No one acknowledged me, and both priests pushed my mother onto her knees. *My mother.* Maeryn held a dagger in her hand beside them and my eyes widened. *Run,* I yelled at myself, *Stop them*. But Cain wrapped a hand around my arm and shook his head.

"You can't stop them, Princess, it's their laws. We cannot intervene," he warned.

"Let me go!" I screamed at him, trying to pull away. Turning back to the stage, I knew I couldn't hold them any longer—the tears began to burst from my eyes. "Please, just wait!" I called to them, *begging* them.

"You may say your last words," the priest said to her.

"Please, just let me go," I cried to Cain.

"I can't do that."

"I'm sorry," my mother said to me. She had stopped crying by now as she stared into my eyes. I saw the love on her face, the only love I had known for twenty-one years. Her lullaby played in my head, the only sound that soothed me through my nightmares. When she looked at Harley, I saw, then, the acceptance of her fate. "Keep her safe, Harley. Don't let them hurt her."

Maeryn stood behind her, a hand wrapped in Guinevere's hair as she yanked her head back. "Mom!" I yelled.

When Maeryn looked down at me, I jerked my arm free from Cain and ran. It took only ten steps for me to reach the platform. And just as my hand touched the wood, Maeryn smiled and slid the dagger across my mother's throat.

And I fell to my knees.

Chapter 35

I screamed.

I screamed louder than I had ever thought was possible. I screamed until my throat burned like my vocal chords were being ripped apart. I screamed until every sound in my body had forsaken me and held my chest as I felt my heart breaking. The rageful tears that fell from my eyes stung like they had burst into flames and burned my skin as they slid down my cheeks.

Guinevere's body fell over, and I watched Maeryn use her foot to push her over the ledge until her limp body landed in front of me. The dagger Maeryn had used fell beside Guinevere, drenched in her blood.

Gathering every ounce of energy I had left, I crawled to her on shaky hands until her blood coated the tips of my fingers. I pulled her into my lap and continued to sob at the weight of her body, and her arm dangling onto the stone floor. Sniffling, I covered her neck as best as I could with my hand. "Eris!" I called, my voice shaking and my throat raw from screaming. "Fix her! You have to fix her!"

He looked at me and his eyes glistened with tears that even *he* seemed to be holding back. "I can't..."

"Yes you can! I *know* you can!" I yelled at him. "I've seen you do it, Eris! Fix her, please!"

"Morrigan..." A soft hand touched my shoulder. "Even if he could, we aren't allowed to interfere," Dez whispered.

They were wasting time. "Fix her!" I screamed. "Please don't do this to me!"

When he shook his head again, I looked down, unable to see my mother through my own tears. "She's dead, Morrigan," Dez spoke again.

The color had almost drained completely from her face. And that's when a different thought occurred to me. I had healed Cass. If I could heal Cass from the brink of death, maybe I could...

I didn't hesitate as I snatched the dagger off of the floor and sliced my own palm, barely flinching from the pain. The moment blood pooled in my hand, I balled it into a fist and tipped it over Guinevere's mouth.

"Come on," I mumbled. "Wake up... Just wake up." Someone grabbed my wrist, attempting to stop me, but I yanked it back. "Wake up!"

She still wouldn't move. Grabbing her face with both hands, I shook it violently.

"JUST WAKE UP!" I screamed.

Someone pulled my arm away again and I looked up to see Kaiden trying to move me away from her. He wrapped a cloth around my hand as I tried to scramble to Guinevere, but he forced me to look at him as he held me back.

"Morrigan! She's *dead*!" he yelled at me. "Look at her! You have to stop!"

But when I turned, the only person I saw was Maeryn as she walked down the steps of the platform—a smirk on her face that made my skin crawl. My own fury blinded me. Blacked out with rage, I gripped the dagger once more, slipping from Kaiden's hold for just a moment as I aimed it at her. But he was quicker than me. His arms wrapped around my waist and held me as I kicked and screamed, slashing at Maeryn.

"I'm going to kill you!" I swore.

I tried breaking free of his hold, but he was too strong. When I threw the dagger at her, she quickly stepped to the side, eyes wide as she barely escaped the impact. She turned to me, horror reflected in her wild stare.

"Good," I snarled. "Look at me. Remember my eyes... Take in every detail, Maeryn. This will be the last face you see when you die, you evil piece of shit!"

Though she laughed, the nervous tremble couldn't be missed as she looked at the priest standing on the platform, but no one came to her aid. Kaiden pulled me closer to him, and he held me until I stopped resisting. Eventually, my fight ended, and the weight of my body fell to his arms.

As he pressed me into his chest, I cried. I cried until I drained my body of its last drop of water. I didn't look at my mother again... I *couldn't*. But I heard Kaiden tell someone, "Take her away."

For a moment, I had forgotten that there were other people there. Footsteps rushed around us as people began leaving, but I didn't want to move. I cradled my head into Kaiden's chest, not caring that it was *him* that held me. I needed grounding... comfort. I needed someone to take all of the fucking pain away that had my head ready to explode.

Someone approached us, but Kaiden's hand went out to stop them. "Not now, Harley..." he said quietly. "Give her some space."

When the footsteps retreated, the room fell into complete, suffocating silence. And I realized that Kaiden and I were the only ones left. The only sound was Kaiden's heartbeat against my ear and our breathing that had somehow synced together.

"Morrigan," Kaiden whispered, moving me until one of his arms slipped under my knees. "Let's get you home, okay?"

Assuming he was going to make me stand, I clutched tighter against him, clinging to his shirt. "Don't," I rasped. "Don't put me down. Don't make me…"

"Shhh," as he stood, he brought me with him and held me in his arms. "I've got you, little dove."

I kept my head hidden in his chest, not wanting to speak to anyone… I didn't want to *see* anyone. The image of Guinevere's body covered in her own blood is all my mind would allow me to witness. Stepping outside, the cold whip of the air made my skin prickle, and Kaiden held me closer.

"I can take her," Dez offered.

"You will not touch her."

No one argued with Kaiden. I felt the familiar lick of shadows against my skin and assumed—at some point—we had arrived back at Eris's castle. Eris tried to intervene, but Kaiden continued walking until we made our way inside and up the stairs.

"Keep her safe, Harley."

… *Her blood sliding down her neck… onto her gown…*

… *Her body falling to the floor, and the sound her head made as it connected with the stone…*

"Oh my… Morrigan!" Eowyn cried, telling me we had stopped at my room.

"Draw her a bath," Kaiden ordered her. Walking us both inside, he began to set me down and panic rose in my chest. I shook my head frantically. "We need to get you out of these clothes, dove. You have to let me put you down."

Lowering me once more, I avoided looking his way as he walked into the bathing room. Instead, I turned to see the standing mirror that hung beside my closet door. My hair had fallen from its pins and the ivory dress I wore now looked like it had been painted a deep maroon. Caked in both fresh *and* dried blood, the soft fabric pressed stiffly against itself. I lifted my gaze to my face and a small drop of blood clung to the top part of my cheek. I tried wiping it, but my fingers left a larger smear of crimson, and I realized my hands were also covered in blood.

Panicking, I searched for a piece of cloth to wipe them and started scrubbing my palms. *Get it off. Get it off of me.* It worked for a moment, until the cloth was suddenly drenched. But I couldn't stop. I couldn't stop scraping it against my hand, scratching it and causing more blood to smear all over my skin. Why wouldn't it go away? *Just go away!*

At the sound of my panic, Kaiden quickly emerged from the bathing room and ran over to me. He ripped the blood-soaked fabric from my hands and I stared down at them in shock. "It won't come off," I cried. "Get it off, Kaiden! Get it off!"

As I sobbed, our eyes finally met, and the smallest speck of color appeared in them for the first time. His eyes... They weren't black... They were *brown*. Had his eyes always been brown?

"Please, Kaiden," I begged him. "Get it off of me. I can't stand it anymore. Get it off!"

With his hand around my wrist, he dragged me to the bathing room and sat me down in a chair. Eowyn rushed inside, but my own shame and fear prevented me from looking her way. I didn't want to know how she saw me. I didn't want to see her face as she took in the blood that covered my body.

That's when I began to shake. It started in my hands, then stretched to my arms and legs. Even my heart raced, making my chest shudder in pain. "I can't…" I panted. "I can't breathe… I can't breathe…"

"Morrigan," Eowyn cried.

"Get out!" he yelled. After Kaiden turned back to me, his voice softened. "You're having a panic attack, Morrigan. I need you to breathe."

"I can't… I can't…"

Taking my hand, he placed it against his chest and inhaled deeply. "Breathe with me, little dove. I need you to breathe with me."

Choking on my sobs, I closed my eyes and tried to focus on his breaths. *Blood. So much blood. All over me. Her blood. My mother's blood.*

"Come back, Morrigan. Feel my breath. Feel my heart."

Kaiden… Kaiden's breathing…

I forced my lungs to mimic his, squeezing my eyes tighter in hopes that it would drown out my own thoughts. I needed him to keep speaking. I needed him to distract me.

"I'm with you, little dove. I'm breathing with you. Do you feel it?" he asked quietly.

I did. Slowly, the heaviness in my chest lightened and I could feel my lungs beginning to open. After a few, deep breaths, the trembling began to cease in my arms. And when I opened my eyes, Kaiden stared back at me as he lifted a wet cloth to my face, wiping it.

He cleaned every inch and wet the cloth in a bucket before lowering it to my hands. We said nothing to each other as he washed them, making sure he didn't leave a single red spot behind. Who was this person? The way he touched me… the tenderness of it. I should have stopped him. I should have insisted that Eowyn be brought back in to help… But I couldn't. I realized then that I didn't *want* anyone else to help me.

Motioning to the bath, he kept his hands on mine before asking, "Do you want me to get Eowyn?"

I shook my head. I couldn't face anyone else right now. My world had been shattered into oblivion and Kaiden was the only thing holding me together somehow. After he stood, he helped me up and turned me around. As he pulled the strings to my dress, he hesitated before pulling it down, allowing me to step out of it.

"Morrigan..." he whispered.

For all of the threats we had made to each other, this was the first time that he had seen my scars—proof of what Maeryn had done to me. *His* Maeryn. I wanted him to look. I wanted him to see it. Truly *see* it.

Finally, I sank into the bath, and Kaiden sat in a chair as I began to clean myself. We continued our mutual silence through it all, but his presence alone seemed to chase away my mind from attacking me any further. And when I was as clean as I could be, he wrapped the robe around me.

I didn't bother dressing myself. My feet were numb while walking toward my bed, and I climbed in, still soaked from the bath. The sheets clung to my skin and I let my head fall onto my pillow, heavy and tired. To my surprise, I felt a dip beside me. He said nothing as he pulled me into his side, resting my head onto his chest, like he needed this as much as I did.

When he moved the blankets over us both, he finally whispered, "I didn't know."

I stayed still, unable to move my body anymore, and closed my eyes, listening to the thrumming of his heart.

"I mean... I *knew*, but I didn't... I didn't know just how bad it was until Dez kicked her out." Exhaustion had kicked in and my body felt drunk as it tried its best to slip into a deep sleep. "I was wrong, Morrigan. So fucking wrong."

Chapter 36

lood.

It's all I could see in front of me. Blood falling from her neck... The sound it made... I couldn't stop hearing the sound. It came from everywhere around me.

"Morrigan, you're dreaming," he said to me.

I knew he was here. I could feel him now. I couldn't do that before.

"I just wanted to protect you," Guinevere whispered eerily. It was her voice but also... wasn't.

"I'm sorry." My cheeks were wet with tears that wouldn't stop falling. "I'm so sorry."

"Morrigan, this isn't real," he said again. "Wake up."

But I shook my head. I didn't want to. This was my fault. If I had just gone with her... "I didn't know," I needed to convince her. "If I had known... I'm so fucking sorry."

I woke up in a fit of sweat, panting as I struggled to catch my breath. Kaiden had left at some point in the night, but Eowyn slept nearby, curled up in a chair. Trying not to wake her, I crept out of bed to run some cold water over my face. But as I threw my legs over the side, she startled awake and quickly stood to help me as if she hadn't just been sleeping.

"Let me help you," she insisted. The skin beneath her eyes was dark and sunken in, indicating the lack of sleep she must have gotten the night before. *My fault.*

"I'm alright... I can—"

"Would you like a bath? Some water? I can run to the kitchen and grab you—"

"Eowyn," I stopped her. With wide and pleading eyes, she looked at me for some kind of direction—any way that she could make this better. But she *couldn't*. "I would just like to get dressed."

"Of course," she said quickly before running to the closet to pick a gown.

I stayed silent as Eowyn helped me dress, and Lyra met me in the hallway when I decided to make my way downstairs. She immediately straightened her back and sucked in a sharp breath. "Morrigan... Are you alright?"

When she reached out, my feet retreated back on instinct. I didn't even mean to. But as her face fell from my rejection, my heart flinched slightly in my chest. *My fault.* "I'm sorry... I..."

"Don't apologize, Morrigan. You have nothing to be sorry for," she tried assuring me. She didn't know just how wrong she was.

We walked down the stairs, and once again, the guys were arguing in the dining hall. It seemed to be all they did nowadays. I had no doubt that Kaiden was in attendance, the source of everyone's anger. This time, they didn't stop when I entered.

Tuning out any noise they were making, I walked slowly toward my chair beside Eris. And only once I sat down, scooting it across the marble floor, did everyone's yelling cease. All eyes turned to me in a loud silence that made me want to light myself on fire.

"Princess…" Dez began.

"Don't ask me if I'm okay, Dez." Picking up my glass of water, I took a long sip, feeling the burn as it slid down my torn throat.

Kaiden's stare all but scratched its way through the side of my face, but I couldn't bring myself to look at him. How could I? He carried me from the palace, washed me, and then stayed beside me as I slept. It only made me all the more confused and I didn't have the emotional capacity to figure that out right now.

"Morrigan," Cass called quietly. "No one should have to see—"

"I don't want to talk about it, Cassius."

I felt Eris's hand touch mine. "If you shut down, it will only feel—"

"Stop… speaking…"

"Princess—"

"What did you do?!" I screamed, slamming my hands onto the table. The chill that ran through my palms now burned against the wood beneath them. "You did nothing! You did *nothing* to stop them! Nothing to help me! I watched my mo—" My voice cracked on the word. "I watched Lady Guinevere bleed out in front of me and none of you—You let her *die*! You all watched her die!"

"Morrigan," Kaiden whispered, placing a hand on my shoulder, but I shoved myself away from it.

"Don't pretend to care, Kaiden," I hissed under my breath. "You don't get to speak to me the way that you have this *entire* time, just to come in as some savior in my time of need. My scars run far deeper than the ones you got to see. *She* caused them. And *you* stopped me from ending it."

Sitting down again, I let out a slow breath and tried to calm the anger that had my head throbbing.

"I would like for you all to leave," I announced loudly. The entire room fell silent in response. And one by one, each of the men left the dining hall—all but Kaiden who remained standing behind my chair.

"That includes you," Eris said to him.

The tension was thick as his feet padded against the floor, toward the doors. I didn't need to be confused. Kaiden and I weren't friends. He *hated* me. And I needed it to stay that way. Because the people I thought had cared for me, sat by and listened to me scream, covered in Guinevere's blood. I meant nothing to them. This meant nothing anymore.

Eris remained quiet and didn't touch his food. Neither did I. We just sat together, listening to the sound of each other breathing until one of his staff came to clear away our plates.

My fault...

It was my *fault.*

I didn't watch as he left; I just waited for the sound of the doors closing and let out a ragged breath. Leaning back in my chair, I stared at the table, letting the lines and colors blur as I unfocused my eyes—looking for any escape that my mind was willing to provide.

Time seemed to blend itself together, and my fourth week passed me by in a blur.

Harley was gone. He didn't even take the time to collect his belongings. I didn't blame him, though. He didn't sign up for any of this. He didn't even know... How could he have known? Eris agreed for Naaz to take over with my lessons, but I paid little attention to them.

I couldn't stop seeing her.

Sometimes, I would walk by a window and see her shadow in the withered gardens outside. My dreams were reoccurring nightmares of her death, an endless loop that even *he* couldn't help me escape from. But it wasn't from lack of trying. As I'd lay there, screaming with Guinevere in my arms, I would hear *him* calling to me—begging for me to wake up.

I didn't understand why he cared so much.

Gods... Listen to me. He couldn't have actually been *real*.

But the flower...

"That's your third glass this morning," Naaz noted, eyeing the wine in my hand.

"Your point is?"

Rolling his eyes, he closed the book that he had been reading from. "Do you remember what we discussed earlier this week? The concept of *spiraling*?"

Everyone had far too many opinions on how I should have been handling my emotions. Lyra scolded me during our target practice, Eowyn kept forcing me to take walks outside... They weren't the ones hallucinating their dead mother in every corner of the castle.

"Morrigan... This isn't healthy."

I finished the wine in my glass and reached for the decanter on the desk before Naaz swiped it away. "Give it to me, Naaz."

"You can't live like this, Morrigan."

Anger flooded my reasoning and I narrowed my eyes at him. "If it had been *my* throat that was cut, would you have stood there and watched as well?"

The clear offense flashed in his eyes. My rational side told me to say something, to take it back. Instead, I quickly swiped the decanter from his hand and turned to leave. Beside the doors stood Guinevere, pale faced and stiff, watching me. Without pouring it, I lifted the decanter to my lips and gulped the wine.

My fault.

My fault.

My fault.

"You look buzzed, Morrigan," Lyra so gracefully pointed out before my Saturday dinner with the guys.

A light chuckle left my lips. *I am.*

With Eowyn not around to supervise my every move, I spent most of the day in my bedroom, lighting up every shadow to keep *her* away. I had even managed to sneak some wine from the kitchen while Eris was held up in his study.

The alcohol made her visits far less frequent. If I drank enough, my dreams were the only things I would need to worry about. But by now, I had grown used to them. I no longer screamed. I just sat there... watching her die... over... and over again. I felt nothing anymore as I held her.

My fault.

I entered the dining hall, noticing that everyone but Kaiden had been seated already. Staring at his empty chair, I tripped over my own feet when I reached Eris. Cain laughed from the end of the table, earning his own, personal glare. "Is something funny?" I asked him.

He only laughed louder and shook his head. Eris snapped, "You think this is comical?"

"I could smell the wine the minute she opened her bedroom door, Eris. She's clearly drunk."

"I am not drunk," I insisted. "I'm just—" My own hiccup interrupted me. "I'm fine."

Cain laughed again, but everyone else stayed silent. "This is just brilliant."

"Morrigan," D said in his usual soft, reserved tone. He had clear worry lines pressing into his face with a frown. "This isn't... *you*."

I tilted my head, making a face at him. "How do you know who I am? You don't know me." Looking around, I locked eyes with every one of them seated. "Actually, none of you do. You've known me for a couple of months—some of you practically less than that." I looked back at D. "This could be who I've been all along."

"It isn't," Eris insisted.

"You know, I'm really starting to dislike these dinners." Slamming my utensils down, I began to stand, but Eris grabbed my hand.

"You will sit, you will eat, and you will sober up. If I have to *compel* you to do it, Gods forgive me, Morrigan, I will compel you." Eris's lips pursed in anger.

Staring back at him, I tried to decipher if he was bluffing or not. "You wouldn't," I tested.

Then, his eyes began to glow. "I would."

I looked to Dez, expecting him to interject. But he only returned an apologetic smile, telling me he had no intentions of doing that. "Princess... Sit down... Please."

With a loud, crude laugh, I sat back in my seat. They didn't understand. No one understood.

"Princess, we just want to help—"

"Don't call me that," I spat, stabbing my fork into the food in front of me.

By the time dinner ended, I breathed a sigh of relief as the last of them left and prepared to retreat back to my room. But Eris had other plans. "We are going to talk about this right now, Morrigan." His eyes held a darkness that I hadn't seen since the encounter in the woods. "You will kill yourself if you continue like this. And I refuse to allow that."

"I need it, Eris." I thought a smidge of honesty might get him to drop the subject, but it only made it worse.

"Why?" he asked. When I didn't respond, he sighed as he stood, bringing me with him. "Use *me*, then." Biting down on his wrist, he raised it as an offering. "It will give you the same relief that you're so desperate to obtain *without* destroying your organs in the process."

I had no restraint as I wrapped my mouth around the fresh cut he made, chasing anything that could bring me even a second of the false pretense of peace. As his blood touched my tongue, what took multiple glasses of wine happened in an instant. The buzz from the alcohol wore off and a gentler one took its place. My brain no longer felt fuzzy, but wired with an invigorating rush of adrenaline.

Moaning, I pulled harder and relaxed my body into Eris. Raising his hand to my hair, he caressed it, pulling my head against his chest. "Take what you need, Morrigan," he whispered. "I won't stop you."

And I did.

I drank like my body had been starved. Until every evil thought that clouded my brain had vanished. And then I drank a little more, just to top it off. When I finally pulled away, Eris shushed me as he tilted my head back, slowly wiping the blood from my lips.

"I would have done it, Morrigan," he said quietly, staring into my eyes that felt heavy with bliss and exhaustion. "I would have fixed her for you. I wanted to. But the amount of energy that I would have needed... I would have had to *kill* another person to get it."

Swallowing the last drop of blood that coated my tongue, my throat suddenly felt dry again at his words. And when I opened my mouth, my lips weighed with burden as I said, "Then, you should have killed *me.*"

My fault.

My fault.

It was my fucking *fault.*

Chapter 37

Though I still saw *her* occasionally, Eris's blood did so much more to ease the hallucinations than the wine had.

It seemed to last for a few days before the headaches would begin again and my nightmares would be almost painful. Another problem the blood solved was the voice in my head. *He* didn't speak anymore. I didn't know if that should have made me feel better or worse. Because without that voice, the only escape I had from my dreams came when the sun would rise.

During one of Naaz's lessons, I felt myself drifting, knowing that I needed to find time to sneak off and feed before *she* made an appearance. I was lucky enough to make it to the end of the lesson before running to his study.

As he held me, his wrist to my lips, pouring into my mouth, Eris seemed more tense than usual. He twirled my hair in his fingers, a routine he had come up with as of late and sighed. "Kaiden will be at dinner tonight," he warned. "Morrigan," he pulled me back, interrupting our arrangement, "you can't tell him about this."

I furrowed my brows in confusion. "Why would I tell him anything—"

"I mean it, Morrigan."

With his wrist at a distance, I was growing frustrated and scared that I hadn't gotten enough to make it through the night. So, I nodded in agreement. "I won't tell him, I swear."

Looking down at my mouth that had likely been smeared with his own blood, he leaned down and licked from my chin to my bottom lip, cleaning it. With the aphrodisiac running through my veins, I couldn't help the shiver of pleasure it caused, snaking down my body.

"You can have the rest after you keep your promise to me."

Entering the dining hall together, I waited for Eris to pull out my seat before sitting down.

I didn't touch my food very much. Truthfully, I had developed a strange *aversion* to it. Food no longer seemed to fill me quite as well as Eris's blood did. And I never really felt *hungry* anymore. Thankfully, I didn't think anyone actually noticed. And if they did, they didn't make any comments. Kaiden, however, stared at me the entire dinner.

I tried my best to avoid looking back at him. A weird guilt hid somewhere deep within my chest. I didn't know *why*. Just because he showed kindness once didn't make him some knight in shining armor. It only further proved that he had the capacity for some form of compassion and simply chose not to show it before.

"You've barely touched your meal, dove," he said from the end of the table.

Sharing a glance with Eris, I looked back down at my plate, returning a tight smile. "I had a filling lunch."

"You look smaller," he continued.

I scoffed. "I highly doubt I've lost a noticeable amount of weight since you've last seen me."

"You have…" Dez chimed in quietly. His eyes held a certain bewilderment, like he had come to some realization in front of me.

"Just leave the girl alone," Cain added. Cain usually egged Kaiden on, enjoying the amusement of our bickering. It seemed even he had grown tired of it now.

"Apologies." I could hear the sarcasm in Kaiden's voice. "Clearly Dez and I are *imagining* things."

Letting out an audible sigh, I pushed out my chair. "Well this was swell, I think I'll be going to bed now." Eris began to stand with me, but I shook my head for him to stay. "I'm alright," I whispered. "I can wait until you finish."

After he placed a soft kiss on my fingers, I left, returning to my room. But in pure Kaiden fashion, I barely made it to my door before sensing a change in the air.

"I should have known," I groaned, turning around to face him.

"What have you done?" he asked, narrowing his eyes.

"I'm sorry?"

"You *did* something, Morrigan. Tell me what you did." He walked forward until my back hit a wall, cornering me with his hands on either side of my face.

"I did nothing, Kaiden. I thought we were done with these stupid games."

He leaned forward, so close that his breath brushed against my nose. His eyes kept shifting between mine, studying me in a way I didn't understand. In that moment, something shifted inside of me. A strange warmth that I had only felt once before, as he cleaned Guinevere's blood from my face and hands. I stared back at him, seeing a small glimpse of that man.

The man I hated... The man that bullied me, taunted me... protected me. Who dressed me and held me until I fell asleep.

He waited, I didn't know what for. It felt like hours had passed before he pulled back and mumbled, "You smell different..."

"Smell different? What is that supposed to—"

Before I could finish my sentence, he vanished into the darkness. I received no warning as the shadows swallowed him and I was left standing alone in the hall. When I finally gathered the courage to move, I slid into my room and pressed my back against the door until it latched shut.

And as I looked forward, a cold, dead Guinevere sat in Eowyn's chair, staring back at me with faded, blue eyes.

Come Tuesday morning, Eris had business to take care of in town, and he planned to be away for the rest of the day.

Rolling my head on my shoulders, I did my best to soothe the headache forming in the middle of Naaz's lesson. It had been three days since I last fed from Eris and I felt exhausted.

"Focus, Morrigan," Naaz said, snapping me from my daze.

"I can't," I mumbled back to him.

Closing his book, he walked behind me and placed his fingers on my temples, moving them in small circles. It helped to soothe the pain pulsing beneath them.

"It'll be late when he returns tonight." With a groan, I leaned into his touch as he spoke. "I noticed you haven't been needing wine since you and Eris started... *spending time* together."

When my eyes opened, I could see him staring down at me. Even my cheeks blushed from the embarrassment of his accusation.

"Don't feel ashamed." He began rubbing harder. "You could ask *me*, you know. Especially if it means you'll stop ignoring everything I try to teach you."

"Maybe I should wait for Eris to come back," I answered with a slight unease.

Laughing, he shook his head. "Is my blood not good for you, *Your Grace?*"

I sat up, moving away from his hands and turned to look at him. It shouldn't have been so uncomfortable for me to consider. Maybe if it had been Cain or D... But Naaz and I spend a lot of time together now. I knew him just as much as I knew Eris, or Dez, or Cass...

As he watched the wheels turning in my eyes, he took the initiative and bit down on his wrist, offering it to me. "Relieve your stress, Morrigan," he said. And as a small drop of blood fell from the open wound, I inhaled sharply, feeling a sudden sense of need.

In that moment, I knew I couldn't resist it. I grabbed his wrist and shoved it into my mouth, holding it tight as I drank from it. Naaz let out a small grunt, stabilizing himself against the chair. He tasted strong and smoky, a vast difference from Eris's rich, savory blood. I drank until the headache subsided and my bones felt strong again. My fatigue had been replaced with a large burst of energy. And after a few moments, he pulled his arm away and I whined at having to release him. But he grabbed my hand and forced me to stand before tilting my head to the side.

"My turn," he whispered, and sunk his teeth into my neck before I could react.

I gasped as a strong bolt of pleasure shot down my body, causing me to squirm in his hold. The last person to truly bite me was Cass... and I had forgotten just how good it felt. A thrumming began in my chest, like a buzzing beneath my skin and it held me tight as he pulled from my veins. Then, as with Eris, the strange tether burst, and Naaz released me at the exact same time.

Licking my wound, I felt it heal as he pulled back to look at me. "You know," I mumbled with a light chuckle. "A warning might have been nice."

As he smiled, my body suddenly sank against him in a strange fit of exhaustion that hadn't been there before. "Whoa," he called out, catching me and picking me up. "I should have remembered that. Let's have you lie down for a little while."

As he brought me back to my room, I heard Eowyn whisper something in question to him, but he ignored it. Relieving Lyra from her watch, he laid me down on the bed and I couldn't stop my eyes from closing.

"We can finish our lesson tomorrow," Naaz whispered in my ear. "Rest, now."

And I fell asleep.

"Morrigan," he called.

No... Why was he here... He was supposed to be gone.

"Morrigan!"

My body shook, forcing my eyes open. Before me stood the same, masked man, but he looked frantic. "What... What am I doing here?" I asked sleepily.

"Morrigan, whatever they are doing... You need to stop,*" he insisted.*

I didn't have a clue what he meant. He wasn't even real. *"Why am I here?" He had his hands wrapped around my arms, holding me tightly. "I don't want to be here. I want to wake up."*

"Look at you!" he yelled. "You're withering away! You need to stop this!"

"Who are you? Why do I keep seeing you?"

He shoved me away in frustration and ran a stiff hand through his ruffled, dark brown hair. As he turned, I could see the markings on his back almost pulsing with a kind of power.

Quickly, he turned back around and rushed toward me, taking my face into his hands. "Listen to me, Morrigan. You need to find me, okay?"

Find him?

"I don't understand—"

"Morrigan, please," he begged. "You're letting them kill *you. I* need *you."*

"Morrigan!"

I woke to someone screaming my name and realized that I had been drenched in water. Coughing, I looked down at my body submerged in the tub, and my lungs felt like they were drowning.

"What..." I tried speaking through the water that kept spilling from my mouth. "What happ...ened?"

"You were taking a bath... I had only been gone for a moment..." Eowyn stuttered through her words, scrambling to find a cloth to clean up the mess that I had apparently made on the floor.

When did I get in the bath?

"Mor," Eowyn began to cry. "I don't... You've been acting so strange... Mor, you're scaring me." Wrapping me in a robe, she sat me down in the chair and knelt in front of me. "Tell me what to do. Tell me how I can help you."

But as I gazed into her blue eyes, I could still see his mask in their reflection. *"You need to find me,"* he seemed to whisper again, clear as day.

Pulling my hands from Eowyn's, I stood and pushed past her. "Morrigan!" she called behind me. "Please! Just let us help you!"

"You can't!" I yelled, ripping a gown from my closet and marching to my bed. No one could help me.

I had officially lost it.

My fault.

My fault.

My *fault.*

Chapter 38

With Naaz now willing to give me what I needed, I saw no reason to tell Eris about it.

I would do anything to keep both *him* and *her* from lurking in every shadow. So, I took whatever Naaz and Eris could offer. Living on a constant high, my days were filled with endless bliss. Bliss that instantly shattered at our next dinner.

Kaiden decided not to come. *Good riddance.* But Dez had been staring at me the entire time I poked at the food on my plate. "You've lost more weight," he whispered. "How is that even possible?"

Rolling my eyes, I made a point to shove a piece of meat into my mouth in an attempt to prove him wrong. I quickly regretted it as my stomach rolled from the taste. "That was rude," I chimed, narrowing my eyes at him.

Dez turned to look at Eris, then back at me and a sudden wave of emotion fell upon his face, causing his eyes to brighten. "Oh, Gods... Are we... Is this because of *us*?" he asked.

Eris's hand froze close to mine on the table. "Dez... Not now."

But the blue in Dez's eyes began to stir. "How often have you been drinking from him, Morrigan?"

Feeling slightly shocked, I looked at Eris to answer for me. "Dez, you're overreacting." Naaz laughed, trying to ease the tension that quickly built across the table. "Just eat your food."

Fast enough to make me flinch, Dez turned to him with a sharp twist, his lips now curling in anger. "You too?! Already?!"

"Naaz?" Eris looked at him.

Before the situation could erupt into chaos, Cass placed a hand on Dez's shoulder. "Why don't we all just take a breath—"

"No wonder she's not eating... She doesn't *need* to. You're practically keeping her high all day." Looking between Eris and Naaz, the two of them stared at one another now that Dez had outed them both, and he let out a crude laugh. "You didn't even *know*, did you? All of this is falling apart and we're just watching her die in front of us! Kaiden was right!"

"Dez," I tried altering my voice to how I used to talk to him, "I think you're being a little bit dramatic. How is it any different than when I drank from *you*?" Then, I looked at Cass. "Or you?"

Dez ignored every word that left my lips as he covered his face with his hands. "What are we doing? This is so fucked up."

His reaction made no sense to me. *I'm fine.* "What do you mean? Why are you overreacting right now?"

"Eowyn is coming home with me," he said under his breath, and the nerve of his assumption lit a fire deep within me.

"She is *not*," I informed him, slamming my cup onto the table.

"You're lucky I don't take Lyra as well, but I know that she can handle herself. Eowyn, however, cannot sit here and watch this happen to you." He looked at me once more, apologetically. "I'm so sorry, Morrigan. I didn't know... We should have known... I can't watch this happen again."

As he stood, I rose from my seat to follow after him, but Eris held me back. "You can't take her from me, Dez!" I yelled.

Without turning around, he made his way to the doors, shaking his head as he lowered it. "Forgive me, Princess..."

"Let him go, Morrigan," Eris insisted. "He won't take her, you know that. Just let him cool off—"

"No."

I shoved free of his hold and ran from the dining hall. But as I reached Eowyn's room, all of her stuff had already been removed. He had to have used Faelar to retrieve it all. He took her.

How could he take her?

"Morrigan?" Lyra called from the doorway. "Are you alright?"

Storming from Eowyn's room, I pushed past her and rushed to my door. "He took her," I answered in a fit of rage.

When I entered my room, I looked for the first thing to release my anger with. Turning to my vanity, a small reflection of Guinevere appeared behind me in Eowyn's chair. So, I wrapped my hands around it and tossed the mirror onto the floor, causing it to shatter into a thousand little shards.

"Whoa!" Lyra yelled. "Morrigan, take a breath."

"He *took* her!"

I reached for the vase on the vanity when Lyra grabbed my arm, stopping me from throwing it. "Bath," she whispered. "Let's get you in a bath before you tear your room apart."

Lyra walked me to the chair in my bathing room and used her hand to heat up the water until it began to steam. "He took her, Lyra," I whispered as my lips began to tremble. "He wanted to take you too."

"No one is taking me from you, Morrigan," she assured me, then mumbled something before leaving the room, but I couldn't decipher it.

My head pounded with an anger I had never felt toward Dez before. How could he do this? He knew what Eowyn meant to me and he *took* her. Shoving my clothes off, I stomped over to the bath and stepped inside.

"I can't watch this happen again."

Watch *what* happen again?

He had been so angry over me feeding from them, but I had done that with both him *and* Cass already. Pushing my mind to think back to those moments, I recalled one strange sensation that seemed to stand out. It always happened during the *first* time I fed from them...

And the first time they fed from *me.*

Why didn't I feel it any of the other times?

"Morrigan!" Lyra yelled, running inside before yanking me from the tub. "I told you to wait! The water is too—"

"What is your problem?" I asked sharply, ripping the robe from her hands and wrapping it around my body. "Gods, Lyra."

She stood still in front of me, frozen in place as she stared at my body. I didn't know how to feel. "How did it not burn you?" she whispered. "Your skin... it isn't even red from the heat."

"Why are you all acting so strange?" I gave up on the idea of a peaceful bath and walked back to my room to get dressed for the night, but Lyra followed closely behind me.

"Morrigan, the water was blazing hot," she insisted.

"I assure you, it was not." Grabbing my hand, she turned me and lifted it between us, wrapping her own around it. "Lyra," I hissed. "What is the matter with you?"

"I don't understand…" she mumbled.

When I looked down, I panicked when I saw flames surrounding her palm, curling over my own skin. I quickly ripped free of her grasp and cradled my hand to my chest. "Lyra!" I yelled at her. "You could have burned me!"

But the bewildered look never left her eyes as she turned on her heels. "I have to go."

"Lyra!" I called to her, running from the room as I chased her. "Why didn't it burn me?! Lyra!"

Slamming into a hard chest, I looked up to see Eris standing in the hall, confused. "I was coming to see you…" He turned back at a retreating Lyra and appeared concerned. "Morrigan, what's wrong?"

"What did Dez mean at the table, Eris?" I asked him.

A mask seemed to fall from his face as he scrambled for an explanation. "He was overreacting, Morrigan. Come, let's just—" He reached for me, but I stepped out of his path. "Oh, come on. Don't be ridiculous."

"They're lying to you, Morrigan."

I jumped at the sound of *his* voice, turning to find the hallway empty save for Eris and I. "It's… It's my blood isn't it? What's so important about my blood, Eris?"

When worry began to swirl in Eris's eyes, I knew I had struck something vital. *My blood.* I knew that they needed to feed, but what was so significant about *my* blood?

"Come here, Morrigan," he insisted, reaching a hand out to me.

"No. I want you to answer my question."

Then, his eyes started to glow. *"Come here."*

I gasped, a part of my chest cracking a little as I gaped at him. "You... Did you just try to *compel* me?" An even better question was... *Why didn't it work?*

Widening his eyes, the light completely faded from them and returned to a deep, royal blue. "Why didn't... That should have worked, I—"

I quickly ran back into my room, slamming the door shut and held it as he tried to enter. "What are you doing to me, Eris?!" I yelled through the wood between us.

"Morrigan, come out. Just let me explain, please."

Looking around, I searched for something to tie around the handles. A leather belt had been conveniently lying beside my dresser. I used my foot to drag it toward the door before wrapping it tight enough to prevent him, or anyone else for that matter, from coming inside.

"Are you ready to listen, Morrigan?" he asked from somewhere behind me.

Turning slowly, I found *him* standing at the center of my room, face covered with his mask. I nodded, pressing my back against the door vibrating from Eris's pounding.

"Okay..." My voice shook with uncertainty. "I'll listen."

The Diary of Daisies and Hellebores

Hellebores!

He loves them. I have planted them throughout my garden now to remind me of him. He was so happy when he saw them the last time he visited the castle. He couldn't show it around the others, but the smile still remained in his eyes. His dark, beautiful eyes.

I could get lost within them.

Chapter 40

KAIDEN

Papers covered my desk in complete disarray.

Something was missing.

I should have stayed that night and been there when she woke. I knew the storm that awaited her better than most. But my own fear ultimately won and pulled me from her arms. I also didn't want her waking to see her sullied clothes. So, I took them outside and burned them before the sun rose. It was best that I hadn't been there. Nothing changed. She remained an absolute nuisance in my life that I never asked for.

Keep convincing yourself of that.

Focusing felt nearly impossible today, though. Staring at the parchment, the only thing I could actually see was Morrigan's face at the last dinner I attended. Her skin looked pale. At the Unveiling, she had already been quite petite, but now she looked almost... sick. Her cheekbones had sharpened and the skin under her eyes appeared dull and almost tinged with purple.

The way she pushed her food around... She hadn't been like that with Cass or Dez. She loved the food there.

I didn't know why I cared so much. But at the bare minimum it was our job to keep her alive. She is a product of the prophecy by the gods. The first, and *only* prophecy to ever be created. So, why were they all watching her kill herself? And when did it become *my* job to fix it?

Pushing my chair back, I decided to step outside for some air. The castle had a peaceful silence to it as I walked through the halls. It had been my decision to relieve most of my staff so long ago. I couldn't handle seeing so many of their faces after... It was just better to be alone. I kept the necessary advisors, a few people to assist with cooking and cleaning, but I didn't need my home filled with strangers anymore.

Solitude felt better... *Safer*.

Why did she *smell* different? And why did it seem so familiar?

The girl got under my skin more than anyone else had in the past. She frustrated me to no end and ignored everything I said to her. And when she saw the smallest lick of my shadows... Most people would have been frightened by them. Most people were. But Morrigan? She barely spared them a glance, and I knew she had seen them.

As I stepped down the steps into the courtyard, I heard the distant sound of yelling coming from the pathway to the gate. It was accompanied by the gallops of horses, and they were approaching fast. My hand flew to the dagger at my side as I waited. That uneasy tug on my skin told me they wanted out, begging to be released. But as I felt the darkness blurring my vision, threatening to take over, I could see the rider racing toward me.

It was Morrigan's guard Lyra.

Why is Lyra here?

Shoving away the shadows, I let go of my dagger and met her at the end of the trail. "My Lord!" she yelled breathlessly.

"What are you doing here?"

Jumping down from her horse, she ran toward me and knelt, keeping her head down to the ground. "I came as quickly as I could…" she panted. "I didn't know who else to go to…"

"That doesn't answer my question." My good-for-nothing guards finally made their way into the courtyard, swords at their sides, and I rolled my eyes, waving at them to stop.

"No one knows I'm here…" she continued. "I… It's *Morrigan*, My Lord. I didn't… I didn't think I could trust anyone else."

"And what makes you think you can trust me?" I had never spoken to Lyra, though I had seen her plenty of times. She stuck to Morrigan like a parasite.

Lyra looked up from her position, her brown eyes swirling with the fire that I could sense from within her. "My Lord… I know the eyes of someone who has lost a person they love." She cleared her throat as those same eyes began to water. "I don't want to lose her, too. Something is happening to her… We don't have time."

Staring up at her horse, I nodded toward the trees she had emerged from. "It's a two-day ride from Eris's castle," I noted.

"I got here in one."

"Tell me *everything*."

I knew it… I fucking knew it.

As Lyra explained to me what she had been witnessing, my blood began to boil. We had spoken about this when Morrigan's existence came to light. We had agreed against it. After what happened... At the very least they knew to be *careful*. They were dragging the girl to her grave and couldn't think straight enough to see it.

When she told me about the little experiment she performed on Morrigan before coming to find me... It put a few of the pieces together in my mind. I didn't know how I hadn't realized it or even accepted the possibility. And I doubted that the gods expected this outcome either.

One problem at a time.

"I'm going to kill them," I growled, balling my hands into tight fists deep enough to cut my palms.

"My Lord," she said quickly. "Lord Dez... I implore you to speak with him. I know he shared a part in it but... He *loves* her. I know he does. Request to speak to him and he will talk, I know he will."

Before making our way to Eris's castle, we stopped outside of Dez's and waited for his guards to alert him. When he stepped out into the courtyard, my anger only increased to a threatening level.

"Think before you react," Lyra whispered beside me.

Too late.

Using my shadows, I disappeared, landing directly in front of him, and swung my fist until it connected with his nose. He leaned over, covering his face, and I grabbed his shirt, pulling him back up before hitting him once more.

"You piece of shit!" I yelled, striking him again and watching his body fall to the ground. "We made an agreement! You all swore you wouldn't!"

"Kaiden!" Lyra yelled behind me in warning, and I could hear the crackling of her fire.

"We said *no,* Dez! She's not some common whore for you all to play with!" I screamed in his face, straddling his body with my legs and leaning down, pulling him up by his collar. "She's a *person,* you sick—"

"I know!" he coughed, spitting up blood from his mouth. "I-I know... We fucked up, Kaiden... It's... It's getting bad."

"Kaiden, put him down," Lyra ordered behind me.

"You could have killed her," I whispered to him.

"I know..."

Throwing him back to the ground, I stepped over and saw Lyra standing close by, palms consumed by a controlled fire.

"She isn't eating anymore. She's lost even more weight." I turned to see Dez standing slowly, wiping his face as his wounds began to heal themselves. "I didn't know that she had been feeding from Eris and Naaz. When I found out, I took Eowyn back with me."

Another wave of anger coursed through me and I marched toward him, stopping inches from his face. "The girl just watched her mother die. Harley abandoned her. And you took away one of her only friends?"

His eyes widened. "Well... When you put it that way." I hit him again, harder than before, hearing a quick snap just above his nose. "Okay," he grunted. "I deserved that."

"We are leaving," I announced before stretching my arm out for them to take. "*Now!*"

When we arrived at the castle, Eris quickly emerged from the doors, heading straight for Lyra. "Where have you been?!"

As he approached, I looked up and found a bright light illuminating Morrigan's room. No... It wasn't just a light... It was *fire.* I grabbed Eris's arm, forcing him to face me. "What did you do?"

"There isn't time," he hissed, shaking me off. "She locked herself in there the same night Lyra left and I haven't been able to enter. It's warded off somehow and even *I* can't penetrate it."

Warded off?

Dez looked just as confused beside me. "How could she possibly—"

An explosion shattered the glass windows in her room, sending smoke and debris falling from the sky. He was right. We didn't have time for this. Transporting all of us inside, I had attempted to bring us into her room, but we landed just outside the door.

After one more attempt at entering with my shadows, I leaned against the door and used every bit of force I could to try and break it down. "Morrigan!" I yelled through it before turning back to Eris. "When did the fire begin?"

"Almost thirty minutes ago. I was begging her to let me in and she kept screaming at someone—like someone was inside with her. I even tried dousing the flames on my own, but Kaiden... This is unlike anything I've seen since—"

"Morrigan!" Lyra yelled, interrupting him. She banged her hands on the door and angry tears had begun to fall from her eyes. "Morrigan! Let us in! Please, it's Lyra!"

"When was the last time you heard her?" I asked Eris.

"I could still hear her coughing a couple of minutes ago, but... She went silent just as I sensed your arrival. I thought with Lyra... I thought she might let her in."

I watched as Lyra placed her hand on the handle, trying to melt it away, but none of our magic seemed to be working. This was far more advanced than I had suspected. It couldn't have been her doing it. She wouldn't even know *how* to.

"Lyra," I said quietly. "Grab my hand." She accepted it, squeezing my fingers fiercely. "If we get in there, I need you to put out the fire as quickly as you can. I don't know if I will be able to open the doors once I'm inside, and I need to find Morrigan."

Once she nodded, I closed my eyes and put every ounce of energy into my shadows. Something pushed us back, a tightly locked door that I had never encountered before. It contained none of Morrigan's essence. I fought against it with all of my strength, willing my darkness to do its job.

Let me in, I called through. *Let me in!*

She couldn't die. She didn't need to die. She didn't deserve it. *We* were the guilty ones and Morrigan had been given to us. We were supposed to protect her. And look at what he had done. What *I* had done.

Let. Me. In!

Finally, I felt that weightless feeling as we pushed through the shadows and my feet landed on broken wood and ash. "Lyra!" I yelled, and within seconds the flames dissipated. Now, I needed to get to Morrigan.

Paintings had been torn from the walls, broken and burned by the fire all over the floor. The bed had been entirely scorched, and the pillows were toppled over, sending thousands of wooden fragments everywhere.

This isn't happening again...

"Kaiden!" Lyra yelled from somewhere behind me.

As I ran into the bathing room, I saw her sitting on the floor, holding Morrigan in her lap. Her gown looked almost black with burns all over the fabric. *No...* Without thinking, I pulled her from Lyra's hold and held her close to me. Her thin face had no color to it anymore, and her cheeks were covered in soot.

"Morrigan," I called to her, holding her face with my hand. "Morrigan, breathe."

This can't be happening again... Not again.

"I shouldn't have left her..." Lyra sobbed from somewhere in the corner. "Fuck, I shouldn't have left her!"

I tried to remain calm as I searched for any sign of life. Bringing my lips to hers, I pushed air in, doing my best to fill her lungs. "Breathe, little dove. Gods, please just *breathe*."

My own eyes stung as I stared down at her body, limp in my arms. Her cheeks were even thinner than I remembered. I left her here. I should have just taken her with me. A part of me knew that something was wrong. Even if she would have hated me.. I should have taken her—locked her in a fucking cage if I had to. At least then she wouldn't be lying on the floor... surrounded by ashes... just like...

Not. Again.

Placing my hand on her chest, I searched for the small buzz of energy that crawled in my veins. I closed my eyes and felt the smoke she had inhaled. There was so much of it. Wrapping an invisible hand around her lungs, I forced it all out. I felt as it moved, making its way slowly up her throat. And when I opened my eyes I could see it escaping her lips. Like tendrils, it rose and lifted into the air.

All I pictured still was *her* charred body in my lap. I couldn't save her. I didn't save her. But Gods... Morrigan... *I'm going to fucking save you.*

"I won't lose you, Morrigan," I whispered for only her to hear. "I won't let this happen again. Fucking. *Breathe!*"

Chapter 41

MORRIGAN

Someone had been screaming my name, a voice that had me believing that I was dreaming.

"What ha—" My throat felt like sandpaper, like I hadn't had a sip of water in weeks. As my eyes began to open, they also burned brutally as I tried focusing my sight.

"You're alive…" was whispered above me.

Suddenly, the sound of a door being kicked down made me acutely aware that my body was on the floor, cradled in someone's lap. *Kaiden's* lap. How had I gotten to the floor? The last thing I remembered was locking Eris out of my room as he banged against the door, begging for me to let him in. After I tied the handles… *he* appeared. But… *Why don't I remember anything else?*

Hovering over me, Kaiden's eyes were red and swollen, like he had been… *crying.* He leaned down and pressed his forehead—which felt hot to the touch—against mine, cupping my cheek with his hand. "What are you doing—"

"Quiet," he hissed, silencing me. "I just need to hear it for a moment longer."

"Hear what?" I asked.

"Your breathing." I had never heard his voice sound so… small, so desperate. "I'm afraid that if I let you go, it might stop again."

What is happening? What happened to me? Why am I on the floor? Why is Kaiden holding me and… Letting my eyes drift toward the sound of sobbing nearby, I could see Lyra curled up in the corner. In the doorway stood Eris and Dez, both panting and frazzled as they stared into the room.

That's when I remembered why I locked Eris out to begin with. Picking up a shard of glass beside me, I shoved out of Kaiden's hold and backed away from them all, holding it out in front of me.

"What's happened to me?" I asked hoarsely.

"Morrigan." On my left, Lyra slowly crawled to me. "Put it down. You're safe."

"No, I'm not!" My eyes remained on the guys, flitting between Eris, Kaiden and Dez. "You've all been using me. I don't know what for, but I do know that Guinevere was right."

As my anger simmered beneath my chest, my body started to heat. Beneath my skin, I felt an itch and used my free hand to try and scratch it. But it wouldn't stop. The itching spread, unable to be soothed by my nails.

"Morrigan," Lyra said quietly. "Mor, look at me."

She stopped as she knelt beside me. "What's happening to me?" I cried.

"Her eyes..." Eris whispered by the door. "Why are her eyes glowing?"

I stared at him in confusion and then back at Lyra as she pulled something from her pocket. "I grabbed this before retrieving Kaiden." In her hand was a chain with a small red ruby hanging from the center. *Fire opal...* I had remembered seeing it when I was with Dez. She quickly placed it around my neck and almost instantly, the itching began to subside. "It'll slow it down... Give you some time to breathe while we figure this out."

"Figure *what* out?" I asked, holding the necklace in my hand. The more my symptoms began to lessen, the stone seemed to shine brighter— glowing like flames within the strange rock.

"You're going through the transition that the rest of us have. Usually for us it's a lot younger but..." As Lyra grabbed a robe and began wrapping it around me, I realized that my clothes looked torn and scorched... the white fabric almost entirely black now. "*You* created this fire, Morrigan."

I didn't remember a fire at all. There was clear evidence of one, but my memory remained locked away, taken from me. How could *I* have created the fire? Why didn't any of them put it out? As Lyra moved to the side, Kaiden stood and approached me, offering a hand. I eyed it cautiously.

"I still don't trust you," I said to him.

"Nor should you," he answered.

And for some reason, it was enough for me to drop the shard and accept his gesture, allowing him to help me off of the floor. Before I could take a single step forward, Kaiden lifted me into his arms and I gasped. "What are you—"

"She's coming with me."

I began to protest, but when we emerged into my room... I had no words. The walls were destroyed... My bed broken and burned. The portraits on the wall were now ash that ruined the perfect, wooden floor beneath us. *I couldn't have done this... I didn't... I could have died... I almost* died...

My fault.

My fault.

"Kaiden!" Eris yelled from somewhere behind us. "You can't just take her! She isn't yours to claim!"

"She clearly isn't safe with any of you. Have you seen her? You're lucky her mortal blood didn't turn yet."

Turn?

"You can't be serious—"

"I'm coming with you," Dez interrupted Eris.

The moment we stepped outside, I sucked in a quick, sharp breath from the winter air. "Fuck, I'm sorry," Kaiden cursed before I felt his body heat against me. "Is that better?"

I simply nodded in response. My head reeled too much for me to form any words yet.

"If Dez is coming, then so am I," Eris demanded nearby.

Turning to look at him, I watched Eris take a single step toward us before black mist shot out from around me and gripped his arms like rope. My lips parted, sucking in a quick breath before I looked up at Kaiden and realized the whites in his eyes had gone completely black. I knew that he could travel in the shadows like a shadow walker... And I knew he had done something to Cain's chair... But *this*... None of their eyes did this.

"Dez is permitted to come with me. *You* are not." His voice sounded far darker than normal. It almost created a chill worse than the air that had my limbs trembling.

"Kaiden," Eris pleaded as he pulled against the shadows binding him. "Let me go, now."

"I may not have any hellebore at my disposal, but I swear to the gods, Eris… If you step one foot near my castle, death will be a mercy for what I have in store for you." In Kaiden's eyes, the darkness swirled like it was alive—like the shadows were a physical extension of himself… taking their own control.

Within seconds, we were shrouded in darkness and it brought us somewhere else. Somewhere I had never been before. It was too dark for me to see the castle, and Kaiden kept it so dimly lit that I could scarcely make out any details. But he held onto me as he walked us through it, like he was scared to let me down.

"Where are we going?" I asked him, my throat still too dry.

After descending some stairs, I noticed the stone walls around us. And I realized that Kaiden wasn't taking me to my room. "I'm sorry," he whispered.

When we stopped before iron bars, I began to struggle. I tried to push against him, hoping that he'd free me, but his strength far surpassed my own. "Kaiden," I begged. "Kaiden, don't."

"If you don't dry out from the blood you've consumed, you'll be a threat to everyone around you, Morrigan."

"Kaiden!" He finally set me down, and I wasted no time standing in an attempt to run, but something wrapped around my wrists, pulling me back. When I looked down, I could see chains locking them in place. I stared in horror and looked up at Kaiden who was already leaving. "Don't do this to me Kaiden, please," I begged. Every memory from my old home came flashing through. The first prison I was ever held in, but at least it had a bed.

"You don't understand, Morrigan," he answered as he stepped onto the other side of the cell. "You still have mortal blood in you. And do you want to know what happens to a mortal when they drink too much of *our* blood?" He turned around to face me, pulling out a dagger from his side. "Shall I show you?

Slowly, he placed his palm out, showing it to me as he took the dagger and began dragging it across his skin. When the blood became visible, something strange seemed to click inside of me. It flipped, forcing a deep craving from within my chest, and I could feel it vibrate in a deep growl. Suddenly, my body lunged forward, forgetting the chains that bound me to the cell.

I couldn't stop myself from thrashing, trying to get to Kaiden... *to his blood.*

I want it.

I need it.

What had likely only been seconds felt like hours as I pushed against my restraints, until Kaiden covered his hand and placed it back down, breaking my trance. "W-What... I..." I stammered, unable to explain my actions.

"It took some time... But we eventually learned that if you dry a mortal out early enough, it stops the changing."

"Changing? Into what?"

Kaiden's laugh held no lightness to it as it echoed against the stone. "Did you really think that Rosina created vampyres, little dove?" My silence only further amused him. "Those little lords of yours..."

Turning, he began to leave and I started panicking again. "Kaiden! No!" I begged with tears stinging my already painfully dry eyes. "Kaiden, don't leave me alone here! Please!"

"I'm doing this for your own good, Morrigan." His voice carried through the hall before I heard his feet ascending the stairs.

"Kaiden!" I called to him, pleading for a miracle. I couldn't be alone. I couldn't be with... Turning, my suspicions were confirmed when I saw the outline of her body in the corner. "Kaiden!" I screamed, backing up until I slid down the stone wall behind me.

Guinevere stepped out, into the light, and sat herself down... Staring at me with pale, blue eyes and a wound slashed across her neck.

My fault.

My fault.

My fault.

"KAIDEN!"

My meals appeared to me from shadows that could only have been created by Kaiden.

I didn't eat them. I couldn't. Not with Guinevere's eyes on me, never blinking. Judging by the amount of food I received, it had been two days since Kaiden placed me in the cell. No one had come down to see or talk to me. I was alone... in darkness... *again.*

Not even *he* seemed to speak to me now.

I should have burned that castle to the ground.

"You don't mean that," I heard a soft, familiar voice call from the shadows.

She wasn't supposed to speak. She never spoke. Turning warily, I saw Guinevere seated as she always was. But this time, her hair had been braided over her head and the wound was no longer on her neck. She looked… almost normal—save for the paleness of her face that hadn't regained any color. "Gods…" I groaned, leaning back against the wall. "I really am going crazy."

"I'm not going anywhere, Morrigan… and neither are *you…*" she whispered. "Not until the blood is completely out of your system. And *not eating* is only going to slow it down. You're starving, Flower."

"Don't call me that." I closed my eyes, trying to ignore her presence. "You aren't her."

She let out a long, quiet sigh. "If you eat your meal, I'll give you some peace."

"You'll leave?" I asked hastily, as if I wasn't talking to a hallucination.

"I'll leave."

I crawled to the tray and picked it up. Though he had placed me in a cell, the food he sent down surely wasn't meant for prisoners. The meat looked rich and the rest of the plate had been filled with vegetables and fruits. It was a miracle that I had made it this long without taking a bite when the smell coated the air all day. Glaring at Guinevere, I took a bite and held back the relieving sigh my body wanted to push out. She only smiled at me, the way she used to, before her body seemed to dissolve into the air.

Leaving me truly… alone.

My. Fault.

The moment I heard footsteps coming from down the hall, I rushed to my feet.

Had Kaiden finally come to release me? Had the blood dried out? It had been two more days already. But when Dez appeared on the other side of the bars, I let out a disappointed groan and sank back to the floor. "I don't imagine he sent you down here to let me out, did he?"

He shook his head, and I noticed he wouldn't raise his eyes to look at me.

"You're okay with this?" I asked him. "Keeping me as a prisoner?"

"You're not a prisoner, Princess..."

"I told you not to call me that anymore." Beside me, Lady Guinevere sat, eyeing him curiously. "What are you here for, then?"

"Just... checking your progress..." A strong scent wafted through the air, springing me to my feet before I could stop myself.

Again, I ran toward the bars, unsuccessfully, and felt the metal gnawing at my wrists. I saw the blood pooling in his hand... I wanted it... I needed...

No.

With every bit of strength manageable, I balled my hands into fists and took a step back. Then, another... until I forced my body to sit back down, fighting against the rage that begged me to go to him.

I don't want it.

I don't need it.

"You're almost there," he said, with a hint of happiness hidden beneath the sad, lonely tone of his voice. "We... We messed up bad, Morrigan. I can only..." Wiping the blood from his healed wound, he kept his head down. "Do you think you'll be able to forgive us? One day?"

"You have me chained to a wall, Dez," I hissed through my teeth. "And you want my forgiveness?"

"There's so much you don't know... but I promise we will tell you. And I will spend every day dedicating my life to earning back the trust I destroyed." He walked away, leaving me to my ghost who said nothing of the interaction. She just turned her gaze to me, and I wasted the rest of my day away with sleep.

Chapter 42

Four days…

That's how long it had been since Dez paid me a visit. In those four days, a lot of my anger seemed to disappear. My thoughts became clearer and I hated myself for it, but I understood why Kaiden put me down here. The way I had reacted to their blood… I was no better than an animal. I didn't want to turn into the creature I saw in my books.

I could feel my strength returning with each meal that Kaiden sent me. What was his motive behind any of this? Why would he have saved me? Why bother? Kaiden made such a point of *hating* me… Nothing made sense anymore. Everything had been turned upside down and I had a feeling that my entire purpose in this world had been nothing more than to be a toy for them. What kind of gods would subject someone to that kind of life? Why the false pretense of becoming a queen? Why not just hand me off to the lords and lock me up at their disposal?

I perked up at the sound of footsteps approaching slowly from the stairs. It was likely another test to see how much progress I had made. When Kaiden came into view, he stopped in front of the cell door and met my eyes. "How are you feeling?"

Making light of the situation, I raised my wrists and shook them, causing the chains to rattle. "Never been better."

Even from where I sat, I could see his lips twitching into a small smirk before pulling the iron doors open and stepping inside. "May I?" he asked, gesturing to the floor beside me. I shrugged and watched him sit down, leaning his head back against the stone wall.

"I'm not upset..." I said quietly. "I... I understand why you had to put me in here. I just wanted you to know that."

Nodding, he lifted his eyebrows as he blinked slowly. "I'm not a good person, little dove," he began. "I've done things that your nightmares could never even conjure. I've killed many men for reasons that should never justify murder. And if you think I regret it, let me assure you—" he turned his head to me and I noticed the emotionless gaze within them. I knew now, by the way his irises swirled, it was his shadows masking how he truly felt. "I would do it all again, Morrigan. There is no redemption for me."

"Why are you telling me this?"

"Because... regardless of the things I have said or done... I need you to know that you are safe here. I will not touch you. I will not feed from you. I will not take your choices from you, as they did. As long as you remain under *my* roof... no harm will come to you, little dove. That's a promise."

Watching him carefully, I looked for any signs of deception—any hint of amusement in his words. But he looked more serious than I had ever seen him. "Why should I trust you?" I asked him.

"You shouldn't."

I stared for a moment longer, unable to decipher the strange feeling that made my heart flutter. "Then, why do I?" As we both fell in silence, I remembered the reason he had likely come here to begin with. Straightening my back, I made myself comfortable and tried to mentally prepare. "Alright. Let's get this over with."

"Get what over with?" He pinched his brows together.

"The test."

Smiling with a warming sincerity, he lifted his hand to reveal a large gash in the center of his palm. As I stared at the blood, I expected my body to have some kind of reaction. But... I felt nothing. I had never been more excited to feel *nothing.*

"When did you do that?" I asked

"Before I even entered the cell." Standing, he waved a hand over me and I felt the chains clink as the locks came undone. Then, he reached his hand out to me. "No more cages, dove."

The room Kaiden provided me with was simple, but beautiful.

It had two large windows on the back wall and between them stood two glass doors. They led to a stone balcony that overlooked the courtyard. His castle was... *different*—quieter. I occasionally saw some of his staff in passing, but they were minimal. The most I would see were guards roaming the castle. I tried smiling at them, yearning for some kind of interaction, but most of them looked too scared to respond.

Kaiden gave me as much space as I expected him to but always seemed to have his eyes on me. We would eat our meals in comfortable silence, the bickering almost entirely nonexistent anymore. And Lyra... she joined us at dinner. She sat directly across from me but still hadn't spoken a word. I knew that I hadn't been the kindest those past couple of weeks... and I hoped she wouldn't be angry at me for much longer. Though, if I could have mustered up the courage to apologize, it might have gone a lot quicker.

Lyra saved my life... How could I ever repay that?

"I can't hold them off for much longer, Morrigan," Kaiden said as he sipped his tea, having already finished his breakfast.

"I don't want to see them, Kaiden." Just the thought of having to speak to any of the guys ignited a flame in my belly. And, of course, the gem laying on my chest began to glow in response.

Apparently, whatever power that had manifested within me seemed to be a lot stronger than Lyra's—And she had been known as their strongest fire wielder since before the gods' ascension. The strange mineral on my necklace had the ability to contain it during a child's "transition" until they learned enough control to no longer need it. But... there had been a few flare-ups here and there.

Usually it only consisted of a small patch of grass catching fire, or a minor burn in the shape of a handprint on the table any time I even thought of the others. There was, however, one night after my time in the cells when Kaiden had to wake me from a nightmare. I remembered being thrown into a cold bath and thrashing around in his arms. Apparently, my body had become so hot that the sheets were completely scorched.

The burns on Kaiden's hands and arms from touching me took an entire day to heal, whereas other wounds would have taken mere minutes.

Beside me, Kaiden's eyes lowered to my chest, observing the light emanating from the necklace. "Drink your tea and center yourself before I need to replace another chair, little dove."

There may have been one time where Kaiden had mentioned Eris's name and my entire chair lit on fire, destroying it completely. Thankfully, Lyra had requested a few training uniforms that fire wielders were given, made with fire resistant fabric. It consisted of a black, loose shirt and black pants. They were comfortable enough and easy to move in, far more sensible than the gowns they had me wearing all the time.

Perhaps the chair should have been made of the same material.

Picking up my cup, I took a long sip of tea in an attempt to clear my mind. I took a couple of deep breaths and looked down to see the glow beginning to dim until it disappeared. "Sorry," I mumbled.

"I know you don't want to see them, but this involves *all* of us. These changes… There is a lot that needs to be discussed now."

Sighing, I took another sip. "I don't want them *here*. In case I… you know." Shame ran through me at the utter lack of control I had over my body.

He nodded, seeming to understand. "I'm sure we can arrange for a meeting in an appropriate setting. Though, I might not mind a burn on one or two of them," he added, smirking.

When the day came to an end, I sat down at my vanity and began removing the braid that I had lazily twisted into my curls. As I stared into the mirror, I tried admiring the way my cheeks were slowly filling out again. It turns out, in *my* case, losing weight was a lot easier than gaining it back. A soft knock came from my door and I gave them permission to enter. But I didn't expect to see a girl with beautiful, oak hair standing in my doorway, sporting the most stunning smile.

"Eowyn!" I gasped, lucky I didn't trip as I raced from my seat and wrapped my arms around her. "You're here... I missed you..." It took everything in me to hold back the tears that my body begged to release.

"I missed this," she whispered.

"I'm so sorry... I didn't know that I was... Oh, Gods." The tears finally began to fall. "I could have hurt you. What if I had transitioned? What if Lyra and Kaiden never—"

"Morrigan," she stopped me. Pushing her arms out, she held me at a length so our eyes could finally meet. And I noticed that hers, too, were glistening. "You didn't, okay? You didn't hurt *anyone*. You would never hurt anyone."

"You don't know that," I cried, thinking of the events that could have transpired. How close had I been to making the change? Who would have been first?

"I *know*, Morrigan." Picking up the half braid still lodged into my hair, her smile grew with a giggle. "I've never seen this style before."

I shoved her playfully and pulled my hair back from her grasp. "I didn't have *you* here to help me."

"Alright, alright." Walking over to my vanity, she pulled the chair out for me and motioned to it. "You can tell me everything while I tame it."

I told her of the feeding, the bloodlust, and just how bad it had gotten. She looked concerned but also hurt as I explained the nightmares and visions of Guinevere. Eowyn insisted that I tell her when I'm struggling in the future. And I knew that I should have. But that day... everything had just shut down. I felt like a fragment of myself drifting into a senseless void. And somehow... *Kaiden*... was the one who brought me back.

I wanted to laugh at the irony.

The only thing I didn't tell her was... was about *him*.

Now that *he* hadn't shown himself... I felt convinced that it was all a major hallucination. I had *finally* been getting better... I didn't need people thinking that my mind was broken as well.

"Will you speak to them, then?" she asked me.

"I should," I drawled, moving to my bed. "Dez wants my forgiveness. And, out of all of them, he's the one I yearn to give it to. But I don't know if I can. I still don't even know what they've done. And I'm frightened to find out."

"Kaiden told Dez you wouldn't even consider a meeting unless I came back with him."

A small smile formed on my lips, and I quickly shook it away. There had to be another reason he allowed Eowyn to come back. There wasn't a world where Kaiden would do anything with the sole purpose alone being *my* happiness.

"Lyra looks humiliated out there," Eowyn sighed. "Have you two spoken?"

Shaking my head, I looked at the door, almost sensing her presence on the other side. "Not yet..."

"Well, you need to, soon. Save her from her misery." Eowyn walked to her chair, plopping down before pulling out a book and smiling at me. "Sit with me?"

"Always," I laughed, before pulling up a seat and finding a book for myself.

The Diary of Daisies and Hellebores

Something has happened… Something
wonderfully horrible…

They could kill us for this, which is why I have
not told him, yet. I cannot condemn him without
a solution…

I have much thinking to do today.

There is an obvious, brutal answer that would
solve this problem… but I do not know if I
can bring myself to commit such an act.

I, indeed, have much I need to think about
today…

Chapter 43

Standing beside Kaiden, my body tensed with anxiety as I waited for them to arrive.

Clearly sensing the energy shift, Kaiden moved in closer to me. It gave off the false impression that he cared about how I felt in terms of this meeting. But I was positive he just didn't want me blowing anything else up.

"Maybe this wasn't a good idea," I whispered, turning to him.

"It's *necessary*."

"We can do it another time. Take us home." His brows pulled together at my words and he stared at me, almost *confused*.

But before he could even consider my request, a familiar voice chimed through the field ahead. "Did you get my gift?" Dez asked.

He had a smile on his face, though it looked tight and forced. I wanted to be angry as I looked at him, conjuring the vilest thought I could respond with. But when his bright, blue eyes met mine, a different emotion swirled in my chest.

"Thank you," I answered him, and his smile brightened just a little in response.

The others funneled in behind him, and a slow simmer spread across my arms at the sight of Eris and Naaz. I didn't need to look down to know that my necklace had begun to glow. The reflection of its light shone bright in each of their eyes. Reaching over, Kaiden removed his glove and placed a chilled hand on the back of my neck. "Cool yourself, little dove," he whispered.

With a deep breath, I let it out slowly and smiled with my many years of practice. "Let's sit."

Kaiden provided a table in an empty clearing, away from any people or things that I could possibly destroy in a fit of anger. As we all sat down, Kaiden pulled out the chair at the head of it and offered the seat to me.

"It's freezing," Eris noted from the other end. "You didn't even give her gloves?"

Lowering myself into the seat, I placed my hands on the table before me and watched the steam rise beneath my palms. Eris's eyes widened at the sight of it. "Seems I don't need them anymore."

From behind me, Lyra let out a light, stifled laugh that made me want to smile.

All seven of the lords were present. Dez and Kaiden sat on either side of me, with Cass beside the former. Cain leaned back in his chair, watching me with a calculated stare and Naaz glared straight ahead at Eris. Poor Dormius looked as uncomfortable as ever and kept his seat at the far end.

I didn't know what pushed me to do so, but I turned my attention to Cass—the first one I stayed with. My first kiss... First trust... First *betrayal*. He would be the first to speak. "I want the truth," I said to him. "All of it. Right now."

Before answering, he shared a nervous glance across the table and then leaned forward onto his elbows. "When the gods created the prophecy, they told us the... well... *your* blood would give us power. We would no longer need to feed from our own people. We could even go longer between feedings." He shifted nervously in his seat, but I remained still and attentive. "You *are* the chosen queen, yes, but... your only *real* duty... is to *us*."

"What do you..." It took just a few seconds for his meaning to truly sink in. "I... Are you saying I'm—"

"The gods couldn't very well tell the people that we would be using one of their own as a blood bag, could they?" Cain interjected in a crude tone. I flinched, not expecting his words to feel so harsh.

"So, I'm just..." On instinct, I turned to Kaiden. "I'm no better than a blood whore. That's what I am. I'm not even meant for—"

"Look at you," he said. Leaning forward, he plucked the necklace and pulled it out, allowing its light to shine up toward my face. "Is this normal to you?" he asked.

"It shouldn't be happening at all!" Cain yelled. "They promised immortality, not *this*." He waved his hand toward me, gesturing at the visible power radiating from the gem. "She's supposed to be mortal. Does this look *mortal* to you?"

"Her blood *is* mortal," Kaiden sneered at him. "Which is why when you *idiots* kept giving her so much of yours, you nearly created a vampyre out of her. All you needed to do was bond. But you had to be selfish pri—"

"Oh please, she would have been fine," Cain scoffed.

"So... you all just... toyed with me? Why did you keep offering it to me? You kept pushing this poison inside of my body... Eris," I turned to him, no longer angry, but hurt, "you could have just let me drink the wine."

"I thought my blood was a safer option for you," he replied, with his voice low and defeated.

"There's something I just don't understand." I returned to Kaiden, knowing he would be the most honest of them all. "If it was *you guys* that created the vampyres with your blood... Why was Rosina blamed for it?"

The way Kaiden's body stiffened at the question seemed to send a wave of unease across the table. "There are a lot of things the gods lied about, Morrigan. And I promise, in time, to tell you all of them."

Too many thoughts were racing through my mind. Too many questions. "You all... You *used* me. Cass..." His face peeked up, shame splattered with each of his freckles. "You told me that your blood made people *feel* things and you... you took advantage of me. You let me—"

Suddenly, Kaiden's hand landed on top of my knee and I didn't realize how heavily I had begun to breathe. They had let me do things... They had touched me and lied to me, convincing me that I had a home. But the entire time I was no better than a—

When he squeezed my thigh, I looked beside me as he placed his own hand on his chest, tapping it to get my attention. I had started to spiral. My lungs were constricting and my chest had tightened already. Laid perfectly across his shirt, I watched his hand rise and fall with the deep breaths he inhaled. *"Breathe with me,"* he whispered, only loud enough for me to hear.

As the seconds passed, I followed his pattern until the glow on my chest lowered to a small dim, and my body calmed down. Then, I turned to Naaz, waiting for what he had to say.

"I won't apologize, Morrigan. I made my choice and I won't grovel for forgiveness."

Rolling my eyes, I looked around at the rest of them. "So, the exhaustion. That was caused by bonding, right? Our blood exchanges?"

"Yes." It was Dez that answered me that time. "Magic can be exhausting, and much is needed to bind you to us and *us* to you."

Staring at Dez, I could feel my body soften at his deflated eyes. "Why?" I asked him. "Why didn't you tell me?"

"I should have. I should have told you and stopped it. Prin—Morrigan, *please*. I can't live like this. Just knowing how badly I've hurt you..." He reached for my hand and I allowed him to take it.

"Pathetic," Cain groaned. "You sound pathetic. I don't see what's changed. If anything, you should *thank* them. The little bird has a new talent." Standing, he puffed out his chest like he truly believed his words were justified. "I say we just complete the bonds *now*."

"Watch yourself," Kaiden warned in a low, deep voice.

"What exactly do these bonds mean?" I asked Dez. "What strings come with it?"

"It ties you to us as it ties *us* to you. I... We can't drink from anyone else now. When we need to feed, it *has* to come from you."

"What happens if you drink from someone else?"

He shrugged. "Truthfully? I don't know. Maybe death?"

This was all too much. I could handle the stipulations of the original prophecy. I had been adjusting to my life. But to be perpetually responsible for their lives... What choice did I have? I would *have* to allow them to feed from me...

Letting out a long breath, I pushed down the growing anxiety that threatened to climb back up—remembering that Kaiden was beside me. "What does that mean for *me*?"

Dez's mouth twitched like he wanted to smile. "You are tied to us as well. You may not feel it now, beneath the anger you're rightfully holding against us, but it's there. Our blood runs in your veins as yours now runs in ours."

And with that, I realized how long it had been for Dez. It meant he hadn't accepted any more offerings. He would need to feed soon... and he could *only* feed from *me*. Standing, I turned to Kaiden. "I'd like to go home."

But as he nodded, Cain let out a rude laugh from his seat. "So that's it? You're just going to leave?"

"At the *very* least, I have earned the right to think about all of this. Have I not?" I hissed back at him. Nobody responded. So, I looked down at Dez and offered a hand. "Will you come with us?"

Cain began to argue again, but Dez spoke before he could. "Anywhere with you."

Kaiden seemed to understand why I invited Dez back, and didn't question it.

When we arrived at the castle, he gave Dez a wary look. "Be gone before dinner," he ordered him, before placing a soft hand on my arm. "You know where to find me."

As Kaiden walked away, I looked up at Dez, who appeared more frightened than anything—like he didn't know what to say or do around me anymore. That wasn't the Dez I had met mere months ago. Wrapping a hand around his arm, I tried to offer a gentle smile. "Walk me to my room?"

"Yes," he breathed in relief, finally relaxing beside me.

When we entered, Eowyn gave us a surprised look as she took in Dez next to me. I gave her a knowing nod and watched her leave, before leading us to the patio. Outside, beneath the setting sun, all you could really see were the withered trees wasting away on the grounds.

"Everything looks so... *angry* here," I said quietly, as Dez leaned against the railing.

"Kaiden has a lot to be angry about."

I looked down at my hands before turning to Dez slowly. "I know you need to feed."

"Morrigan, I can't expect you to—"

"I *want* you to." Placing a gentle hand on top of his, I gave it a light squeeze. "I don't know where I stand with the rest of them. I don't even know where I stand with Kaiden anymore... But I know where I stand with *you*. Feed from me. Take what you need. After, we can work on mending the bridge between us. It will take time but—"

"I'll wait forever if I have to, Princess," he answered quickly.

Laughing, I shook my head. "I know you would." I moved his hand from the railing and held it with my own. "Feed, Dez."

After swallowing, he took a step closer and wrapped his other hand behind my neck, pulling me toward him. I angled my neck to give him more, and I could feel his breath on my skin. "Are you sure?" he whispered.

The sensation alone sent butterflies fluttering through my stomach. I couldn't remember the last time he had touched me, and I feared just how much I missed it. "Yes," I exhaled.

Lowering his lips, he placed a gentle kiss on my neck before biting down, and I gasped, clinging to his chest. I couldn't help the pleasure that began to stir, and I tried fighting against it. But it was inevitable. As he pulled from my veins, I succumbed to the blissful sensation causing my entire body to warm. Why did it have to feel so good? Why did it have to make me want him?

He only drank for a few seconds before licking my skin and kissing it again. As he let go, I tried to hide the slight disappointment I had been met with. "I'll see you soon, Princess," he said before walking away and leaving my room.

After a couple of minutes, I walked to my door and knocked softly against the wood, knowing Lyra stood behind it. She opened the door and peered inside. "Can we talk?" I asked her.

She appeared nervous as she nodded, but slipped inside and closed the door behind her. Together, we sat on the edge of my bed in silence, each waiting for the other to speak first. Before I could begin, Lyra turned to me with tears in her eyes.

"I'm so sorry, Morrigan. I should have come to see you. I was scared... I thought if I saw you like that... I would just let you go. I couldn't see you in chains... I'm sorry—"

"Lyra," I said softly, trying to get her to stop speaking.

"I watched you breaking before me and I took too long to do something about it. You could have *died*... Please, forgive me. I'm so sorry." Her tears had broken into sobs and I placed my hands on both of her cheeks, trying to wipe them away.

"I don't deserve you," I whispered as my own eyes started stinging.

With no more words, she pulled me into a hug and held me tightly. I didn't know how long we sat there together, but as each minute passed, another part of my heart had begun to heal. Maybe I didn't have my mother... *or* my father... but I had finally realized that this... Lyra... Eowyn...

They are my family.

And if love equated to wealth... well... I was absolutely rich with it.

Chapter 44

KAIDEN

Morrigan's steps held a new… lightness to them.

She ate a little more food at each meal. And I could usually hear laughter resonating from her room as she would read with Eowyn. She didn't need to know that I had made a point to take several walks throughout my day just to hear it. Lyra knew, however. As I passed Morrigan's door each day, Lyra's eyes would become a little more knowing than I was comfortable with.

But I was grateful that she had people here who could offer her something that my presence alone never would. I would make sure she felt safe and that she was cared for… loved by the right people. I would make sure she had everything that she could want and more. As long as I was never one of them.

Though, on occasion, it didn't stop me from pretending. That for the fleeting fifteen seconds of hearing her laughter, it was *me* making her laugh. Because in the rare moments of peace we had been given lately, something stirred in me when my words earned a smile from her. I could pretend, as I passed her room, that I hadn't allowed her to go through the torture that she did. That her scars weren't of my own doing, intentional or not. I could pretend that, in a different world and under different circumstances, there would have been a chance where she might have considered me.

Morrigan held a beauty that remained unmatched by anyone else in this world. She harbored a kindness that had yet to be snuffed out by the darkness that I knew lurked beneath the false light.

Even within the hatred and anger we bore toward each other, something entirely different continued to scratch its way to the surface. And pretending became far too easy nowadays. The worst of it being that we could have loved each other... Especially when everything about her undoubtedly screams that the stars wrote her name for *me*. Her eyes... Her hair... Even my own shadows seemed to agree.

But by the time her laughter would fade behind me, the pretending would begin to change. I would have to continue on as if our souls didn't call to each other in a way the others didn't seem to understand. I would have to pretend that holding her that day didn't... heal a part of me that I thought had died all those years ago.

I would *have* to pretend.

And for her?

I would.

But, even beneath the happiness that I knew to be genuine, something still held her back. I put relentless effort into finding Harley, who had completely disappeared. Morrigan longed for a home, a true home. And now that the guys had ruined the original plan—the idea of her choosing one of us—well, it all seemed a bit confusing now. No one had discussed it since the day they all came clean with her. We had no plan moving forward, and I could see that it was affecting her.

There had also been the slight issue of what their blood actually *did* to her—the ripple effect that it had caused. The change made her blood stronger, more potent. I found myself needing to feed more in her presence in order to mask the need that kept drawing me to her. With so many uncertainties, I knew of one place that might bring her a small fraction of the peace that she deserved. So, I asked Lyra to tell Morrigan to be ready after breakfast, and set aside the remaining duties I had for the day.

When she stepped out into the courtyard, my breath seemed to be taken with the wind as it flew through her curls. They hung loosely down her back, grazing against the long-sleeved, black gown with one of my fur-lined cloaks around her shoulders. I had to turn away so she didn't catch me staring so intently.

What the fuck is wrong with you, Kaiden?

"Where are we going?" she asked, stopping beside me.

"I'd rather show you than *tell* you." Reaching out, I waited for her to grab my arm, and slightly shuddered as she did. The warmth that radiated from her hand... I quickly allowed the darkness to consume us and pushed through the shadows until we stood before a large, iron gate.

"Where are we?" she asked, almost breathless as she looked up at the intricate designs engraved into the red rocks.

"Place your hand on the bars."

Narrowing her eyes, she looked at me with mistrust. I had to stick my tongue in my cheek to stop myself from laughing. *Smart girl.*

"It will only open for you, little dove," I explained. "Just… trust me. This once."

With a leap of faith, Morrigan looked forward at the gate again. She seemed to be examining it closely, trying to look through and see what was inside. But she didn't know the glamour that it held.

"Okay…" She sighed and slowly reached out, placing a gentle hand on the iron. And the moment she touched it, I could feel the pulse of magic as it recognized her.

I was right…

MORRIGAN

The gates pushed out, revealing a cluster of trees before me.

But as quickly as I saw them, their image began to fade. Similar to Kaiden's shadows, everything distorted until the scenery changed and revealed a large garden in its stead. "How did it—"

"A glamour," Kaiden finished for me.

Though the flowers and leaves had been taken by the winter spell, it was easy to imagine how beautiful it had been when it bloomed. There were stones that encircled different parts of the gardens, likely separating different species of plants. And at the center of it all, stood a three-tiered fountain with algae taking over the beautiful structure.

Behind the fountain, I could see stairs that led up a steep hill but couldn't quite make out what hid at the top of it. I turned to Kaiden behind me with wide eyes. "Where did you bring me?" I asked him.

"Home."

I had no idea what he meant as I looked around again before walking toward the fountain. It had been sculpted from marble and even its cracks were majestic. Running my fingers over small traces of gold, Kaiden stepped in behind me. "What is this place?"

"Garden of the Gods." He gazed around with a comfortable familiarity. "It *was* beautiful once. But it died when the gods ascended." His eyes made their way back to mine, the sun shining on the small hint of brown within them. "The gods lived here. No matter the season, it always shone with vibrant colors. We haven't been able to step inside once they abandoned it. So, this is the first time I've seen it in, well... *centuries*."

"Then, how was *I* able to open it?"

Kneeling down, he twirled the colorless leaves in his fingers. "You are the *chosen one*, in case you've forgotten."

I smiled and tried to hide the creeping blush on my cheeks, when I noticed one, small, bright flower. The tips of the petals were pink, and it faded into white toward its center. A lotus flower. "How strange," I whispered, catching Kaiden's attention. Lowering down, I examined the only flower alive in the entire garden. "Harley always said his favorite flowers were the lotus flowers because they represent rebirth."

Kaiden chuckled. "Fitting it would be the only flower standing in such a dark place. They were the gods' flower after all."

Something strange bubbled inside of me, like a breath that wasn't my own. As I stared at the flower, I could suddenly feel the energy pulsing from it... calling to me. It felt like I had been here before—like it recognized my soul and had been waiting for me. I reached down, hesitating slightly before plucking it from the ground. And that same energy vibrated between my fingers. That's when a warmth overcame me and a breeze blew through my hair, causing Kaiden to rise from the ground.

"Morrigan?" he asked quietly.

"Hmm?" I brought the flower to my nose and inhaled the calming aroma as it swept through me like rushing water.

"Morrigan," Kaiden called again.

When I looked up at him, I realized that everything had begun to change all over again. The leaves regenerated on the trees that surrounded the gardens. The branches grew taller. And the gardens were now filled with flowers of every color. Behind me, the sound of water made me jump, and I turned to see that the fountain was no longer covered in algae. It glistened with the sun's light reflecting off of the golden specks that decorated it. Water ran down the fountain, beautifully clear, and its mist cooled my skin against the sudden heat in the air.

Winter had disappeared in the blink of an eye.

My eyes were wide with wonder as I stared at the most breathtaking place I had ever laid eyes on. And when I faced Kaiden again, the same expression reflected in his own gaze, but it had remained on me.

"I don't understand," I whispered.

But as he took a slight step toward me, my heart skipped a single beat, raising even more questions. "I think I'm starting to," he answered quietly. Then, he shook his head, like he was chasing away a thought within it. "There's something else I'd like to show you."

It took us a good while to climb the stairs, and Kaiden looked utterly unfazed by it, of course.

The man had the body of a god. He could likely run for miles and barely generate a drop of sweat. *Stop thinking about what sweat would look like on him.* Our forced proximity had been confusing every cell in my body. *That...* along with his newfound kindness... I was still just a *girl*, after all. It was perfectly acceptable to acknowledge that someone looked pretty without falling in love with them.

I ignored the slight sting in my feet as we reached the top. And once again, we were met with another amazing sight. A large castle sat before us, the walls made of red stone. And where the trees cleared, a wide peak overlooked a vast portion of Andonia.

"This was their private home," Kaiden whispered, leaning into my side. "There were no staff, no guards. Their own, private escape."

"Are we allowed to go in?" I asked him.

"It's *your* home, Morrigan. It opened for you, and *only* you. You don't need anyone's permission."

The castle's walls were falling apart. The courtyard had been covered three-fourths of the way, and carved into the floor was a map of Andonia. Each territory had been labeled with the name of the god that had been worshipped most there. With my foot, I traced part of the map beneath me and looked up at the sky, not a cloud in sight. I wondered how beautiful it might have been to see the stars above while lying on the cool, stone floor.

"Why did you bring me here?" I called over my shoulder, admiring the different hues of blue above us. The silence felt so peaceful.

Kaiden blocked my view as he moved in front of me. And instead of answering my question, he held out his hand to me. "Dance with me."

I couldn't stop the laughter from blurting out. "Dance with you? Gods, I..." Nothing but sincerity reflected back at me in his eyes. "You... There isn't any music."

But as he waved a hand beside him, I watched vines twist around themselves. They carved and wove until a harp was created. "How did you—"

"Dance with me," he repeated.

I swallowed the lump in my throat and gave him my hand. As the harp began to play a beautiful, slow melody, he spun me once before pulling me into his chest. With his free hand, he held my back, keeping me close, and I tilted my head up to look at him.

Why are we dancing right now? I asked myself. But I couldn't stop moving with him. And with our feet gliding across the floor, Kaiden's eyes never lost contact with mine. We held each other there, stuck in time like the world had paused with us. I shouldn't have been enjoying it as much as I was. Kaiden was cruel. *Mean.* I *hated* him...

But why couldn't I look away?

Why, with every ounce of hate, did I feel closer to him than anyone else? Did he feel it too? The idea that we could have been kind to each other... *happy* even, forced its way through my mind like a parasite... That, if things had been different... this is what I could have chosen all along...

"Kaiden," I breathed, watching his eyes lower to my lips. My stomach began flipping, not knowing where to land. "What are we doing?"

A pained expression crossed his face. "I... I don't know."

Our feet moved together like we were two pieces of a puzzle—like our bodies had taken over and we no longer had to think for ourselves. And I found myself believing that the feelings inside of me were valid. What if... What if this had been the plan all along? What if every decision in our lives had led us to this... exact... moment?

"Kaiden..." I hadn't realized just how close his face had lowered down to mine. I could almost feel him breathing against my lips.

"Morrigan..." The heat radiating between us could light a fire.

I didn't know when things had changed with us, *if* things had changed with us. But the intensity that clashed between our bodies made me dizzy. We had stopped moving at some point, standing utterly still as we stared at one another. And just as I unintentionally licked my lips, he sucked in a sharp breath of fresh air before breaking our trance and stepping back.

"We-we should probably get back," he said nervously.

The space in front of me felt empty, lonely. I tried my best to hide the flush of embarrassment on my cheeks and nodded. It was for the best. Turning back to the castle, I could see the harp still sitting beside the wall, but its music had stopped.

"Can we come back sometime?" I asked him.

"You need only ask, little dove."

Chapter 45

Eowyn helped me dress for dinner, but my mind remained distracted.

I couldn't shake the feeling that something had… shifted after our visit to the Garden of the Gods. Kaiden seemed more present than normal. He would even join me in the library on occasion while Eowyn and I sat together, reading. There had been one time where he found me alone and shared the space with me on his settee. It was late, and I couldn't sleep. So, when exhaustion *did* overtake me, I remembered waking to a blanket delicately placed over me.

What is happening?

"Morrigan," Eowyn gasped. "You're biting your nails. Since when do you bite your nails?"

With a fit of exasperation, I dropped my hands into my lap. "I don't know," I whined.

Smirking at me through the mirror, Eowyn tilted her head in consideration. "You know. I think I have just the dress for you to wear tonight."

She brought out one of the fancier gowns in my closet. It had yet to be worn. An occasion hadn't called for it yet. "Why on earth would I need to wear this?"

Eowyn rolled her eyes and ignored my protest, getting the gown ready to wear anyway. "I don't mean to be so intrusive, but you both really need to stop fighting this before the tension alone causes you to blow up the castle."

"Excuse me?" I scoffed. "Fighting *what*?"

But the look that she gave me appeared anything but amused. "You watch each other basically all day. Everyone can see it but the two of you. Even Lyra told me about—"

"Lyra, too?!" I huffed.

"Mor…" Letting out a sigh, she picked up my hand and held it. "Sometimes… Sometimes the things that we *need* aren't necessarily the things that we *want*."

"Well that was really specific, Eowyn. Thank you for your counsel."

She laughed and shook her head. "I just mean… I don't know anything about Kaiden's life. Nothing can excuse his behavior, but something has switched in him, too. And that's because of *you*. That day… when he took you home after they… Morrigan, you truly can't be that blind."

Shaking out of her grasp, I tried to convince myself that her words held no bearing. "Your assumptions are wrong," I told her.

When I walked out of the room, Lyra stood there waiting for me. And with one look at my dress, she let out a low whistle. "Who are *you* trying to impress?"

A deep blush spread across my cheeks. "I'm going to eat dinner alone tonight... If that's alright."

With a light chuckle, she nodded. "Right..." She winked. "I'll see you in the morning, then."

As she walked away, embarrassment flushed me. "You two are wrong!" I yelled at her. But she only continued to laugh, making her way through the hall, and disappearing into the darkness.

They have no idea what they're talking about.

Keep telling yourself that.

Gods dammit...

With another puff of air, letting out my frustration, I walked down to the dining hall.

By the time I arrived, Kaiden had already sat down with a cup of tea in front of him.

As I walked into the room, he looked up and nearly spit out his drink at the sight of me. That sure did wonders for a girl's ego. "Morrigan," he rasped, wiping the tea from his lips.

His eyes seemed to trail down my dress as I walked toward my seat. "Eowyn wanted to dress me tonight," I answered shyly.

Before I could reach my chair, Kaiden moved quickly to stand, pulling it out for me. "You... The dress is beautiful. I mean, Eowyn has great taste." His entire face cringed after he spoke.

When our dinner had been placed before us, I couldn't help but stare at my plate. I knew that he was looking at me. His eyes practically burned a hole into the side of my face. But thinking of what Eowyn had said to me, I feared facing him. What if she was right? I couldn't risk having these feelings. Kaiden *hates* me. He would never...

But the Kaiden I knew these past few weeks... wasn't the Kaiden I had first met. There were no taunts, no insults. And even the pet name I had once loathed seemed to grow on me. It felt more endearing than offensive now. The way that he said it... That is what made the difference. It flowed from his tongue with meaning. Finally, my eyes met his, and he hadn't touched his food either. I sat there, frozen, unable to move or even *think*. Did he feel it too? Was he restraining himself as much as I was?

Breaking our gaze, his eyes moved to my neck and I watched his throat bob. "Morrigan," he warned.

My necklace had lit up like the sun, blazing against my chest. Groaning in frustration, I hid my face into my hands. "This damned necklace." If it wasn't already obvious what had been going through my mind, it most *definitely* was now.

"Dove..." he whispered. When I turned back to him, he had his head lowered, staring at his cup in front of him. "I can't... I need you to know that I can't give you what you want."

Stupid. You're so fucking stupid.

"What have I done to make you hate me so much?" I asked blatantly, trying to hide the small amount of pain behind my voice.

"I don't hate you, I..." He sighed as he rubbed the back of his neck nervously. Then, he pulled back and straightened himself out. "Maybe you should go and stay with Dez again. I know you care for him and he—"

"I've lost my appetite." It felt as though he had taken his dagger and stabbed me in the heart. I had been a complete idiot. Eowyn and Lyra were fools for even insinuating... I pushed out my chair and stood.

But as I walked out of the dining hall, I could hear Kaiden cursing behind me, following close by. "Wait! Morrigan... Shit."

His footsteps grew louder, but I ignored him. I didn't know where I was going, but I needed to be far away from Kaiden. I could only pray that he would give up his chase.

"Morrigan, fuck. Please, I didn't mean that."

"Nope. I think you very well *did* mean that, Kaiden," I called out behind me. "You don't want me here. You never wanted me here. You've made that abundantly clear." I lowered to a whisper, scolding myself. "Gods, I'm so stupid.. How could I even think..."

I somehow found myself in the throne room and realized the only exit stood right behind me. But when I turned, he had it blocked. "Let me speak," he insisted.

"Why should I?" I crossed my arms over my chest. "You're right. I *should* go back to Dez. At least he was kind to me."

His lips formed a sharp, thin like as he ran a hand through his hair. "You don't understand. When I saw you, I thought that they... I was angry and I needed to stay as far away from you as possible."

"Wow. This is great. I'm leaving now." I tried pushing past him, but he grabbed my shoulders, keeping me still.

"I avoided the dinners, praying to the gods I wouldn't have to see you."

"I get it Kaiden, you hated me from the start. You don't need to repeat yourself." I tried again to shimmy out of his hold, but he gripped tighter and began closing the space between us.

"No, Morrigan. Fuck, just listen," he begged.

"Spit it out, Kaiden!"

"Because the second I saw your face, I fucking loved you." My whole body tensed in response. "There was no escape. I saw your face, and in an instant, you had this hold on me—this connection I had no control over. I couldn't even stop it if I tried. I saw you and it felt like nothing else had made sense until *that* specific moment. I don't know how to describe it, Morrigan. I saw you and I was ready to kill the rest of them if it meant they would never touch you. But I knew I harbored too much rage, too much resentment, for you to ever choose me. I couldn't bear the idea of losing you, Morrigan. I've lost too much already."

His eyes swam with so many different emotions—so much sadness and guilt. But that wasn't a good enough excuse for me.

Actually... How *dare* he.

"How can you say that?! You *tormented* me! You teased me about Maeryn, constantly reminding me of my pain. How can you have the nerve to say you *loved* me? That isn't love, Kaiden."

"There are things... things I'm not ready to tell you. And you need to understand that when I saw you... it brought back memories that I wasn't ready to face. Maeryn—she was an asset for me. She had never been cruel like that, and when we learned of your existence, I knew she would keep you safe *and* report back to me. I didn't know her jealousy would lead to..." His voice shook a little. "I needed you to hate me. I needed to keep you far away from me. I'm surrounded by death, Morrigan. I can't fucking love you. I can't go through this again—"

"Kaiden has a lot to be angry about." That's what Dez had told me. Something broke him long ago, just as *I* had been. Maybe even worse. Kaiden had devoted so much time to helping me, and I wanted nothing more than to repay him somehow.

"I forgive you," I whispered.

Our foreheads met as he closed the distance. "Don't say that. Don't do this to me, please."

Cupping his face with my hands, I whispered again," I forgive you, Kaiden. For *all* of it." I lifted his face until I could see his eyes. "Share your burden with me, whatever it is. I'm not the same, innocent girl that you first met. I can handle it. Share your burden and I'll share mine."

Before I had the chance to react, Kaiden's lips were on mine, devouring me. I had never felt such raw passion, so much *need*. His hands grabbed my hips, forcing me against his chest. "Tell me to stop," he panted.

"Don't stop."

Breaking the kiss, he cursed as he lifted me into his arms. "Tell me no," he pleaded.

And as I watched the small flicker of darkness beginning to swirl in his eyes. I answered, "Yes."

In mere seconds, we were transported to what I assumed to be his room. He twisted me around, placing kisses along my shoulder as a groan rumbled deep within his chest.

"The dress," I said breathlessly. "It's too hot. I need it off."

It only took him a moment to undo the back, yanking it down to my feet, but when he stood up, he paused. His breathing picked up frantically, and I turned around, placing my hand on his chest.

"You didn't put those there," I reminded him.

"I did."

Ignoring his words, I pushed up onto my toes and kissed him. And he melted into my mouth. He returned the kiss with a fierceness as I began undoing his shirt, and then his pants. With a couple of steps, he backed me up against the bed until I fell onto my back, and I moved myself onto the pillows.

As he crawled onto the sheets, staring at me with his dark, menacing eyes, I could see the light of my necklace blazing in their reflection. "I don't know if I can control it," I admitted quietly.

But he continued to my thighs where he spread my legs, wrapping them over his shoulders. "Then, let my castle fall in flames. I gave you plenty of chances to tell me no, little dove..." He lowered his head, placing it perfectly above my center and smiled. "Now? You're *mine*."

Before his tongue could touch me, I placed my hand in his hair to stop him. "Wait," I said breathlessly, feeling my heart ready to explode. "If we... What happens when you change your mind? Kaiden, I can't just—"

His lips brushed my center, lodging my words in my throat and making my eyes flutter as I looked down at him. "You've got it all wrong, Morrigan." The next time he placed a kiss, he stuck his tongue out and gently swiped it along my center. He groaned, the sound vibrating the bed beneath me. "There's no leaving, now."

I attempted saying his name once more, scared of what it meant. Unfortunately, the only sound that escaped was a moan as he dragged his tongue against my core, placing a hand on my stomach and shoving me back down. As he pushed his fingers inside of me, my body began rocking against his mouth, begging him for more. He tasted me like he *needed* it, and by the gods... I needed *him*. I had never needed anything more in my life.

There was no going back. The kiss alone ignited a dark craving inside of me that I didn't know I had. There's a thin line between love and hate... and somewhere along the way, we crossed that line. Even if I hadn't admitted it to myself, my worst moments were when Kaiden didn't show. Any time I made it to my room without a disturbance, my heart would sink just a little. Even if our interactions were volatile, I *needed* them... They kept me alive, even in my darkest moments.

Kaiden was pushing me to a level of desire that bordered obsession, and every time my body would come close enough to its climax, he would stop. "Kaiden," I whined.

"I've never told you, but I love the sound of my name on your tongue. You've always said it like you wanted to *kill* me." He gently nipped where his tongue had been, making my body jerk beneath him. "Say it again," he pleaded.

Daring to look at him, I opened my eyes and lost every part of my breath. His shadows were creeping along his skin—an extension of himself. And his eyes... They were begging to take over. It should have frightened me. It *would* have frightened anyone else. "Kaiden," I answered with a slow exhale.

He softly bit my thigh and left kisses along my skin as he crawled up my body. Kaiden... he's *beautiful*. If looks alone could kill, he would have stolen my breath any number of times he cornered me in that hall. I would learn every inch of his body so that I could trace it by memory.

He began moving his fingers inside of me again, and as his face hovered above mine, I wrapped my hands in his hair. Yanking him down toward me, I kissed him like I had been suffocating. I needed to taste him, every part of him. Everything just felt... right.

My arms were meant to be around him. His lips were made for me.

Pulling his fingers out, he released me from the kiss and whispered, "Look at me."

I opened my eyes just as I felt him enter me, and I gasped as I held onto his neck. I could feel him stretching me, filling me completely. And as he brought his forehead to mine, keeping our gazes locked, it was a moment we shared together. Having him, like this, completed me in a way that I didn't understand—like the final hole in my heart had been mended.

Everything just... clicked. I was *his* now. This man could ruin me in the blink of an eye.

Our bodies moved together like a dance we already knew. I couldn't look away from him, from the beauty that hovered above me. The eyes I had once feared now held me, safe inside of their darkness. He poured himself into me, sharing every heartache, every ounce of pain, and I would take it all if it meant I could have him. If it meant I could keep him, just like this.

The whites of his eyes turned completely black, and I could feel him tense above me. But I captured his lips for another kiss. "Let go, Kaiden."

A deep growl escaped his chest and his pace quickened. The headboard crashed against the wall and I dug my nails into his back. That's when I felt them, his shadows slinking along my hands. They were making their way up my arms, surrounding me in their own blanket of protection. At the same time, I could feel the fire within me igniting in response. They were calling to each other in a way.

"Kaiden," I panted, feeling my release building like a storm inside of me. "Kaiden, I—"

"*Mine*," he growled.

The sound of his voice alone is what sent me over the ledge—my release washing over me like a landslide. As we both finished together, I felt the surge of power that exploded into the room. It was like my body had been relieved of every bit of tension I had held onto for weeks.

His head collapsed onto my shoulder, and I looked down to see his shadows slowly leaving my skin. They felt cool, brushing through the small hairs on my arms. And as they retreated back into Kaiden, I almost missed how they felt against me.

After a couple of seconds breathing together, he lifted his head and looked around, laughing as he stared at the bed. "What is so funny?" I asked him.

Finally, I looked down at the sheets and realized there was a large burn mark that spread across the bed. It even seemed to reach the wooden floor below. Kaiden shook his head and lowered it back to my chest, directly above my heart. "I'll have them changed into something a little more… durable."

He laughed again, and I wished that I could bottle up that sound so I could save it forever—the most beautiful sound I had ever heard.

I think I love you too, I thought to myself… too scared to let the incriminating words slip from my mouth.

Chapter 46

Kaiden and I began spending far too much time tangled up in bed together.

My room had all but been forgotten, now that I stayed with him in his. And it was never a question. He barely wanted to allow me out of his sight anymore. I truthfully felt a little guilty about it, in regards to Lyra and Eowyn. But the sly smiles they would give me any time Kaiden walked into the room showed me they didn't take much offense to it.

Sitting down in the dining hall, I sipped from my tea as I mulled over the ridiculousness of Kaiden's suggestion. "Absolutely not," I said blatantly. Beside me, Eowyn snickered a little and Lyra pressed her lips together, forcing herself not to smile.

Most of the formalities had all but flown out the window among the three of us. There were no titles, just friends. Both Eowyn and Lyra ate most meals with us, unless Kaiden wanted *alone* time with me at dinner. I would never admit to the two of them just how many times I'd been spread out on that table. It was a secret I planned on carrying to my grave.

I had been surprised with how close Lyra and Kaiden had become. He seemed to trust her more than his own men. He requested that she train his soldiers, and he would seek counsel with her on certain matters.

Kaiden ran a frustrated hand over his face and sighed. "I understand that you don't want to see them—"

"And she has every right to feel that way," Lyra added.

Giving her the fakest smile he could manage, he turned to her. "Thank you, *Lyra*. But now that you're bonded, they literally rely on your blood, Morrigan."

"Then, let them starve." I shrugged, returning to my tea.

But I felt Kaiden place his hand on mine and instantly turned to him. "As much as I would love to see *most*, if not *all* of them dead… We don't know what will happen to *you* if they die." His eyes softened, and I knew that I would have to give in to his request. "I can't risk losing you, dove."

Gods dammit… He played you good.

I sighed, placing my cup of tea down on the table. "Fine."

"We'll get it over with and then we will have time to figure out a better plan moving forward." He stood, bending down to place a soft kiss on my lips, and my heart fluttered from his touch.

When he left, I sat there in my chair for a little while longer. I imagined the smoke that filled my room that day when Kaiden and Lyra rescued me. I pictured Eris's face when he tried to compel me… Disgust made the tea sit heavy in my stomach at their lack of self-control… their carelessness with my life. But, in the end, I knew that Kaiden was right.

Dez had fed recently, but Eris... Naaz... even *Cass* would need to feed soon.

"Do you want us there?" Eowyn asked me.

"No." I leaned back in my seat in defeat. "I think I'd like to do this alone."

She nodded in understanding, and gave me a quick hug before leaving the dining hall. Eowyn had taken up my room now that it was no longer used. She enjoyed sitting on the balcony, reading in the brisk morning air. Although the outside of the castle looked like death itself, its silence offered a certain peace. I would often join her in the evenings before returning to Kaiden's room.

"I don't like the idea of you being alone with them," Lyra added as she finished her food. "At least make sure Kaiden is in the room with you, please."

Biting the nail on my thumb, I couldn't help but feel anxious at having Kaiden watch. Neither of us had brought up the topic of bonding together, and I felt some shame having to share my blood with the others in front of him. I had asked Kaiden how he handled the Offerings, knowing how the aphrodisiac is released with their bites. But he assured me he never drinks from someone directly. Usually one of his guards volunteers, and they pour their blood into a chalice for him.

It made me feel better, selfishly so. I couldn't stand the thought of him touching anyone... of his lips on anyone else's skin but *mine*.

He... is mine.

They arrived just before dinner, and I felt incredibly eager to get it over with.

Walking into the throne room, I saw Eris, Naaz and Cass all standing together. Eris and Naaz tried to look unfazed by it all, but I could see the nerves in Eris's face. Cass, though, looked like a wreck. It almost made me want to smile. Seeing the person who took the most, feeling the brunt of it, well that felt like justice handed to him by Fate herself.

They all turned to look at me as I approached them, Kaiden following closely behind.

"Morrigan," Eris acknowledged.

I simply raised my chin slightly and clasped my hands at my waist. "We can skip the pleasantries. I'd like for my dinner not to be spoiled before I have the chance to enjoy it." I eyed each of them, trying to decide the best way to handle this before turning back to Kaiden. "I don't know how it'll affect me, giving so much blood at once."

He nodded, placing a hand on my lower back. "I'll give you a small amount of my blood to heal you after. As long as I don't feed from you, it won't complete the bond."

"You haven't bonded with her?" Cass asked, clearly surprised.

Kaiden glared back at him. "No, Cassius. I haven't." He rolled up his sleeve, exposing his wrist for when they were done. "Turns out, I'm fully capable of pleasuring a woman without *drugging* her first."

Immediately turning defensive, Cass took an unfriendly step forward, his fists clenched at his side. But Naaz stopped him. "If you would like to starve, be my guest. But I'd suggest not antagonizing the only one of us that holds her trust right now."

Walking toward the center of the room, I stopped at the table that held three glasses. "I don't think it's entirely necessary, nor appropriate, for your lips to be anywhere near my body any time soon. So," I moved to stand behind the table, showing it to them, "you can drink from *these*."

Displayed on the table was a dagger, perfectly placed behind the glasses. I stared at it nervously, and Kaiden instantly appeared at my side. "Allow me," he whispered in my ear.

Taking my hand, he turned it so that my palm faced up. He didn't look at me as he brought the dagger to my skin, giving no warning before pressing deep and dragging it across my hand. My lips flinched from the pain, but I muffled it, closing my eyes to ignore the radiating heat from the wound. Once he finished, he moved my hand toward the glasses.

One by one, I squeezed my palm over them until they were full enough. Each glass made my head lighter. By the time the third one had been filled, I wavered, with Kaiden holding me up. The walls around me looked blurry as they spun across my vision. After wrapping my hand with cloth, he raised his wrist and quickly placed it against my lips.

I hesitated with the blood settling across my tongue. I was scared. What if it happened again? What if I couldn't control myself? "I'm here." His words caressed me, protecting me. "I won't let anything happen to you."

I allowed the blood to flow into my mouth, swallowing it and stifling the moan that wanted to escape. Each of them tasted so different. Kaiden's... it was sweet, but *strong*. I could feel his power as it coated my tongue... the darkness that swirled inside of him. The dizziness began to fade, and it took all of my courage to pull away the moment I felt the skin on my palm stitch itself back together.

Kaiden's eyes shone with approval and he kissed my head before removing the cloth from my hand.

I offered a glass to Eris first, and he made no eye contact as he drank it. I wondered if it tasted as bitter as his expression looked as he set down the glass. Next was Naaz, and he didn't look away from me, even though I could see the resentment in his brown eyes. When Cass stepped forward, I pulled the glass back, stopping him. He gaped at me, confused.

"I trusted you, Cassius."

His throat looked tight as he swallowed. "I know."

"I was alone. Inexperienced. Ignorant. And I *trusted* you."

"I'm sorry, Morrigan." So much desperation was present in his voice, and I almost pitied him.

I looked him dead in the eyes. "Beg."

"What?"

Taking a step back, I motioned to the floor. "Get on your knees… and *beg*."

Beside him, Eris and Naaz exchanged glances with each other. But Cass's eyes were wide with embarrassment before turning to Kaiden. "You have to be joking. Kai—"

"Beg!" I demanded, my voice echoing off of the walls.

Looking ashamed, he lowered himself down slowly until he knelt before his *queen*. And it was the most beautiful sight that I had ever seen. A rush of power and importance ran through my body like a wave. I brought such a large man down to the ground with a simple word. As he looked up at me, with defeat in his eyes, it fueled the fire in my chest, causing the gem to glow.

"I couldn't care less what the gods claimed my duty was to you all." I turned to each of them, showcasing the fury in my eyes. "The next time *any* of you decide to fuck with me again…" I looked back down at Cass. "Remember that *I* hold your lives in my hand now."

After handing Cass the glass, I turned back to Kaiden, who looked ready to devour me. "You can all leave now," he called to them, not moving his eyes from mine. No one said a word as they left, and I wrapped my arms around him. As he cupped my face, pressing his forehead against mine, he said, "Don't get too hasty. I'm not doing anything while you're under the influence of my blood."

I let out a long sigh. I knew he was right. "Okay, fine." Letting go of him, I pushed up and placed a quick kiss on his lips. "I promised Lyra I would visit Hagen today, anyway. I owe him quite a few apologies."

"That works out well, then. Dez called Lyra back this morning to help him train some of the younger fire wielders for a few hours. She can meet you there once she's done." He pulled me in for one more kiss, groaning as he let me go. "Leave before I tie you to our bed and keep you for myself."

Our bed.

The Diary of Daisies and Hellebores

I decided to tell him.

It is becoming hard to hide from the others. He wasn't angry with me, but I know he is scared. I cannot blame him. I am scared as well. This has never happened before, and we must proceed with delicate caution. Together we have casted an illusion so the others cannot see. It is a temporary solution, but it will give us more time to find a permanent one.

Chapter 47

Hagen pulled me in for a tight hug, squeezing me to the point that I thought my lungs might actually collapse.

"I'm glad you're alright." He stepped back, looking me over as his face dropped a little. "Lyra told me…"

"I'm fine," I stopped him. "Well, I *will* be fine. I'm sorry it's been so long."

"No apologies," he said as he wrapped an arm around me. "You've been away for so long, some of the villagers would like to see you before dinner, if that's alright. I figured while we wait for Lyra—"

I smiled brightly at him. "I would *love* that."

We made our way through the town center, where I was greeted by familiar faces. Many wanted to shower me with gifts, which I politely declined as much as possible. Until Hagen decided to grab baskets for them to load it all into. As I rested by the fountain, its water frozen in place, I watched the children playing around me. They threw small pebbles onto the ice, laughing together, and I had forgotten how peaceful it felt here. I was home again.

Behind the children, an older couple stood nearby, watching the little ones with wide smiles. I thought of what it would be like to have little ones—being able to love them with the same compassion I craved for so many years. Would Kaiden want children? Would he want them with *me*?

I should have told him how I felt. And as I watched everyone passing by, I decided I would do just that when I got home.

Home.

Our home.

In the corner of my eye, I saw someone approaching. I turned to see a beautiful, tall woman with silky, blonde hair. *Gwenyth*. Her face looked pale and broken, where it had once been full of color. "Y… Your Grace," she stuttered, lowering her head to me.

"Can I help you, Gwenyth?"

She extended a hand with a small smile. "Walk with me?" she offered.

I felt hesitant to accept. But the way she had acted toward me held little weight after everything the lords had done. Nodding, I stood and accepted her hand, walking through the market at her side. Some stared at the two of us, likely taken aback by the knowledge of what Gwenyth *used* to be to Dez. But I knew his feelings for me. And I trusted them.

We made our way to the lake that had iced over and I let go of Gwenyth, leaning against the pier. "It's so peacefully quiet."

"I think… I wasn't exactly kind to you when you first arrived. And…" I watched Gwenyth fiddle with her fingers nervously. "I would like to start over, if you'll accept it."

I had to hold back my surprise. "You... You want us to be—"

"Friends." She smiled.

I had been doing a lot of forgiving lately. And if I could move past the betrayal I felt with Dez, surely I could give an innocent woman a chance as well. "I think I would be alright with that," I said to her.

Beside me, her eyes began to water and she turned, hiding her tears as she wiped them away. "Thank you, Your Grace."

We stood together for a while, quietly admiring the glistening sun against the ice on the water. It glimmered like stars shining across the lake. Then, I heard footsteps walking along the pier and looked up to see Hagen approaching. "Seems Lyra may not make it in time for dinner, Your Grace," he said smiling.

So, I looked at Gwenyth. "Would you like to join us?" I asked her.

"Y-yes... I would love that."

We started a small fire in the pit outside of Hagen's home, facing the trees. Hagen walked to the other side of the house to retrieve more wood while Gwenyth and I huddled close to the embers. The flames felt different to me now. It was as if the fire had become a part of my blood—like I could sense its heat under my skin. If only I had known how to regulate this power... call it to me instead of allowing it to take control. Fire was so unstable, so untrustworthy. But Lyra could wield it as smoothly as her lungs controlled her breath. She promised we would start training after the week ended.

"I didn't love him," Gwenyth said beside me. "Not really." I looked at her, but remained silent, giving her space to speak. "I've always craved love. My parents adore each other and they've always looked at me like I was such a disappointment. All I wanted—all I *want* is someone to look at me the way my father looks at my mother... The way *he* looks at *you*."

I shook my head and returned to the flames. "It's not love."

Gwenyth laughed. "He loves you, Your Grace. He hasn't come back here since you left. He sends his guards to handle everything, and anyone that *has* seen him... Well... he's lost without you."

Even if I didn't want to admit it, I felt lost without him, too. Dez had a gentle soul, so much love to give. He made me feel like I was floating on air most days. His kisses were passionate. And when he touched me, it was like he needed me to be able to breathe on his own. I didn't have the will to stay angry at him for long. That much I knew.

But then, there was Cain and Dormius. Was it right to deny them of what the gods promised? If that truly is my only purpose... did they not deserve the same? Cain had a right to be angry and jealous when we all met that day. It wasn't fair that four of them reaped the benefits of my blood while the other three were left waiting—forcing them to feed on their own. They didn't ask for this curse.

And what if I *did* love Dez, too? Would Kaiden accept it? Could he set aside his own wants and needs to share me with another? How could I ask that of him?

"Your mind is racing right now, isn't it?" Gwenyth asked. "I can see it in your eyes."

"I have a lot of decisions to make, with so little time to make them," I admitted with a sigh.

The smoke shifted as she moved closer to me. "I couldn't imagine being in your position. So much weight on your shoulders. If it brings you any solace, know that you are truly loved by everyone. Your people adore you, Morrigan." The last part of her words felt almost bitter. "It's a shame."

Pulling my brows together, I turned to her, confused. "A shame?"

But before she could explain, loud explosions erupted throughout the village. I jumped up as I watched arrows fly, striking bystanders nearby.

No. This isn't happening. I spun around, ready to grab Gwenyth's hand, but she was gone. She likely ran to safety and I would need to do the same, but not until I found Hagen.

DEZ

EARLIER THAT DAY

Lyra's yelling filled my ears, enough to give anyone nearby a killer migraine.

"Focus. On. Your. Breathing!" she screamed at the recruits.

Rolling my eyes, I recalled the same scared expression on *her* face during her training. She grew into something fierce in the years I had known her. She would have been a soldier worth remembering during the war. A fire broke out beneath the feet of one of the young wielders and Lyra marched over to him, putting it out before it could spread.

"If something as small as being yelled at sets you off so easily, how will you handle being *shot* at? How are you going to protect your family? Your lords? Your *queen*?" She stepped up to his face and the poor boy cowered beneath her.

Releasing a long, tired sigh, I stood from my seat. "Let's take a breath. Let them refuel and after lunch, we can pick it back up."

The recruits couldn't have been faster in their escape.

As Lyra pulled out her pocket watch, she checked the time and looked anxious as she placed it back down. "You should come tonight," she said to me.

I shook my head. "She doesn't want me there."

"You don't know *what* she wants."

In that, she was correct. The last time I had seen her, she was so caring and gentle with me. I wanted to remember that. I didn't want to risk seeing any more disappointment in her eyes when she looked at me.

"Listen, you fucked up," Lyra said crudely. If it had been anyone else speaking to me like that, my dagger would have found itself lodged in their throat. But Lyra was different. She had become family now, as much as the rest of us were. "But she needs you just as much as you need her. Come tonight. For her."

I smirked as I turned back to the castle. "I'll think about it," I promised her. "Come, let's eat before we return to your unyielding torture."

After lunch, we remained outside for quite some time, conducting more training. I had never seen a greener set of soldiers before. It seemed like, as the years passed, the potency of their magic faded within the gifted. Their mortal blood had been diluting whatever part of them descended from the gods. But, before long, the sun had set. And we didn't realize just how late it had gotten until Lyra pulled out her watch again, letting out a loud curse.

"We'll continue tomorrow," she called out. "Everyone leave." Gathering her things quickly, she grabbed my arm and pulled me into a fast walk. "Hagen is going to kill me for being so late. Let's go."

"I never said that I was going," I laughed, trudging along with her.

"I decided for you."

We came to a halt when one of my guards ran toward us, frantically. "Henri? What's wrong?" I asked him, noting the fearful look in his eyes.

He looked to be out of breath, and his face had gone pale. "Faelar, My Lord... I was doing one of my rounds and... One moment he had been sitting on the stairs... The next..."

"Spit it out, Henri!" Lyra hissed, grabbing his shoulders.

"H-He's dead. An arrow… Right through his head… My men are searching the grounds now."

Chapter 48

MORRIGAN

Am I breathing?

I couldn't tell if I was breathing. In front of me lay a stiff body, covered in blood that had splattered onto my dress. She had been shot with an arrow through her head as she tried to run to me. They were here… *They* were here… Hagen. I had to find Hagen.

"Hagen!" I screamed through the cries of agony around me. "Hag—" A hand covered my mouth and I could feel the tremors now in my arms. They were going to take me. They were going to kill me.

"Your Grace," a familiar voice whispered into my ear. "You must be quiet and come with me." Hagen. It was *Hagen's* voice. I turned to him with wide eyes, struck with horror, and he looked down at the body beside me, mirroring the same fear. "Hurry. We must hide you."

Hagen pulled me, running to his home and slamming the door shut behind him. "Hagen," I panted. "What's happening?"

"Hush now," he warned, placing a finger to his lips. More screaming poured in through the windows, and I made the mistake of looking outside. People were dropping like flies. Those who had been dancing and laughing only hours before, were dead now. That's how quick it happened. They were gone.

Kaiden, I thought to myself, as if he could hear me. Tears welled in my eyes as a sinking feeling cracked inside of my chest. I wasn't going home. I wouldn't see Kaiden again. Lyra... Eowyn...

The people... They were all dying because of *me*.

My fault...

My fault...

I ran to the door, ready to open it, but Hagen grabbed my arm, shoving me back against the wall. "No, Your Grace. If you go out there you will die."

"They want *me*, Hagen. I can't let everyone die to save myself. Let. Me. Go," I ordered him.

But he moved himself in front of the door, barricading me inside. "You'll have to kill me before I let you out of this house, Morrigan."

The screams... They were burning into my mind. Men, women, children... So many people were dying and I couldn't stop it. "Hagen," I began to cry. "*Please.*"

A heavy pair of footsteps ran toward the house, and I quickly smacked my hand over my mouth as Hagen placed a board over the door. Then, he grabbed me once more and rushed me into Lyra's room. Lyra had a small area in the back corner with a loose piece of wood. She used to hide the bows she would make as a child so Hagen wouldn't confiscate them. Hagen shoved me inside of the small opening and quickly replaced the board over me, trying to keep me hidden.

By the time he turned around, I heard the sound of glass breaking and knew that they had come through the windows outside of the room. "We know she's in here, old man! Don't think I won't burn this house down just to smoke her out!"

My fingers twitched, desperately wanting to shove myself out of the cramped space and let them have me. If Hagen died too... I wouldn't be able to live with myself. "She isn't here," he called back to them.

"Did you think you could hide from us forever, *Princess*?" the man taunted.

I quickly had to stifle my scream as the door to Lyra's room flung open, and Hagen took a defensive step forward. Through the cracks, I could see the man standing before him. He was covered in blood that surely hadn't been his own, and it even stained his blonde locks that hung wild from his head. "Tell me where she is, old man, and I *might* let you live."

"I told you. She isn't—"

The moment the man's hand struck Hagen in his face, I could barely contain the cry that crawled up from my throat. And he heard it.

Turning his eyes to the board that covered me, his grin widened into something sinister that I would likely never forget. "There you are." I had nowhere to go as he stalked toward me and ripped off the wood. "Let's have a good look at you."

Giving it my best effort, I clawed at him, trying to give me enough space to make a run for it. But he grabbed my face with his hands, pinching it tightly before slamming me back against the wall. *Kaiden... Kaiden, please.*

My skin began to crawl as he brought his face close to mine and sniffed up my neck. "This is going to be fun, Princess," he whispered and then dug his fingers into my arm, dragging me out of the house.

"Hagen!" I screamed back at him, begging to know that he was okay. "Hagen!"

I was quickly shoved to the snow, my face taking the first impact. It took all of my energy to push myself up onto my hands. But I quickly regretted doing so. Bodies surrounded us, bleeding into the snow. And against the walls sat women, cradling their crying children, all huddled together.

My fault... Oh, Gods... This is all my fault.

They were staring at their loved ones, dead on the ground. And that's when I noticed another, smaller body that had fallen victim to their slaughter... A *child*... His eyes were closed... and he... he looked like he was sleeping... I felt a sob building in my chest before two pairs of feet stood before me. One pair of boots, and one pair of feminine shoes that I had seen only minutes ago.

Trailing my eyes up, I looked first at Gwenyth who stood above me, sporting a menacing smirk. But beside her... I couldn't believe what I was seeing. "I don't... I don't understand."

He smiled as he knelt down, rubbing his thumb along my chin. "Gods... I could paint that look on your face and hang it in my throne room, Princess."

"I told you she would be here," Gwenyth sneered.

"How... How could you?" I cried, aiming my anger at her. "These are your *people*. Your *friends*. Your *family*."

"And *you* were taking it away from me! Everything was fine until you got here! Now, Dez will have no one else to turn to." She spoke as if she truly thought that this would solve her problems. But everyone here...

They *saw* her. The only way she could get away with any of it is if they… No… They were going to kill them all.

Nausea swirled in my stomach and I swallowed, keeping it down as best I could. "Why would you do this?!" I yelled at him.

Looking around, he let out a laugh. "This is *nothing*. You should have seen the war. This? This is child's play." He returned his icy gaze to me. "You look so beautiful beneath me, Princess."

"I gave you what you wanted. Now it's your turn to hold up your promise," Gwenyth hissed at him. "They all know I brought you here. They need to be taken care of."

"No!" I cried. "Please. I'll go. I'll do what you want. Don't hurt them."

"So eager to protect everyone." He smiled and pinched my face harder. "You've always had such a bleeding heart, haven't you?"

"What are you waiting for?" Gwenyth whispered.

But as he looked into my eyes, he let out an exasperated sigh and gripped the dagger at his side. "Only because you asked nicely," he said to me before turning around and shoving the dagger into Gwenyth's chest. "I'm not interested in slaughtering an entire village—not when I already have what I want. Snakes shouldn't trust snakes, Gwenyth."

A look of shock froze on her face as the light faded from her eyes and her body fell to the ground. "You're a monster." My voice sounded rough as I swallowed the cry still stuck in my throat.

When he leaned back down, I felt the first tear slip down my cheek. And the bastard pulled my face to his, licking it. He let out a moan, pulling back with his eyes closed. But when they opened, they were devoid of any possible emotion. "You haven't even *seen* the monster yet, *Your Grace*." Standing, he pushed my face away, a sting left in the wake of his fingers. "Bring her."

"He'll come for you," I warned him as hands gripped my arms. "He'll stop at nothing. He will *kill* you for this, Cain."

Cain laughed wickedly. "Princess... He would have to find us first."

Before I could mutter another word, someone else's voice whispered in my ear. *"Sleep."* And everything turned black.

My body bounced around, swaying as I laid against someone's chest.

Even with how groggy my mind seemed to be, I could tell that we were on a horse. Cain rode in front, so I knew that it wasn't him holding me. And beside him was the blonde man that found me in Hagen's home.

Okay, Morrigan. Now you need to think. You need to get away somehow.

I tried to keep my body still and limp against the stranger as I used my eyes to survey the area. We were in the woods somewhere. I didn't know how much time had passed either. Looking down, I saw the necklace still hanging around my neck.

You can do this. Just take it off. Maybe without it you'll have a chance.

My movements were painfully slow. I couldn't let the person know that I was awake. I tried to keep it in rhythm with the rocking of the horse, making my hand barely noticeable. The moment I felt the tip of the gem, I pinched my fingers around it and pulled carefully. The string stretched against the back of my neck, scratching at my skin. But I bit down on my tongue, ignoring the pain.

Just a little more...

With one more thud from the horse, I yanked it gently and felt it snap. The energy that surged within me buzzed like a rush of power, and I inhaled it all. *Help me*, I thought. *Anything. Do anything.*

It started in my fingertips—a low hum that seemed to expand into my fingers. Then, the itching began again, but I fought the urge to succumb to it. *Let it happen,* I told myself. *You just need a head start. Kaiden will already be looking for you.* The sky still appeared dark, so it couldn't have been that long since we left. But it would have been long enough for someone to notify Dez. And Dez would have retrieved Kaiden. They were looking for me.

"My Lord," the man said behind me. "She's... Something's not right."

I knew he felt the heat radiating from my body. I channeled every ounce of anger that I had within me, willing it to come out. That's when Cain's horse came to a halt and he turned slowly, evidently annoyed. "What are you going on about—"

It clicked. Like a wave of heat, bursting through my body. It wasn't much, but the reins on the horse caught fire and the man behind me yelped, dropping the rope. It was just enough for me to toss myself to the side and dismount before breaking into a sprint.

Kaiden. I have to get to Kaiden.

I ran as fast as my feet would take me. The wind whipping my hair masked the sound of men yelling at each other. And I knew if I stopped for even a second, Cain would have me. So without any knowledge of where I was going, I let the earth guide my every step and prayed to the gods that someone would find me.

"Princess!" someone yelled. It wasn't Cain. It sounded more like the other man. The blonde one. "This isn't going to end well for you!"

It was too dark to see anything with the branches blocking out the remaining light of the moon. But I grabbed onto every tree that I could, thrusting myself forward. As if by some kind of miracle, I heard voices. They were far away, but I recognized them well enough.

"Morrigan!" a female yelled, the sound of it barely carried through the wind. It was Lyra. I just knew that it was Lyra.

"Thank the gods…" I whispered to myself. "Lyra!" I threw my voice into the night, begging for her to hear me.

She called my name again, still so far away. And I tried to push even faster than my feet could handle, hissing at the stones scraping my soles.

"Lyra—" My voice had been cut off from someone slamming my head into a nearby tree. Even with the darkness around me, bright stars seemed to dance in my vision.

"I thought Aamon's compulsion would last longer than that," Cain said quietly. The only parts of him that I could see were his eyes glowing a sinister, emerald green. The way it slithered around in his irises resembled the snake that he was. "But this…" Something sharp pierced my neck, long and thin, and I gasped as I felt a stinging pain burn through my veins. "Good luck fighting this one."

The last thing I heard before my vision went black was Lyra, calling my name once more from somewhere nearby.

Chapter 49

KAIDEN

Red.

It was the only color that I could see… Red spewing in front of me as I shoved my dagger inside of the soldier dangling in my arms… Red dripping from my blade, as I yanked it from his chest… Red from the blood pooling beneath my feet as I threw his body to the side. I would paint every inch of this castle with it if I couldn't find her soon.

The few guards that remained gaped at me with terror striking like lightning in their eyes. "Where is she?" I asked in a low growl, barely able to contain my own shadows that burst from me like black flames. I grabbed one by the collar, hauling him to his feet until our noses practically touched. "You will tell me where she is or you will meet the same end as your brothers. Where. Is. She?"

He trembled in my grasp, shaking so hard it caused his teeth to clatter against each other. "I-I... I don't know, My Lord... Lord Cain... He's b-been gone..."

"You lie!" I yelled in his face, watching him flinch back as he closed his eyes. In a fit of anger, I thrust my dagger into his heart, hearing his gasp for air. "I will kill all of you. Do you understand me?"

The remnants of life left from his eyes and I dropped him onto the pile of bodies beside me. Then, I turned back to the rest of them. They all looked frightened, exactly how I wanted them. But no one would tell me what I needed to know. They took her. I know they did. The entire town saw Cain.

They took Morrigan.

Morrigan...

"Tell me where she is!" I demanded.

He won't hurt her, I continued to tell myself, praying I would start believing it. *They need her. She'll be safe.*

"Tell me!" The shadows could no longer be contained. They spread out like webs, grabbing hold of the guards and slamming them each against the walls around us. As the darkness tied itself like ropes around their necks, I watched them kick and claw at the smoke, trying to release its grip.

"As long as you remain under my roof... no harm will come to you, little dove. That's a promise."

I lied to her. I swore I would protect her. This was *my* fault. I should have seen the lies in the accusations of her mother. I allowed her to leave the castle...

"Morrigan..." I panted, chest heaving from a night spent with slaughter.

They thought they had seen me angry. They thought they felt my wrath all those years ago. But they knew nothing of the fury inside of me—of the darkness I harbored. They would see it now.

With Morrigan's face in my mind, I let out the darkest, most guttural scream that my body could release. Feeling my rage, the shadows clenched together, slicing their heads clean off. As they dropped to the floor, echoing thuds bouncing from the walls, I fell to my knees with them.

"I'll find you…" I whispered.

By the time Dez had arrived, there were only a few lingering guards remaining on the grounds for him to interrogate.

They wouldn't receive any form of apology from me. I'd kill them too if it meant getting her back. And with the look in Dez's eyes as he took in the bodies that lingered in the castle, he didn't seem too sorry for it either. The problem was that their minds seemed to have been tampered with. Even I could smell the dark magic imprinted in them. And that meant only one thing.

Cain had a Mind Renderer at his disposal—a forbidden gift as strong, if not stronger than our own compulsion. They could make you think or do *anything* they wanted you to. The main difference being, when people are under *our* compulsion, they remain lucid. But the moment a Mind Renderer so much as whispers in your ear, you are under their full control. There was a reason that having these kinds of gifts ended only in execution.

"I don't think Cain has been here for quite some time," Lyra assessed.

The Holy Palace had been left in ruins. No living priests or priestesses remained inside. The bodies… I may not be a holy man, but to kill innocents… especially as young as they were… It hurt to see. And to know that Cain had the ability to carry out such orders... I now had true fear for Morrigan's life. I *needed* to find her.

How could the seers not have prophesized this? How could they not have known of the evil brewing inside of him? Their job was to protect Andonia with their knowledge.

The only small piece of hope that remained relied on Cain's obsession with bonding with Morrigan. He wanted it. Which meant he would need her alive to do so.

"What are we going to do with them?" Lyra asked. Very few of his people were left behind. The rest seemed to have been killed off at some point—likely due to whomever else he had hidden away with more forbidden gifts. Now, only a few hundred were here. And with no one to care for them... they were doomed.

Behind us, Dez had spent the rest of his night burning the dead. There was no time for burials with no leads on where Cain had taken Morrigan. "We'll find room for them," I assured her.

But with each second that passed, my pulse would quicken its pace. How could I have been so stupid? I needed to think. I needed silence and privacy. When the bodies were completely disposed of, I wasted no time in returning home.

What if he's hurting her?

What if he's touched her?

I'll kill him. I'll fucking kill him.

The thought of seeing a single bruise on Morrigan's skin... another scar... I couldn't breathe. I ignored Dez and Lyra upon our arrival, feeling my own shadows unraveling, and transported to my room.

You've ruined her life.

Why couldn't you be kind?

Why didn't you protect her?

I tried… I thought I tried…

Why couldn't I breathe? Why couldn't I control myself? Losing my balance, I fell against the side of my dresser, hanging onto it with my hands.

She'll end up dead, too. And it's your *fault*.

No.

The light in my room began to dim—like the sun had been doused of its flames. It was my shadows. They began circling me like a storm, slowly closing in and suffocating the space. I should have protected her from the start. I should have seen the change in Maeryn. I should have known she would be cruel.

"Warriors like us? We hold no space for love, Kaiden," Ryuk had said to me once. *"Love is weak. A burden to us all. Without it, imagine what kind of power you could yield. You could rise above them all. Take this as a blessing, son."*

He would have said the same now. He was the one who trained me after my loss… He trained me to remove emotions from my life—to put my own ambitions first. But why couldn't I do that now? Just picturing her eyes again held enough pain that brought me to the floor. And the darkness that Ryuk had gifted me with was swallowing me.

"I'm sorry…" I whispered to her, wherever she was. "I did this."

Someone called my name, but the shadows swirling around me muffled the sound. It didn't matter. I did this. I let this happen to her.

"Morrigan…"

"Kaiden!"

I could feel someone enter the funnel that now separated me from the world. But even if I wanted to, I couldn't stop it. I could never stop them. They were a curse that I barely had the strength to contain. But as someone grabbed my shoulders, I turned to the side and saw Dez drop to his knees.

"Dez…" I said quietly. My chest had tightened so much that it felt like my heart would implode. "I did this… I—"

"We'll find her, Kaiden." His hands dug into my shoulders as he shook me, and I could see tears in his eyes. "Do you hear me? We will find her."

"I have to, Dez," I pleaded. "I…"

"I know."

And for the first time in my life, I dropped my head onto his chest and felt a tear escape. My shadows fell, disappearing the moment the tear slipped from my cheek. And my heart felt as though it had shattered. Dez didn't stop me. He stayed, sitting with me there on the floor as I cried.

"I love her too, Kaiden."

Chapter 50

MORRIGAN

My head throbbed as I tried to peel my eyes open.

It felt like I had been asleep for ages, and every joint in my body ached. The world was a blur as I came to my senses. But wherever he had taken me, the lights were too dim for me to see much. As I shifted myself, I felt a rocking sensation, causing my head to spin. Beneath me, cold, abrasive iron scratched my arm.

Why would I be laying on bars?

As my vision finally came into focus, I could see torches placed along, what looked to be, a stone wall. But they were… below me. My heart rate picked up as I turned my eyes slowly to the bars under my body. And they shook as I scrambled into a seated position. I was hovering in the air... I was in...

"Princess!" Cain called from below. "You're awake!"

The sound of his voice struck my body with fear. I spotted him on a throne, the blonde man beside him with a distinguishable smirk on his face as he looked up at me. Cain stood and walked, stopping just beneath me, chuckling as he tilted his head up. Raising his hand, I felt a jolt near the bars and felt myself being lowered. Once he could touch the iron, the entire thing shook, coming to a stop again.

"I made this for you, you know," he purred. Hooking one finger around the metal, he pushed it, causing the cage to twirl. "What did Kaiden like to call you? Little bird? No... Ah!" He grabbed the bars, bringing it to a sudden halt and my stomach leapt into my throat. "*Little dove*."

"Don't call me that," I hissed at him, closing my eyes to soothe the dizziness in my head.

"Don't you like your cage, Princess?" Cain's laughter ignited the tears in my eyes, but I did everything to keep them from falling.

Kaiden's coming, I reminded myself. *He'll find me and kill Cain for what he's done. He's coming.*

I heard the quick sound of a latch opening and my breath was torn from my lungs. I didn't have time to grab anything as my body fell through the air, landing with a hard smack against the floor. I screamed from the crack of a bone breaking in my arm and turned over, clutching it to my chest.

Cain's hand wrapped into my hair and he yanked me up, causing a flush of heat to shoot from my wound. "You would have come to *me* next if Kaiden hadn't taken you for himself." He brushed his nose up my cheek and I tried not to flinch. Every inch of movement made my arm throb even worse. "I bet he couldn't wait to taste you. Fucking hypocrite."

"We never bonded," I blurted through clenched teeth.

His eyes went wide before he threw his head back laughing. "And here I thought *Dez* was the bleeding heart."

Dropping me back down to the floor, a quiet whine escaped my lips from the pain. There were no windows around us. It almost looked as if we were underground. Several people stood around, staring, but I didn't recognize a single face. They weren't dressed in uniforms and didn't look like soldiers. I tried searching for an exit, but the only pathways out of the room were hidden in darkness.

Suddenly, a hand gripped my hair again and lifted me to stand. The pain was so intense, I couldn't stop myself from crying as Cain shoved my back against a nearby wall. He grabbed my face and forced me to look at him, but the coldness in his eyes turned my blood to ice.

"W-What are you going to do?" I asked him, unable to stop the shaking in my voice.

His eyes strayed from mine and trailed down to my throat. Then, he licked his lips. "Take what's mine."

It only took a second to feel his teeth piercing my skin, and I screamed from the fire that shot into my veins. No part of it was gentle. My skin tore apart and each pull he made felt like needles slithering down my throat, into my shoulders. I could barely breathe through it. When he let go, the pull was violent and tore even more skin from my throat.

Something wet touched my mouth and my eyes widened when I noticed his wrist. "No…" I begged, trying to shove him away. "Please—"

"Sit *still*," he ordered.

"Cain, plea—" He forced his wrist into my mouth and his blood poured onto my tongue.

I couldn't stop myself from swallowing, and that's when I felt it… *snap*. Now that I was aware of the bonds, I could feel the energy connecting us two. It felt violating. A wave of magic rushed through my body that, in any other circumstance, would have given me pleasure. But I only felt pain, betrayal, and fear of what I had become the last time I bonded with one of them.

"Good girl," he whispered in my ear. And a tear fell from my eye in defeat.

I'm sorry, Kaiden. I'm so sorry.

Cain finally released his wrist from my mouth, and I felt slight relief as the pain in my arm faded. But then he forced his lips on mine and I panicked. I tried shoving him off of me, punching at his chest as hard as I could. And when he wouldn't budge, I bit down on his bottom lip until I felt his flesh tear.

When he drew himself back, I spit his own blood onto his face.

"You *bitch*," he yelled and I let myself smile. When he noticed it, I watched in slow motion as he raised his hand and struck me across my cheek. The force of it sent me down to the floor. "You want to act like a brat? *Fine.*"

Grabbing my ankle, he began dragging me across the floor, and I looked back at the cage placed on the floor, with a door opened wide on its side. "No!" I pleaded. "No, Cain. Please!"

"I want my meals where I can see them," he sneered before shoving me into the bars and latching them behind me. I ran to the door and shook it, praying they would open. Then, I closed my eyes and searched for any sign of the flame that I knew hid within me. "Don't bother with that, Princess. I've been giving you just enough hellebore injections to keep those embers at bay."

The cage shook as it began to rise and I sank down onto my knees, feeling the ache of them rubbing against the iron. "You can't keep me like this," I cried. My tears fell, dripping down the cage and dropping to the floor. But that exhaustion had begun to kick in—the same one I felt when the others bonded with me.

"Sleep, love."

I didn't know how long I had been asleep for, but I remembered seeing Kaiden's face.

I felt his hands on me, holding me like he did each night. And for a moment, I had accepted that it was all a nightmare. I convinced myself that I had been in bed, with him… *safe*. But as my eyes opened, and I saw the floor beneath me, nausea crept into my throat once more.

Groaning from stiff joints, I tried stretching them out. But every inch of me hurt.

"Lovely!" Cain's voice resembled nails scratching against a chalkboard. I flinched just at the sound of it. "You were asleep for an entire day, Princess! I was beginning to worry!"

Go back to sleep… Dream of Kaiden again… But my stomach rumbled with a debilitating hunger.

Cain stood from his throne, and I sucked in a breath when I noticed him flick his wrist. The bottom of the cage disappeared again and I cried out as I fell to the floor. Without time to brace for the impact, I landed with my hands in front of me and felt the snap in my wrist. I writhed in pain, clutching my hand close to me.

It took him only a few steps to reach me. And once he threw his leg over my body, he yanked me up by my hair, pretending to examine me. "*Tsk, tsk.*" He looked at my wrist with insincere worry masked on his face. "You should *really* be more careful, Princess." When he dropped me to the floor, I bit my tongue to stop from crying as tears stung my eyes.

"Why are you doing this to me?" I hissed. Even my voice sounded dry with how badly my body yearned for water.

He knelt beside me, and I winced, pulling away as he moved a curl from my face. "The idea of *sharing* you... with all of *them*?" He shook his head, clicking his tongue. "That just wouldn't do for me. The moment I saw you, I knew I wanted you all to myself."

His finger slid down my cheek and stopped just above my pulse on my neck.

"The *power* in your blood..." Closing his eyes, he inhaled deeply. "I can feel it in my veins, Princess. They were fools for not keeping you for themselves."

Standing, he walked back toward his throne, not even offering to heal my wrist. "I need food," I called to him. "Water... *something*. You-You can't continue to use me like this if I'm dead."

He seemed to think for a moment as he paused before throwing his head back with an annoyed sigh. Then, he looked over to the blonde man from the village. "Get her some water, Aamon." Aamon nodded and began walking away. "Not a lot, though!" Cain turned to me. "We need the little fire-starter weak."

A moment later, Aamon returned with a glass in his hand. He squatted in front of me, holding it out for me to grab. But as I reached for it, he quickly pulled it away. A slow grin spread across his face and he tipped the glass over, pouring it onto the floor. Once it was half-gone, he handed the glass to me again. Behind him, Cain let out an amused laugh.

They were toying with me.

Regardless of the shame I felt, I drank the water, needing all the strength I could get. But looking around, I couldn't believe the amount of people standing there. They looked at each other, whispering quietly as they stared at me. There was something strange about them. An aura that I couldn't quite understand seemed to emanate from their direction. I had never felt such power before, not even from Lyra.

Cain must have noticed me and chuckled, grabbing my attention. "Welcome to my Court of Monsters, Princess."

"I don't understand…"

"You're aware that anyone born with a forbidden gift is put to death, correct?" he asked. When I nodded, he stood and began approaching them. "People consider them *cursed*."

I watched nervously as he grabbed a small boy by the collar, thrusting him forward. He had a blindfold placed over his eyes, but he didn't seem to be injured in any way. The boy appeared as frightened as I was, grabbing at Cain's hand blindly.

"Now, now, Azrael…" Gripping the boy's shoulders, Cain held him still as he stood behind him. "Don't you want to impress our guest?" He nodded to Aamon again. "Bring her."

Aamon disappeared into one of the tunnels, and when he reemerged I clamped my hand over my mouth when I saw who he dragged in with him. Her bottom lip had been cut down the middle and a bruise painted the corner of her eye. Even her cheeks looked swollen. *No.*

He shoved Shae to her knees and she turned to me with exhaustion in her eyes. "Your Grace," she said. Her face begged for mercy, some inkling of hope that I could save her.

"Let her go, Cain," I begged him. "You have me. I'm not going anywhere. Please, just let her go."

He hushed me like I was a child. "Don't interrupt. It's *rude*. Didn't your mother ever teach you any…" My chest cracked a little as he stopped himself. And his smile made me feel faint. "Oh… How silly of me to forget…"

"It was you, wasn't it," I sneered. Guinevere had no memory of what she had done. "You forced her to kill that priest."

"Yes, well. That's all in the past now," Cain sighed. "She was a fighter, though, if I must say. Her love for you held such strength... I actually needed Aamon to compel her for me." Cain let out a single laugh and then straightened himself again. "Back to the matter at hand."

Turning back to Shae, I could see the fear in her eyes. "Shae..." I said quietly. "Shae, I'll get you out of here. I promise, I'll—"

"Be. Silent!" Cain yelled. "Say another word to the hag and I'll have Aamon cut her throat before the show can even begin. Do you understand me?"

I nodded, swallowing my pride and pushed myself up to sit. Even with the pain radiating from my wrist, I could barely focus on it as I kept my eyes between Shae and Cain. The little boy shook beneath his grasp.

Slowly, he lifted the blindfold from Azrael's head and I held my breath when I saw the child's eyes. There was no color to his irises. They looked faded, save for the black ring that circled them. "Alright, Azrael," Cain drawled. "Go on."

"M-my L-lord. Please d-don't..." Azrael's voice sounded so tiny... He couldn't have been more than seven or eight years old.

"Don't make me repeat myself, boy."

In an instant, Shae let out a pained yell. She clutched her head, bending over in pain, and her screams pierced my ears, imprinting the sound into my mind. As she curled over, landing on the floor, her cries grew louder. Ignoring Cain's warning, I raced over to her and pulled Shae onto my lap. "Stop this, Cain!" I begged. But his smile only widened.

I tried my best to soothe her, pushing her hair out of her face. But I couldn't stop it. I didn't even know what was happening to her. Then, blood began to pool in her eyes, leaking from her nose and ears. It looked black.

"Cain! You're killing her!"

And as quickly as Shae had begun screaming, she went silent. I heard Azrael gasp and groan in pain, but I couldn't take my eyes off of her. Bringing my fingers to her neck, I felt no pulse. Shae was dead. Death. Death is all I brought to these people. First Guinevere... Then, the villagers... Now, Shae...

"Oops," Cain mocked. "There *is* a reason they're forbidden, Princess. Sometimes, in the little ones, they just don't know when to... *stop*." I could sense Cain approaching me, and Aamon pulled Shae from my lap. But my arms felt numb as I watched her body get dragged away. "A *Blight* is what they call people like Azrael. A single look from them and they can poison your mind, killing their victims almost instantly."

"I'm sorry," Azrael cried from behind us. "I didn't mean to hurt her!"

I turned to see someone else wrap the fabric over his eyes again before hauling him out of the room. A boy. He was just a boy.

With all of my fury, I looked up at Cain. "You're insane."

His smile fell instantly and the coldness returned to his eyes. "I think it's time to go back to your cage, *bird*."

As he grabbed me by my hair, I scratched at his hands. "No!" I yelled. "Cain! No! Please!"

I thrashed as hard as I could and turned my head just enough to reach his arm before biting down on it. He released me with a curse and I jumped to my feet, ready to run. But another pair of hands touched my head and I felt lips beside my ear.

"Sleep."

The Diary of Daisies and Hellebores

It's almost time, and it is painful. Writing is the
only thing that is keeping my mind from the
stabbing sensation that keeps coming and going.
I have seen my handmaidens push through it, but
our Priestess's would always assist them with
their pain. I cannot afford that luxury, as the
others would then
find out.
I am in our secret home, waiting for his return.
It's almost time.

Chapter 51

DEZ

Kaiden had insisted we all meet together in his library, explaining that he found something.

When everyone arrived, he escorted us there where Eowyn had been waiting for us. I was surprised to see her and couldn't fathom the reason she would need to be present. When I made her Morrigan's handmaiden, I never expected their relationship to blossom in the way that it did. But I couldn't have been more grateful.

Eowyn seemed to be one of the only people that Morrigan truly trusted—someone that wouldn't dare lie to her in the way that we had. Beside her stood Lyra. She wouldn't even look at me. I knew she blamed me for her not being there to protect Morrigan, and I couldn't find any flaw in her conclusion. I was the one who took Lyra away that day. If I hadn't… well, maybe Lyra *would* have stopped it.

Even if Lyra didn't speak about it, I knew she loved Morrigan. We *all* know. Morrigan was impossible not to love—a pure drop of sunlight that attracted all types of people. Her smile alone could brighten the night, chasing away every dark corner of your heart.

"Are you well?" I asked Eowyn. She had chosen to stay with Kaiden after Morrigan went missing, even after I invited her to come back home. She said it made her feel closer to Morrigan and wanted to be there when she came back home.

Home.

The irony in Morrigan considering this place *home* didn't pass me by. But after seeing Kaiden break down the way that he did… I understood it. In some strange way, I could see why they might have been made for each other. They had both lost vital pieces of themselves due to the actions of others. And even while they clashed together, forcing themselves to hate one another, I would notice the small shift in Morrigan's eyes as she searched for Kaiden at dinner. I knew of every encounter he had with her in the halls.

"I miss her," Eowyn answered quietly, and the pain in her face said enough.

Kaiden walked past me and tossed a book onto the desk beside us. Looking down, I read the title: "*The Diary of Daisies and Hellebores*? Isn't that the book Morrigan was reading?"

"Have any of you actually read this book? Even *heard* of it before?" Kaiden asked.

I looked around and realized we were all collectively confused. For as long as I had been alive, I had never actually seen the book before. It never seemed strange to me since, truthfully, I would rather spend my free time doing anything but reading. Even Naaz, the scholar of our group, stared at the book without recognition.

Eowyn stepped forward. "Morrigan gave it to me after she read it." Picking up the book, she ran her hands along the cover. "Bits and pieces started to sound familiar, like a story I already knew. But this story was far different than the one that *I* knew... as a child, I mean."

After Eowyn opened it to a specific page, she handed it to Kaiden who began reading it to us. "Hellebores. He loves them. I have planted them throughout my garden now to remind me of him."

"Rosina," I exhaled. "I don't understand. Everything associated with her had been burned after the war. How did this—"

"We came up with a solution to see each other in private," Kaiden interrupted, continuing to read. "A place where only *we* can go. A perfect escape."

The tunnels... Kaiden returned the book to Eowyn, who held it close to her chest like a piece of Morrigan came with it.

"She's speaking of the tunnels that stretch underneath the two castles they both ruled from. One entrance for *her* and one entrance for *Ryuk*," Kaiden explained to the others.

"That's why they took her on *my* land... He knew he'd never get to her on yours..." I sat down, letting the weight of the blame drag me into my seat. "I don't understand. I thought they had been destroyed. How have *none* of us seen this book?"

More importantly, how did *Morrigan* find it? Who gave it to her?

"This *has* to be where Cain took her. It's the only thing that would explain their ability to come and go so easily. The way they disappear... Cain had to have found the entrances to them." Kaiden's voice held so much anger and rage.

"The entrance only opens with blood from a god, Kaiden. How could Cain have gained access?" I asked.

"I'm beginning to think Cain has a long list of secrets he's been hiding." Kaiden's eyes flashed with knowledge that I didn't seem to be picking up on.

Shaking her head, Eowyn stepped forward. "Is it true? Is what Rosina said... Did they really..."

Kaiden sighed, leaning onto the desk and shared a glance with me. "Eowyn. There are a lot of things that the gods—"

"The baby?" Eowyn looked at us with accusation in her eyes that made me still.

"Rosina never had a child," D said beside me. But Kaiden looked at me—a silent conversation passing between us.

A truth only *we* knew.

A truth that would certainly destroy everything we had built.

And one that Morrigan would never forgive.

MORRIGAN

I had no way of knowing how much time had passed since Cain brought me here.

If I had to guess, I had been in that cage for a week... Maybe *two*. Without any windows or light, the days blurred together far too easily. Sometimes, when I fought a little too hard, Cain would inject more hellebore into my neck. I could have been asleep for days and I wouldn't be able to tell. He only allowed me a single meal and glass of water a day.

But, like the first time, Aamon continued to pour out half of my cup. I no longer felt human, but more of a pet for them. An animal. A *bird*.

If Cain wanted me, he'd drop me without warning. Sometimes, he'd make sure I hovered high enough to cause an injury, just to force me to drink his blood and heal it. He wanted to break me.

Maybe he already had.

When Cain released the bottom of my cage, I didn't have the strength to try and prepare myself. My shoulder took the brunt of it before my head smacked against the floor. My shoulder had definitely dislocated itself and a small trickle of blood began to fall from my ear.

As I heard footsteps approach, I didn't bother to turn and look at him. He grabbed my arm and shoved it back into place, ripping a scream from my throat before it turned into a sob. "Please," I cried. "Cain—"

The words faded when I saw who stepped over me. *No... No, no no....*

"Hello, dove," he cooed.

It sounded like his voice but also... *didn't*. His dark, tousled hair fell over his brows as he stared down at me. And the sinister look in his eyes hurt me more than any injury could.

"You're not... You're not Kaiden," I whispered.

"Are you so sure?" he asked. Reaching down, he fisted the collar of my dress and lifted me. Every part of his face resembled him, even down to the small freckles on his nose and forehead.

"K... Kaiden..." When I raised my hand and touched his cheek, I knew. I didn't know how, but I knew it wasn't Kaiden's face. "Stop this, Cain," I begged.

"You never asked me what my gift was, Princess." Bringing my face closer to his, he brushed his nose against my cheek and made my body tremble. "I can make you see *anyone* I want you to see, *little dove*."

Oh, Gods...

"Imagine the fun we could have—forcing you to see the man you love." When he lifted his head again, my eyes widened as Dez stared back at me. "The *men* you adore."

"No!" I screamed, grabbing his hands and shoving them off of me. When I fell back down, I turned away from him, squeezing my eyes shut. I wouldn't be able to withstand that kind of torture. I couldn't see Dez's face as he... Anyone but them.

Put me out of my misery, I all but begged the gods. *Just kill me, please.*

"I promise, Morrigan," Cain whispered in my ear, returning to his own voice. "If you continue to fight me like you have, I will make the very faces you love be the ones that bring you the most pain." My chest hurt as I cried, hugging myself as I willed my heart to stop beating. He pressed his wrist to my mouth. "Drink."

"*Fuck you*," I seethed, turning away from him.

I squealed as he grabbed my hair and forced me to look at him. "You're an ungrateful bitch." Beside us, Aamon had approached with a plate of food. But Cain shook his head and looked down at me in disgust. "Let her starve today."

I couldn't stop the tears as he dragged me back to my cage again, shoving me inside and raising it once more. Then, I watched him walk to his throne and sit down, eating the food that was meant for me. I glared as he ate every last bite and watched him drink the glass of water beside it.

It hurt. Every part of my body wanted to scream. Kaiden would come for me... He would find me. I *knew* he would.

"And if he doesn't?"

I tensed at the familiar voice in my head. Turning, I saw *him* sitting in the cage with me—the mask still hiding his face. Leaning against the bars, he watched me with a frown. It made sense that I had started hallucinating again. With the malnutrition and dehydration, my body was being deprived. My brain probably stood on its last legs, ready to give out.

"Go away," I whispered to him.

"No, Morrigan. You no longer have the strength to push me out." He looked around, examining the cage we were both in. *"You need me."*

"You're not real," I said louder. "Leave me alone."

But as his hand reached out and stopped on top of mine, I felt it. It warmed my palm and made my tears fall harder at the small token of affection that I didn't know I needed. *"I won't leave you again,"* he promised me. *"We'll get you out of here."*

The Diary of Daisies and Hellebores

He's so beautiful... I cry every time I look at him.
They look just alike.
He... hasn't returned yet, but I am counting the
seconds until he does. I am certain that he will
love him as much as I do already.
My heart is so full. I can feel his cries as if they
are my own. He looks at me like I am his world
and he is mine.
I hope he returns soon.

Chapter 52

Two days had gone by since Cain allowed me to eat or have any water.

I only knew this by keeping close attention on the others. In the morning, they'd all move to a separate room, I assumed for food. Then, Cain would speak with Aamon on his throne, seeming to send some of them off. One thing I couldn't quite understand was when he would place a small amount of his own blood into a tiny glass tube for them. I didn't know what it meant.

But on the third day, he lowered my cage instead of dropping me. I could scarcely hide my surprise as he opened the door, gesturing for me to get out. Everyone that remained in the throne room just stared at me. My dress looked filthy. I hadn't been allowed a single bath or even a change of clothes. The fabric had begun to tear and the color faded from the dirt that stuck to the gown. *I can't continue like this.*

He ordered everyone to leave as I stepped out of the cage. "I have a proposition for you, Princess," he said, from behind me. After snapping his fingers, Aamon appeared from one of the tunnels with a plate full of food. My mouth watered at the sight of it. "If you promise not to fight me. I might reconsider your sleeping arrangements."

Unable to stop myself, I took a step toward the scent that wafted in the air, and my stomach cramped with need. But Cain placed a hand on my arm and stopped me from moving any further.

"Not so fast," he ordered. "I want your word, Princess." Aamon brandished the dish in front of me, waving it around in a way that made me feel like an object. But I didn't care. I *needed* that food.

"Play into his game, Morrigan," he whispered from somewhere nearby. *"You can't escape if you're dead."*

"Yes," I blurted, my eyes stuck in tunnel vision as I looked at the assortment of fruits in front of me. "I promise. Please."

Cain chuckled and released my arm. Without thinking, I ran to Aamon and snatched the plate from his hand, digging into the food. I didn't care how I looked. He had starved me for days and my body was on the verge of shutting down.

"Slow down, Morrigan," he insisted, but I didn't listen. *He* couldn't understand how badly my body needed this.

"Water, Princess?" When I turned, Cain held a full glass in his hand. I reached out hesitantly before taking it. But when he didn't move it away, I swiped the glass and gulped it down as fast as I could—scared that Aamon might interfere. With the last sip, I nearly choked. "Easy, love," Cain warned. He retrieved the empty glass from my hand and passed it off to Aamon. "Let's take a walk."

Entering one of the many tunnels nearby, we passed several rooms that had been built into the walls. Some of the people from the throne room sat in them, eyeing me as we continued on. I wondered which room Azrael might be in, if this was where they slept. How did he get all of them down here? *Why* did he?

We stopped at an empty one, and on top of the bed lay a folded, plain maiden's gown. It fairly resembled Eowyn's dresses. I took a tentative step into the room, and Cain moved to the other side where I noticed a large tub placed near the wall. *A bath*, I thought to myself, letting out a sigh of relief when I saw Cain dip his hand into it, warming the water.

Just when I felt the smallest flame of gratitude, Cain stood and nodded his head at me. "Take off the dress."

My lips parted and I nearly forgot how to breathe. "I... Aren't you going to—"

"You can't possibly believe that I would trust you in here by yourself. You're my lifeline now, Princess. If anything were to happen to you... Well, then, I'd be dead as well. Now, I'd move a little faster than that before I change my mind."

Clenching my jaw tight, I took another step forward and jumped at the sound of the door closing behind me, and a lock sliding into place. *"I'm going to kill him,"* he said. *"I swear it to you, Morrigan."*

As my eyes began to sting, I slowly slipped the dress off of me and quickly covered my chest with my arms, lowering myself into the water. I refused to look Cain in the eyes. If I pretended that he wasn't there, then, I could get it over with.

He handed me a cloth to wash myself, and I swallowed every tear that wanted to shed. Even as he stepped behind me and slowly began cleaning my hair. He untangled every knot and did it so gently that the act almost confused my body into enjoying it. That's how deprived he had made me.

Kaiden... His name almost caused a tear to slip by. *I just want to go home.*

"You will."

"Alright, Princess. Let's get you dressed." Cain insisted on assisting me, and by that time, my tears had all but dried out. By the time he tied the gown behind me, I had finally come to my senses.

Kaiden wasn't coming. Kaiden didn't even know where to find me. Cain had spent this long preparing.. *whatever it was* that he had planned. Kaiden wasn't...

The door unlatched, and I watched as Aamon stepped through—fear immediately causing my body to shake. He wanted to compel me. Turning, I grabbed onto Cain's shirt. "Please," I begged. "Please, I don't want to sleep."

But he smiled softly at me, grabbing hold of my wrists and removing them. "You promised not to fight," he whispered.

A second later, another set of hands touched me before I felt a pair of lips beside my ear. "*Sleep.*"

I felt like I had fallen from the sky before opening my eyes.

I stood in a garden, one full of daisies. But above me, the sky looked dark. I didn't see any sign of a moon—not even a single fleck of stars shone above. But past the garden, something seemed to light up the horizon.

Had I gotten out? Had someone finally rescued me?

Somehow, I sensed him *without hearing a single sound.* "I'm dreaming aren't I?" *I asked, shoulders deflating a little with my breath.*

"Yes and no," *he said, moving to stand beside me.*

Kneeling down, I ran my hand through the flowers. They felt real. "What is this place?"

"Somewhere I like to go when I need to escape." *He dropped down as well and plucked one of the daisies before offering it to me.* "I thought you might need to escape."

I turned my head to look at him and wished more than anything that I could see the face beneath the mask. But maybe that's what my mind needed. A savior. I had been through so much that I created my own hero somehow. If only he had been real. *I accepted the flower but didn't look away from him.*

"I'm scared." *My voice cracked on my words.* "When I wake up, I'll be… He'll…" *The tears I couldn't shed earlier began to fall, and he brought his hand to my cheek to catch them.* "I don't want to be alone. I want to go home. I'm going to* die *here. I can't—"*

"I'm here," *he whispered.* "I'll be with you for every second of it, Morrigan. And the moment we find a way, I'll get you out of there. I won't let anything happen to you, okay?"

Forgetting that this was, in fact, just a dream, I fell into his chest and cried. He held me tight and I only sobbed harder, needing every bit of affection that his fantasy could offer me. It was a distraction, and it would all be gone in the morning, but I could live in it for now.

"Don't leave me," *I begged him.*

Pulling me tightly, he whispered quietly, "Never."

The dream ended abruptly, and I opened my eyes to the sound of the door opening.

Bracing myself, I expected to see Cain stepping inside. But Aamon's face greeted me instead, under the dim light the torches offered. Sitting up, I rubbed my eyes with the palms of my hands. "Is it time to eat already?" I asked, a little more hopeful than I intended to sound.

"It's the middle of the night, Princess. You have hours before your next meal." He approached slowly, but the look in his eyes frightened me.

A lump began to form in my throat. "Then why are you here?" I asked him.

I tracked his every movement as he stalked closer, searching frantically for anything to defend myself with. Scooting back on the bed, I tried keeping distance between us, but my back hit the wall. And before I could yell out, Aamon's eyes began to glow. "*You will not make a sound and you will not move until I leave.*"

I tried speaking, but it felt like the day I had been lost in the woods. My lips were practically sewn shut. Panicking, my entire body began to tremble as he crawled onto the bed. With his hands on my ankles, he yanked me down until I lay flat against the mattress and hovered over me. Using his finger, he pulled down one of my sleeves, revealing my shoulder to him, and I felt the sharp end of a knife pierce into my skin.

Internally, I was screaming as loud as I could. But no one could hear me.

"All this talk of your blood," he whispered, admiring the cut he made. "Don't worry, Princess. I just want a *taste*."

He leaned down, licking the blood that had begun to slide down my shoulder. Tears were welling in my eyes, but I couldn't make any sound.

"You taste so good," he mumbled against my skin.

Kaiden, I thought to myself—willing for him to hear it somehow. *Please... Kaiden... Dez... I need you.*

"Cain wasn't kidding about the power." When Aamon pulled back, his eyes seemed to glow even brighter than they had before. My blood stained his teeth as he smiled, and squeezed my shoulder, making more seep through the cut.

I couldn't kick him—couldn't push him. I was completely helpless against whatever he wanted to do with me. *Kaiden, please...*

He finally pulled back and looked at me. "*You will say nothing of this. You will not tell anyone that I was here or what I did.*"

Standing, he straightened his clothes and licked his lips. The moment he left, I sucked in a sharp breath and felt my chest tighten. I was going to die. Whether it came at the hands of Cain or Aamon, I wasn't making it out of these tunnels alive.

And I wasn't sure that I even wanted to anymore.

Chapter 53

The next time I opened my eyes, I realized that someone was sitting on my bed.

I felt the divot in the mattress, and I quickly sat up expecting to see Aamon again, but instead, found Azrael, equally startled. "I'm sorry," he said quietly. "I didn't mean to scare you."

Looking around, I realized we were alone and couldn't hide my confusion. Why would he be here? As I remembered what he had made Azrael do... Shae's face... I felt guilty when I pulled my feet away from him. Could Cain have sent him to do it again? Who would it be this time?

"Everyone's scared of me," he whispered, lowering his head. "I'm sorry. I didn't want to hurt your friend. Lord Cain, he..."

My heart physically hurt... He was just a child.

"How old are you?" I asked him.

He shrugged. "Six, I think. Maybe seven... I don't know when my birthday is. I've always just been... here."

Had Cain tried breeding them? Using those with forbidden gifts to create children with similar ones? He's been here... Had he even seen the sun before? Felt its warmth? How could a child survive like this?

"You should know firsthand what a child can withstand," his voice answered from somewhere within my mind.

Ignoring the fear, I sat up and inched closer to Azrael. "How long have you worn that cloth?"

"For a couple of years," he said quietly. "My gifts came earlier than normal... And one day, when I got really upset with my mom... she..."

My heart instantly broke for him. Cain allowed this to happen. He probably celebrated when he found out just what gift Azrael possessed. "And your father?" I asked him.

He shrugged again. "Lord Cain had sent him somewhere not too long ago and, well... he never came back."

Azrael had been left here alone... No mother to care for him... No father to guide him. *"He's strong, though. I can sense it. A fighter."*

I felt inclined to agree. Reaching forward, I took a chance and gripped the ends of the fabric holding the blindfold together. Azrael immediately flinched, scooting back. "M-May I?" I asked.

"I don't want to hurt you." His bottom lip trembled as he spoke, and I didn't want to push him. It wasn't my place to do so.

"Well... is there a reason you're here, Azrael?"

Nodding, he reached to his side and pulled out another folded gown. "Lord Cain asked that I bring this to you." I accepted it but kept my eyes on the boy. "He asked that you change and meet him in the throne room. I-I can walk you there." He jumped from the bed and ran to the door, sneaking out before I could respond to him.

When I looked down at the dress in my hands... I cocked my head to the side. Why did it feel so... *familiar?* Unfolding it, I stood and let the hem of the gown drop to the floor before realizing what he had given me. It was the blue gown that I used to wear in the cottage—another form of humiliation, I quickly assumed.

Masking the disgust on my face, I followed Azrael to the throne room and was surprised by how empty it looked. Even Aamon didn't appear to be anywhere in sight. Cain sat on his throne and his face lit up when he saw me.

"Look how lovely that is on you!" he exclaimed, walking toward me and Azrael. When he moved the boy away from us, Azrael took that as his cue to leave and darted back into the tunnels. Did Cain know what Aamon had done the other night? Did he send him to do it? "I have something for you," he sang. A wide smile spread across his face, and his excitement scared me.

In the corner of my eye, a woman approached. She had long, blonde hair and wore white robes as she walked beside Aamon. Blind rage filled my body, clouding my vision as I gaped at Maeryn. "Morrigan," she said, her voice as unpleasant as ever. I wanted to kill her. I was *going* to kill her.

"Come, Maeryn," Cain waved.

She stopped directly in front of me. *So close. I could do it. If I could just wrap my hands around her throat. I would only need a minute or so.*

"Morrigan," his voice warned. *"Not here. Not now."*

"Maeryn will tend to you daily. She'll help you dress... Help you bathe... Just like old times!" he laughed, and Maeryn smiled with him. But it only fueled the already raging fire that continued to build inside of me.

As I glared into her eyes, the memory of her slicing Guinevere's throat played like a shadow in their reflection. The way she smiled as the Lady fell... Her blood spilling everywhere... I felt a quiet spark in my hand and noticed Maeryn's eyes flash toward them as well. Then, something sharp pinched my neck.

"Now, now," Cain whispered as a warm, burning sensation crept through my veins. "We'll have none of that here." My body swayed, and he caught me in his arms. As quickly as the power had returned, it disappeared entirely. "Gods, she really hates you, doesn't she?" he teased at Maeryn.

"Maeryn," I hissed, though my words felt a bit slurred. *Hellebore*, I remembered. He had to have lowered the dosage since I still had the ability to stand.

"Let's play nice, Princess," Cain warned. "I would hate to have to dispose of my next surprise." He waved Maeryn off before dragging me into a tunnel.

I was forced to use the walls in order to keep myself upright. Even the light of the torches were hurting my eyes. We passed several doors with rooms like my own and I couldn't fathom just how many people he had here. Depending on how far the tunnels reached... This could hold an army. We eventually stopped in front of a closed door, and Cain grabbed my arm, pulling me to him.

"You're going to *love* this," he chided before opening it.

Inside I saw a bed like my own, placed against the wall, with someone sitting on it, chained. His clothes looked torn and dirty. With how deep his knees were bent, I knew he was tall. But as my eyes trailed up and took in his black hair, with grey striping the sides of his head, I placed my hand over my mouth to stifle the gasp.

Noticing us, he stood quickly and tried to run to me, but the chains held him back, forcing him to fall to his knees. "Morrigan," he called. So much pain weighed down a single word. He looked like he had aged over ten years, from the bags under his eyes.

I thought he had abandoned me... I thought he left... "Harley?" I asked, shaking in Cain's grasp.

"What a wholesome father-daughter reunion I've provided for you both," Cain said. He shoved me inside, letting go of my arm and causing me to fall over. As if the hellebore wasn't enough. "I'll give the two of you some privacy. Maeryn will fetch you when it's time for your meal." He quickly left, closing and locking the door behind him.

After a couple of minutes filled with painful silence, Harley's chains rattled as he shifted. "Morrigan," he whispered. But I couldn't stop looking at the ground. The last time I had seen Harley was when... "Morrigan, please look at me."

"I... I thought you left me," I whispered softly. "You were gone when I woke up. I thought that you—"

"No, Morrigan. I didn't leave you. How could I? You're my—"

"Stop," I interrupted him. "You don't have to—"

"Morrigan." I finally looked up and his eyes were red. "I have no one. I have no other children. Ernmas... *Guinevere*... She was the only woman I ever loved." He inched closer to me again, mere inches separating our hands. "You're the only family I have left in this world, Morrigan. Don't take that away, please. I didn't know. You have to believe that I didn't know. If I had known—"

"What if you had?" Sniffling, I wiped away a stray tear that slipped down my cheek. "What could you have done?"

"I would have given my *life* to give you a better one. A *worthy* one." His own voice trembled as violently as his hands. "Maeryn, she's..."

"I know."

After a few more beats of silence, I moved closer to him, closing the distance between us, and stared into his tear-filled eyes. He didn't leave me. My bottom lip shook before I broke down. "I'm so scared," I cried.

Harley quickly reached out, pulling me against his chest as he held me. "I know. Your mother... She asked me to keep you safe and I... I'm so sorry, Morrigan."

Tears cascaded down my cheeks, drenching his shirt as he pulled me tighter. He didn't leave me. He didn't—

"He didn't leave you," he whispered nearby. *"See? You aren't alone, Morrigan. You've never truly been alone."*

Maeryn retrieved me from Harley's room.

She bore a fake smile that looked personally stitched into her face as she opened the door, causing Harley to stiffen like a board. "Maeryn, I swear to the Gods..."

"Oh save the semantics, Harley. Don't think I'm against making an orphan out of her," she warned.

I removed myself from Harley's embrace quickly. I couldn't handle another death. "It's okay," I told him. "I'll be okay."

As we walked the tunnel, Maeryn chuckled beside me. "Cain warned me that I couldn't lay a hand on you. Though, *Aamon* was quite pleased when I told him about your blood."

I stopped walking and looked at her. I tried to speak, but due to Aamon's compulsion, I couldn't mutter a single word about it. They stayed glued to the tip of my tongue, unable to leave my lips.

"Did it hurt, Morrigan?" she pressed on. "He's taken quite a liking to you, hasn't he?"

She started to laugh at my silence and brought me back to my room.

My power had sparked when I saw her. That meant it was there. Somewhere deep and barely obtainable, but it was there. If I could just eat a bit more… drink a bit more… If I could muster up just enough energy to make that spark a flame… perhaps I could escape.

But even if I did manage to leave, where would I go? How would I get out? There was no way of knowing how deep these tunnels stretched, or which one led *where*. So, I needed a plan.

And who better to formulate one than the scholar Cain so foolishly placed into my hands?

Chapter 54

My mornings had become almost bearable now that I could visit Harley.

It helped a lot more than I thought it would. With Aamon deciding to visit me almost nightly, forcing me to abide with his compulsion, at least with Harley I was safe.

"And me." he said beside me.

I rolled my eyes. "You never used to talk this much."

"I'm sorry?" Harley asked.

Closing my lips together, I shot him a look and realized that I had spoken out loud. And with my masked stranger being only in *my* mind, Harley just listened to me talking to myself. *Why, yes, Morrigan. You have gone mad.*

"Nothing," I lied and returned to the small stack of books Cain had allowed me to read in my endless free time. "Harley? Do you know where we are?" It was a long shot, but if *anyone* could put the pieces together, it would be Harley.

He let out a long breath and closed his own book, keeping his head down. "I do." I joined him on the bed and leaned back against the wall, hoping that whatever information he had would lead us to a way out of here. "When Rosina fell in love with Ryuk, they knew it was forbidden. So, they met in secret. They built these tunnels to be together without the others knowing where they were. Only the blood of a god could permit them to enter. And only Ryuk and Rosina knew where the entrances were."

"But how did Cain get in?"

He shook his head, just as puzzled as I was. "That... I still don't know. Though, I have my suspicions." He turned to me. "I'm surprised you didn't put it together yourself."

Why would I... *The diary.* That's why it all sounded so familiar. But how would Harley know that— "*You* gave me that diary." The small smile he gave me confirmed it. "So it's true, then? *All* of it?"

"The world is cruel, Morrigan. Our history has been told through a web of lies and deceit. One person's enemy is another person's friend." He closed his eyes and let his head hit the wall behind us. "Rosina had always been kind to me. She was beautiful and innocent and... You remind me a lot of her. She would have adored you."

Sitting up straighter, I leaned in and lowered my voice a little. "Then, you must know how to get out. If you *knew* her. Maybe we could—"

His door opened and we both turned to see Maeryn standing in the hall. "She's barely been here an hour," Harley complained.

"She's been here plenty," Maeryn hissed back at him. Something seemed to be bothering her more than normal. I knew that look on her face. Growing up, it usually meant I was long overdue for a *lesson.*

Not willing to risk Harley being placed in the center of their wrath, I stood from the bed and picked up my book. "It's okay," I told him. "I'll see you tomorrow." I gave him a short smile and turned to Maeryn, prepared to deal with the aftermath of whatever angered her that morning.

But when we arrived at my room, she entered with me and closed the door behind her. I knew that it couldn't mean anything good. The only comfort I had was that she stated Cain wouldn't allow her to touch me. Turning slowly to face her, I found she had her back pressed against the cell door with her hands balled into fists.

"Maeryn?" I asked.

"What *is* it about you?" It was only then that I smelled the alcohol on her. Maeryn was drunk. "Kaiden wouldn't touch me... and I knew it was because of *you*. But Cain..." Her words were slurring, but it didn't mask the hate within them. "You know, I've never been called another woman's name before."

Fuck. "I don't want Cain," I tried assuring her. "Believe me, Maeryn. I wouldn't touch him to save my life." As she laughed, her fingers slipped into her pocket and removed a small dagger, clenching it in her hand. "Maeryn, if you touch me, he'll be furious. Y-you know that. I'll tell him," I warned.

She barely registered my words. Lifting the blade, she pointed it at me and her lips curled back. "You're *no one!*" she yelled at me. "*Why,* Morrigan?! Why must you ruin every single part of my life?!"

She ran at me quicker than I had time to think and I backed up until I hit the wall. Before the tip of the knife reached my chest, I grabbed her wrist. The stone behind me rubbed against my skin, scratching me as we struggled together. This is what my life had become. Everywhere I turned, death waited for me. It would never end.

"You took him from me!" Her spit sprayed against my face, burning with every bit of her anger. "You don't deserve this! You don't deserve *him*!"

"Don't listen to her, Morrigan," he pleaded. *"You're too good for this—too good for* them.*"*

She's right, I wanted to answer him. *I'm not strong enough for this.*

Perhaps… Perhaps I could let her. I could easily release my hand and let the knife sink into me, killing me. It would all be over, then. No more Aamon… No more Cain… I might even see… I might see my mother again.

"Do you remember what you told her, Morrigan?" he asked me. I couldn't see him anywhere, but I knew he was here. He was *always* here.

What I told her…

"Look at me. Remember my eyes… Take in every detail Maeryn. This will be the last face you see when you die, you evil piece of shit!" I listened to my own voice playing through my ears like a raging melody.

No. Maeryn wouldn't be the one to kill me. "You're pathetic, Maeryn," I seethed through clenched teeth. With my own fury building like a storm within me, I slammed my head against hers, causing her to stumble back a few steps. The moment she dropped the knife, I swung at her, landing a blow directly across her nose.

"I'm going to kill you," she growled before running after me again. I quickly moved to the side, missing her by an inch, but as I turned toward the door I felt her grab my hair.

"Upper hand, Morrigan," he told me. I kicked back, slamming into her leg and she released me as she fell down. *"Knife, Morrigan. Grab the knife."*

I looked around for it, spotting it on the floor just beside the wall. But just as I ran, Maeryn's hand wrapped around my ankle and pulled. With my chest against the floor, I turned and kicked her as hard as I could against her nose. *I hope that fucking hurt.*

Then, I quickly crawled toward the blade. I was so close. The knife barely inches from my hand. Until Maeryn flipped me onto my back and straddled me. She pinned me down and hovered above with her nose obviously broken and bloody. This was her true face—ugly, damaged and evil. All of that beauty… and for *what*?

"You're pathetic, Maeryn! A waste of space!" I yelled at her. And then I felt her fist hit me across my cheek. I didn't care. I turned my face back up to look at her. "They'll *never* love you. Nobody could ever love—"

She hit me again and I felt blood pooling in my mouth. I spit it onto the floor beside my head and couldn't help but laugh. I didn't know *why* I was laughing. But it wouldn't stop. So much pain… I had been in so much pain. "You really *have* gone insane," she sneered. "Why are you laughing?! Stop laughing!"

I only laughed louder as she hit me again, unable to control myself anymore. The whole situation… It was so ridiculous. The gods chose *me* to be a *blood whore* to seven men. A *blood whore*. Not a *queen*. The person chosen to raise me beat me relentlessly. I fell in love with the one man who treated me worse than the rest of them. And now I had been kidnapped, placed into an underground tunnel, where no one could find me.

"This isn't funny," he hissed nearby.

Oh right, and I was hallucinating a complete stranger.

"Oh, but it is," I laughed. "It really is." I began coughing up the blood that started dripping down my throat.

"Who are you talking to?" she asked, then she shook her head. "Let's just get this over with."

Her hands let go of mine and wrapped around my throat. Grabbing her wrists, I tried to pull them off as the airflow completely closed off. I squirmed and kicked, but I was too weak. I had always been so fucking weak.

Before long, my eyes began to blur as my lungs burned. And the tips of my fingers started to tingle. Looking to the side, it wasn't *him* that I saw. It was *her*. My mother. She sank down in the corner of the room, her hands covering her mouth as tears fell down her cheeks.

It's okay, I wanted to tell her. *I fought. I tried. I can be with you now.*

But as I closed my eyes, accepting the fate that Maeryn offered me, *his* voice crept into my mind in a quiet whisper. *"This will be the last face you see when you die. That's what you promised her. It wasn't your fault, Morrigan. None of it was. The gods thought they could create a puppet."*

I opened my eyes.

"Show them who holds the strings."

I quickly stretched my arm out as far as I could until I touched the handle. Then, staring Maeryn in the eyes, I pierced the knife into her throat. Her hands loosened as blood sprayed across my face. But I didn't care. Every ounce of bottled rage poured from me as I threw Maeryn to the side and climbed on top of her.

Removing the blade from her throat, I grasped the handle with both hands. "You *tortured* me!" I screamed. "For *years!*"

I brought the knife down, stabbing her chest over and over again. I couldn't stop myself. I screamed at her as I mauled her body. Screamed at the walls. Screamed at the gods for ever creating me to begin with.

"I WAS A CHILD!" My throat burned from how loud I yelled. But still, the blade found its way into the wound that only grew larger with each thrust.

"Morrigan," he said. *"Morrigan, she's dead. You have to stop."*

"No!" I wouldn't. "You took *everything* from me!" I yelled at her. "EVERYTHING!"

Someone ran into the room, but I didn't see them. All I saw was Maeryn's pale, crimson-stained face falling to the side. Then, my body was being pulled off of hers. Panting, I kicked and swung my arms, trying to break free of their hold. But they wrapped their arms around me, forcing me to hug my chest. "What did you do, Morrigan?" Cain said behind me.

Aamon passed us and stopped beside Maeryn's body. It lay on the floor, mutilated and bloody, barely recognizable anymore. *I* did that. *I* killed her. "I kept my promise."

The Diary of Daisies and Hellebores

He…

They know.

He returned with them.

How could he… What has he done? They looked at the baby in disgust and he would not even acknowledge it. What could they have said to him? What has made him change so drastically?

How could he bring them to this place?

How could he betray me?

They… They wouldn't stop looking at my baby…

Chapter 55

DEZ

Kaiden and I prepared to leave together so we could speak to one of the seers at the Palace.

One of them *had* to know something. They claimed they couldn't foresee Cain's actions, which made absolutely no sense to any of us. But even so, now that we had an idea of where she could be… they might have known how to access it.

When we arrived at the Palace, we were greeted by one of the elder priests, Priest Orin. "My Lords!" he exclaimed. "How pleasant to see you both. I must offer my sincere condolences in regards to the—"

"Don't waste your breath, Priest," Kaiden hissed as we trudged up the steps. "Bring me your oldest seer."

Kaiden hadn't been himself since she left. He was never really *himself*, but even after... It didn't hurt him this bad last time. The effect it had on him was contagious. He reeked of anger and rage and could barely hold a long enough conversation without wanting to hurt someone. But I understood it.

I could *feel* her still. I could hear her heartbeat in my sleep. I knew she was alive, though I didn't know how I knew that. And sometimes, I felt other things as well. Some nights I woke screaming, drenched in sweat. I would get random pains all over my body—my wrist, my shoulder— stinging like small cuts. Cass, Eris, and Naaz thought I was becoming manic. They weren't feeling any of it and it made me feel like I had gone insane. But Kaiden believed me.

He didn't understand it, but he never thought that I was lying.

"I cannot see her," the old woman said. Her face appeared withered from age and she was likely a blink away from death. "We have *never* been able to see her."

What?

Kaiden's brows pulled together. "What do you mean you can't *see* her?"

She simply shrugged in response.

"The tunnels, then. You can't expect me to believe that you don't know where the entrances are," I added, hoping to save the woman from the wrath brewing in Kaiden's black eyes.

She turned her grey stare to me. "The entrances will only open to those with the blood of a god."

"Then, how could Cain have accessed them?!" Kaiden screamed, pushing his face into hers as he hovered above her chair.

"Your questions have already been answered. I don't know what more help I can give that you don't already have."

Frustrated, Kaiden stood and threw his glass of wine against the wall, shattering it. But still, the seer looked unfazed by his outburst. "I want to know where the fucking entrance is!" he screamed, leaning onto her chair again.

Smiling, she nodded. "I will take you to the entrance." I breathed a sigh of relief. "In two days."

"Two days?! We might not *have* two days!" I could see Kaiden's knuckles turning white as he gripped the arms beside her.

"That is all that I can offer you. All that *any* of us will offer you."

Kaiden looked at me. "Two days," I whispered. "We can make it two more days."

"But can she?" he asked. The rage in his eyes had simmered into nothing more than pain. His question was genuine. He needed hope, as we all did. But Kaiden looked like he might die without it.

Two days. That's all we needed.

We're coming, Princess.

MORRIGAN

Red.

So much… *red.*

Cain took me from my room, and the moment I stepped through the doorway, my world seemed to crash. All I could see was *red.* Red on my hands. Red on my dress. Red on Cain's shirt from where he held me against him. What had I done?

"Morrigan!" I heard Harley call my name before I felt his hands against my cheeks, but I could barely register him in front of me. "What did you do to her?!"

"I didn't do anything, old man," Cain hissed.

I'm covered in blood...

"Morrigan, you need to breathe."

Why am I covered in blood?

"Your little girl got carried away with herself." He handed something to Harley, clothing maybe. "Clean her up. Her room is..." Cain gagged. "She needs to stay here for a while."

What's wrong with my room? Is that where this blood came from?

When Harley's hands left my face, I slowly trailed my eyes down until I looked at my palms. They were drenched. You couldn't see an inch of my own skin beneath the dark, sticky crimson that covered them. *What did I do?*

"What you had *to,"* he whispered.

"I killed her..."

Harley appeared before me again and brought a cloth to my face as he wiped it. But I could hear the gulp of his swallow. "We need to change you, Morrigan. Your clothes are... Can you get changed?" Change? Why did I need to change? *Right... My clothes, they're... They're covered in blood. Her blood.* "I'm going to help you, Morrigan. Okay?"

I nodded, barely able to remain in my own reality. My mind kept straying, trying its best to forget what I had done. But quick images flashed through my mind. The knife in Maeryn's chest... Her blood spraying on me when I stabbed her throat. I lost my footing just as Harley removed my dress and he caught me. "I killed her," I whispered.

"We need to get the blood off of you."

I felt my body being submerged into water. And as I sank in, it became muddled with red liquid. It spread like vines, filling the tub. Even more poured out the more he lowered me down. Clinging to his arms, I kicked and tried to jump from the bath. "No," I cried. "There's too much!"

"Morrigan, please," Harley pleaded. His voice sounded almost as pained as mine. "Please, we need to get this off of you."

I held onto one of his arms, turning my eyes away from the water as he rinsed it all off of me. *I killed her. I killed someone. Her blood is on me.* It wasn't long before he pulled me from the bath and wrapped me in something. When I looked down, the red was gone from my skin, but it had become a part of me. It would never really leave. I took someone's life.

"She deserved it, Morrigan," he said to me. *"She would have killed you if you hadn't."*

She deserved it. Yes. It's okay.

My feet touched the floor and I no longer felt Harley's arms around me. "Harley?" I called, staring down at my hands that looked perfectly clean now. "Harley!"

"I'm here." He guided my feet to step into a new gown, lifting it until he covered me and tied it in the back. "I'm here, Morrigan."

"What did I do?" My voice cracked as he stood in front of me and cradled my face with his hands.

"What you *had* to," he assured me. But I couldn't breathe anymore. My lungs were closing in on themselves and my chest had a knot tied around it. "Morrigan, breathe."

A panic attack. That's what Kaiden called it. I was having a panic attack.

"Breathe, Morrigan," Harley said again.

But it was Kaiden's voice that I heard in my mind. *"Breathe with me, little dove. Come back to me, Morrigan."*

Sinking to the floor, I landed on my knees and could feel Harley drop down with me. He pulled me against his chest. "Why won't this end?" I panted. "I want to go *home*."

What were Dez and the rest of them going to do? What would happen when they needed to feed again? Would they die, too? "I'm here, Morrigan," Harley cried as he held me. "I've got you."

Harley.

My... *father*.

He didn't leave me. He didn't abandon me. He's here... holding me. "Dad," I wept. And his chest shook even harder. "I can't do this anymore, please." I was begging, but I didn't know what for.

Why did they have to choose *me*? So many people are born every day, but they had chosen *me*. I wasn't strong enough for this.

"I'm here, Morrigan," Harley whispered. "I'm not going to leave you. I'm going to get you out of here."

"We are here, Morrigan."

The Diary of Daisies and Hellebores

They took him.

They took my baby.

They took my baby.

They took him.

THEY TOOK HIM!

What has he done?

They...

They took my baby.

Chapter 56

Harley stared at me but hadn't spoken for a couple of minutes. I had to shut out what happened with Maeryn in order to protect myself. I couldn't fold now. Too much was at stake, too many lives, and I needed to find the strength in me to keep going. So, Harley and I filled a few days with me catching up on what happened while he was gone. It helped to clear my mind.

"When's the last time you felt your... *magic*?" he asked, like he wasn't quite sure if that had been the correct word for it.

"When I saw Maeryn," I told him. "But I think Cain's been lacing me with hellebore to keep it at bay. I can't even feel it anymore."

He nodded, considering something. "But it all started when you had been consuming blood from both Eris and Naaz, correct?"

This had been the most uncomfortable conversation that I could have been participating in with my *father,* of all people. "Yes." But as his brows scrunched even further together, I could see the inception of a plan beginning to form in his eyes. "You're thinking of something. What are you thinking about?"

"Do you trust me?"

I nodded. "Of course."

"You're not going to like it."

He was right, I didn't.

But I would do it. However, I had my own conditions. So, when Cain came to retrieve me, I looked back at Harley as I walked to the door. He appeared so calm, I didn't know how he did it. My nerves were racing like a wildfire spreading throughout my heart. What if I never saw him again? I knew none of that mattered in his eyes. He would be happy if I was the only one to leave, but that wouldn't be enough for me. I would spend every second finding my way back to save him.

In that moment, the words left me before I knew what I was even saying. "I love you," I said to him. Then, I quickly turned and walked away, knowing that if he said it back to me, I wouldn't have the heart to carry out our plan.

We walked together to the throne room in silence, and when Cain grabbed my arm, I didn't pull away. I needed him to believe that my will to fight was gone now—that I had truly given up.

"You're lucky I'm in a *giving* mood today," he said as we entered the small dining hall. "But, since you've been a good girl, I thought I would humor your request." Seated at the table was Azrael, still with his blindfold on, looking confused. *Thank the gods...* Seeing him gave me enough courage to do what I needed to do.

"Thank you," I whispered to him, and I didn't need to fake the sincerity in my voice. I meant it. He just had no clue as to *why*.

While we sat together, I looked at all four tunnels that were masked in darkness. *"They all lead to the same place,"* Harley had explained. *"They'll feel never-ending, but if you keep running, you'll find the exit. Once you hear the wind, run and don't look back. They'll find you, Morrigan. One of them will sense you."*

There weren't many people here today—the tunnels were quiet. Cain said that the food stash had been getting low, so he sent some people out to collect more. When our plates were placed down, I helped Azrael with his.

"Are you okay?" I asked him in a low voice, just enough for him to hear.

He nodded slightly, trembling in his seat. He didn't know why he was here and looked frightened beyond belief. *Just a little more time,* I wanted to say to him. *Please, trust me.*

"He'll slow you down," he warned.

This isn't negotiable.

I moved to my plate, prepared to eat, when Cain stopped me. "A deal's a deal, Princess." Pressing my lips together, I took a deep breath. The *other* part of my plan. I didn't really need this food. I just needed to make sure that Azrael had enough.

"Remember what your father told you," he said.

"It has to be real. You won't be able to get enough strength from his blood if you're too focused on fighting the bond. Don't be scared and don't *feel ashamed. You do what you need to do and take all that you can."*

He escorted me to a room just outside of the hall as Azrael ate. And when I approached Cain, I held out my wrist for him. He drank, not bothering to make it gentle—likely a reminder of my place with him. Then, he shoved me against the wall, pushing his body against mine like he owned me. But I let the pain fuel the fire within me. His greed would ignite every flame he had doused. When he finished, he bit his wrist and offered it to me with a challenging glint in his eyes.

Make it real.

I licked his skin and let go of my inhibitions. Allowing the bond to take over, his blood no longer tasted sour. As I pulled from it, Cain's chest vibrated with a deep moan. *Make it real...* even if every part of me wanted to puke. I took a wary step forward, watching him take several steps back until he hit a chair nearby.

Sinking into the seat, Cain quickly took his dagger and cut a line down the side of his neck. "More," he pleaded, and I could see the lust on his face blinding his actions.

Make it real.

Climbing on top of him, I latched onto his neck and pulled even more. I drank more blood than I had ever taken in before, and my skin buzzed from it. That flame sat in my belly, rising slowly to my chest. *Just a little more.* But Cain placed his hands on my hips, attempting to push me away.

"Princess," he groaned.

More. Just a little more.

Needing to distract him, I moved my hips against him and placed my hand on his chest, fisting his shirt. It was just enough to redirect his mind as he dug his fingers into my thighs. My skin began to itch... Then, it started to *burn*.

Just... a little... more.

"Morrigan," Cain said nervously. "Morrigan, let go." I ignored him and sucked harder, using my teeth to keep his wound open. Then, his hand moved to his side, where the dagger was.

"You can't kill him," Harley had reminded me. *"Not without hellebore. And we don't know what would happen to you if he* did *die. You just need a head start."*

As his fingers wrapped around the knife, I released his neck and placed both hands on his head. His eyes widened, and in them, I could see the reflection of my own, blazing with a light I had never seen before.

"Who's the monster now, Cain?" I hissed before twisting it as hard as I could, listening to it snap.

KAIDEN

"Absolutely not."

She was out of her mind if she thought I would allow her to accompany us. We spent the entirety of the morning arguing over it. We had no clue what we were walking into. No idea on how many people he had with him—or if they had hellebore.

"Morrigan would kill me if I allowed anything to happen to you," I reminded Lyra. "And I quite enjoy being alive, thank you."

Cass scoffed from his seat. "Are you not the very same person we assigned to protect Morrigan? Look where that got us—"

Before anyone could blink, Lyra had removed her dagger and drove it into the table beside Cass's hand. "And did you not use her as your *blood whore… My Lord*?" Cass visibly flinched next to her. "She was safer with me than she was with you. I can promise you that."

"Lyra," I warned calmly. "I need you *here*." She removed her dagger and turned back to me. "You're the only person I trust to keep matters handled while I'm gone. Please."

Her shoulders slumped. "I'll go check on Eowyn," she groaned, and left the room.

Once the door closed behind her, Cass stood and faced me. "You're going to allow her to act the way she did?"

I shrugged. "Don't act as if Morrigan wouldn't have had your balls for speaking to her that way."

Beside me, Dez chuckled and Cass looked almost offended by it. Dez… He's someone I never truly saw coming. Before the war we had an… acquaintanceship of sorts. We weren't exactly *friends*, but we were thrown into the same, unwanted task that we shared in secret. When it came to all of us as a whole, Dez held the heart. In truth? He was likely the only one of the bunch that actually deserved her.

I knew she loved him. She may not have said it, but I saw it in her eyes on the day we met with everyone. But I also knew that there was no way I would be letting her go, not now. So, somehow, we would need to figure out a way to live with this. A way for us *both* to be in her life. If there was anyone I had to share her with, I trusted him the most.

"So, what exactly *is* the plan?" D asked. He hadn't been very present since Morrigan disappeared. Though, I supposed, he never really was to begin with either. He had always kept to himself.

"The seer will lead us to the entrance first thing in the morning. She'll get us inside, but she won't go any further than that," Dez answered for me.

"Kaiden," Naaz whispered. "I think we need to prepare for what… Morrigan might not be the same. We don't know what's happened down there."

My insides felt like they were being stabbed. Just the idea of someone laying their hands on her... but I knew that Naaz was right. Cain had always been, well... *passionate*. Out of all of us, his temper was the worst. But his tastes? They were disturbing. I had seen him once, during one of his Offerings. He was too quick with her, too forceful. She screamed as he fed and I could have sworn I watched him smile as he did.

Closing my eyes, I shook the thought from my mind as the girl's face began morphing into Morrigan's. "We'll be cautious," I assured him.

That's when Dez stepped into my side, lowering his voice as well. "Do you... The dreams, my nightmares..." His face fell. "Do you think he's hurting her?"

I placed a hand on his shoulder. "I promise you, Dez. Any person who's laid a single finger on Morrigan will get what's coming to them."

Chapter 57

MORRIGAN

I gasped as his head fell back against the chair.

He looked almost lifeless, but I knew that he wasn't. He wouldn't stay out for long, which meant I didn't have time to think. Swiping the dagger from his hand, I jumped off of him and ran back to the dining hall.

"Your Grace?" Azrael called from his chair, looking around beneath his blindfold.

"There's no time to explain," I rushed out before snatching him from his chair and grabbing his hand. "Azrael," I warned. "I need you to trust me."

Before he could say anything, I picked him up, into my arms, and looked for the first tunnel to run down. "What are you doing?!" he yelled.

"Hush!" Even though there weren't many people that I had seen around, with as many rooms as there were, I knew *someone* had to have been left behind. And I didn't have time to waste.

I pulled a torch from a nearby wall and held it with my other hand, keeping Azrael close. But when I heard a few voices yelling behind us, the fear finally outweighed my adrenaline. I ran as fast as I could down the dark hall, with zero knowledge of where it would lead me.

"Where are you going?" he asked me.

"I don't know!" I yelled, making a turn at the end of the pathway.

"You're going to go in circles if you aren't careful," he warned.

"Well then *you* navigate the tunnels for me!"

"Who are you talking to?" Azrael asked me.

For the love of the gods...

"Tunnels?" he went quiet for a moment. *"Morrigan, you need to follow my voice."*

What do you mean, follow *your voice?*

"Listen to it. Let it guide you."

"Princess!" Cain's voice echoed across the walls, traveling through the darkness from wherever he was. He had barely been out for more than a couple of minutes, but it at least gave us a small head start.

"The string between us. You feel it, don't you?"

He was right. Though it was barely there, I still felt it—an invisible cord that always drew me to him in my dreams. It's how he would pull me from my nightmares. If I clung to that tether, he would drag me out of them.

"Follow it. Let it lead you."

I could smell Cain's blood nearby. How did he get so close so fast? "I can feel you, Princess!"

Pushing through the fear, I continued running and held Azrael a little tighter. He had begun to tremble against my chest. His tears landed on my shoulder, soaking the fabric below his face. I couldn't stop. I *had* to find a way out. Seeking out the tether, I let it guide my decisions. I turned down whichever tunnel it seemed to call to and ran through the darkness. But with each tunnel, I had been greeted with longer halls and dimmer torches.

Eventually, I heard a whistle through the shadows. It was Cain, taunting me. He began humming the tune of my mother's lullaby. "It'll be quick, Princess. I swear it!" His laughter bellowed through the darkness. "He won't feel a thing. And after, you're going right back in that cage."

"I don't want to die," Azrael cried.

"You won't," I promised. And as my feet began to ache, that tether pulled again. But this time, it led me to a room nearby. I opened the door and slammed it shut, locking it for good measure before placing Azrael down.

"He's coming," he whispered and I placed a finger to my mouth to shush him.

But just as we took a step into the shadows, the door pounded with rage behind us. Azrael jumped and clung to my side. "Your father spent all of this time teaching you… and you're still just as foolish."

"I followed it!" I yelled. "Why aren't you talking now?!"

The empty room didn't respond. The only sound that could be heard were Cain's fists slamming against the door. *Oh Gods… I* was *crazy… I* am *crazy… and I just… I just led us to nowhere…*

I looked down at Az who stared in terror at the small light pouring through the bottom of the door. Picking him up again, I wrapped his legs around me and stepped back into the darkness. "I won't let him hurt you," I whispered, trying to convince myself that I could keep him safe.

I expected to hit a wall, but I just kept going back. *How large is this room?* I thought to myself. But I jumped again when Cain pounded once more. "You're making this harder than it needs to be, Princess!"

Whispers... I could hear whispers, just as I did when Maeryn would lock me in that room... Then, the hairs on my arms stood straight and it itched like something had started to crawl on them. I swatted whatever it was away, swinging my arms as the sensation increased.

"Your Grace," Azrael cried.

The air around us felt thick. It's how Kaiden's shadows sometimes felt when he took us somewhere—like the darkness was hugging me, tightening around the both of us.

"What's happening?!" I yelled.

After another step back, the room burst with light.

Azrael lifted his head from my shoulder and gasped. "Where are we?" he asked.

Turning around, I saw a room that I knew I had seen before. The floor beneath me looked dark, and in front of us stood a long, skinny bridge. "I don't know..." I answered him truthfully. "But I've been here before."

I walked forward, and a sound began to rise from the light below the bridge. They were screams. We were out of options now. It was either walk across the bridge, and risk what lay at the end of it, or wait for Cain to find us. So, I took a step onto it, balancing myself out as I held Azrael.

"Your Grace..." he said warily. But I ignored him. Each step made my heart pound like thunder. I could feel the blazing heat from the fire under us, and I feared a single movement could send us into it.

Aside from the light that emanated from the flames, it caused too much smoke for me to see ahead of us. The screams grew louder, and even

Azrael covered his ears to protect them. I made the mistake of looking down, staring into the endless lake of fire, and under my feet, I could feel it. But it didn't burn me. I welcomed the heat, allowing my own fire to rise. Without any knowledge as to *how,* I knew my soul belonged here.

I didn't allow myself to worry as we continued forward, hoping there would be an end to my path. And just when it felt like I had been walking for hours, I saw something emerge from the smoke—a figure. I quickly stopped, scared to death that Cain had finally found us, and pulled Azrael even tighter.

But the figure looked taller than Cain, and my heart pulsed as he began walking right toward us.

"Hello?" I called to him.

The man stopped and stood deathly still. "Morrigan?"

That voice... It was... "You're... *real?*" I whispered.

I didn't think before taking a hurried step forward, not paying attention to where my foot landed. And in the midst of the excitement, thinking we were free, I had forgotten the heat and the sweat the fire had caused. When my foot touched the stone...

I slipped.

"MORRIGAN!" he screamed, as I felt my breath leave my lungs.

Azrael dug his fingers into my shoulders, clinging for his life as we fell, and the flames consumed us. The last thing I felt was my back hitting a hard surface below before the light disappeared, and I blacked out.

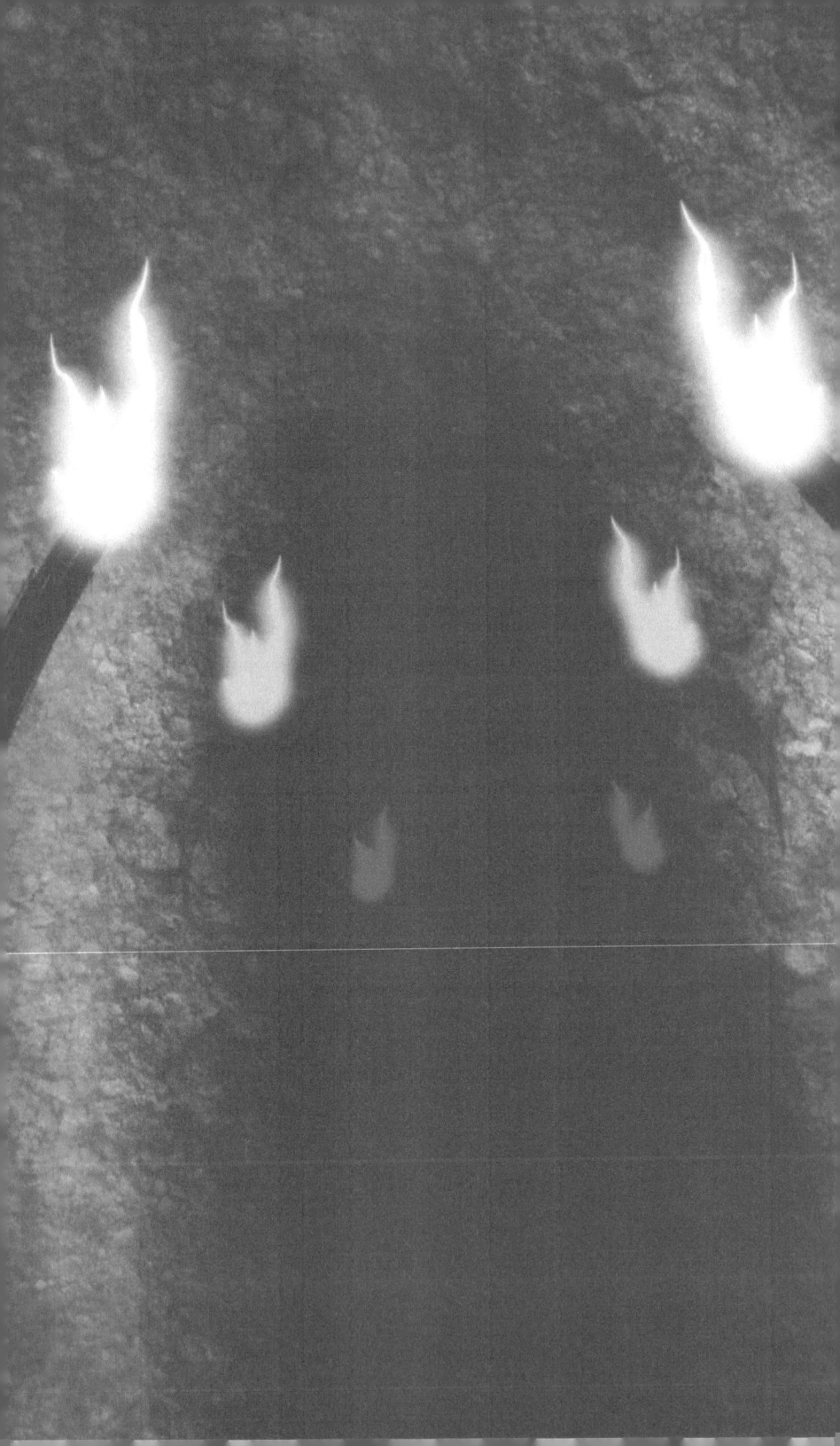

<u>*The Diary of Daisies and Hellebores*</u>

I will kill them all.

To be continued...

DID YOU NOT LIKE MY ENDING?
MY POOR, LITTLE DOVE…
WELL… SINCE YOU ASKED SO
NICELY… I'LL GIVE YOU A LITTLE PEEK.

THE EIGHTH SIN

Prologue

300 YEARS AGO

The echoes of her feet could be heard along the stone walls, swallowing the sound of his cries and sending them through the tunnels.

"Please," she begged him, holding him tight against her chest as she maneuvered her way through the darkness. The only thing that lit up the path was the power that shone in her eyes, almost as bright as the sun. "Please, you have to be quiet."

She had trusted him. He told her he would protect them both but ran to the rest of them the moment he got scared. He betrayed her, and now they had come to collect the only thing keeping her shattered heart from crumbling. The baby cried in her arms, not understanding what was at stake if she couldn't soothe him—or better yet, find a way out of this nightmare.

Behind her, the shadows were slithering along the walls, creeping toward her at a deadly pace. The only thing stopping them was her *own* light, but she had used so much of it already to slow them down. Soon, her light would dim and they would catch her.

She paused at a wall, placing her hand against the stone and pushed. The rocks split, collapsing onto the ground, and revealed a small, hollow space. After running inside, she turned around and quickly raised the pebbles, aligning them back together. The baby wailed, flinging his arms as she clutched him, surrounding her child with every ounce of light that she could manage. But she *sensed* him. She felt every pulse of his heart as he approached, feeling their tether pulling at one another.

It was then that she regretted allowing him to convince her of the soul bond. They found a way to tie their light together, making their hearts beat as one. He promised eternity, but now, she knew he did it with malice. He did it to keep her wrapped around his finger like a puppet. He was too strong—his power far deadlier than her own. And now, she knew that *he* could feel *her*, too.

"My little daisy…" He meant the words to sound loving, filled with his felonious affection that was never truly real. "We can fix this."

"I won't let you hurt him!" she yelled, her baby flinching from the sound. Lifting the child, she pressed her forehead against his and smiled sadly at his own light connecting with hers. She could feel it—the pulsing energy that ran through his veins. "I won't let him hurt you. I won't let them take you."

"He'll be safe, my daisy," he lied. She knew he was lying. She could feel his emotions burning through her chest like a wildfire, ready to explode.

"You can't have him!" she said again, stepping back until they hit a wall, and sank down to her feet.

Pounding began as he slammed his fist, trying to fight the wards she placed the moment the stone had stitched itself together. But they wouldn't last for long. No, she knew he would get in eventually—just as she knew that he *would* take him. Looking down, she placed the baby against her lap, removing his blanket so she could memorize every inch of his face. She soaked in the piercing blue eyes, with white, iridescent light that streaked his irises. He inherited them from her.

She jumped at another bang on the wall, listening to the rocks tremble as they began to crack. Tears swelling in her eyes, she hugged the child and let them fall. "I love you so much," she whispered to him, the words alone beginning to soothe him. "You're the only good in my life…" Her cries shifted into heavy sobs as she heard pebbles falling to the floor. "I'll kill them. I'll kill *all* of them. If they touch you I'll burn the fucking world to the ground, do you understand me? I will *destroy* every inch of their precious earth if I can't keep you safe."

"You can't stop this," he growled. Then, the rocks flew apart, his shadows covering every inch of space between his silver, glowing eyes and her light. He finally resembled the true monster that he was. "Give me my son."

Lips quivering, she placed a shaky kiss against his head and cherished the sound of his heart as long as she could. "I'm begging you," she cried. "Please… Don't—"

Before she could mutter another word, the shadows pierced through her light, wrapping like vines around the child and pulling him from her embrace. She screamed as she reached for him, but more of the dark tendrils slinked around her arms, holding them against the stone like chains.

"No!" she yelled, willing every bit of strength she could to fight his power, but she was forced to watch in the darkness as the shadows brought the child to him. The baby's eyes shone bright, illuminating the room as *he* grabbed him.

But there was a pause as he stared into his eyes... Like, for a single second, he contemplated his actions. "He looks just like you," he whispered. Then, any bit of kindness that she could see, faded into his silver glow. And from her distance, she watched as little black webs crawled up the baby's arms, slithering toward his face, until they reached the child's eyes. The light that shone, blue and beautiful, snuffed out with his darkness encompassing her baby. "It didn't have to be this way," he sneered at her.

"I'll kill you," she growled, feeling every bit of her rage twisting into a fire, deep in her belly. "I'll fucking kill *all* of you."

With a small twist of his lips, he gave her a crooked smirk, before disappearing into the darkness. When her arms fell to the ground, she ran at the last remaining shadows, but it was too late. He took him. *They* took him.

"No," she whimpered. "No, no, no..."

All of her fury and anger bubbled beneath her skin. She could barely contain it anymore. The light that had begun to dim, now burst like a star exploding in the sky. She let out a scream so guttural that it tore from her throat like venom, defiling every ounce of love that he left behind in her heart. The light grew... and grew... destroying the rocks beneath her hand… exploding the hollow cave around her… until the only thing left that she could feel was a blazing fire that had enveloped her. Her cries echoed, morphing into the screams of a thousand souls that she planned to *burn*.

The *world* would burn.

And *she*… would kill… them *all*.

Acknowledgements

There are so many people who have walked beside me on this journey, and I couldn't let this book go out into the world without pausing to say thank you. Writing can often feel like a solitary act, but this story—this dream— was shaped and strengthened by the incredible people in my life.

*First, to my **husband**, my heart, my anchor. Thank you for being my constant. You've been my biggest supporter, my sounding board, and my gentle reminder that love is the most powerful story of all. Thank you for every cup of coffee, every late-night pep talk, and every quiet moment of understanding. You've seen me at my best and my worst, and still, you've stood by me, loving me through it all. Your belief in me has carried me through the moments when I doubted myself most. You are my forever muse and my greatest love story.*

*To my **children**, who remind me every day that it's okay to dream. You see the world through eyes full of wonder, and you've taught me that imagination is never something we outgrow. You've inspired me to keep reaching for magic, both on the page and in life.*

*To **Nicole**, my wonderful editor and now one of my dearest friends. You didn't just help polish my words—you breathed life into them. You took my tangled thoughts and helped me mold them into something that felt whole and alive. Your patience, insight, and endless attention to detail pushed this book to be the very best version of itself. But beyond the work, you became someone I could trust, laugh with, and lean on. You gave so much of your time and heart to this story, and I'll never be able to thank you enough for that.*

To **Ashley**, my best friend and constant source of light—you have listened to every plot twist, every "what if," every emotional breakdown, and every wild idea that came rushing into my brain. You've been there through the excitement, the frustration, and all the in-between moments that make up the creative process. Every morning call, every encouraging word, every shared laugh reminded me why I love what I do. You've supported me without question, and your faith in me never wavered. You're the kind of friend every person dreams of having.

To my incredible **Beta Readers**, thank you for being the first to step into this world with me. You caught things I couldn't see, asked the right questions, and helped shape the story into what it is today. Your passion, honesty, and care have meant more to me than you know.

To my **ARC Readers**, you reminded me why I write in the first place. Reading your reactions, seeing your excitement, and feeling your love for this story made all the long nights and endless edits worth it. Your feedback filled me with pride and gratitude, and your words gave me the courage to keep creating.

And finally, to my **readers**... you are the heartbeat of this journey. You've given me a safe space to tell my stories, to pour out my imagination and creativity without fear. Knowing that my words find a home in your hearts is the greatest reward I could ever ask for. Thank you for believing in me, for sharing in these worlds, and for reminding me that stories truly do connect us all.

From the bottom of my heart...

Thank you.

PLEASE CHECK MY SOCIAL MEDIA
ACCOUNTS FOR UPDATES ON FUTURE
WORKS AND OTHER PUBLISHED BOOKS.
(LINKS BELOW.)

Tik Tok: Crystalcrist.author

Instagram: Crystalcrist.author

Facebook group: Crystal's Sinful Readers

OTHER WORKS BY CRYSTAL CRIST:

- **"The Delectable Sins Series"** – *A spicy series of interconnected, standalone demon romance novellas.*
  - A Forbidden Encounter (Book 1): Az and Lilith's story.
  - A Forbidden Sin (Book 2): Draco, Lucifer and Lena's story.
- **Taboo romance**
  - Blackbird: A Stepbrother Romance
    - **Blackbird: Carry You Home releases 2026**

www.ingramcontent.com/pod-product-compliance
Lightning Source LLC
Chambersburg PA
CBHW021939110726
47901CB00003B/898